OTHERWORLD

A NOVEL

JARED C. WILSON

David C Cook
transforming lives together

OTHERWORLD
Published by David C Cook
4050 Lee Vance View
Colorado Springs, CO 80918 U.S.A.

David C Cook Distribution Canada
55 Woodslee Avenue, Paris, Ontario, Canada N3L 3E5

David C Cook U.K., Kingsway Communications
Eastbourne, East Sussex BN23 6NT, England

The graphic circle C logo is a registered trademark of David C Cook.

This story is a work of fiction. All characters and events are the product of the author's
imagination. Any resemblance to any person, living or dead, is coincidental.

Romans 6:23 and 1 Corinthians 13:53-57 in chapter 12 are taken from the Holy
Bible, New International Version©, NIV®. Copyright © 1973, 2011 by Biblica,
Inc. ™ Used by permission of Zondervan. All rights reserved worldwide. www.
zondervan.com; John 3:16 in chapter 12, Timothy 4:3–4 in chapter 14, Psalm
62:1–4 in chapter 17, and Psalm 64:1, 10; 66:8–11; and 68:1–2 in chapter 18 are
taken from the New American Standard Bible®, Copyright © 1960, 1995 by The
Lockman Foundation. Used by permission. (www.Lockman.org.); 1 John 4:1–3
and Romans 16:20 in chapter 13, Psalm 68:3 in chapter 18, and Revelation 5:12 in
chapter 19 are taken from the King James Version of the Bible. (Public Domain.).

ISBN 978-0-7814-1116-5
eISBN 978-1-4347-0704-8

© 2013 Jared C. Wilson
The Team: Alex Field, Nick Lee, Caitlyn Carlson, Karen Athen
Cover Design: Nick Lee
Cover Photo: Shutterstock

Printed in the United States of America
First Edition 2013

1 2 3 4 5 6 7 8 9 10

082113

For Becky

"But do you really mean, sir," said Peter, "that there could
be other worlds—all over the place, just round the corner—like that?"

"Nothing is more probable," said the Professor.

from C. S. Lewis' *The Lion, the Witch and the Wardrobe*

CHAPTER ONE

She was dead before she knew it. Before she toppled to the unyielding earth with a dull thud, she was dead. A bone snapped, maybe two, but she didn't feel or hear them. Just before it happened she knew it was very cold. But it had been cold for days, days she didn't and couldn't keep track of, so she never thought to complain. Then she heard the footsteps, quick and heavy on the frosty ground. Then a piercing pain. In a hip? She couldn't be sure. A searing heat. Then darkness. Had she the mental capacity to philosophize, she would have thought, *So this is it*. But she didn't, so she didn't. If she had been the least bit wise, and of course she wasn't (it was impossible), she might have realized that what was happening to her was the bizarre beginning to the most terrible story the small town she didn't know she lived in had ever seen.

CHAPTER TWO

The old man cursed his neighbors' pathetic aversion to the cold as he began his routine morning trek across his land, semifrozen turf crunching beneath his brown work boots. The news reported eighteen degrees. One would think it a definite sign of the apocalypse from the way the locals were acting. Ice on windshields became top news stories, just like every winter, but Pops Dickey didn't know what all the fuss was about. He had moved to Trumbull, a small town attached to the Texas mecca of Houston, about five years ago, and every year the Texans, used to the sweltering hundred-degree temperatures in the summertime, became prophets of woe when the weather turned chilly. Pops was a Wisconsin native, so besides putting up with all these Southern oddballs, he had to put up with their moaning and complaining about the cold. He had been through much worse. Much, much worse.

Pops owned a small bit of land on the Myrtle side of Trumbull to the north, not the Houston side. Pure country. He had some woods, a little pond, some animals. The sound of his cow bellowing became audible as Pops latched the gate on his chicken coop.

"Even the freakin' cows are complainin'," he muttered, his breath fogging in the crisp air. *Wisconsin cows don't complain*, he thought.

When he'd purchased the farm, three cows came with it. He'd sold one of them two years before but held on to the other two for no particular reason. He liked the milk, but he had no ambitions of expanding his operation to supplying dairy or raising beef cattle. He just liked the thought of having cows on his farm. "What's a farm without cows?" he had said. "Still a farm," his wife, Gertie, replied, but Pops kept them just the same. He was beginning to have second thoughts as the animal's lowing seemed to change pitch, nearing an almost shriek. He was in the little barn now, and it struck him that only the mooing cow was present.

"For crying out loud, ya stupid cow, what's got your tail in a grinder?" Pops examined the animal up and down and from end to end. Nothing appeared to be physically wrong. "Where's your sister?" he asked aloud. Pops had been around cows all his life. He'd never heard one of the docile creatures make such a ruckus. Her moo became unbearable, and he exited the barn, made a left, and walked around to the rear of the brown wooden building. There on top of a thin patch of ice and scattered hay lay the missing animal, lifeless and stiff.

"Well, dang."

Something caught his eye. *You gotta be kidding me*, he thought. He crouched, touched a gloved hand to the animal's side, and sure enough, there was blood there. It was black and hard, coagulated by time and the cold, dry air. *Coyotes?* Maybe. It was possible, but there weren't that many in this area. Plus, he'd never heard of coyotes attacking a cow anywhere around here. Chickens, maybe. Maybe even a pig or two. He admitted to himself that it wasn't out of the question, though. It was probably the best explanation short of human mischief. He got down on his knees, gripping her belly with his hand firmly. He ran it along her underside and looked for tearing or ripping. It was a pretty clean kill for coyotes, or any animal, for that matter. There was no pool of blood, no obvious damage to the beast, no evidence at all that a coyote—or pack of coyotes—had attacked her. Wouldn't she be strewn about, her insides dashed all over the place? Or maybe they would have eaten the evidence or dragged it away. Or maybe the blood had seeped into the ground. The latter was a tough one to believe. The ground was bone-dry, even frozen in places. It could not have swallowed up water, much less blood.

Pops positioned himself where he could grab her with both arms from underneath, squeezing them between her heavy carcass and the ground. It was a tight fit, but he reached under as far as he could and attempted to turn her over. It was futile. Pops was a seventy-one-year-old man, and thin to boot. She was immense, and the stiffness of death had long since set in. A young weight lifter would have left the task incomplete. Pops was straining, aged muscles tight, his teeth clenched. He managed to bring more of her belly into view, though, and what he saw cleared it all up. No coyote had touched her.

He rose to his feet, spit, and began a slow trot back to the house. He had to tell Gertie, and he supposed he should make a phone call. Somebody had cut his cow open.

* * *

Six o'clock came very early for Graham Lattimer. He had been up all night with a splitting headache and collapsed into bed at four in the morning only to wake at half past five. He would have called in sick, but the Trumbull Police Department had a light morning shift. He was their captain, and his presence was imperative. He didn't shower and didn't shave. As he removed his uniform from the closet, he began a somewhat frantic search for his car keys. They lay on the kitchen counter next to the refrigerator, and he discovered them only when he decided to give up the search for a while and get a glass of orange juice. He downed it quickly, wiped strands of pulp from his mouth, and stepped into the frigid Trumbull morning.

It was only after settling into his creaky office chair that he realized his headache was still present and promising to make the day as excruciating as the previous night. He dug in his desk for aspirin. No dice.

"Kelly!" he yelled, then winced at the self-inflicted pain. He pressed the intercom button on his telephone. "Kelly? Are you there?"

"Right here," came the reply.

"Have you got any aspirin?"

"Just a sec. Let me check." A pause. "Yeah, right here."

"Bless you. Could you spare a couple?"

"Sure. I'll be right there."

Graham released the intercom and picked a clipboard up off the corner of his desk. He scanned it, reading the names of those currently out on patrol. Kelly entered.

"Here you go," she said, handing him the bottle of generic headache medicine.

He removed the cap and dumped out a handful of pills.

"I don't think you're s'posed to take that much."

He just looked at her blankly, and then lifted his palm to his mouth, devouring its contents. Struggling to swallow them all dry-mouthed, he continued to peruse the shift sheet. He held the clipboard limply with one hand and buried the other in his brown mop of hair as he massaged his head. When he had downed the last pill, he asked, "Is Petrie still out?"

"I think so. He hasn't checked in, but I could be wrong. He was due back at five-thirty."

"Yeah, that's what it says here. Is Lane in?"

"Yes, sir. He came in about fifteen minutes ago."

"Good. Would you have him and Petrie, when Petrie gets here, meet me in the office?"

"Yes, sir." She retrieved her aspirin bottle and exited, but a minute later Graham's intercom sounded.

"Yes?"

"Um, Captain Lattimer, I forgot to tell you."

"Tell me what?"

"A Mr. Dickey called about forty-five minutes ago and filed a report."

"Mr. who?"

"Mr. Dickey. Pops Dickey. The old couple who own the farm off Trace Road."

Graham searched his memory. The search came up empty.

Kelly ended the silence. "Anyways, he called about forty-five minutes ago and filed a report about a ... well, a vandalism, I guess."

"Somebody key his truck or something?"

"Uh, no, sir. Somebody ... um ..."

"Yes?"

"Somebody killed his cow."

"Killed his what?"

"Yeah, his cow."

"Well, okay."

"Anyways, he just filed a report. You know, over the phone. I said we'd send somebody out."

"Yeah, okay. Thanks, Kelly. Don't forget to tell Petrie and Lane whenever Petrie manages to get himself here."

"Yes, sir."

Graham closed his eyes and breathed deep. His attempts at relaxation only made the intense throbbing in his skull more pronounced. The *Houston Chronicle* lay on his desk, the banner headline in bold lettering calling attention to the cold weather. THE HEAT

IS GONE! it read. *You don't say*, the captain thought. He was only on the second sentence of what he considered a pointless article when a rapping on the glass of his office door drew his attention away. He saw Petrie and Lane through the translucent panel.

"Come in," he ordered.

The two police officers filed in, both yawning conspicuously.

"Tired?"

"You bet, Cap," Mark Lane answered. He was the taller of the two.

"How'd the shift go?"

Officer Sam Petrie offered, "Like a Sunday drive, sir." He was the more muscular of the two, but also the more awkward. "A couple of kids were out goofin' around. Otherwise, pretty uneventful."

"Same here," Lane added. "I didn't see nobody out, 'cept the newspaper guy this morning."

"Good," Graham responded. Then he remembered: "Either of y'all out by Trace Road last night?"

"Not me," Lane said.

"Me neither."

"Where were the kids you ran into?"

"Out by the high school," said Petrie. "They were just hangin' out, though. Weren't even drinkin' or nothin'. I told 'em to get home or I'd call their parents. They said their parents knew they's out, but I told 'em to get to goin' anyway, and they left."

"Follow 'em?"

"No, sir," said Petrie.

Graham leaned back in his chair. He stroked the inside of his cheek with his tongue and rubbed his temples with his forefingers.

"What's up, Cap?" Lane asked.

"Somebody's cow was killed last night."

"Whose?"

"Oh, some old couple. That's why I was askin' about Trace Road. Name's Dickey."

"Pops and Gertie Dickey?" said Petrie.

"Yeah, I guess. You know 'em?"

"Yessir. They go to church with my folks."

"Well, good. Since you know 'em so well, you can check out his dead cow on your way home."

"Sir?"

"You heard me."

"Right. Dead cow."

"That's all, fellas."

The two police officers turned and vacated the captain's office. Lane headed home as Petrie navigated his car toward Trace Road.

* * *

Like all trips between two points in Trumbull, the drive was short. Officer Petrie arrived at Pops and Gertie Dickey's small farm and parked in their dirt driveway. He watched the old man in a red flannel shirt and faded overalls emerge from the house and peer out from the porch.

"Howdy," Petrie called out.

Pops groaned, then said, "Didn't think you guys would make it out this quick."

"Well, you know."

"Uh-huh. My cow's over there around the back of the barn."

It was an odd coupling—a young cop, clean-shaven and hair slicked back and parted neatly, wearing his starched police uniform, following the old, gruff farmer with gray whiskers poking out of his wrinkled and leathery face and clothed in his weather-beaten attire. They commenced the hundred-yard trek to the barn and remained uncomfortably silent the entire way. Only when they had rounded the building did Pops break the quiet.

"There she is."

"Yep." Petrie approached the animal and crouched down. He didn't know exactly what to be looking for. He had never investigated a dead cow. He had never investigated a dead *person*, for that matter. He didn't know what to say. "Yep. She's dead all right."

"Yeah. She's dead." Pops gave him a look like, *You're a regular Sherlock Holmes.*

"She a prize cow?"

"Pardon?"

"A prize cow. You enter her in contests and such?"

Pops looked at Petrie like he'd just passed gas. "No. She's just a regular cow."

"That so?" Petrie asked mostly to himself. He inspected more closely, touching the blood dried into the animal's hair and the short cut in its underside. He still didn't know what to say. "Anybody sore at you?"

"Sore at me? No, I don't think so. I don't know hardly anybody anyway."

"You go to Tabernacle Faith, right?"

The perturbation was radiating from Pops's face now. "The wife's the churchgoer."

"My folks go there. Bill and Paula Petrie?"

"Don't know 'em," Pops responded matter-of-factly.

Dismayed, Petrie shook his head. He had hoped the conversation would cover his failure to find anything substantial to say about the cow. "Can't think of anybody who'd wanna kill your cow, huh, Mr. Dickey?"

"No. Like I said, she's just a regular cow."

Petrie surveyed the dead animal. "I'll get a specialist out here right away, Mr. Dickey."

"Say what, now?"

"A specialist. A veterinarian or somebody to look at this cut. Inspect the animal."

"Listen, no big deal. She's just a cow. I just wanted to file a report and see if you guys could maybe find out who did it. Cows cost quite a bit. Sure, I'd like to catch whoever did her in, you know. But I don't need a specialist or whatever."

"It's okay, Mr. Dickey. It won't be a problem. I think somebody more qualified could get more answers here than I could."

* * *

Two hours later, Captain Graham Lattimer was still fighting off the pain in his head when Petrie's call came in to the station.

Kelly got his attention. "Captain? Officer Petrie's on the radio."

The headache played with his comprehension. "On the radio?"

"The police radio, sir."

"Oh, right." He had to exit his office to answer the call. He used the receiver on Kelly's desk. "Petrie?"

"Sir," came the reply, "I think you need to come out here."

"Out where?"

"The Dickey farm on Trace Road."

Graham looked at his watch. "Shouldn't you be at home?"

"Um, sir. We have a situation here."

"What are you talkin' about?"

"The dead cow, sir …"

"Yes?"

"Well, sir, we have a doctor here, and he says the cow's missing several internal organs."

Graham waited for more. It didn't come. "Okay. So?"

"Well, um … the cut. The cut in the animal is very small and very precise."

"I'm not following, Petrie."

"Sir, the doctor here says the cut wasn't made by any knife."

"What was it made by?"

"He says it was made with heat. A laser, probably."

"Come again?"

"The doctor says this cow was cut open with a laser, or something like it, and that certain specific organs were removed in some peculiar way."

"What are you trying to say, Petrie?"

"Well, sir … have you ever heard of animal mutilations done by … um, well … You should probably come out here, anyway. It's like a UFO kind of thing."

Graham didn't answer. He paused to make sure he hadn't imagined Officer Petrie saying what he thought he had. And then, glancing down at the police radio receiver and realizing that anybody could hear the exchange, he realized he needed to get to the farm before any of the kooks with police scanners could.

CHAPTER THREE

Landon University seemed every bit as large as the city of Houston itself. The campus ran endlessly in every direction, connected by thousands of yards of meandering sidewalks leading to thirty-six different buildings. There were technical complexes, art halls, history centers, and that odd hybrid *cafetorium*. Nestled in a nook of woods in the northwest part of the fourth-largest city in America, the place was a labyrinth.

In the southernmost parking lot, thirty-six-year old Mike Walsh, whom stress had made appear several years older (he'd been pondering the creases in his face and flecks of gray in his hair while contemplating the mirror that very morning), emerged from his old import, its original beige gleaming from the recent wash of melted frost, and looked up at the imposing structures. An uneasy sensation of déjá vu rushed to meet him. He struggled to reconcile the fact that he never liked school yet had decided to make a living studying, researching, and writing. It was his editor's idea—no, it was his editor's *mandate*—that the writers of *Spotlight Magazine* take a few midsemester fast-track courses at the university. So after years of freedom from the strife of academia, Mike found himself back in college. He glanced down at the schedule clutched tightly in his sweaty hand. He'd been signed up for something called Cultural Anthropology. He made careful note of the room number for the hundredth time that morning and set out to find the Smith Building on the narrow white cement pathway, watching his step, as the path was still a bit icy. Once in the Smith Building, he would search for the Study Wing. He'd been warned that nearly every building housed a Study Wing, so it was of paramount importance that he find the right one. He had called ahead of time. "Smith Building, Study Wing. Room 144 is on the first floor," the nice lady on the other end instructed.

"Yes, but can you tell me how to find the Smith Building?" he countered.

"From the southern parking lot, stay on the main sidewalk. It will be the fifth or sixth building on your right."

"What if I can't find a parking space in the southern lot?"

She sighed. "You'll find a space."

And he did. He was nervous, probably more so than when he had entered college for the first time, but recently, more and more, he managed to find a way to be nervous about everything. The minutiae of his life took center stage. Every detail was pored over, studied, contemplated, and worried about. Insomnia, like a disease, slowly overtook him, stealing more and more hours of sleep away from him every night. His job ruled his day. Cable television infomercials and YouTube searches ruled his nights. It had been this way a long time. It had been this way since Molly left.

She'd complained about his lack of attention. He was "devoted to his job, but only fairly acquainted with his wife." He knew this. He realized it, even saw her resentment coming, and he pretended it was petty. It was easy to justify ambivalence, and he fooled himself into thinking everything would work itself out. And then (he wished he could've thought, *Out of the blue* …), she'd packed up her things in the luggage given to them at their wedding and went to live with her sister in Dallas. She'd been gone nearly a year. He had called every day the first few weeks, but she wouldn't speak to him. He surrendered full pursuit and reduced his efforts to one call a week, but he'd only made genuine contact twice.

He said all the right things, but then again, so did every man in his situation. Saying the right things was saying the wrong things. He couldn't begrudge her wariness. He just wanted her back. He offering to do anything—counseling, self-help books, date nights, going to church—everything. He missed everything about her, but mostly he missed her being the consolation of his very existence. In the soul-searching through her absence, he had pretty much realized that more than missing her, he missed what she did for him. When he didn't pity himself, the reality of his selfishness appalled him. He wanted to tell her this. He desperately wanted to inform her of his breakthrough. He knew she would be skeptical, but he would ask for one more chance. He had to have one more opportunity to make things right. He saw it clearly. He could not entertain even the consideration of leaving her, and the fact that she had left him made him realize what a poor excuse for a husband he had been. Many men, perhaps, would criticize her for forsaking her marriage vows, and in his fits of self-justification, he had fixated on this fault as if it was *the* fault, but he knew he could really place no blame on her. He had done that too many times before. It was his turn to shoulder it, right or wrong. He would rather die than divorce, and he had to believe that, in her heart, she would too.

Now he floated, like an astronaut off the line, minutes from suffocation, his source and safety miles away. In Dallas.

The Smith Building was indeed the fifth building, but it lay on the left, not on the right as the telephone lady had claimed. In broad block letters of gold to the right of its glass-door entrance, it announced its name (and underneath, FUNDED BY THE CECIL SMITH FAMILY). He took a deep breath and strolled into the pungent aroma of ammonia.

His shoes squeaked shrilly at every step, which of course did wonders for his profound sense of self-consciousness.

After one wrong turn (in the course of which he took the long way around, even pausing to drink from a water fountain so as not to draw attention to his misdirection), he discovered Room 144. He was the first person to arrive, and he immediately busied himself with debating whether to sit near the front or the rear. He settled on the front.

An older man with silver hair entered, took a seat at a metal desk beneath an expansive whiteboard, and began rifling through papers that were tucked into several manila file folders. He said nothing—didn't even acknowledge Mike's presence.

Mike glanced down at his hands. They were thin and pale, ghostlike, barely distinguishable from the white desktop.

The class trickled in slowly. The instructor began the roll call, and Mike's name was called last, as always, and like always he took its alphabetical placement personally.

✳ ✳ ✳

Not far from Landon University, Captain Graham Lattimer pulled into the driveway of Pops and Gertie Dickey's humble farm. It was a tricky maneuver, what with the staggered position of three vans and an assortment of pickup trucks. He could see at least one camera crew standing in the dirt in front of the front porch. Several people held up video cameras and recording devices of various kinds to two figures atop the porch like they were presenting flowers to players on a stage. One fellow on the porch was a thin old man in overalls, and the other fellow belonged to Graham.

"P-e-t-r-i-e," Officer Petrie instructed the press as Graham approached. They gazed at the young man intently, and he was beaming.

One reporter turned to Graham as he wedged his way into the crowd and ascended the porch steps. "Are you the chief?"

Graham ignored him and positioned himself nose to nose with Petrie. "Nobody authorized this powwow," he said.

"Uh, sir, I," was all Petrie could muster. Graham grasped him firmly by the elbow, spun him in an about-face, and entered the Dickeys' home through the screen door, leaving the farmer to field inquiries alone.

Graham barked, "What do you think you're doing?"

"Captain, I didn't expect all this."

"What did you expect? You blabbed on a public frequency about UFOs and sheesh. You know how many bored weirdos we got out here."

"Cap, they just showed up and started askin' questions. I just thought someone should answer 'em."

"What did you tell them?"

"Well, nothing, really. They just got here. Just a few minutes before you did. I only got as far as my name."

"Good."

"Pops is still out there, Cap. Should I bring him in?"

"No. It's his house. I can't keep him from talkin' to nobody at his house." He paused to listen. He couldn't hear what Pops was saying outside, but he feared the worst. "Now, what's this all about, Sam?"

"The cow, sir. Like I told you, Doc Driscoll looked at the cut and all."

"Doc Driscoll? Who's he?"

"A vet."

"A vet? What's with the"—he lowered his voice—"UFO stuff?"

"He reads about it in books."

"Sheesh."

"Granted, sir, he's no certified expert or nothin'."

"He's a certified *somethin'*, tell you what."

"Granted, but he looked real good at that cut. He said nothing on earth made that cut."

"Least nothin' on earth he's seen." Graham could hear Pops out on the porch say something about aliens. "We gotta get the old man in here."

* * *

As Mike Walsh's cultural anthropology class made its way down one of the Smith Building's many hallways to the resource center, his phone began to vibrate. He'd had the forethought to turn off the ringer. As he guessed, it was work. He hated to abandon the trip to the center on his first day, especially since he was positive he would be unable to find it later on his own, but he was only there by his boss's orders to begin with. If boss calls, boss gets called back. Finding a quiet corner, he called the number.

"*Spotlight Magazine*, this is Robbie Jensen's office," came the answer.

"Tina, this is Mike."

"Sure, Mike, hold on a second." Then, her voice laced with sarcasm, she added, "You're gonna love this."

A classical concerto filled the earpiece for approximately seven seconds.

"Mike. This is Robbie."

"Yeah?"

"Look, something just came up. A story not far from you."

"You realize I'm right in the middle of a college class *you* sent me to. You realize that, don't you?"

"Yeah, sorry about that, but forget the class." For the first time in a long while, Mike Walsh was genuinely happy. His editor continued, "I want you to head out to Trumbull."

"What for?"

"You're not gonna believe this, but some Trumbull cop just radioed in a report of alien mutilation."

"Come again?"

"Alien mutilation. Some old farmer … I got his name right here. Lucas Dickey. Twenty-four Trace Road in Trumbull. You know where that's at?"

"Whoa, slow down. What'd you say?"

"You heard me. Alien mutilation."

"You gotta be kidding me. What are we, *The Star*? TMZ?"

Robbie laughed. "Don't joke; they'll probably be there."

"This is all kinds of stupid."

"Yeah, but it's all kinds of cool, too. Twenty-four Trace Road, okay? Get on down there. I want this story."

"A story on aliens. In Trumbull."

"Mike, I'm not joking, dude." Robbie's voice hinted at annoyance, but then again, he always seemed annoyed. "We're a special-interest magazine, and this is definitely special interest. Right in our own backyard. Move it."

"Okay," Mike replied, though his disbelief remained. He managed to say, "And forget about the class?"

"What? Oh … yeah, forget about it for today."

Now Mike was unhappy all over again. He ended the call without saying good-bye and retrieved his gloves from his oversized winter coat. The drive to Trumbull would not be very long, but the heater in his car was a poor performer.

✳ ✳ ✳

Graham left Officer Petrie in the Dickeys' quaint country living room and went to steal Pops away from the horde of reporters. He found them not standing in front of the porch as before but moving in one large group toward the old man's barn. The old man himself led the way, talking all the while. Graham ran. He covered ground quickly and came up on them in time to invade their circle and get close to Pops.

He spoke in the farmer's ear. "Excuse me, Mr. Dickey, but could you come answer some questions for us?"

"Right now?" Pops asked. He wasn't looking at Graham but at his audience.

"Yes, sir. We'd really appreciate it." And then, to reassure the man, "Then you can talk to these people all you want."

Pops seemed to want to talk to all these people now, but he relented. "Okay."

Graham escorted him back to the house, amateur reporters in tow, all asking questions. He ignored them and held open the creaky door for Pops, let him enter, and then turned to face the crowd himself.

"Okay, you people. Just hold on to your horses and whatnot. Mr. Dickey'll be back out, and you can ask all your questions soon enough."

"It's a cover-up!" one man called out.

Graham gave him a look that said, *Die. Right now, just fall over.*

"Could we have your name, sir?" another person asked.

"Captain Graham Lattimer of Trumbull Police."

A young guy with his phone held aloft to record video pressed forward. "Captain, was this the work of a *chupacabra*?" He was laughing as he spoke.

"What?" Graham had no idea what the man was saying. "Nobody's chupin' anything, the heck that means," he answered. "That's all." He stepped into the house, leaving the reporters behind him.

Gertie Dickey was handing Officer Petrie a basket of corn bread. Pops was perched on the edge of an easy chair, leaning forward, peering toward the screen door, probably to make sure that the reporters weren't leaving.

"They'll stick around," Graham assured Pops. He turned to Petrie. "Did you get ahold of that vet of yours?"

"Yes, sir. He's on his way back."

"Good."

Gertie Dickey extended her basket to Graham. "Would you like some corn bread, Captain Lattimer?"

"No, thank you, ma'am. I'd appreciate some aspirin if you got it, though."

* * *

By the time Mike Walsh arrived at the Dickey farm, his beige import was one of just four vehicles in the driveway. One was a rusted pickup, and the other two were Trumbull police cruisers. Mike removed a small recorder from the glove compartment and walked to the front door. It was open, leaving only a screen door through which he saw four men seated. They saw him before he could knock.

"Ship has sailed," admonished a man wearing a police uniform. He was the older of two officers in the room and bore the put-upon countenance of one in charge.

"Excuse me?" said Mike.

"Everybody's already gone. You're a little late."

"Sorry." But he wasn't. He was irked by the officer's tone. "My name's Mike Walsh. I'm from *Spotlight Magazine.* Do you mind if I come in?"

"Yes," the older cop said. "Interviews are over."

"You know, I just drove from Houston. I have a right to ask some questions."

"I don't care if you drove from Baton Rouge or the Bay of Pigs. We're asking the questions right now, and you'll have to wait."

Mike pondered the officer. He looked like he'd slept in his uniform. The cop's brow seemed permanently furrowed, the creases deep crevices of stress, the brown thicket of his eyebrows contorted into Spanish tildes. He gave the impression of a walking migraine.

"I can wait," Mike said. "I've got nothing but time."

The cop pursed his lips like he wanted to spit and held Mike's gaze.

Mike looked down. Calling through the screen door was comfortable enough. It held the impression of a barrier. But now he felt sure this policeman would gladly push it open onto his face.

The cop shook his head and muttered, "Sheesh."

An old man in overalls piped up. "Come back later," he said.

Mike scrutinized the four of them. The younger police officer and the fourth man, a middle-aged fellow in a collared golf shirt tucked into khakis, seemed embarrassed to be there. Mike remembered he didn't want to be there himself.

"Whatever you say," he said, and he left.

* * *

Inside the Dickey home, the four men resumed their conversation. Still seated in his green upholstered easy chair, Pops spent most of it listening. So did Sam Petrie, slumped in a wooden dinner chair, looking scolded and worn. The bulk of the exchange took place between the captain and Dr. Lewis Driscoll, a local veterinarian.

"So, tell me, Doc," Graham began, "what leads you to believe aliens were involved in the death of Mr. Dickey's cow?"

"Well, let me tell you. That cut was so even, so perfect. No ragged edges. Nothin'. And it looked a little burnt. The cut was small. Real small. And too small to remove the organs through it."

"How do you know the organs are missing?"

"I examined it."

"You cut it open?"

"Yes."

"I see." Graham was dumbfounded. He was certain an alien hadn't killed Pops Dickey's cow, but he couldn't explain how organs were missing when the wound to the animal was too small to have been their exit point. There would be no way to further examine the animal, though, now that Driscoll had widened the original puncture.

Doc Driscoll continued, "The amount of blood was unusual as well. There was an uncommonly small amount of blood inside the animal, like it had been drained. But there was hardly any blood on the ground."

"Soaked it up."

"I don't think so, Mr. Lattimer. The ground's practically frozen. It couldn't soak it up. If anything, it would've frozen it."

"Maybe animals, then. Maybe raccoons or something drank it up."

"Maybe, but animals don't usually come out after blood. They may come out for the internals, you know, but not for blood. They'd get into Mr. Dickey's trash before they'd get into animal remains."

Driscoll began a rather compelling argument, explaining to those in the Dickeys' living room how he had started out interested in UFOs as a hobby but eventually became a serious researcher. He'd read all the books and articles, seen convincing film footage, and even attended a few seminars on the subject when they came to Houston. He was a believer.

An hour later, the two police officers walked to their cars together.

Petrie spoke. "What do you think, Cap?"

Lattimer stopped. "I think that man's fruity."

And that was that.

* * *

The sun idled into the horizon, putting itself to sleep, casting a kaleidoscope of ambers and oranges and violets onto the lower evening sky, the fireworks of day's end.

Mike sat in a flimsy lawn chair on the roof of his parents' house, admiring the view. He was spending more and more time at his old homestead, finding the familiarity comforting when he could take his mind off of Molly. He sipped sweet iced tea from a plastic Houston Astros cup his dad had gotten at a home game with a five-dollar soda. It had been an interesting day. A day complete with first-day-of-school jitters (at age thirty-six, no less!) and mad dashes for a story on aliens from outer space. He chuckled. He pictured the headline: E.T. KILLS A COW. He chuckled again and poured some tea down his throat. His teeth ached, and he wondered why he was drinking iced tea on a freezing winter night.

The sun drifted down and vaporized, and Mike sat alone in the darkness. He gazed at the sky and the few stars that were visible. The landscape of infinity before him, Mike's mind drifted. Mike thought of his life and how empty it had become since Molly left. The last year was an eternity. Eyes fixed on the firmament above him, he mentally connected the dots, creating his own constellations, and dreamed of his wife. He remembered lying with her on the cold roof of their Colorado cabin on the first night of their honeymoon. They watched the stars. The night sky outside Colorado Springs was an infinite panorama. Endless space and endless time. Molly reached out and clasped his hand, and they felt so close to heaven and so close to each other. A light snow began to drizzle down, so they cuddled.

Their love felt primeval, primordial. Love did not seem to exist anywhere but between the two of them. And yet in the gnaw of this memory for Mike, in the draining flood of many memories, many aches, buried in the endless onslaught of moments both precious and regrettable, he could see the germination of his possessiveness and thus his inevitable neglect. He'd made an idol of his wife, and she'd withered under the weight. We always neglect the gods we presume to possess. Now he was sure he'd fallen from grace.

Time flew.

When Mike began to shiver, he tossed the chair into the back lawn and shimmied down the ladder. He left a "thank you for dinner" note for his mother, who had long since turned in, and had started for the door when his father's gun cabinet caught his eye.

As a kid, Mike had spent countless hours staring into the cabinet at his father's weapons. He'd always wanted to touch them, to cradle them in his hand, to somehow soak up their power through his skin, but he never did. They were forbidden fruit. He did not have the kind of father who wanted to pass on the interest to his boy. The cabinet stayed locked, his father's hobby a solitary pursuit. He often warned Mike about the dangers of firearms. "The only time a policeman draws a gun is when he intends to take a life, and that's what guns do, Mikey," he said. "They take lives. Guns make death. Don't ever forget that." Mike never forgot. Even before he saw a dead body in the river by his home, he had seen death in his father's gun cabinet.

He peered into the cabinet, much like he had as a child, eyes wide and mind racing. He wanted to hold one of the guns. He threw a guilty glance over his shoulder to his parents' bedroom. They slept soundly. He could hear the drone of his father's snoring. Mike tried the latch to the cabinet and found it unlocked.

Of course. No kids to worry about anymore.

The hinges on the cabinet door squealed. Mike tensed. Immediately he was angry that he should be thirty-six and scared, ashamed to hold a piece of a collection his father had begun when he was much younger.

He opened the door further, but slower this time, and winced, waiting for it to creak again. It didn't, and the opening of the door felt like the opening of a tomb. The smells of oil and leather and metal wafted out. Tentatively, he reached out and touched one of the pistols. Its sleek silver looked like it would feel hot and slippery, but it was hard, dry, and cold. He slipped his hand around the gun's grip and lifted it from the cabinet, plucking the fruit from the forbidden tree. He read the words on its side: LLAMA 45. He wanted to look down the barrel but could not bring himself to do it, to peer into its death eye. The gun sat heavy in his hand, and he admired it. He assumed it was loaded, and he pushed it carefully into his inside coat pocket.

He closed the cabinet and walked to his car. The lump in his coat pocket swung against him on each step, and he felt strangely powerful, inflated, delirious.

✳ ✳ ✳

Arms outstretched, tense and taut, a man sat alone in the dark room. All lights were extinguished. A candle, lit an hour before, had gone out. Despite the below-freezing temperature outside, the man wore nothing but his underwear. The circulation had long ago left his legs, the tingling of limbs asleep long passed. Now, his legs simply did not exist. The organ of life pulsed strong within his chest and seemed to hammer against his rib cage with every beat. Loud. He could hear it, but not like the people who say they hear their heart beating, when they really mean they *feel* it beating. He heard its *sound*. It was a bass drum steadily pounding on, like the rhythm kept by the man who conducts the rowing of a slave ship. And deep in the bowels of the ship, he drummed faster to produce his desired effect: to speed up the rowing. To speed up time itself. Breaths came short but quick, keeping time with his heart. He sweated profusely. Eyes wide open, bulging out and quivering every which way for a sign, adjusting to the blackness, seeing through it. All was eerily still, with the room draped in the quiet that accompanies darkness, a quiet that is a sound all its own. A silence so stark it *hums*. Dark, dark, all was dark ...

And then the abyss crept in.

✳ ✳ ✳

Morning came, and the sun brought no warmth with its reappearance. Temperatures were in the low twenties, and the overnight forecast called for the middle teens. But for the first time in weeks, a weather-related story did not make the top headline.

"Have you seen this?" asked Robbie Jensen, *Spotlight Magazine*'s editor in chief. He was a short, skinny, balding, bespectacled man. He was perpetually on edge, and he further fueled this with an always-present and always-full coffee mug clutched in his left hand.

"What?" Mike asked. He had just arrived and had not even sat down.

Robbie held the morning paper's Lifestyle section. The headline read, CLOSE ENCOUNTER IN TRUMBULL.

"Is this for real?" Mike asked primarily to himself. He took the paper. "They could've at least tacked a question mark on the end to add some speculation."

"Read it. You'd think I bought it in the grocery-store checkout line."

Mike scanned the article. It gave the entire what's what and who's who. Pops Dickey. Sam Petrie. Lewis Driscoll. Police Captain Graham Lattimer (whose only statement was his name). In full color, to the right of the piece, was a photograph of Pops, Officer Petrie, and the dead cow. The caption stated, FARM OWNER "POPS" DICKEY AND TRUMBULL POLICE OFFICER SAM PETRIE WITH THE ALLEGED VICTIM OF EXTRATERRESTRIAL VANDALISM.

Hmm. At least they wrote "alleged."

Mike looked at Robbie blankly.

"You got this, right, Mike? You never called me back. Did you get it?"

"No. Everybody was gone when I got there. I got lost, and then the sheriff or somebody told me to leave."

All Robbie could say was, "Oh, man."

"Robbie, by the time we print anything, this'll be old news. We're a monthly mag, you know. In two weeks, Goober the idiot neighbor will fess up. You know how this works. 'It was just a pie tray hanging from fish line.'" Mike acted it out with his fingers. "Et cetera."

"Yeah. Maybe." Robbie seemed to calm down.

Mike said, "I'm saving your life here, man. We woulda looked like morons."

"Right," said Robbie. "Okay, look. We can get the basics from the stuff already in print, but I want you to do a UFO story for next issue. Special Report: UFO Phenomenon, or whatever. Okay?"

"You're killing me."

"It's special interest. Interest that is special. Suck it up. It's not like I'm asking you to find Bigfoot or something. Treat 'em like morons, I don't care. I just want to see the story. Yes?"

"Yeah," Mike said. "Okay."

It was a story. He began telling himself it might even be interesting. As a child, he was one of the many who read H. G. Wells and Ray Bradbury and thought, *Maybe ...*

Science fiction or not, it was work, and, really, it was all he had left.

✳ ✳ ✳

The Landon University library was hidden among the many buildings on campus. After numerous wrong turns, two slips on the icy
sidewalk, and a few curse words, Mike discovered it nestled in its
own section of forest on the west end. It was identical in structure
to every other building at the college, and Mike wondered about the
lack of architectural creativity. Its only distinguishing characteristic
was the black letters, too small to read from the main sidewalk, that
announced, LANDON LIBRARY AND RESOURCE CENTER.
The inside was just as drab as the outside. All the shelves were metal,
and no art hung on the walls, only school-related posters and flyers.
One announced the theater department's latest production of *Our
Town*. Another invited all young Democrats to an organizational
meeting. Others were for various clubs, seminars, or classes. No
sculptures. No paintings.

He was surprised to find that Landon Library possessed a vast selec-
tion of offerings on UFOs, aliens, space travel, and the like. He noted
that they rested between books on cryptozoology and books on the
occult and witchcraft. *Interesting.*

He laid a few titles on a table in a neat stack: *The Roswell Incident*,
In Search of UFOs, a few standard texts by Whitley Strieber, *Alien
Impact* by Michael Craft, as well as numerous books on sightings and
abductions. He recognized the name of Erich von Däniken, author
of *Chariots of the Gods*, *Gods from Outer Space*, and *The Gold of the
Gods*. He searched indices for references to animal mutilation and
found information only in Craft's book. He skimmed and perused.
After a few hours of mind-numbing reading, he replaced the books
and, after finding nothing else of interest in the stacks, plunged into
the periodicals subject catalog. He found a few articles on so-called
close encounters, mysterious animal mutilations (these usually

came hand in hand with stories of crop circles), and a relatively new trend in mutilation reports, the *chupacabra*, roughly translated from Spanish as "the goatsucker."

The whole thing was utterly ridiculous. The photographs were blurry and completely ambiguous. *Pie trays on fishing line*, he thought as he looked at the grainy purported photos of UFOs. No real pictures of the *chupacabras* existed either, just crude sketches directed by alleged witnesses. On the Internet, there were countless grainy photos and videos and skeletal remains, most identified as coyotes with mange and the like.

Mike read for hours, beginning a process of fast-track education on the subject. He paused to look at his watch when his stomach growled. Half past two and time for lunch. He checked out two books to glance over at mealtime and returned them within the hour. He found his table still unoccupied, and he sat down to read some more. When he felt he'd exhausted all the academic offerings, he opened his laptop and began throwing key words into Google. Within the pages and pages of crazed ruminations documented in large fonts, all caps, and eye-scorching neons, he found only a few articles of interest, mostly from skeptics. The true believers' integrity was impugned by their incompetent design skills and lack of Internet savvy. But hours consuming hopeless videos and blog posts were hours he had not spent maddeningly clicking "Check Mail" in his email program, as if each next click would summon a message from her.

✳ ✳ ✳

The clock alarm did not sound. If Mike skipped a shower and breakfast, he might make it to class on time. He was determined to do this since he had abandoned it halfway through his first day. He dressed speedily, grabbed his computer bag, remembering to put his borrowed library articles in it, and ran out the door. The ice on his windshield was thick. After turning the defrost on, he chipped frantically with a plastic ice scraper, a cheap giveaway from the insurance company. It was slow going, so he retreated to the house and emerged with a bowl of hot water, which he poured over the glass, hoping it wouldn't crack. The ice fell away, and the windshield escaped unscathed. He discarded the bowl in his backseat and revved the engine. It clanked mysteriously. As always, Mike became flush with nervousness, but he pulled into the university parking lot on time, ran frantically to the Smith Building, and seated himself in his desk with two minutes to spare.

It was the professor's first lecture. The man had seemed amiable enough on the first day of class, going over the syllabus and sending the class down to the resource center to begin the first exploratory stage in the papers that would become their final exam, but as Mike had been drawn away then by Robbie's call, he hadn't the chance to see the man in professorial action. He was a whirlwind of information. He was going on and on about the evolution of morality from culture to culture, spanning continents and centuries, summoning an electric winsomeness as if from the ether. He used no notes. He made none on the whiteboard. Nobody dared interrupt him with a question.

"What we are seeking—and by 'we' I mean you—is gnosis. Special knowledge from the heavens. And by the heavens, I mean the nether regions of the universe, that point of original origination. The celestial crater that marks the big bang. Whatever constellation is made up by the stardust in your bones, people, whatever your DNA is silently summoning you to recognize, is the secret world unlocking all the secret worlds. If you want to know where mankind is going, you've got to trace it back, all the way back-back-back, to where it's been."

Mike was sure as anything that nobody, including himself, had the slightest clue what the man was talking about, but he was just as sure they were all enjoying it. One young lady surreptitiously pulled out her phone and snapped a photo of the prof mid-gesticulation, undoubtedly destined for some quippy Instagram post.

At the end of the class, Mike jotted down the homework reading assignment in a little notepad. He also scribbled the title of the textbook he had yet to purchase. He set out for the library.

The Landon Library and Research Center was bustling with activity. At each photocopy machine, long lines formed and were continuously dissected by students frantically darting here and there. *Semester's first research paper*, he assumed. He hoped he could find an open table. He did not look forward to sharing space with giggling, note-passing, gum-smacking college students. He discovered a table with a lone occupant. A young man in a high school letter jacket pored over a sports magazine. His lips mouthed the text as he read. Mike lay his computer bag down to secure his seat and went to return the articles he had borrowed the day before. On his way back, he hunted through the catalogs and found some more. At the table, he finished entire volumes of *Science Fact or Fiction?*, *UFO Hunter*, *Roswell Scrapbook*, and *Space Digest* before his companion at the table had finished an article on arena football.

Mike began to notice something. The more he read, the more it all sounded the same. There was nothing new. In a matter of two days, he had really completed his fast-track education on the subject of UFOs. Sure, there were new stories to hear with new eyewitnesses and new twists, but generally they were the same stories, only with different people and different places. They usually concluded with harassment by government agents. These stories eventually led to the UFO folklore of mysterious men in black who arrive unannounced and pressure witnesses into silence. Mike decided he had seen it all.

He rose, maneuvered his way through a seemingly endless mass of aimless collegiates to find a quiet space to use his phone and called Robbie.

"Look, I think I've run into a rut here with this story."

"You're such a baby," Robbie said. "I knew you'd do this again, you big baby."

"Man, I've read all there is to read. All these stories sound exactly alike, and I'm getting tired of reading the same story over and over again."

"*You* are, but the public ain't. While you're wasting time reading, the story is passing you by. Did you know Pops Dickey was on the *Today Show* this morning?"

"The NBC *Today Show?*"

"Is there another one?"

"I didn't see it."

"And the Chronicle is still running stories. Pops ain't gonna make the *New York Times* or anything, but our little Trumbull farmer is reaching for the stars Honey Boo-Boo style, bro. Time to get with the program. Are you listening to me?"

"I'm listening," Mike said.

"Look, I don't care what you write. Just do a brief history of UFOs or something. We'll tack on this dead cow story to the beginning to make it current. But people are eatin' this up, man. Let's just give the public what they want. Journalism shmournalism. We are in the business of selling magazines, right?"

"Yeah, okay. I can do that."

"Hey, maybe you can get back out there and get some interviews."

"Yeah, sure."

Mike hung up the phone and returned to the table to discover his computer bag on the floor, leaning against a table leg. Three girls were seated, and the young sports fan was no longer interested in arena football. Mike picked up his bag and removed his research from its place on the table under the nose of a gawking college girl. If she noticed, she gave no indication.

* * *

Night. Another cold one. Just as predicted, the temperature hovered in the middle teens. Wearing an old blue sweat suit and a quilt wrapped around him like a superhero's cape, Mike Walsh stared into his laptop and worked on his article. Across the room, Miles Davis wailed from the stereo. The article was coming along slowly. Maybe he wasn't such an expert after all. He decided on one more jaunt to the Landon Library. Maybe he'd missed something.

FROM "LIGHTS OVER TULSA" BY SID BENTLEY IN *UFO HUNTER* MAGAZINE:

> To this date, no serious investigation has been conducted by any government or official organization. The truth, it seems, will remain hidden in Darla Belford's hazy videotape and the many still pictures taken by amateur photographers. What are these lights? Experts have testified that they are moving

in patterns contradictory to known laws of physics. Are residents of Tulsa being visited by extraterrestrials or top-secret military aircraft? The evidence is overwhelming. Something is happening ...

* * *

The phone's ring woke Mike from a deep sleep. He was in the middle of a dream about Molly. His clock read 8:00 a.m. Rising from the womb of comforters and quilts, he set his bare feet on his cold bedroom floor. The shock was enough to launch the drowsiness clear from his head. Within three rings, he answered the phone and muttered, "Hello."

"Mike?"

One word. One single word, and it was his name. The voice was so familiar, and his body filled with longing in one glorious instant. Wide awake now, hoping against delusion, he ventured, "Molly?"

"Yeah, it's me. Listen ..."

His dream became sweet and real.

"... I'm going to be in Houston today. Vickie's showing some of her paintings, and I was wondering if maybe we could have lunch or something."

Shocked. Overjoyed. "Sure, sure. What time?"

"Well, we're leaving in just a minute, and we should be there no later than noon, wouldn't you think?"

"Yeah, it shouldn't take you much more than four hours, if that."

"Okay, so we'll be there around noon, I guess. Vickie's going on to the gallery, but I won't have to be there till three or so. Could we do it before then?"

"Sure, yeah. Do you have my cell number?"

"Is it still the same?"

"Yeah."

"Yeah, I've got it. I'll just call you, then."

"Sure. Just call me, and I'll come right from work or wherever I am." He would. He would drive his little beige import as fast as it would go to get wherever she was.

"Okay. I'll see you later, then."

"Okay. Bye."

"Bye."

He hung up. His body throbbed with exhilaration. A lunch. He had lived a year without her, without even seeing her (*barely even spoke to her*, he thought), and now she would be here within four hours. A lunch. This could be his chance. A window of opportunity. He could get her back!

He looked at his clock. Eight-o-four. *Time enough to even get some work done*, he thought. He bundled up and started the drive north to Trumbull.

✳ ✳ ✳

Not for a lack of pounding, no one answered the Dickeys' front door. Mike decided to drive to the police station.

The Trumbull Police Department's building on Highway 2920 was neither small nor large, but adequate. Mike entered feeling a bit nervous. He recalled being told to leave by one of their officers at the Dickeys' farm the day Pops found his cow lying behind his barn, allegedly attacked by beings from outer space. He approached the front desk.

"Excuse me, but could you tell me where I could find Officer Sam Petrie?"

The man looked up at him. "You a reporter?"

"Uh ... yeah." He didn't know if this would get him in or out.

"Hold on a sec." The man called out behind him. "Kelly, get Captain Lattimer, would you, please?"

Mike could see a woman in the back respond by picking up her telephone and speaking into it.

✳ ✳ ✳

Kelly's voice came into Lattimer's office. "Captain? The front desk is asking for you."

"Sheesh," Graham responded. He walked to the front and confronted the reporter.

"Sam Petrie?" asked the man.

"No. Who are you?"

"Mike Walsh. I work for *Spotlight Magazine*."

"Never heard of it."

"Well, all right. Anyways—"

"Petrie ain't here. He's got leave. Probably starting his world tour or something."

"Is there someone I could speak to?"

Graham hesitated. He knew what Mike wanted to talk about. Things were fairly slow right now. No *real* crimes. Trumbull had been pretty peaceful in that sense.

"You from one of those *tacky* magazines?" Graham asked.

"I really don't think so, no."

"All right. I guess you can come on back."

The two men retreated to Graham's office, the policeman leading the reporter. Once inside, the former sat behind his desk and the latter sat on a faux leather couch.

"I'm one of the captains—Graham Lattimer."

"Nice to meet you."

"Hold on just a second." He pressed his intercom button. "Kelly? Got any aspirin?" He released it and returned his attention to Mike. "*Spotlight*? What kind of paper is that?"

"It's a special-interest magazine. Kinda like *People*, only not as popular. And not just about people. We tell true stories we think people will want to read."

Graham laughed. "True stories."

"Yeah. Could I ask you a few questions?"

"I'm sure you could."

"Well, I was kinda wondering about Mr. Dickey's UFO sighting."

"Load of bull."

"Pardon me?"

"That's a load of bull. At least, I'm pretty sure it is. All we got was a call from the man asking to file a report about his cow. Found her dead. Cut open behind his barn. He wasn't even in a rush or anything. Even said that. 'No big deal,' or something to that effect. One of my guys goes out there on his way home ..."

"That's Petrie?"

"... Right. Petrie. Well, he looks at it and gets the idea to call a vet out. See, what no one's getting from this, Mike, is that neither Pops nor Petrie had any inclination of believing aliens killed that animal. This vet shows up—name's Lewis Driscoll—and he declares without a doubt that poor Elsie was the victim of alien mutilation." Graham rolled his eyes.

"I take it you disagree?"

"You bet. Quote me on that, too. Doc Driscoll—he might be a good vet an' all; I'd probably take my dachshund to him—but where he gets the idea he's some kinda alien expert, I don't know."

"So Pops's claims of seeing an actual UFO …"

"Shoot, he and the wife are down in California right now for some TV show. You see where this is going?"

"Sure."

"Yeah. He's gonna give some press conference sometime here in Houston. Petrie will probably be there. Doc Driscoll, too. What you gotta realize is that there isn't any forensic protocol for this kinda thing. Shoot, Driscoll made his own cut in the animal before any expert investigation took place. And the whole lot of 'em—Pops, Petrie, and Driscoll—done rolled her all around. Anything they coulda done to destroy any evidence, they did. Whatever killed that man's cow is still unidentified, but take it from me: it wasn't no alien."

"Okay."

"Like I said, quote me on that, if you want."

The encounter ranked as one of Mike Walsh's shortest interviews ever, but he believed he gained a great understanding of the people involved. A naive cop. An old farmer eager for his fifteen minutes. A veterinarian whose obsession clouded his better judgment.

FROM "UFO IN TEXAS" BY JOHN JORDAN IN *NEWSDAY*:

> The deceased bovine, allegedly the victim of alien mutilation, was secured yesterday by forensic experts, as well as authorities in various fields of

biology and a handful of investigators popularly known as ufologists. Inspection is underway, but the verdict is still out. Meanwhile, the animal's owner, Lucas "Pops" Dickey, is scheduled to appear on the syndicated television show *Encounters*. In the near future, however, the case's best evidence will reveal what really happened, and Mr. Dickey's story may secure its place in history as one of America's more obscure hoaxes. Only time will tell ...

✳ ✳ ✳

A cacophony of murmurs and whispers, shuffling feet, and rustling pages filled Landon Library. Mike Walsh was back among the university youth, studying books on the subject at hand. This time, however, he didn't look for the standard fare. He found *Studies in UFO Mythology*; *Dreams, Visions, and Paranoia*; *UFOs in Hypnosis*; and other works considered extraordinarily speculative even by ufologists. The authors' views were unorthodox in that they attributed the UFO phenomenon to anything and everything *but* visitors from outer space. Much of it was psychology or analysis of mass hysteria or exposure of organized trickery. Spread open before him lay a particularly interesting volume alleging that UFOs were physical manifestations of a witness's subconscious desire acting out through unwilled telekinesis. He studied it intently. He was startled when a voice interrupted his pursuit.

"Chariots of fire, eh?"

Mike looked up. It was his professor. *Am I supposed to be in class?*

"I've read that one. It's decent," the professor noted.

"Yeah," Mike said, and then he added apathetically, "It's very interesting."

The professor's face tilted. "Aren't you in one of my classes?"

"Yes, sir. Cultural Anthropology. Mid-semester."

"Right, right. You sit in the front row."

"Right."

"I'm sorry. Please excuse my short memory, but these mid-semester classes always seem to get lost among my regular classes. I have a lot of students. Could you tell me your name?"

"Mike Walsh." He shook the professor's hand.

"Pleased to meet you, Mike. I'm Dr. Bering. I'm a bit of an ufologist myself, actually."

"You're kidding."

"I never kid. Bad for the chakras."

"Yes, definitely," Mike said, although he didn't know what chakras were. "Well, I'd love to get your take on this stuff."

"My take's been published, Mike, believe it or not. Some of my work is in the library. Would you like me to find some pieces for you?"

Before Mike could answer in the affirmative, Dr. Bering disappeared into the periodicals section, returning shortly with an article in hand.

"Here you go, chum. This should start you off properly."

Dr. Bering laid the photocopied article, "Aliens from This World," on the table.

"Thank you much, Professor."

"Not a problem. If you don't mind … why the interest?"

"Well, I'm a writer, and I'm doing a piece on the Trumbull story. Well, partly that and partly a history of UFOs."

"Well, if you'd like, I wouldn't mind discussing the matter with you. Are you free?"

"Sure …" But then he remembered. "Uh, well, actually no. I'm supposed to have lunch with my wife sometime soon. I *would* like to meet with you, though."

"Of course."

* * *

Twelve twenty-two in the afternoon. Mike pointed his car on the freeway toward downtown Houston. Molly paged him at twelve-o-six. He headed to Lily's Grill, their meeting place. He felt nervous, like a boy on his first date. The sheer anticipation of seeing her again caused sweat to bead on his brow. He struggled to remove his jacket and maintain control of the car. The bank sign gave the temperature at thirty-four degrees, but Mike was burning up. Off came his gloves.

Lily's was a popular place, and finding a parking space proved a challenging task. He hurried inside and found her waiting for him. She was beautiful.

"Hi."

"Hi."

He hugged her, but not tightly. He felt unsure of himself and was determined not to foul things up.

CHAPTER FOUR

The temperature began dropping around four o'clock in the afternoon. The big city was not accustomed to such a period of winter, especially so early in the season. Houston had its share of freezes. It had even snowed once or twice in recent history, though not usually the kind that stayed on the ground. Just little flakes that floated down and disappeared at foot level. Everyone kept busy remarking about the unique nature of this cold spell.

The pastor remarked too. Four days, and the church had been without heat. The maintenance crew was unequipped and unskilled, and the budget was tight. The church couldn't muster funds for repair. The pastor, hunched in his study, decided that they'd have to take a special offering during Sunday's service. *At the end*, he thought. *Let them shiver and shake for an hour or so. Then they'll pay anything to get the dumb thing fixed.* He smiled to himself, but then wondered if his strategy would constitute manipulation of the congregation. *No, just skillful shepherding.* He smiled again. On his huge oak desk lay his sermon outline for the upcoming service, and he gave it scant attention. He gazed outside, through his window, at the sky. Time had moved so fast for him. Four years of college. Three years of seminary. Seven more in various churches in several Southern states. And then, two years ago, he had answered a Houston church's invitation and brought his wife. Sixteen years, and it was a blur.

He thought back to the beginning of those sixteen years. Recently licensed for ministry by his home church in Louisiana, he began his freshman year of college. From there, the only direction was up. He never looked down.

Outside, two boys were performing death-defying stunts using skateboards and the parking barriers in the church's front lot. They laughed and punched each other, falling down only to get back up and try some other daredevil trick. Pastor Steve Woodbridge watched as they flew. They never rose more than two feet off the ground, but they were flying. Arms out like tightrope walkers. Baggy shirts waving in the wind. All smiles and skinned knees. He watched … and wished. Then came reality.

* * *

Each day after his lunch with Molly ended with a restless night. His brief bouts of unconsciousness were hard-won and occupied with vague nightmares, memories of which he could not summon in the daylight. The weekend was a blur of television and beer and the dark rising tide of depression. Monday he skipped work. But Tuesday he went to school.

Class seemed more satisfying than before, perhaps due to his library encounter with Dr. Bering, and when it was over, the professor approached.

"Mr. Walsh. Time today? Care to chat?"

Dr. Bering's office was surprisingly large and surrounded with bookshelves, achieving a pleasing symmetry with a mahogany desk at the end opposite the door, a desktop computer on a credenza behind it, and two plush wingback chairs for visitors in the center. Mike scanned the spines of the books nearest the door. He recognized many of the same authors he'd encountered in Landon's paranormal selections and counted twelve written by Dr. Bering himself, when the professor interrupted:

"Please, make yourself comfortable."

Mike did, planting himself in one of the wingbacks.

Bering sat in a rolling leather chair behind his desk and crossed his legs. Propping an elbow on the arm of the chair and leaning his chin on his fist, he said, "Well. What would you like to know?"

"Well, UFOs, I guess," Mike said.

"Right, right. And did you read my article?"

Caught. Mike responded sheepishly, "Um, well … no, I didn't get a chance to." A lie. He'd had plenty of time. He just hadn't read it.

"Oh, well, I understand that." Dr. Bering leaned back in his desk chair. "I guess I should begin by saying that flying saucers from outer space are one hundred percent bunk."

"Sounds about right."

"Right, right. I know exactly what you're thinking. And I'll tell you, I've read every book that matters, even written a few of my own. I've talked to witnesses, and I've seen government documents and videos and photos and radar readings, both classified and public. They're all very interesting *and* amusing to me, but what it all adds up to is not the popular conclusion."

"And that is?"

"Crafts from outer space, Mr. Walsh. Little bug-eyed humanoids flying around in disks. Visitors from other planets."

"Are they all lying, then?"

"Not necessarily. Not everybody. But, tell me, Mike, did it ever strike you as funny how the only people who see these things are farmers in the middle of nowhere?"

Mike nodded. Of course it had. Every skeptical mind thought that at one time or another.

Dr. Bering continued. "However, I do believe that some reputable folks are telling the truth."

"What are they seeing?"

"Let's back up a few paces. Maybe I should tell you why I don't believe in them." He leaned back in his chair. "Do you believe in the big bang?"

"I believe in God," Mike said, though not at all with confidence.

"Okay, okay. You believe in God, and that's your right, but can you see how this thing you call God and this event called the big bang could coexist? I mean, one doesn't necessarily cancel out the other. The thing you call God—some designer or force with some intention, conscious or not—could have very well lit the fuse. Are you with me?"

"Yeah, I guess."

"Okay, God or not, those of us who have dedicated ourselves to science, to the pursuit of the origins of our universe, have found this to be the most logical resolution to the problem of beginnings. Follow?"

"Sure."

"Now, even the most devout materialist will admit that what happened in the beginning was a ... well, a long shot. For the explosion to happen at the right place at the right time, and for that explosion to bring about a prototype for life—this planet, I mean—and then, for the atmosphere and ingredients and the catalyst, lightning or what-have-you, to all be in place ... well, the odds of all this are beyond astronomical. The chances of all this happening in one huge cosmic accident are virtually nil. But it did. How can anyone believe it could happen again someplace else? Even in another galaxy across the far reaches of the universe, it exceeds plausibility."

"So you're saying what happened here was so impossible it couldn't have occurred anywhere else."

"Exactly. I'll use the standard argument of intelligent design against this very scenario to illustrate. If you set off a bomb in a junkyard, the result will not be a working automobile. Well, I say it very well might be. It might produce a Rolls Royce, even. Given enough time and enough parallel dimensions, it would certainly happen. And it did happen. But it didn't happen twice."

"But," Mike said, "wouldn't the same logic that says such a thing could happen—given enough time and parallel dimensions—also provide that it could happen more than once?"

"Certainly. That is entirely logical. But it's not very reasonable. And by reasonable, I mean, it's not a very good matching of both logic and the available evidence."

"Then what are people seeing?"

"A multitude of things, I suppose. Queer reflections of earth-based light shimmering in the sky. Airplanes. Experimental military aircraft. Perhaps nothing but illusions, tricks played by the mind. Some, though"—he lowered his voice dramatically—"are *real*."

"But you just said—"

"I know what I said!" Bering smiled big. "Are you hearing me?" He wasn't scolding. He was drawing Mike in.

"I guess not."

"Some are real, Mike. Some are very, very real. And they are aliens. They are aliens from another place."

"Okay, now I really don't think I'm hearing you."

"I don't either. But I'll put it to you plainly. When I say 'aliens,' I don't mean aliens like the kind I've just laid a case for disbelieving. I mean visitors from *this* world."

"You mean people."

"No, not people. Not people like us, anyway. Not human beings." Dr. Bering hesitated, and the look on his face seemed to say, *You probably won't believe this, but* ... "It's not even fair to call them aliens. This is more their home than ours, really. I'm talking, Mike, about beings who travel to our world from within our world."

"What?" Mike asked, simultaneously skeptical and intrigued.

"Another dimension. A world within our own, on this very earth, but invisible and unreachable by us."

Mike fumbled in his computer bag for his pen and notepad. He *had* to write this stuff down. "Okay," he prodded.

"Mike, I believe there is another dimension connected to our own planet, maybe even on it, with beings very similar in most respects to ourselves. Their civilization or world is far more advanced than our own, and they are able to enter our dimension at will. They appear and disappear as they please."

Mike was writing, but his incredulity was showing. "All right."

Bering understood the tone. "Is it really so strange a proposition?"

"I remember watching a Superman cartoon as a kid, where Superman went to prevent a volcano from destroying a village. When he got there, the volcano exploded violently, blowing him into another dimension where everything was backward. At the same time, an evil Superman was blown into this dimension. They spent the whole show trying to switch places and get back."

Dr. Bering looked insulted. He plowed forward. "Interesting. But I'm afraid it's not quite the same concept. I'm not sure how they do it, whether by machine or some other technology, or whether it is an ability intrinsic to their physiology. Some visit in craft. Some in person."

Dumbfounded, Mike remained sitting, bewildered and convinced he was facing an honest-to-goodness quack. The professor said things as preposterous as those said by the people he refuted. "Is there any way to figure out how?" Mike finally asked.

"It's doubtful. This thing is far more advanced than any place we could ever hope to be. I don't think any scientist at the top of his field in quantum mechanics or theoretical physics, or anybody else for that matter, could figure this out. There are only a few scientific principles behind it as far as I know, but all are highly speculative. Have you heard of the Kaluza-Klein theory?"

"No."

"Well, I won't bog you down with details, but it is a scientific theory of hyperspace. Higher dimensions above and beyond our own four-dimensional senses."

Mike wasn't sure what to say. He felt like he'd heard enough. The two looked at each other, each scrutinizing the other's face. The reporter looked for signs of kidding in the professor's eyes. The professor was still smiling, but not coyly, not with a wink. He had the pleasant confidence of the utterly convinced. Mike broke the silence.

"Dr. Bering, I appreciate this very much. Thank you for your time. You've definitely given me a lot to chew on."

Bering's smile broke. "Oh. Well, my pleasure. Stop in any time, friend. And I'll see you in class Thursday."

Mike reflected on his conversation with Dr. Bering during the cold walk to the university parking lot. He deliberated, weighing whether to lend the professor's views any credence. Dr. Bering was an intelligent man, after all, but beyond that, he had the charisma of the most ardent of true believers.

FROM "ALIENS FROM THIS WORLD" BY DR. SAMUEL BERING IN *SCIENCE QUEST*:

> The proposal is that a relationship exists between the sightings of unidentified craft and the divine visions and apparitions witnessed by the devoutly religious around the world. Neither group sees what it thinks it does, but both are seeing *something*. In early California, Paiute Indians shared a traditional tale of an advanced race they called the *Hav-Masuvs*, who floated about in silver "flying canoes." Can these accounts be reconciled? Yes. What is witnessed undoubtedly comes from a dimension apart from our own, but parallel to it …

Captain Graham Lattimer survived a rough Friday. The previous few days had been peaceful enough. The press had mostly managed to steer clear of the police station. They found Sam Petrie at home and asked all the questions they wanted to. Pops Dickey was harder to locate. In person, anyway. If people really wanted to get his story, all they had to do was turn on the television in time for *Encounters* or some other tabloid program. The farmer's story dropped a position in the *Chronicle* every day, but no one sitting in the Trumbull police station would have doubted its popularity. Graham's headaches would not go away, and the persistence of the reporters with their tendency to arrive in great numbers and shout different questions all at once, each trying to drown out the others, only made the pain worse. They showed no satisfaction with his opinion on the matter. Branding Pops a "kooky nutcase" didn't make for good news. Truth be known, most everybody was convinced that Pops was off his rocker, but no one wanted to face the facts. They wanted the centuries-old mystery solved. They wanted to get up in the morning, shuffle out the front door, and pick up the newspaper to read the headline: ALIENS ARE REAL!

Ain't gonna happen, Graham thought. He lay motionless in bed, his temples throbbing intensely, and waited for sleep to come. The pounding in his head was as much noise as it was pain, and he wondered if he would ever doze off. The television flickered in his dark bedroom, the volume muted, of course. The meteorologist announced the forecast for the next day. Another chilly one. The closed captioning was producing unintelligible gibberish along the bottom of the screen. Graham attempted to read the man's lips. He couldn't make any of it out, but the on-screen graphics clued him in. At the end of the forecast, the captioning program suddenly became coherent, and the weatherman's parting words glared at him from the TV screen, white letters against a black background: "Be assured, it's gonna be nasty." Graham clicked the set off with his remote control and removed a worn King James Bible from the nightstand. *Be assured, his mind echoed. It's gonna be nasty.*

None of the *Spotlight Magazine* staff favored late-night meetings, especially on Fridays. Nonetheless, all arrived in the downtown office prepared and on time. Gathered around a long conference table, they each presented their work to Robbie Jensen, editor in chief, and to the staff as a whole, and they all began laying out a schedule of stories for the next several months. The task was long and tedious but six hours later, as Saturday's light began creeping through the office windows, the task was complete. Robbie accompanied Mike out to his car.

"Your piece turned out great, Mike."

"Yep. Thanks."

"Something the matter? You don't look so good."

"You mean besides the fact that we were here all night on a Friday?"

"Yeah. Besides that."

Mike gazed out past his friend. For once, the hurt came through. A wall came down. He felt just short of tears. "I saw Molly last week."

"Oh yeah? That's great. How's she doing?"

"She's doing okay, I guess." He breathed deep. "I messed up pretty bad, Rob. Real bad."

"What do you mean? What'd you do?"

"I freaked. I don't know. I went in totally cool. Just wanted to take it slow, you know. Didn't want to jump right into everything and mess it all up. I just wanted to gauge the situation, you know. Just be a good guy. Not come on too strong."

"And?"

"I screwed up. I acted like I didn't even miss her."

"Well, that can't be that bad. I'm sure she knows you do."

"I don't know. It wasn't just that. I just said all the wrong things."

"Was she mad at you?"

"No, just real quiet. And then she left real quick without really saying good-bye, you know? I mean, she did say it, but it wasn't really … I don't know. I don't know even what I'm talking about. I just feel like I made the situation worse."

"I think maybe you're just too worried. It'll be okay. Everything's gonna work out good for you guys."

"I don't know. I feel like I've already lost her." *I feel like I've lost everything.*

"What are you gonna do?"

"It's five o'clock on Saturday morning. I'm gonna go home, eat some sugary cereal, and try to get some sleep."

✳ ✳ ✳

Steve Woodbridge performed a balancing act on the street curb in front of his church. His arms wavered up and down, preserving his equilibrium as he stepped, one foot in front of the other. Slowly. He reached the end of the curb and willingly collapsed into the grass of the parking median. Looking up at the sky, he tried to count the stars. Like a child. Just like a little boy in the backyard.

His thoughts drifted to the time of adolescence. Stickball with his neighborhood pals. Campouts. Tackle football in the abandoned lot. That was a time of innocence, a time when life was on hold. When life was carefree. The only expectation was to be a good boy. No grand ambitions. No long-range goals to mold your existence around. Not then.

"Pastor Woodbridge? That you?"

The inert figure sprawled out in the cold grass of the parking median revived and turned toward the voice. Max, the custodian, had arrived for his morning shift.

"Yeah, Max. It's me."

"What're you doing down there?"

"Just thinking."

Max was baffled. "You been here since yesterday?"

"Yeah." The pastor rose to his feet and brushed the grass off his pants and coat. "I guess I should call my wife and tell her I'm okay."

FROM "THE UFO RIDDLE" BY MICHAEL C. WALSH IN *SPOTLIGHT MAGAZINE*:

> The best bet is that no resolution to the Trumbull alien mutilation will be found. After years of documentation from every conceivable geographic point on the globe, the mystery of UFOs remains unsolved, and for good reason. The burden of proof lies with those who make these outrageous claims, and not one throughout all of history has had evidence solid enough to support them. The solution to the riddle of UFOs has been with us all along in the oft-heard, but oft-dismissed, voice of the skeptic: they don't exist.

Mike Walsh succumbed to sleep with one recurring thought in his head: *I've lost everything.*

Graham Lattimer woke, pain still clanging in his skull, with a phrase left over from the previous night's news: *Be assured …*

Steve Woodbridge fought off sleep during the drive home. A thought remained with him as well: *The wife's gonna kill me.*

In the fall of 1972, a twelve-year-old boy walked along an unpaved road, holding the strong, wrinkled hand of his grandfather. The elder led his grandson down a path they took routinely every week. Decaying leaves crackled at their steps, scattering brown and orange and red autumn confetti. The morning was young, and the walk was brisk. A cool breeze nipped at their faces when they turned the corner at Main and Versailles. They passed a row of stores. Each was closed and would be for the rest of the day. Sunday. Church day.

The boy swung his arm, taking his grandfather's with him in each pendulum stroke. He looked forward to this time every week. Not so much for church but for the walk. He raised his head and studied the old man's face. It was toughened and creased by hard work and time itself. They wore matching slacks, and the fabric swished with each stride. Still gazing upward, the child watched as a smile materialized on his grandfather's face.

"Why are you smiling, Grandpa?" the boy asked, but he knew why.

"Because I know *this* is about to happen!" his grandfather declared, promptly attacking the boy with tickles.

The boy squirmed around, flailing his arms wildly, and let the laughter billow from his mouth. Tears began to stream from his eyes, but they were *good* tears. Tears of laughter. Tears of joy. After a good minute, the man released him, and they resumed their walk.

The little country church stood on the top of a hill. Its white-washed wood appeared to glow in the morning sunlight. There were scatters of people all around, dressed in their Sunday suits and dresses. Children scampered about, and some shot marbles in the dirt. When the boy and man reached the peak of the incline, they saw a reflection of the sun occurring someplace unseen, casting its beam directly through the round stained glass window that was set in the steeple spire atop the pitched roof. The boy marveled at it. Each color came alive and pulsed.

That very morning, at the end of the church service, the preacher gave his customary invitation: "Anyone wishing to make a decision this morning, just come down this aisle. There are friends here who would love to talk with you and share with you the wonderful love of Jesus Christ." The choir and congregation sang Hymn 282. It was not a slow hymn, which would tend to depress anyone considering answering the altar call, but a lively one: "Blessed Assurance." And that morning, the young boy made another walk with his grandfather by his side. They didn't need a "friend" from down front. Just the front pew. And there, Graham Lattimer, age twelve, prayed with his grandfather to receive God's gift of salvation. *Blessed assurance, Jesus is mine! Oh, what a foretaste of glory divine! Heir of salvation, purchase of God, born of His Spirit, washed in His blood. This is my story, this is my song, praising my Savior all the day long; this is my story, this is my song, praising my Savior all the day long.*

Two years later, his grandfather lay in bed in the home they shared and approached death's door. Graham brought him dinner. Toast and jelly and a glass of milk. His grandfather wouldn't accept it.

"I won't need that," he said simply.

Graham knew why. The man took his hand. He had been the boy's guardian nearly all the child's life. Graham's parents passed away when he was only six, and his father's father took him in and raised him.

They sat in silence for a while. Outside, a bird chirped, and the sound came into the room unusually loud, as will happen when two people are frozen in quiet, each acutely aware of every breath, each lingering uncomfortably, anticipating a word from the other. The rise and fall of Grandpa's chest slowed.

"What did you do this afternoon?" the man asked.

"I was here. I didn't do anything."

"Why?"

"I wanted to stay with you."

"You should've gone out and played with your friends."

"I can do that some other time."

They quieted again and accepted the realization that death was near.

"Does Aunt Faye know?" the boy asked.

"No, no. You'll need to call her, I guess. I didn't want to worry her. I'm sure she'll be upset for not knowing, but I'd rather it be this way." He paused. "You'll have to live with her, you know."

"I know."

"She's a good lady. You'll like living with her."

"I know."

They both bowed their heads as if they'd rehearsed this moment. Graham was thinking. Grandpa whispered a prayer under his breath, but the boy could not understand it.

Blessed assurance …

The boy began to cry.

Jesus is mine …

Then the old man breathed his last and passed on, still clutching his grandson's hand. He left without any last wishes or parting words or dying speeches … just a legacy. A legacy of faith and prayer and devotion.

This is my story, this is my song …

Graham went to live with his aunt Faye and grew into manhood in her care, but he attributed any good that was in him to the love his grandfather showed him and the Love he found in a little country church one autumn morning.

Praising my Savior all the day long.

* * *

"Looks like he's been dead awhile," one of the crowd announced matter-of-factly.

The men gathered together on the muddy bank of the river. Some stood. Others squatted down for a closer look. One man with a long pole in his hand stood in the river itself, knee-deep in the murky water. He had a body snagged on a hook attached to the pole's end and drew it to the shore. The body was that of a middle-aged man with a full beard. He was puffy, bloated, translucently white with blotches of violet from the water and the weather. When they rolled him over, his eyes were open and bulging, glassy and swollen. The flesh on his face and skin had separations, rifts from the gradual sloughing off.

They quickly went to work putting him inside a large black bag. They sealed it with a zipper and struggled to carry it to an ambulance waiting up on the shoulder of the road that ran along the riverbank. They slammed the doors shut and drove away.

A few yards from the men's deep footprints, a boy sat cross-legged in the mud. No one had thought to shoo him away from the gruesome discovery. His eyes remained wide open, and he stared at the river. It flowed lazily, carrying limbs and leaves with it, and he half-expected to see another body come floating along. He had discovered the body while fishing. He looked out and saw what appeared to be a man floating on his back. He was just riding the current. His buddy Len went to notify the proper authorities, who arrived and left before Len's return.

A summer fishing expedition was cruelly interrupted. And now, alone, the boy was consumed with thoughts of the events that had transpired before him. He saw it. A blue-skinned, mouth-open, drifting for who-knows-how-long corpse. He had only wanted to catch a few bass with his friend, but he had come face-to-face with … well, with death. And the image lodged in his mind, braced against his sense of adolescent well-being, forever haunting him. The trauma was real, heavy, big. It was all-caps: DEATH. That was the shadow memory trailing him. Something hit the ground beside him, splashing mud onto his pants. Then something struck his arm, and it hurt. It stung. Looking up, he saw Gary Newsome, the neighborhood bully, standing on the embankment, a brand-new BB rifle in his hand.

"Got you now, Michael Walsh!" Gary shrieked.

When someone calls you by your full name, they're either an authority, a stranger, or an idiot, Mike decided, but he didn't sense the urge to approach Gary and decide which category he fell into. He just assumed *idiot* and, leaving his fishing rod in the mud, ran as fast as he could toward home.

His feet sloshed in the wetness of his shoes. He was already blaming Gary for the blisters he knew he'd get. But he ran. He brought his feet down over and over, pounding the pavement, leaving muddy footprints and hoping Gary would slip on them. His little-kid mind remembered winning third place in the hundred-yard dash on Field Day at school, and he had the hysterical thought that if they had sent Gary Newsome after him with a BB gun, he may have won first. Gary, in hot pursuit, managed to get three or four more shots off. Two struck Mike in the back, and he yelped and arched his back and ran faster. Mike could feel the other BBs whiz by his ear. Gary had a good aim, that's for sure, but it was difficult to run and pump up the air rifle at the same time.

"I'll get you later," Gary said, and he gave up the chase, likely heading to the woods to hunt squirrels or rabbits or any other small forest creatures unfortunate enough to encounter this adolescent madman.

Once safe inside the security of home, Mike checked his wounds. The BBs left red welts, but none had penetrated the skin. He sought the comfort of his bedroom and sprawled out on the floor to read a comic book. He read not a word, though, and registered none of the pictures. All he could see was the body of the man in the river.

The year was 1988.

Eight years later, Mike Walsh began his study of journalism in college. He joined the staff of the school newspaper, and his first assignment was to interview the star of the theater department's latest play. Her name was Molly, and she was beautiful. She had the most glorious hair he had ever seen, long and wavy hair of amber that caressed her shoulders, and she had blue eyes he could only describe as beguiling. A clunky camcorder on a tripod recorded the interview. He didn't want to miss anything. He wanted to see every wonderful blink and every word formed by her red lips.

He kept the videotape and played it back over and over in his dorm room just to hear her voice. He asked her out on a date, and she accepted his invitation. They went out for Italian food and caught a movie at the local multiplex. At the end of the evening, he knew he was in love, and he hoped she was too.

Four years after their first date, they married and began a new life in Houston. They loved each other very much, but as the years progressed, their relationship underwent times of stress. They always worked it out, though.

They spent thirteen years working it out, but the solutions came to a halt without warning. And now Mike Walsh recovered from his all-night meeting with the *Spotlight Magazine* staff by lying in bed, under attack from the memories.

The contents of that tape replayed in his dreams, and then the scene dissolved to another. He saw Molly walking out the door of their home, suitcase in hand, over and over and over again. Then he was running frantically from Gary Newsome, who was firing his BB gun at him. Each bullet found its target. And then he would tear into his house, scamper down the long hallway, and open the door to his bedroom, only to find himself standing in the mud by the river. The body drifted slowly to the shore.

Here was a man who learned a brutal lesson as a young boy. The impermanence of life. A man who sought the love of a woman who was gone. A man who faced a life of loss. Of pain. A life of staring down the deep, deep hole ...

I've lost everything.

... that lay in his soul.

※ ※ ※

June 29, 1995. Two long buses pulled into the First Church parking lot, screeched to a halt, and opened their doors to spew a hundred or so road-weary teenagers onto the hot asphalt in Drury, Louisiana. All were tired and hungry and very eager to go home, shower, and go to bed forever. All, that is, but one. A nineteen-year-old boy, hair and eyes chocolate brown, emerged refreshed. He, like the others, had been awake for close to twenty-four hours, but unlike the others, he loved every minute of it. He was the only teenager smiling.

His parents stood waiting for him by their wood-paneled station wagon. He ran to them hurriedly.

"Did you have a good time?" his mother asked, as if it wasn't evident already.

The words *good time* didn't exactly describe it.

"Well, let's get on home, and you can tell us all about it."

They gathered his bags and put them in the rear seat—the one that faced backward. The "back-back," as they liked to call it. The boy's mouth ran the entire trip home and for quite a while once they arrived.

"I'm just glad you all came home before your birthday. I hated the thought of you spending it over there," his mother said.

"It would have been fine by me," Steven Woodbridge responded. "I could have stayed another whole week." He changed his mind. "Another whole month," he said, but something inside corrected even that, saying, *My whole life!*

"Well, your dad and I are glad you're back, and we have a surprise for you."

Surprise. They had a party scheduled for him that same night, but he had been tipped off weeks ago by a friend who "just couldn't keep a secret." When evening came, they drove to the Drury West Community Center. The marquee read, HAPPY 19TH BIRTHDAY, STEVEN! and had balloons and streamers tied to it. All of his friends from school, work, and church were there, as well as the friends of his parents. In Drury, birthday parties were community affairs. They were big to-do's, and everyone was invited, no matter how distant a relation or acquaintance. Steve's parents spared no expense, because they were proud of their son.

His father's boss, Mr. Whitten, shook his hand. "Congratulations, Steven," he said, and he grinned from ear to ear.

"For what?" Steve asked. *Congratulations* seemed like an unusual thing to say to someone on their birthday.

"For the licensing, of course."

"Oh, right. Thanks."

The licensing. Nearly a month prior, Steve graduated from high school, and a week later, his church presented him with a Certificate of License. It was a diploma-sized piece of parchment bought at the local religious bookstore. In Old English calligraphy, it made its declaration: THIS CERTIFIES THAT STEVEN J. WOODBRIDGE, WHO HAS GIVEN EVIDENCE THAT GOD HAS CALLED HIM INTO THE GOSPEL MINISTRY, IS LICENSED TO PREACH THE GOSPEL AND EXERCISE HIS GIFTS IN MINISTRY BY FIRST CHURCH OF DRURY, LOUISIANA, ON THE 17TH DAY OF MAY 1995. At the bottom, the church clerk and the pastor signed their names. Technically, this meant Steve could perform marriage ceremonies or funeral services, "the ol' marry and bury" as he liked to call it. Other than that, though, it was little more than a status symbol, at least to the people his parents concerned themselves with. Steve never really gave it much thought. At the age of sixteen, he had gone down the aisle one morning at church. He had just returned from a trip with the youth group, and he somehow had this incredible feeling that he was being *called* into something. Invited. Drawn, even. The counselor near the altar explained to him that this was God calling him to be a preacher. What did he know? He accepted, and his parents were overjoyed.

The day of his nineteenth birthday, he returned from a trip where all week he experienced a similar feeling.

"Hey, Steve. Tell me about Mexico," said Tom D'Amato, the Woodbridges' neighbor.

Steve did not hesitate. "The single most awesome experience of my entire life."

"Get out."

"No, really."

"It's probably the water."

"Ha, right, the water."

"Wasn't it, like, *dirty*?"

"Well, yeah—"

"Well. Glad it was good," Tom said.

That night, after the party guests had all given him their best wishes and shuffled on home, the Woodbridge family sat around their dinner table and talked.

"We are so proud of you, Son," his mother said.

"Thanks, Mom."

His father slid a pile of papers across the table and left them in front of his son. "Your application to Brantley came in. I went ahead and filled it out for you. Everything but the essay part, that is. I guess you just need to do that and then sign it."

Steve looked over it.

"I filled it out just the same as the other ones you did yourself. It should be the exact same," his father said.

"Yeah. It is."

"Something the matter, Son?"

Steve glanced at the blanks next to MAJOR and MINOR. They were filled in with the words *Christianity* and *Music*.

His mother joined the inquiry. "Steve? Is everything okay?"

"Yeah. Everything's good."

"You look like something's wrong."

"Well …"

"What?" his mother asked.

"I was thinking …"

"About what?"

"About maybe concentrating on Spanish."

His father spoke up. "Spanish? What for?"

"Well …" He knew they were not going to like this. "I've been thinking about maybe going back to Mexico."

"What do you mean?" his mother said. "Another mission trip?"

"Well, yeah, I guess. But, like, I was thinking about the missionary training school some of the guys were telling me about. I think I might like to see what it might take to go into Mexico. Like, long term."

His mother looked like she might cry.

His father chose a different line of objection. "Steve, I know you and the kids just got back from having a great time down there. I'm sure the Lord really moved." He said this as if he had no idea what it really meant. "I'm sure you did a lot of good things for a lot of people, and naturally, you're real emotional about that. You feel good about it. But I think maybe you're confusing that with something else. You don't want to alter your entire life from a week's worth of a good feeling." The truth was, Steve knew, it was his father who didn't want him to alter his life. His father's plans.

"What about being a preacher?" his mother asked.

"It's still being a preacher, I guess," Steve said. "Just different."

"It's not just that," Father interjected, but it *was* just that. "I just don't think you should forget about your goals, here."

"Yeah," Steve offered lamely. "I guess you're right."

He could not convince them. He knew it was pointless. They lorded his uprightness over him, used it against him. He was a good kid, compliant, passive. Always had been. His respect for his parents was used against his own best interests but he was too respectful to point it out. Any protest could find no purchase. His dad was a master convincer and his mother a master at passive aggression, a veritable maestro with the martyr complex. Trying to convince them that full-time missionary work was what he really aimed to do was like trying to shove a wet piece of paper through the cracks in a brick wall. It wouldn't go.

As he aged, matured, he could actually see more of his parents' perspective, could feel its sensibility take shape in his mind. If he'd had a kid who came home from a short-term mission trip to announce he was going to be a missionary, he would scoff too. What do kids know?

Except that kids know a lot. No, not about what's prudent and what's practical, but much, much more about what's spiritual, intuitive, what lights up the angelic senses in their souls, what gives life its groove. Kids have faith. Adults have the facts that make faith seem like kid's stuff.

So Steve Woodbridge pursued their goals as if they were his own. College. Seminary. Looking back, the only truly fulfilling thing about it all was finding and falling in love with his wife. When those goals were accomplished, he became *Pastor* Steve Woodbridge, and his life's work and mission became climbing the corporate ladder of ministry. Knowing the right people. Knowing the right words to say and the right way to act. Moving to another church only if it had a larger congregation and a higher salary (although he would never admit this to anyone, including himself). He played the part and worked his way to the top.

But others were playing the game too. Which is how he found himself in Houston, lured by a nice salary and a nice building, *horn-swaggled*, as it were, by what turned out to be a congregation mired in conflict, sunk in debt, and primed to vote a tremendous pay cut for their new pastor in his second year.

And yet, the financial situation was not his regret. His pursuit of the American pastoral dream had come back to bite him, but his lament was not *this* decision but *every* decision since 1995. Every day, he could not help but think about that village in Mexico.

CHAPTER FIVE

The meteorologist's prediction proved accurate. The coldest day of Houston's unusual cold spell hit with a vengeance, encasing the Bayou City in an icy cocoon.

Pops Dickey, back from his journey to the West Coast, made his customary morning rounds on the farm. There would be no reporters on the Dickey farm for a while, no photographers to pose for. (The results from the panel of experts' inspection of the deceased cow were inconclusive.) Stepping into the barn, he almost hoped he'd find her surviving counterpart flat in the hay, maybe even with a little gray alien standing over her, smoking ray gun in hand. His little metallic shoulders would be hunched innocently. "No beef on Mars," he would say. But the animal had managed to survive the bitter cold of the preceding night and any attempts on her life by otherworldly invaders.

A few miles away, Graham Lattimer arrived at the station, wearing his police blues under a windbreaker and khaki trench coat. He had received a scarf for Christmas two years prior, and he wore it for the first time. He wondered how it could be so cold and, given Houston's humidity, not snow. He noticed the sky lacked for clouds. Then he wondered how the sun could shine so brightly on such a clear day and yet offer no warmth.

* * *

In the early hours of the morning, Dr. Leopold Sutzkever sat in his tiny office in Landon University and read the newspaper. He sipped hot cocoa from a #1 TEACHER coffee mug, a gift from a former student. On Saturdays, classes didn't begin until 9:00 a.m., so the doors remained locked, and the only illumination in the hallways came from the emergency fluorescents in the hallway and the meager light cast by Leo's cheap desk lamp. The building was relatively dark and completely silent. He separated the Local News section from the other pages and had begun to peruse the articles when he heard a crash down the hallway. It was not loud. It didn't have to be. One could hear the mechanical whispering tick-tock of the clock on the wall outside. The crash was muffled and seemed to come from another room a ways down, not from the hallway itself. Leo was not the sort of man to let something so seemingly insignificant go without inspection. If someone was injured, he intended to help.

He emerged from his office and had not taken more than two steps when a blinding fury of light escaped from under the closed office door belonging to Dr. Samuel Bering. Though emitted from a crack less than an inch in height between door and floor, it set the entire hallway ablaze for nearly three seconds. Leo's eyes filled with a brilliant white that promptly dulled into black as his vision failed. He rubbed his eyes vigorously with his wiry aged-spotted hands, desperately attempting to restore sight. When it came, he found himself sitting on the floor, and he immediately stood and cautiously approached his colleague's office. No hint of light appeared from within. He knocked.

"Dr. Bering?" he called. "Dr. Bering, are you in there?" No response. "Samuel, are you in there?"

He checked the knob and found it unlocked. He slowly turned it and opened the door to reveal Bering's office. He stepped into the darkness and looked around. No one. He flipped the switch on the wall, and the light revealed a vase on the floor at the base of the desk. It lay in a thousand broken pieces and pottery dust. He thought it strange detritus for such a short fall. But he couldn't figure out how it would have fallen. There were no open windows for a strong wind to come through. And no one in his right mind would schedule the air conditioner to come on in the middle of winter, ruling out the possibility of a brisk breeze from the vent. Even stranger, there was nothing to explain the blinding light. At least nothing visible. And the room … yes! It *was*. Despite the cold without, the room within was easily twenty degrees colder. And it smelled musty, like a years-neglected attic.

Sutzkever found the smell, the sensation, the whole not-as-it-seems environment eerily familiar. His thoughts now concerned Dr. Bering.

Mike Walsh awoke shortly before noon and was happy to escape the tyranny of sleep. He was a miserable fellow. Sleep for him had been hard to find, and when found, it presented a cavalcade of horrific dreams. He sat for a minute, trying to let the drowsiness and the dreams seep out of him. When full consciousness arrived, he put the coffeepot on and sat at the table.

He sorted through the accumulation of mail and magazines and other papers on the table, separating them into two piles: keep and throw away. In the heap of paraphernalia, he came across "Aliens from This World" by Dr. Samuel Bering.

The professor's theory seemed preposterous, something out of *The Outer Limits*, but then there was the problem of the professor's pitch-perfect congeniality. Perhaps he was an eccentric, but Bering didn't seem crazy. Mike hadn't read the professor's article. He felt it had nothing important to add to his story. His assignment was simple: UFOs. Throwing in some crazy bit about other dimensions or parallel universes or whatever the professor called them would have been a needless tangent. Had the science of it not had the potential to confuse the average *Spotlight* reader, it would have made a suitable story on its own.

He began to read the article, and it *did* appear as if the professor knew what he was talking about. It was heavy with bits of scientific data and research done by cosmologists and theoretical physicists and other academics who spent their time doing nothing but contemplating the whats and hows of pseudoscientific pursuits like time travel and telekinesis. The professor neglected to cite this research and data with Mike in their talk, but Mike knew he wouldn't have understood it in the least anyway and that Bering probably knew it. But even from his layman's perspective, Mike thought the article laid out a fairly convincing case for Bering's theory. The professor made it sound possible. He made it sound *probable*.

FROM "ALIENS FROM THIS WORLD" BY DR. SAMUEL BERING IN *SCIENCE QUEST*:

> In the early '80s, Kaluza-Klein theory reemerged with researchers aggravated by the task of unifying gravity with other quantum forces. Under this theory, forces are reconciled with each other

because there is much more space with which to work. Expanding to an nth dimension allows the unification of Einstein's field of gravity with the electromagnetic force and the Yang-Mills "weak and strong" forces. Kaluza-Klein may provide a reason to file away the heaps of papers Einstein left unsolved on his desk when he passed away. It is his holy grail. It may reveal how we may reconcile all forces, known and unknown, and though its full understanding is beyond our present capabilities, it can be manipulated mathematically. In essence, its propositions are extremely ludicrous but can be proven on paper. Kaluza-Klein holds the secrets to higher dimensions and even the unwanted stepchild of theoretical physicists—time travel. Arguably, Kaluza-Klein theory and its revelations contain answers to the proverbial "meaning of life" ...

* * *

Captain Lattimer sat at his desk and dug through the drawers in search of relief. Without notice, Kelly entered and deposited an aspirin bottle in front of him.

"Thanks," he said. "I left mine in my glove compartment."

"No problem."

He unscrewed the lid and devoured three tablets.

"I guess I should tell you," she said.

Graham studied her face. He was in pain and wasn't sure he wanted to hear what she was on the verge of saying. Her countenance, all scrunched brow and bitten lower lip, only deepened his apprehension. Graham sighed.

"Do I want to hear it?" he asked.

"Probably not."

He rubbed his forehead and then responded, "Okay. Shoot."

"We got four calls last night reporting sightings of mysterious lights in the sky."

He groaned. "You gotta be kiddin' me," he said, not really to Kelly so much as to the air, to the invisible spirit of aggravation he had, until this time, only acknowledged subconsciously.

"No, sir."

"Anybody check them out?"

"Yeah. Lane drove out to each site. He said he didn't see anything. He took down some statements. Also, there was a camera crew here."

"Camera crew? What for?"

"Not here at the station, but here in town. They're from some TV show. Lane said they followed him around from site to site."

Graham nodded knowingly and smiled. He wondered at first why the townspeople had waited so long to make their calls, but he realized that the TV show's presence in Trumbull was too much for some to bear. They, like Pops Dickey, wanted their day in the spotlight. Tired of anticipating the reality shows no one knew lay on the television horizon, they wanted their fifteen minutes now.

"Anybody get any photos of these lights?" he asked.

Kelly only smirked.

"Of course not," he said, and he smiled back at her.

"Lane's reports are out here on the table if you'd like to look at them." She was still smiling.

"No, that's all right." He was still smiling too.

Kelly exited, closing the door behind her. Graham settled deep into his chair and thought about the events of the past week. What should have been a simple case of one unknown person killing a local farmer's cow had blossomed into a national media event, and all thanks to one veterinarian. One crazy veterinarian who had read too many science-fiction novels and had seen one too many alien autopsy videos. The panel of experts who investigated the crime did nothing to squelch the publicity, despite their vague conclusions, the obtuseness of which, in fact, only provoked more crackpot theories to fill in the gaps. The people of Trumbull wanted flying saucers and nothing else. Just like the urban myths of the inner cities (alligators in the sewer or a ghostly woman who appears when you say "Bloody Mary" five times into a mirror in a dark room) or the stories of sea serpents from sailors who had spent too much time on the ocean, the bored people of Trumbull (schoolteachers and widows and waitresses and retirees and, of course, farmers) shared an imagination collective enough that it eventually became truth. All of the hoopla disappointed Graham. He had hoped his fellow citizens would cling to their better judgment, a practicality and a simple empiricism common in rural folk. He didn't like the eagerness with which they had lapped up the media attention. It sickened him, all of this strange talk diverting people's attention away from the concerns of real life.

Mike read Dr. Bering's article four times, and each time it made more sense. He was sure there was a lot of data left out. Bering alluded to many theories and studies and researchers' findings without fully elaborating on them all. The magazine the article appeared in, *Science Quest*, was intended for mass audiences, not scholars or the intellectual elite. Mike assumed Bering was writing for people like himself—people who would have great difficulty understanding complex physics without the proper education, yet who had, as hobbyists perhaps, studied up enough to both expect and appreciate the supporting science. There was enough advanced material to make Bering's claims appear credible, and Mike decided he'd like to meet with him to discuss the matter further. In their original meeting, Mike was intrigued enough by the theories to take interest, but he had been dismissive, considering them overly speculative despite the mental amusement they offered. But subsequent readings of the article hinted at something deeper. At times, Bering's writing seemed to be not hypothetical posturing but the ideas of a man who knew of what he was speaking. A man who knew his subject very well. He moved from theories and "research suggests" to making bold statements as if he had firsthand experience.

Mike combed the pockets in his computer bag for his course syllabus. He found it and located Dr. Bering's office number on the cover page.

"Hello, you've reached the office of Dr. Samuel Bering. If you are one of my philosophy students, please call the alternate number listed on your syllabus. If you are a student in any of my other classes or need any other information from me, please leave a brief message after the tone."

"Dr. Bering. This is Mike Walsh. I was just wondering if maybe we could get together again sometime and talk about your article. I hated to leave so abruptly on you the other day, and I just wondered if we could meet again. If you can, please call me at home any time.

If you can't, I'll see you in class Tuesday. Thanks. Bye." He hung up. Mike always felt stupid leaving voice mail. He hated leaving recorded evidence of his being a complete moron.

After a long shower and a little more coffee, Mike left to meet Robbie for a late lunch. At the Dixie Shack, he found his seat opposite Robbie in a window booth.

"So, man," Robbie said. "After this morning, I gotta ask. How you been?"

"Oh, all right." His voice, as much as his choice of words, gave him away, and he was not entirely disappointed. He wanted to talk about it.

"No, like, for real. How are you? Am I gonna pick up the paper some morning and see a gruesome story about you or what?"

Mike faked a smile. "No. I'm ... getting by."

"You didn't really tell me what happened when you met up with Molly."

"Nothing happened. I was an idiot. I tried to play it cool, like I said, but I guess ..."

"She wanted it warm."

"Yeah. I don't know."

"Talked to her since then?"

"No. I wanted to, but it didn't feel right. I guess I felt like I messed it up when she was here, and I want to give it some time."

Robbie didn't seem to know what to say. He said, "You miss her."

"Of course." Of course he missed her! Wouldn't you miss your center of gravity? It was hard to do any writing without drifting off into a daydream about her that seemed to last for a few minutes. But he would glance at the clock and be shocked to see an hour had passed. He couldn't sleep at night. He was paranoid. Easily upset.

Simple pleasures like a cup of coffee on the back porch or a football game on TV offered no solace, especially since she was not there to share the coffee with him or yell for joy with him when Arian Foster battled across the goal line. Only two days ago, he awoke from sleep and turned over in the bed, fully expecting to see her all bundled up in the sheets and blankets. When he registered her absence, he began to cry, and Mike had not cried since ... well, since the day she left. *Of course* he missed her.

"What's she been doing?" Robbie asked.

"She's still staying with her sister in Dallas."

"The painter?"

"Yeah."

"She working?"

"Who? Molly, or her sister?"

"Molly."

"No." He was encouraged by this. If Molly went out and landed herself a job, it would only solidify the permanence of their separation.

Robbie seemed to realize this as well. "That's good," he said. Then he changed the subject. "Hey, your piece turned out really great. I wish you could've got ahold of that Dickey guy in Trumbull. But it was still good."

Their food arrived, and Mike was sure the jalapeños on his burger were going to give him heartburn. The talk of Molly had soured his spirits. They stayed for a while after they finished eating, sipping coffee and talking.

"So what else is going on?" Robbie asked.

"Nothin' much. There's not much to do. I read or watch TV."

"What about cultural anthropology?"

"Pretty interesting, actually. This professor? Bering? A pretty interesting guy."

"Oh, yeah?"

"He's one of those tweed-suit types. Older guy. He teaches *everything*. Philosophy, physics, anthropology. Crazy published."

"Don't say? What does he write about?"

"Everything. Religion and literature and history. Most of them are science-related or philosophy-related, though." And then he remembered. "And UFOs."

"He writes about UFOs?"

"Yeah. I was in the library the other day doing research for the article, and he just shows up and starts talking to me. Next thing I know, he's telling me he's an ufologist, and he goes into the periodicals stacks and gets me some piece he wrote."

"What was it about?"

"Craziness, man. He doesn't believe UFOs are aliens from outer space. But he doesn't think they are hallucinations or natural phenomena, either. He thinks they are people from another dimension."

"Oh-kay."

"He seemed to know what he was talking about. His article is full of research and studies done in prestigious universities and the theories of Einstein and other scientists."

"Another dimension?" Robbie said.

Mike nodded.

Robbie hummed *The Twilight Zone* theme.

"Yeah, that's what I think." Mike chuckled. "But he *really* sounds like he knows what he's talking about."

"Are you saying you believe him?"

"No, of course not. But it makes a lot of sense. And it's *new*. I hadn't heard this sort of thing before. And it's halfway intelligent, with the hyper-dimensional stuff. I mean, it's certainly out of the mainstream. But it's slightly more respectable than most of the crap out there."

"Yeah," Robbie said. "Sounds totally respectable."

Mike chuckled. "Seriously, though. A lot of scientists are starting to come around on this stuff. Not the UFOs, I mean, but hyperspace. Supposedly, at the time of the big bang, two universes split apart. One was our four-dimensional world, and the other is a six-dimensional world. It sounds stupid, I know, but Einstein's own theories and the formulas of his successors all seem to support it. It's pretty complicated. I don't understand it all, but it sounds like there's some truth there. I mean, who am I to argue with some of the greatest minds in science?"

"You got me," Robbie answered.

✳ ✳ ✳

Sunday arrived, and Pastor Steve Woodbridge stumbled through his sermon. His memorization of the text he usually wrote out word for word offered no help. He didn't forget anything. Anything, that is, except the zeal. The fire. The eloquence his congregation had come to expect from him. He was a dandy of a preacher and usually earned a generous share of "Amens" and "That's rights" from the crowd. But they were not into it that morning because *he* was not into it. He usually roamed the stage, addressing each section of the sanctuary, making each listener feel as though he were right there sitting face-to-face with them alone, giving them sound biblical advice. He could even make those in the back pews feel that way. This morning, however, he remained behind the broad wooden pulpit. The fuzzy end of the pulpit microphone, which extended from the lectern in a flexible metal rod, obscured the view of his face, so all anyone could see was the red end of it and the top of his head. It looked like a clown nose. Yes, gone was the fire. Gone was his unique brand of homiletical intimacy. He was drained of urgency, charm, warmth— it was all gone.

The warmth was gone in more ways than one. The congregation sat huddled together, a huge mass of shivers and chattering teeth. They were bundled up in jackets and coats, the older ones in shawls. They resembled a gathering of winter football fans in the bleachers more than a gathering of churchgoers. The heating system was still out, and by the end of the morning's service, they'd be happy to shell out whatever it took to get it repaired. By the end of the service, they'd be happy to hear a sermon on hellfire and damnation if it would put a little warmth in their bones.

There was no hellfire, though. Just a message on the peace of God dressed up in some lame pastoral pun. Steve hadn't put much thought into this one. Something like "Get a Piece of God's Peace," which was extraordinarily lamer than usual. He closed with prayer, and the ushers were called forward to begin the offering. Pauline Kaas, an old lady in a wig that fooled no one, played a song on the organ as the plates were passed and the offering taken. (It was the church's largest of the year.) Each loud bellow from the pipes reverberated in the frozen air and gave Steve a shudder in his chair atop the platform. Directly behind him, in the front row of the choir, stood his wife, Carla. She leaned forward and whispered, "Good job, honey."

He nodded but didn't believe her one bit. It was probably the worst of his sermons in recent history. He knew that. Every freezing church member knew that. His wife knew that too. He had gone through the motions. It was a rehearsed event and had been for a long while. The hymns full of words and phrases hardly anybody understood were sung over and over until they were just habit, and those who did understand them no longer cared what they said. The songs had become rituals to them; they were on the liturgical auto-pilot to which he and his seminary colleagues had sworn they would never fall sway.

Hymns were just the tip of the iceberg of things Steve had grown callous about. Sunday school was social time. Prayer meetings were gossip sessions. The lukewarmness of his parishioners had spread to him. Or … had it begun in him? *After all,* he had been taught, *ninety-nine percent of church problems are based in leadership issues.* He had learned that at some leadership seminar conducted by one of the nation's megachurches. He couldn't remember which one. He had been to so many. Conference attendance was just one of those things that came with being a religious professional. Like an executive's business trips. He had finally begun to reason within himself that there was nothing inherently wrong with cryptic hymns or pain-fully dull organ music or obligatory lunches with church elders who routinely (though not overtly) threatened his job. It was all part of the deal. A deal he had accepted many years ago. One thing could be said for sure, though. Disillusionment, the child of passionless routine, set in.

Steve stood at the exit in the church lobby right next to a potted ficus and shook the hand of each person who waited in a long line to have some face time with the pastor. The line stretched all the way into the sanctuary, and Steve could not see the end. He answered what seemed to be a hundred "thank you's" to a hundred people's "Wonderful sermon, Pastor" and then headed to his study to pray. This was one custom he had not come to abhor. Every Sunday, after every service, he would meet in his study with one of his only friends. He was a man he trusted and valued and appreciated as a confidante and a leader in the church. This man was what old pastors would call a "prayer warrior," before the term became passé. Prayer seemed to be the man's natural instinct, his way of being. If any man had come to be so heavenly minded the ways of earth had grown wearisome to him, it was Steve's friend Graham Lattimer.

Mike Walsh had a poor aim. On Sunday afternoon, he slouched in a tattered fold-up lawn chair borrowed from his mother and, in the middle of a vast vacant lot near the woods, held his father's forty-five caliber Llama pistol perpendicular to his body. His targets were four empty beer bottles, the contents of which happened to be picking a fight with his stomach at that very moment. He squinted with his left eye, keeping the right tightly shut. He squeezed the trigger and fired his last bullet. Another complete miss. That made eight. He wondered how Gary Newsome had been able to pull off the spectacular feat of firing (and hitting his target) in the course of a brisk foot race. So many years had passed, and Mike still believed he could feel the bruises on his back. The punishment came not from being in the wrong place at the wrong time, but from just being himself—Mike Walsh, perpetual victim. Everybody's doormat, footstool, scapegoat, what-have-you. The born loser. And it hurt. It hurt so bad. Worse than pellets in the back. Worse than the nightmares, the vivid night-mares where he was a child again, watching the bloated corpse drift to shore right in front of him, floating on the currents of the river. Floating on the cyclical currents of his mind. It even hurt worse than the fact that the wife he thought he adored left and, for all he knew, was gaining a tan on a thin band of white flesh around her ring finger and was getting a job and was scouring the personal ads for a man who adored her and actually *proved* it. The overwhelmingly painful epiphany was this: he hated himself.

He slowly lowered the gun, and it fell from his hand to the with-ered ground. The winter sun cast its brilliant gaze downward but offered no warmth. He laid his head down upon his own shoulder and breathed deep, the chilly air tingling in his lungs. It was thin and suffocating. He looked out at the lot before him. It was an intermi-nable expanse of browns and whites, and the sun's glare gave it the illusion of a field of ice. And so he stood alone in this tundra, a fitting natural reflection of the desolate landscape of his life, and wrestled with overpowering thoughts of self-loathing and self-depredation.

The Sunday evening service was cut short due to the lack of heat in the church building. The offering from the morning service would handle that problem in no time, though. Steve took advantage of his night off and lay on his couch, safe and secure in the comforts of his own Victorian home, watching a news program on television. It was one of the major networks' overproduced news magazine shows with exclusive interviews and hidden-camera investigations, and he was not even half-interested. Carla was in the kitchen but had joined him briefly when she overheard the anchorman introduce a segment on supermarkets that pasted false expiration date labels on meat and dairy products.

"Can you believe that?" she asked.

"No, I sure can't," he replied, not caring in the least.

And then she walked back to the kitchen, shaking her head. (Steve heard her rustling through the refrigerator, and he had no doubt she was inspecting the contents and taking care to smell each package of meat.) Steve looked at the screen but did not receive its signal. He pressed his remote control's CHANNEL UP button and held it down, watching the stations blip by in one-second intervals. The incoherent noise of channel surfing, each channel emitting a split second's worth of dialogue or music (like the effect achieved by quickly rotating a radio's tuner), filled the room. Steve caught a bit of bass fishing. A tiny moment of the Sunday Night Movie. A splinter of what might have been a rock video. One special second of "a very special episode" of some sitcom. An infomercial. Many commercials. A dozen images unregistered. He was miles away. Away from the television screen. Away from his Victorian house on the corner of a block of Yard of the Month winners in a suburban subdivision in the northwest part of the big modern city of Houston, Texas. He and his wife stood together, away from what he had become, and in the middle of the treasure he, in his days of youthful naiveté and innocent aspirations, once sought.

✴ ✴ ✴

The cold night hung over Houston like sackcloth. Over one house in the city, the air was electric and thick with miserable darkness. It was the darkness of back alleys inexplicably darker than the streets around them despite the same night overhead, darker because of the passing of strange, ominous shadows and the presence of fear, as abundant as the very atoms in the air. And inside the house, a man waited in the stillness of a room that filled with the black air from outside.

Across the room, a candle instantly lit from the effort of an unseen hand, and then the visitor appeared. He was hard to make out, for the candle illuminated only a portion of his figure from the waist up. A nasty glow was cast on his face. The bottom half of him seemed to not be there at all.

"Hello, Samuel."

Samuel Bering, the one seated, shook with excitement and fear. He rose to his feet and responded, "Hello."

"This is all becoming quite unnecessary."

Bering didn't understand.

The visitor continued: "This ritual, I mean. It's not necessary at all. The candle, the silly posturing. You're practically naked."

"Well, I … I," Bering said. "I thought that's what you wanted. You told me—"

The visitor interrupted, "I know. I know. Just a test, you see. A test for you, dear Samuel. Would you honor my presence? I didn't know. I couldn't know until you showed me. Until you could prove yourself."

"Prove myself what?"

"Prove yourself not a bore, friend. My colleagues and I aren't at all interested in those who are merely interested in us, if you catch my meaning. We are gluttons for intelligence. What lengths would dear Samuel go to in order to request the pleasure of my company? I knew you were a wise one, but I had to talk to you to find out if you were worth talking to. Very practical, I know, but I'm afraid we haven't devised a machine or system to individually classify you people as worthy or unworthy. It must all be checked out, friend. And I, for one, don't even check someone out who isn't up to satisfying a few unusual requests."

"Taking my clothes off?"

"Yes, taking your clothes off. Everything. I hope you're catching on. I must attribute your apparent lack of mental swiftness with the awe you must be experiencing at this moment. Or fear. Is it fear that dulls your brain, chum?"

"I ... no. No, I'm not afraid."

"Of course," the visitor said, grinning an unpleasant grin. "Believe me, I understand."

Bering's eyes began to adjust, and he could see that the visitor wore a black suit jacket that covered a pristine white dress shirt and crimson tie. The bottom half of his body still appeared empty. Empty, that is, except for a murky mist or smoke, or what Samuel imagined as mist or smoke. It was difficult to tell if there was nothing there at all, or if the visitor's pants gave an odd impression, an illusion of vapor. The visitor's lips curled into a wide, toothy smile, and the undulating glow of the candlelight created weird contortions of shadow in the creases of his face. His brow darted in, capturing two dark eyes beneath its furrow. His forehead was cloaked mainly in shadow, and if his hair was not jet black and slicked severely back, then he had no head at all (no top of the head anyway).

The visitor continued, "I'm here to show you great things, Samuel. You've proved yourself to me, and that is what I asked. I can show you great things. Tell you great things. Teach you. Share with you the secrets of time and space and the invisible unknown. In my world, the average fellow on the street is immensely more intelligent than you, and you are a many-degreed man, are you not? You learned with the best at the finest institutions. You are a master of many arts, many things. If I dare say it, chum, you are a genius. But there are many more things for you to learn. Yes ..." The visitor moved in close, and Samuel could smell his breath. It was sweet and bitter at the same time. "... there are many more things for you to learn."

CHAPTER SIX

The Dickey farm suffered another frigid Trumbull morning, and Pops enjoyed it. The endless days of frosty winter reminded him of Wisconsin. He remembered sitting on the porch of the corner grocery up there with his good friend Stu Hidell. Pops ran the old guy's name together and called him "Stewadell," but Stu didn't care. Pops was his good friend. His only friend, for that matter. The two of them would perch themselves on the grocer's porch swing and survey the monotony of the small town square, like buzzards taking waiting for carrion. Anything they saw—be it a gaggle of schoolchildren, two young sweethearts, or an old maid—would be subject to criticism. They were like Statler and Waldorf, the two old men in the Muppet movies, two cynical puppets commenting on a cast of characters (of which they were a part), pontificating from a position of false superiority. Pops and Stu weren't nearly as comical, though. Pops looked back on that time with fondness and recalled one particular exchange distinctly.

"Not so cold today as yesterday," Pops commented blandly.

"Yeah," Stu replied.

"Bothering you at all?"

"Affects my arthritis a bit, but not bad beyond that."

"Yeah," Pops mimicked.

"Can't imagine what those Texans do down there in the heat all the time. In the God-forsaken desert, ya know."

"Buncha idiots."

The two knew absolutely nothing about Texas, but Pops had found most of his suspicions confirmed upon moving there. He was convinced they *were* a bunch of idiots. But he didn't exactly live in a desert. And it wasn't exactly hot at the time. He got the notion to write ol' Stewadell a letter and let him know it almost felt like Wisconsin, minus the snow of course, but his better judgment ruled it out. He didn't want Stu to think he was actually *enjoying* the place. And letter writing, as everyone knew, was for sissies.

Pops stood near his small pond and looked wistfully up at the tree line. Thin sheets of ice hemmed the rim of the pond. He was desperately trying to get his story together and organize the facts, all of which were completely untrue, into one coherent and, above all, believable incident. A reporter was due any minute to record Pops's terrifying encounter with a flying saucer. He loved the attention, but Gertie, his wife, had asked him why, if he hated all these Southerners so much, he wanted so many of them around all the time. She also had a problem with his dishonesty, but she was an old woman and would not summon the audacity to confront him with it (although if she had tried to, she might not have found any there to summon). Pops only grumbled, and, in the end, Gertie seemed content to let her husband do things his own way. He had, after all, done that every day since they had met.

When he felt like he had his tale all straightened out, he began his morning rounds and made for the barn. Approaching its wind-beaten door, he couldn't help hoping once again for the discovery of alien mischief. He paused for a brief moment and then opened the door in a dramatic fashion, stepping back to allow it room to swing wide. Looking inside, his face turned pale with horror, and had his hair not turned white gradually many years ago, now would have been the proper time for it to do so instantaneously.

His cow was lying on her side, her body mutilated hideously in all ways imaginable. Pops reeled back, leaned over, and threw up his breakfast.

The reporter pulled his blue sedan into the Dickeys' dirt driveway, and his first glimpse of the farmer was as he approached the car, an exuberant smile on his wrinkled face. Pops's initial shock was over. His story began.

✳ ✳ ✳

Graham and Officer Petrie sat in the captain's office and ate breakfast. A doughnut for Petrie. A doughnut and aspirin for Graham.

"Head still botherin' ya, huh?"

"Ever since this cold weather started. I think maybe I'll go see a doctor today. Can't be normal to have headaches for this long, can it?"

"Can't say I know."

They sat in silence for a while, and it was comfortable, the way two men who know each other well can sit for the longest time without saying a word and not feel like they *have* to say a word. The only sound was the din of roaming busybodies wafting in from outside the office door and the occasional popping of Petrie's jaw as he munched on his doughnut. The sound would have been annoying had Graham not been annoyed enough by the miserable pain in his skull. They finished their breakfast, and Graham asked, "How'd the press conference go?"

"Okay. Didn't say much. Pops really took it away. He went on and on. Lewis Driscoll even got up and walked off."

"That so?"

"Yeah. He said"—Petrie straightened up for his Driscoll impersonation—"'The old man's tall tales do a disservice to serious UFO research.'"

"That so?"

"Yeah."

"Sheesh." Graham wiped away the powdered sugar he knew had gathered on his upper lip. "Got a call from New Mexico last night."

"New Mexico?"

"Yeah, Albuquerque. Anyways, this lady says she investigates cattle mutilations. Says they been getting 'em all over the place up there. Every rancher around had problems with 'em. Same deal as here, too. Surgical cuts. Blood drained. Same organs missing. This lady says that in 1989 she went out to Hope, Arkansas, where some farmer's pregnant heifers were found dead, all layin' in a line."

"Hope, Arkansas. That's where Clinton was born."

"Yeah? Anyways, she says one heifer had an eye missing. One was missing a large section of its belly, and they all were drained of blood and had bloodless oval-shaped incisions in their rectums."

Petrie shifted uncomfortably. "Sheesh."

"Well, that's what I said, pretty much."

Petrie was looking down at the office's drab mustard carpeting. Graham could see the conflict in the young man's face. It was exciting to have some action for a change, but he wanted to please Graham too much to take too much pleasure in it. "What do you think about all this?" Petrie finally said.

"Don't know for sure," Graham replied. "But I've got an idea."

The opportunity to elaborate did not present itself, because the intercom sounded, and Kelly's urgent voice relayed a message.

"Captain, we got another call here from Pops Dickey. He says his cow's dead."

"Tell Mr. Dickey we know that already."

"Uh, no, sir. His *other* cow."

* * *

Graham floored the gas pedal in his police cruiser, determined to arrive before anyone else. The car hummed just short of eighty miles per hour, dodging potholes and passing other drivers like a flash. He did not turn on the siren. It would only draw attention, and the sight of Trumbull's finest tearing up the country roads like a drag racer earned enough attention of its own. Petrie was gripping his door handle like the whole thing might fly off.

"Think you could slow down a bit, Cap?" he said quietly.

The harrowing drive lasted no more than four minutes. Graham skidded into the farm driveway, narrowly avoiding dinging the fender of a news van. There were several of them. They had been waiting. Waiting and hoping, just like Pops had. And they were as ready as he was for the news. *ALIENS VISIT DICKEY FARM A SECOND TIME.*

The two cops saw men in the distance snapping photographs of the barn. Graham and Petrie jogged toward them, and when they got close, Petrie's foot made unbalanced contact with the icy ground and sent him sliding forward. His arms wavered out, and he fell hard face-forward into the grass, cracking his nose against the tough earth.

Graham watched the incident, and at first, seeing him skidding along like a figure skater, thought Petrie had done it on purpose, but when he hurtled forward, he was hoping no one had seen. *Here's Graham Lattimer, bringing his good buddy Barney Fife,* he thought.

Petrie got up. A line of blood drifted from his right nostril.

"Sheesh," Graham said. "You all right?"

"Yeah." Petrie smirked.

"What's so funny?"

Petrie said, "I thought for sure I was gonna die on that ride over here, and here I go busting my face just walkin'." He smiled, and Graham gave him a courtesy grin in return, but started for the barn door.

A mess of people stood inside, all shouting at once and waving microphones and audio recorders and video cameras around. Pops Dickey stood on a bale of hay and fielded their questions. When he saw Graham come through the wide entryway his face tensed. He began yelling over the crowd at Graham, and the crowd did not quiet down. "Captain! Captain! These people are gonna stay right where they are! This is my farm, and I have every right to do *my* business on *my* farm!"

Graham nodded and, strolling up to the bale of hay and cupping his hands to his mouth, yelled to the farmer, "Just wanna see the cow, that's all."

Pops pointed to an area behind him.

"Mind if I take a look?" Graham yelled again.

Pops shook his head.

Graham noticed the resentment on Pops's face. "Does that mean, no, I can't, or does that mean, no, you don't mind?"

Pops made the thumbs-up sign and jerked it back, gesturing to the area again, and Graham took this to mean he didn't mind.

He and Petrie walked back around into a little stall. The scene was horrific. Blood still seeped from the deep gashes in the side of the animal and was spread all over the place. It didn't resemble the first mutilation at all. Graham remembered the absence of blood in the previous killing and the clean precision of the cuts that Doc Driscoll had said were performed with a laser. This animal was anything but clean.

"Whoever did this is one sick puppy," Graham said.

"Hey, Cap, check this out." Petrie stooped to the ground in a corner of the stall and picked something up. It was a small card. He brought it to Graham.

"Playing card?" Graham asked.

"No, sir."

He handed it to Graham. Branded on its slick surface was a black-robed skeleton holding a sickle. Its thin bony fingers cradled the sickle's long handle, and it smiled cruelly at Graham, a sinister, evil smile. A thought from a wholly different source reminded him, *Be assured.*

Petrie said, "It's a tarot card. That there's the card of death."

Mike Walsh awoke and immediately realized that it was Molly's birthday. It felt strange for him to remember. He never did before. She always reminded him, dropping subtle hints that weren't that subtle. But this day, he woke up and remembered, probably because she was gone and, naturally, consumed his thoughts.

He rolled out of bed and stepped into the shower stall. He sat over the drain, legs crossed, and let the shower head pour its hot rain upon him. He always bathed this way in the morning. It helped him wake up. He feared getting into the stall and standing up only to somehow doze off to sleep and crash through the shower door. When he sensed the ultimate arrival of consciousness, he stood and began washing.

The first floor of the downtown office building that housed *Spotlight Magazine* had a little gift shop in the back. Mike thumbed through hundreds of cards and replaced them all. They were either too trite or too serious. He didn't want to express insensitivity to his estranged wife, but he also didn't want to be too pushy. He found a blank one with a picture of a rose on the front. It took him fifteen minutes to come up with his own simple message: "Hope you have a very happy birthday. Miss you very much and hope to see you soon. Love, Mike." (The absence of I's was not conscious.) He paid for it, sealed it up, and addressed it. He had Vickie's address scribbled in a five-year-old pocket book, and he hoped she hadn't moved. Mike put the envelope in the outgoing mail basket in the magazine's office. The minute the mail-room boy picked it up, and it was impossible to take back, Mike had the overwhelming feeling that he had said the wrong thing. He didn't add *belated* to "happy birthday," and he regretted writing "hope to see you soon." Certainly, she would assume he was being presumptuous and would hate him all the more. Then he regretted the fact that he had sent her a card at all. Why not call? But he couldn't remember Vickie's number. He probably would have found it somehow, but he didn't like the idea of sending a card *and* making a phone call. He figured she'd think the card was a desperate measure from a desperate man, and indeed it *was*, but the feeling was there nonetheless. It couldn't be wrong for him to love her after she left. What was the point of leaving him if it wasn't to wake him up. *To LEAVE, you idiot!*

He sat at his desk and proofread somebody's story about a Santa Barbara woman who rescued sea turtles. His phone buzzed.

"This is Mike," he answered.

"Mike?"

"Yes?"

"This is Dr. Bering. From the college."

"Right, right. How are you?"

"Doing good. I got your message and just wanted to let you know to stop by my office any time this week. I'd be delighted to discuss anything you'd be interested in."

"Sure, that'd be great. How'd you get my number here?"

There was a pause, and then, "Oh, I found it in one of the school records," which sounded reasonable enough, but Mike got the odd feeling that the professor was lying.

"Oh, okay. Well, I'll be in class tomorrow. Can we meet after?"

"Love to."

"Okay, then."

What was it about the man that Mike found so compelling? Bering had an *aura*, was the only thing he could figure. The UFO and hyper-dimensions stuff was just the surface. Mike was only barely interested in that stuff, anyway. But there was something else there, something indiscernible, some undercurrent to his every word and gesture, some secret gravitas. It was speaking to Mike's void.

Mike scribbled "Meet with Bering" under the next day's date on his desk calendar even though he knew he wouldn't forget, and he read a section in the article before him about the turtles being released into the wild.

FROM THE JOURNAL OF DR. LEOPOLD SUTZKEVER:

… There are several existing conditions that would typify the phenomenon that I fear may be present in my colleague, Dr. Bering. They are, if I recall correctly:

1. Continued compulsions or habits
2. Chronic fear
3. Mental anguish
4. Unnatural sexual desires
5. Involuntary actions or spasms
6. Unorthodox beliefs
7. Recurring nightmares
8. Insatiable appetite for attention
9. Unexplained physical infirmities.

I have witnessed a few of these in encounters with Bering but have no manner with which to observe them all (even if I wanted to) without asking him outright. (Imagine what drama might occur if I happened to inquire of him: "Excuse me, Dr. Bering, but do you harbor any predilections for unnatural sex?" It just wouldn't do.) These signs aren't necessarily a foolproof litmus test. They are symptoms found in those merely suffering psychological trauma. But there are other signs as well. My hallway experience was much like my "adventure" in 1979, and the atmosphere of his office gave me such a queer sensation. I am almost certain that my suspicions are correct.

✳ ✳ ✳

In the Trumbull police station, Graham held the tarot card, secured as evidence in a clear plastic bag, and turned it over and over in his hand. The Grim Reaper mocked him. Several of his best men, Officers Petrie and Lane among them, sat in his office and watched him.

"Petrie, I don't want anyone touching that animal. I don't want anybody to step within six feet of it. Not Doc Driscoll, not any TV people. Not even Pops. I wanna keep it clean. It's about time we find the idiot doin' all this and restore some common sense to this town. Lane?"

"Yes, sir?"

"Go through the case files for every vandalism we've had here and in Myrtle in the past year. Call every last person on those sheets, including the investigating and arresting officers. Get ahold of the suspects and suspects' friends and the suspects' ninety-year-old grandmothers, if you have to, and ask them all where they were last night and the night of the first killing. Got it?"

"Yes, sir."

"The sooner we catch 'em, the sooner we can get some peace and quiet in this town and get rid of all these reporters. The rest of you guys: one of you find any stores that sell these cards and ask around. See if the shopkeepers remember selling any recently. One of you guys go to Trumbull high school, one of you to the junior high, and talk to the principals about any kids that may stand out. Past problems with vandalism or picking fights. Cross-reference that list with any kids who might wear Satanic or occult T-shirts or jewelry. If you see any kids around, ask 'em if they know anything. Got all that?"

The group nodded and turned to leave.

"Wait, one more thing. One of you guys ask Kelly to bring me some aspirin." And as they shuffled out the door, he shouted after them, "And don't talk to any reporters!"

* * *

Bering remembered the visitor's instructions. No candle. No need for nudity. The lights were only dimmed, not switched off completely, and he waited expectantly, seated not on the floor, but in his recliner. As before, he called aloud for his visitor, the invisible guest whose eyes and ears saw and heard Bering's every movement. He saw into Bering's world from his own. He influenced Bering's life with a subconscious guiding hand. Bering knew the visitor held the keys to unsearchable wisdom and impossible technology. His mind harbored the secrets and the reasons and the meanings of life.

Bering continued to call, but there was no sign of stirring. But then …

He believed he saw a shadow on the far wall, but not one of a man. Of something larger. It appeared briefly, in half a blink's time, so he attributed it to delusion. *A child will see a monster in a pile of clothes. The danger of the closet or under the bed. An apparition of expectancy.*

He beckoned again, louder this time …

… Nothing.

"Are you here?" *There! In the corner!*

A small saucer and teacup seemed to quiver. The vibration of porcelain on wood floor was vaguely audible. And then it ceased. Again, just a splinter of a second in time. Just imagination.

"Hello?" *Imagination still, or are the lights growing dimmer?* "Hello?"

A footstep? Again, a shadow?

He was shaking vigorously, throwing a shower of perspiration off his face. The drops gathered into a thin puddle on the floor below. He gazed down. And there was no sweat at all, but a round, rippling puddle of blood. He squeezed his eyelids shut tight. He heard a sound, much like the scratching scamper of a rat's claws, as *something* scurried across the floor behind him. It was not a light trample like a rat, though, but the frantic scritch-scratch of *something larger*. His body tensed, every vein, artery, and nerve straining, tightening, and testing capacity. He opened his eyes, and the pool on the floor was sweat.

The room began to gleam, the lightbulbs emitting blinding fury. He squinted and could feel his body temperature rise. Tremulous panic had thrown a thousand coals into his internal engine. And then ...

"Hello, Samuel."

Bering jumped.

"Did I startle you, chum?"

"Y-yes. I didn't know if you would come."

"Well, I'm here. Don't fret. I came as soon as I heard your call."

"Was the little show necessary?"

"Show?"

"I thought I was losing my mind."

"Well, now. Wouldn't that be a shame? What exactly did you see?"

"The lights, the saucer, the whole bit."

"Dreadfully sorry about that, chum. My colleagues can be a bit mischievous from time to time if the moment grabs them right. Please accept my apologies."

"Sure. Scared me pretty good, I must admit. The footsteps, the shadow."

The visitor appeared confused. "The what?"

"That huge shadow on the wall. Your friends always go to such lengths to frighten people?"

The look of confusion vanished from the visitor's face as anger washed over it. "I see," he said, gritting his teeth. His scowl diminished, and the anger dissipated from his countenance. He was jovial once again. "The shadow," he murmured. "Yes. Sorry for the scare."

Samuel relaxed a bit more. "God, you scared me pretty good."

The visitor raised an eyebrow. "God? How *interesting*."

"I hope I didn't offend you."

"No, no, Samuel. I understand the expression, chum."

The visitor stepped forward and sat down in the air as if a chair had appeared directly under him. But it didn't, and Samuel was amazed.

"I realize," the visitor began, "that you are a man of great understanding."

"I mean to be," Samuel said.

"Yes. I'm very certain that you are. I want to teach you, Samuel. I want to teach you about ... *reality*."

"This is my only ambition."

"Let me refer to a friend from my past. He and I were secret companions. Confidantes. He was a great mind too. I introduced myself to him in much the same way that I have introduced myself to you. Are you familiar with the work of Heinrich Gorschbrat?"

"Yes," Bering said, and he understood immediately. "Like Nietzsche, he said that God is dead."

"Precisely, chum. Precisely."

FROM THE TRANSCRIPT OF THE VIDEO
INTERVIEW OF MOLLY HOLLAND, CONDUCTED
BY MICHAEL C. WALSH; OCTOBER 21, 1996

Mike: ... So, tell me about the play.

Molly: Well, it's Rodgers and Hammerstein's *The Sound of Music*, and I play Maria. It's about a carefree nun who goes to work as a governess to care for the children of a widower. It takes place in Austria during World War Two, and so there's a secondary plot about Nazis and the family's escape from them. Maria teaches the children ... well, I guess about how to be kids, and they even form a little singing group. It's also a love story.

Mike: What's your favorite part of the production?

Molly: You mean a certain scene? Or aspect of the play?

Mike: Well, *both*, I guess.

Molly: I like the musical aspect of the production the best, because I love to sing. But I love to act, too. But I think I more enjoyed the singing. My favorite scene is where Maria and Captain von Trapp dance on the patio during the big party.

Mike: Why'd you like that scene so much?

Molly: I don't know. I guess because it was a fun scene to do. And also it's sort of magical, because it's the first time they really look into each other's eyes and get a glimpse of the feelings inside.

Mike: Oh—

Molly: It's just so romantic. Two people thrown together by chance, who actually sort of conflict at the beginning, but who, I guess, wear each other down and fall in love. Neither of them knew such a common occurrence as hiring a governess—a governess who's a nun and not supposed to fall in love—would result in the love of a lifetime.

Mike: Isn't that what happens in most love stories?

Molly: What? A nun?

Mike: No, two people meet under common circumstances and then fall in love.

Molly: I guess, but I'm not in one of *those* love stories. I'm in this one.

Mike: True.

Molly: Why are you smiling?

Mike: What? Oh, no reason. Let's see ... [shuffling of papers]

Molly: You're not very organized.

Mike: Yeah ... sorry. Let's see ... have you had much acting experience?

Molly: In some church Christmas pageants when I was a kid. And in high school.

Mike: Did you sing in any of those?

Molly: Yeah. We did *The Music Man*, and I got to sing in that. And I was in the glee club, so I sang in that, too.

Mike: Okay ...

Molly: You're smiling again. Why are you smiling?

Mike: I didn't know I was. Sorry.

Molly: No big deal.

Mike: Sorry. Okay, tell me about your life, now. Do you want to go into acting as a profession?

Molly: I don't know. It'd be neat, but there are just so many people out there, and it takes a lot of time and effort and patience to be successful at it.

Mike: What do you plan to do, then?

Molly: Good question. I don't know. I guess graduate and find a job. Fall in love and get married.

Mike: Like Maria von Trapp?

Molly: Yeah. Like that. You're smiling again.

Mike: Is it wrong for me to be smiling?

Molly: No.

Mike: Now *you're* smiling.

* * *

The heavy doors of the Regal Theater, one of the few in Houston that showed movies late into the night (that you didn't have to be twenty-one to view), swung open, and Mike Walsh staggered out like a cowpoke exiting through the swinging batwings of a saloon. He stepped into the icy 1:00 a.m. air. He had watched Clint Eastwood in Sergio Leone's *The Good, the Bad, and the Ugly* alone in the empty theater, and that was a good thing, because for some reason, he brought his pistol. It was stuffed into the inside pocket of his thick winter coat, and he had brandished it during the film's shootout scenes, playing along like he was in that world. He pointed it at the screen and fired it several times, but there were no bullets. Just an empty click. He shot nothingness out of a little gun, and it was good that no one had been present to witness his little game. If there *had*, he most certainly would have been finishing his night in a jail cell. He was alone in a room with a classic Western and his own delirium.

He was drunk. He walked slowly with erratic steps and stared intently at the ground. His beige import waited for him around the corner, but he wandered in the opposite direction, either forgetting about it or not caring about it. He meandered into and out of the street.

Uptown Houston sat empty as a ghost town. A biting winter wind stung his cheeks, but he hardly noticed. There were no bums out on the stoops. None huddled together under handout blankets or warmed their hands over barrel fires on the street corners. He heard the faint hum of traffic in the distance but saw no cars. Not that he was looking. His eyes glared down at the shuffling of his feet. Overhead, stretching on into the night before him, the streetlights lining the sidewalk were the only signs of life around, pulsating bluish gas and drawing in orbits of dying moths. Mike stuffed his numb hands into his coat pockets. The fingertips of his right hand encountered the butt of the pistol and rested there. He caressed it with his index finger.

The sky frowned darkly upon him. There was no moon. Only a trail of streetlights. And darkness.

He stepped off the sidewalk into the street and did not notice the car that was speeding toward him. The lady inside punched the horn, and Mike awoke, though still heavily dazed, and spun to face two searing headlights that had joined into one blinding force. He stiffened, frozen like a scared deer in the mesmerizing shaft of light. The lady slammed on her brakes, and the tires screeched against the pavement, bathing the moment with the pungent odor of burned rubber. Her scream was muffled because her windows were up, but Mike could still hear it: "What do you think you're doing?" The car lurched forward and grinded to a halt ten yards from the human obstruction in the road.

It seemed so unreal to Mike. Vivid, but unreal. Like a movie. Like a Western movie. Facing a showdown, he promptly whisked the pistol out of his coat pocket in one fluid motion and pointed it at the windshield of the car.

The lady freaked, screaming and stomping the gas pedal, launching the car dangerously forward and into Mike. He tried to jump up (*just like in the movies*, he thought), and he landed hip down on the hood, denting it heavily, and slammed into the windshield with the entire left side of his body. It groaned inward, cracking down the middle, but it did not shatter. The lady slammed on the brakes, and Mike tumbled off of the hood onto the cold, hard asphalt. She jerked the wheel harshly to the right and sped off, no doubt in search of a telephone or a policeman, whichever presented itself first.

Mike's body jolted with adrenaline, which accomplished two things: to mask any feeling of his injuries and to force him to run. He ran as fast as he could, fueled by the sudden flash of energy and by fright. For the first time in hours, clear thought dominated his brain, and his head turned right to left and left to right, eyes darting in frantic search of shelter. Someplace to hide. *And maybe to die.*

The police would never find him, though.

Mike didn't know that, though. He kept running, lungs working in overdrive, as if the chase was already on. He imagined a searchlight scanning the walls along the sidewalk and his feet always staying just out of its scope of illumination. Four miles and an infinite number of chest-burning breaths later, he collapsed in the gutter near a drainage opening in the street curb. The TransCo building loomed above him, gothic and haunting. The fountain sculpture everyone called The Water Wall sat in the building's shadow, in the middle of a lonely park, but the flow of water had been turned off a long time ago. The Wall just stood there. Mysterious. Houston's own Stonehenge. Steam from the sewer eased out of the drainage slit and drifted over him. The fog of the moors. He looked at his hands. They were shaking. A dull throb of pain began first in his hip, the onset of recognizing his injuries, and then spread throughout his frame, as if charting the course of impact. The hip. The rib cage. The shoulder. Then, his entire body, foot to skull, ached furiously. He glanced back at his hands. His wedding ring!

Where is it?

He began to sob and scrape the rough pavement with his bloody hands, hoping to find it. He scrambled around on his hands and knees, searching the area around him. He dug in his pockets. The manhole cover atop the sidewalk caught his eye, and he thought for a moment of ripping it off and diving down.

It could've fallen into the drain.

The wildness of the notion itself urged him to do it, but it was the wildness of the notion that jerked him into reality and made him decide against it.

Tears and sweat dripped down his face and deposited in his mouth, a place where blood had already taken up residence. Once again, he collapsed to the ground, a heap of sobs and sniffles and fear of broken bones and internal hemorrhaging. A heap of broken man.

I've lost everything.

A car pulled up, and its door opened. Mike heard the click-clack of footsteps approaching. He expected the police. Instead, a concerned voice, familiar yet unidentifiable, spoke out, shattering the chilly silence.

"Mike. Mike, are you all right?"

Mike turned and squinted his vision into focus. "Dr. Bering?"

"Yes, it's me. Come on, now. Let's see if we can get you up and into the car."

The professor helped him to his feet and half led, half carried him to the passenger side of his car. He helped Mike in, fastened the safety belt around him, and shut the door. He crossed to the driver's side and got in.

"How did you know where I was?" Mike asked.

"A little bird told me," Bering replied, and he drove the car off into the night.

CHAPTER SEVEN

Sitting comfortably on the couch, Mike had buried his hand in a bowl of Crunchy Cheese Twisters and was watching television. The Texans were losing. Again.

In the ongoing world behind him, a world from which he had excused himself at opening kickoff, his wife, Molly, was milling about. Cleaning. Or looking for something. Mike wasn't sure what she was doing, but he didn't give it much thought. Doors opened and closed. Drawers slid in and out. There was a sound resembling the working of a zipper. None of these registered. Like a tree falling in the woods without a witness, it wasn't really happening.

It didn't occur to him that all the noises were telltale signs of someone who was packing (and from the extent of the carrying-on, packing for a very long trip). No, it didn't occur to him until she was standing before him, blocking his view of the television screen, a leather suitcase in hand (HOPE YOU HAVE MANY WONDERFUL TRIPS WITH THIS! CONGRATULATIONS! YOU'LL SHARE A BEAUTIFUL LIFE TOGETHER! LOVE, AUNT JENNY).

"Bye, Mike," Molly said.

"Huh?" he said.

He did not recall hearing anything about a trip. Or had he? He wasn't sure, but he thought that if she had a vacation planned, he would have known about it. For goodness' sake, he would have had her freeze all of his meals for him in plastic containers if he had known she wasn't going to be around to cook. He would have had her wash all of his clothes before she left, so he would have them ready to wear while she was gone. But something in her eyes did not hint *vacation*. Nothing indicated *trip*. Her eyes said, *I'm LEAVING, you idiot!* And then, her mouth said: "I'm leaving" (sparingly, without the *you idiot*).

"What do you mean?" he asked.

"What do you think? I'm leaving. I'm going."

"What? Why?"

"*Because*, Mike!" Her eyes filled with tears.

"I don't understand."

"Of course you don't understand. You never understand. You never understand anything. I'm leaving you, and that's what I'm doing."

"What? Why?" he asked.

"Because you're never *here*, Mike!"

What was that supposed to mean? She clutched her hand to her chest upon the word *here*, like she meant "in her rib cage."

"What are you talking about?" he asked.

"I'm talking about you and me and how you're never here."

"I'm right here!" he yelled. He always ended up yelling in times of conflict with her, and he always regretted it immediately, but he never stopped.

"I don't mean here at the house. I mean with me." Now *she* raised her voice. "I want you here with me!"

Why do women always have to speak in code? "I'm right here!" Then, he added, "I've been right here all freakin' day!"

"That's what I mean. You've been here and not with me. I want you to *talk* to me. To come *be* with me."

"I've been right here!" He started to feel like a parrot now. *Repeat the line; everything's fine!* "I've been right here!"

She said nothing. Maybe she couldn't explain. Maybe she already had, maybe she'd tried in all of their other arguments. Maybe all the resolutions of all of those other arguments amounted to no resolution at all. Her tears came down endlessly, and she sniffed and gasped.

"I've been right here," Mike said. "Right here on the couch. If you wanted to talk, why didn't you come to talk to me? Why didn't you come tell me?"

She gasped out, "Because I want you to come to me. Because I've *been* wanting you to come to me. You've changed, Mike. You're not the same anymore. You used to want to be with me."

He still wanted to be with her. Why couldn't she see that? He loved her. Couldn't she see that? Didn't *she* love *him*? Why was this happening?

"Now you just watch TV or read or work—"

He lashed out. "I *have* to work, Molly! You want me to just give it up? To quit? How do you think we even live in this house if I don't work?" It was a stupid counterattack that got him nowhere, and he knew it.

"I know that," she cried. "It's just … you do all *that* and you never have time for me! You never *make* time for me. You're devoted to your job, but only fairly acquainted with your wife!"

"What's that supposed to mean?" He was going in circles now. He had to. He had to do anything to keep this argument going. It was certainly better than watching her walk out the door. The suitcase, still in her hand, had done its job very well. It was a sign, a symbol, a signal. He began to stare at it. The suitcase.

HOPE YOU HAVE MANY WONDERFUL TRIPS WITH THIS! *Yeah, well, thanks a lot, Aunt Jenny! As a matter of fact, Molly's about to take one now!*

The suitcase was the exclamation point. Her mind was made up, and she was going.

"I've been living in this house *alone* for the past few years," she cried, "and I can't stand it anymore!"

He could think of nothing to say, so she ended it:

"Bye."

And she was gone.

He couldn't say a word. He just watched the door close, and a feeling of coldness spread out from the center of his chest.

He sat on the couch—motionless, dazed—for hours and hours and hours …

… Slowly, winding back in a counterclockwise spiral, came consciousness. Light. Then darkness. Light. Then dark. Light …

… And the smooth sailing of music on the waves of the air.

Mike opened his eyes and found himself in a room he had never been in before. Panic began to set in, and he tried to move, but when he did, every nerve in his body screamed, and pain lit up his bones and muscles and flesh with a violent fury. He stopped. Looking straight out, he saw a wall … no, a ceiling, and he realized he was lying down.

Now consciousness filled him completely, and he recognized the music as Beethoven. The sharp pain in his body reminded him of the events of the night, and he realized he lay either in a hospital or in Dr. Bering's home.

"Dr. Bering?" he called out, though rather weakly.

"Right here," came the man's voice. It was smooth.

"What … what … Am I okay?" he finally asked.

"Amazingly, you've nothing but bruises and scratches, although you've got a good helping of them."

"Shouldn't I be in a hospital?"

"You don't remember?"

"Remember what?" Mike asked.

"When I picked you up?"

"Yeah, I remember that."

"Well, I took you to a friend of mine, a physician. I wasn't quite sure if I should take you to a hospital. You had that gun with you. Your eyes were open, and you were responsive, even answering questions. He examined you and released you into my care. You even walked to the car. You don't remember that?"

"No," Mike said. "I don't remember that at all."

"Do you remember anything?"

Did he? "Yes," he said, pausing. "The, uh—football."

"I see," said Bering, apparently not seeing at all.

"Yeah. But I remember … I remember Molly."

"Is Molly your wife?"

"Yes."

"Well then, we'd better give her a call."

Yes. We'd certainly better. She'll be quite concerned. So, why don't we? Oh, yeah … "She … she no longer lives here. She's moved."

Dr. Bering offered a simple, "Oh."

"What did you tell your friend?"

"The same thing you told him. You had a motorbike accident." He smiled. "Would you like to tell me what really happened?"

Mike told him the entire story. The movie. The pistol (which Bering had recovered and secured). The lady and her car. The wedding ring. The unfortunate background for the story, which concluded with Bering's rescue of Mike from the gutter and the dream he had just escaped from (although it had really happened, and there was no escaping *that*).

Mike slept for another hour, and when he awoke, Dr. Bering had some vegetable soup for him. It was warm and filling and seemed to melt away the spreading cold that had lingered in his chest since the dream. They sat together, saying nothing for a long time, listening to Beethoven, then Brahms, then Wagner, then Mozart—just bits and pieces of each, according to Bering's taste.

Mike felt comfortable and somehow whole. He felt, although he would never have described it this way, *loved*.

"Dr. Bering?"

"Yes?" he answered, and he looked very much like a man who had guessed exactly what Mike intended to ask. He had poised himself as if ready for it.

"Talk to me about hyperspace."

"Sure, Mike. I'd be happy to."

✳ ✳ ✳

Molly Walsh sat in her sister Vickie's living room and stared at a painting on the wall. It was one of Vickie's works, an original, and it was in impressionist or expressionist style (Molly never could remember the difference), but she was not quite sure what it meant. To her, it looked very much like a big finger painting. She recognized the vague shape of a person, swirled about in broad, colorful strokes, but the area around it was formless. Just huge swirls and swishes of yellows and blues mixing here and there into vibrant greens, all swimming about and splashing into waves of thickness that had taken days to harden. Whatever it was, Vickie had many more just like it, and people were buying them left and right. She'd recently done a showing of her work in a private gallery in Houston—her first foray outside her local network of artists. Molly went with her. There were hors d'oeuvres, obnoxious and erudite art collectors, and walls and walls of Vickie's giant finger paintings. And then, of course, there had been lunch with Mike.

Dear Mike. Molly felt bad for him. He seemed to be trying very hard not to try at all. He kept the conversation clear of talk about their relationship. He didn't mention getting back together. He had tried to put on a cheery face and failed miserably. Molly assumed that Mike did not want to come on too strong, to scare her away. But in the process, where she had sought his needing of her, had been silently reaching for him to *say* something to the effect that he desired her, she found him only able to *do* something. And that something resembled the actions of a wounded animal strutting about in an attempt to fool his predator.

But she was not a predator. Couldn't he see that? Couldn't he see how much she wanted him? How badly she wanted him to tell her he had changed? That was all she needed. That's all it would have taken. At least, that's what she told herself as she numbly watched the finger-painted lady drown in the finger-painted seas. But Mike always felt attacked.

Sitting across from him in the restaurant, she wanted to reach across and take his hand … no, she wanted to slip over to his side of the booth and give him a big hug. A long, lingering embrace that would put an end to the whole wretched situation. When she left the restaurant, though, she was glad she hadn't. She did not want to torture him. Leaving was not intended to hurt him. She knew that it would, but it was not her reason. She really did not know what her reason was, if she ever even had one. Perhaps waking him up was a reason. Nevertheless, she had decided long before she left that she could not live that way. Mike knew this, because she had told him. Several times. And every time, he would say things would be different, and they were not. Ultimately, she left to authenticate her words with truth. She could not live like that, and when he decided she would have to, she decided to make good on her warning. And she left. It was the hardest thing she had ever done, but it did not bother her as much as she had thought it would. The fact that he said nothing as she walked out, only sat on the couch with a blank expression on his face, made it easier for her.

She knew he missed her. She could feel it. From so many miles away, she could feel it. She hated herself for not taking his calls for so long. Vickie would say she couldn't come to the phone or she had just stepped out to go to the grocery store. It felt like the cruel game teenage girls play when an unwanted suitor calls.

"Who is it?"

"Mike."

"Tell him I'm not here."

Finally, he had given up. No more calls.

* * *

Less than ten miles away, the driver of an overloaded tractor-trailer fell asleep on a Dallas straightaway. At the incredible speed of ninety-five miles per hour, the truck began to drift across the lanes.

Coming from the other direction, unaware of the monster rocketing across the yellow center stripe, a lady bopping along to the Goo Goo Dolls in a small Volkswagen took a seemingly harmless break from her attention to the road ahead of her to look down and adjust the radio volume. When she looked up, it was too late.

At the point the two paths intersected, the small car exploded in a loud blast of crunching metal. The truck sent it flying in all directions, its frame disintegrating throughout its short and abrupt trajectory. When it landed, already crushed and stripped of most of its parts, the truck hit it again, this time pushing it with deadly velocity up over a sidewalk and through the glass and brick of Tom's Hardware.

Two lives. Two vapors. Both here and then gone in the blink of an eye.

✳ ✳ ✳

Dr. Bering led Mike into his study. Every step shot lightning bolts of pain up Mike's legs, and so it was slow going. Once in the room, Bering sat his wounded friend down in his own recliner.

The study was a warm, inviting place. The walls were shelves filled with books that reached to the ceiling. It was quite a substantial library, and Mike sat wide-eyed, scanning the spines of the thousands of books, catching titles and authors he recognized. Bering's fiction shelves groaned under the weight of the collected works of nearly every literary master, old and new.

Bering pulled up a chair across from Mike and sat down.

"It's an admirable collection, I know."

"It is," Mike said.

There was a vintage movie poster matted and framed on the wall: Billy the Kid's Women. Clearly some pulp flick from the dustbin of post-war cinema. Mike looked for the year on the print.

Bering smiled. "I was in that."

"You were in this? The movie?"

"Yep. I played Kid Number Three. That was 1957."

"How'd you do that?"

"I grew up in California. Here, sit down. My mother was a Hollywood hanger-on of sorts. Never really amounted to much, but here and there somebody owed her a favor, and putting her kid in a few terrible movies was one of them."

"You in any others?" Mike asked.

"Just one other. *Men From Venus*. A fantastic piece of sci-fi garbage that made Ed Wood look like Godard."

"This one any good?" Mike said, gesturing at the print.

"No, not really. I enjoyed being on the set, but we all knew even then we weren't making anything worth anything. It's not available even on video today. Every now and then, I'm told, it pops up on some Sunday TV matinee in some backwater markets. But I've never cared to watch it again. The poster was one of the few things of my mother's that I kept."

"Did you know any famous people in Hollywood?"

"Oh, plenty," Bering said. "They were nearly all boring. Some of the most uninteresting people to ever exist. For all the glitz and glamour, Hollywood stars were but shadows of real human beings. But I did grow up around a few famous folks who were a bit different."

"Who?"

"Well, I could tell you about Ron Hubbard."

"The Scientology guy?"

"Yes, the Scientology guy. My mother was one of his many mistresses. He was one of the prime figures in the Rosicrucian commune my mother and I were a part of for a while in Los Angeles. A few has-been actors and actresses flitted through. But Hubbard and the writer Robert Heinlein were probably the most integral names you'd recognize today. And the rocket scientist Parsons. They had a good little something going patterned on the work of Aleister Crowley."

"The Satanist guy?" Mike asked.

Bering glanced away, pained. "That's an unfortunate designation. Crowley was a mystic, Mike, a conjurer of the inner human spirit and its outer connection with the invisible, primordial life. He was the discoverer of the Themelite perspective, which to this day is probably the closest religious approximation of true gnosis."

The professor propped his feet up on an ottoman. Mike did the same.

Bering was close now. He continued:

"These men in this community were striving after something each in their respective trades had been searching for. Through art, through rocketry, through magick. Each lost his own way. They lost the gnosis, the essence. They lost the science and so lost the art. Hubbard of course went for the therapeutic approach and made himself the great cult. The others left the pursuit and went after science fiction. They diverged. Do you see? What they didn't look for was the science. The reality. The facts under the fantasy."

"Which would be what?" Mike said.

"In 1919, an unknown German mathematician from the University of Konigsberg wrote a rather spellbinding letter to Albert Einstein. His name was Theodor Kaluza, and in his short letter, he made the proposal of uniting Einstein's theory of gravity with James Clerk Maxwell's theory of light. Maxwell, you'll recall from my article, is the man who recorded the basic laws of the electromagnetic force, which, of course, brought us into the era of electricity. Anyway, Kaluza reconciled Einstein and Maxwell by introducing a higher dimension. He said that light itself is not a wave, but a *commotion*, if you will, caused by the rippling of that dimension. Now, Einstein's field equations for gravity are written in four dimensions, but Kaluza wrote them down in five. Then, he mathematically calculated, within these five dimensions, Einstein's theory *and* Maxwell's. Well, you can imagine Einstein's shock. The old fart was dumbfounded, I'm sure.

"What this obscure German mathematician had done was unify the two biggest field theories known to science. And Kaluza's field theory was like a well-crafted puzzle. Take the pieces apart, and there you had both theories—Einstein's and Maxwell's—still completely whole.

"Einstein, though astonished, was probably more than a little unnerved. Two years passed before he even decided to submit an article outlining Kaluza's findings for publication. It was indeed groundbreaking, but scientists became fed up with it. Most physicists didn't believe in a fifth dimension, and furthermore, its existence couldn't be tested as even Kaluza admitted, since it had to be 'balled up' into a tiny circle totally invisible. The energy needed to examine this ball would be one hundred billion *billion* times greater than that locked in a proton. An amount amazingly beyond what we will be able to produce even in the next few centuries. Kaluza-Klein theory was abandoned for several years.

"But then, as you read in my article, the eighties saw its resurrection. By this time, though, scientists had discovered more forces in the universe than light and gravity, and they were astonished to find that Kaluza-Klein had room for them all. Kaluza-Klein is just the launching pad, though. It opened the door for super-gravity and super-strings. Mike, super-string theory unites everything!

And Kaluza-Klein opened the door for the study of black holes and wormholes and other mysteries.

"The trick is to go back and see just what exactly happened before the big bang. At the onset of creation, what was going on? Really, the only theory that can propose to know is the ten-dimensional superstring theory. It supposes that our four-dimensional world split with a six-dimensional twin."

"Where's the twin?" Mike asked.

"Remember the tiny circle? That's it. But you see, it may not be all that tiny. I mean, in its world, everything seems normal just like ours, but in the grand scheme of the entire universe—or universes— our planet, and even our solar system or galaxy, may seem like a tiny invisible ball. Somehow, though, beings from our twin are able to manipulate time and space, perhaps using wormholes, to manifest themselves right here as if they were ordinary human beings like you or me."

"How?"

"Good question. I don't know exactly, and I don't know if anyone will ever know. They are light-years ahead of us, technologically speaking. And, on top of that, if we had the means to do it, we still would find it unbearably impossible. See, we can only think in three-dimensional space, or four, if you throw in 'time' as the fourth dimension. Do you know the Pythagorean theorem?"

"Uh, yeah. A squared plus B squared equals C squared, right?"

"Right. That gives us the length of a triangle's hypotenuse. The sum of the squares of the smaller sides equals the square of the longest side. It works three-dimensionally, as well. The sum of the squares of three adjacent sides of a cube is equal to the square of its diagonal. If A, B, and C are the cube's sides, and D is its diagonal length, then A squared plus B squared plus C squared equals D squared. And it works in N dimensions. An N-dimensional cube can have an unlimited number of sides—a 'hypercube,' if you will. You can't picture it, because your three-dimensional mind can't picture it, but mathematically it works. Every letter, A through Y, when each is squared and their sum found, will equal Z squared. And it goes on infinitely. I'm getting away from my point here, but as you can see, what is entirely possible can be beyond the realms of our comprehension. Hyperspatial beings can travel to our world with relative ease. The fact that we do not understand their methods does not hinder them at all.

"Imagine soap bubbles floating in the air, distinct worlds oblivious to each other. Somehow, a pixie can hop from bubble to bubble. Or imagine a rubber basketball that is worn down from constant play. In some areas, the rubber may be very thin, allowing air to pass through from the inside of the ball to the outside. This world may have thin, worn-down areas that allow for passing through. The worn areas could be wormholes. Gateways from one dimension to another. Here on Earth, they abound in areas prevalent with magnetic energy. Places the Native Americans would say are mystical. They could be present near catastrophic geological phenomena or cataclysmic meteorological events where the magnetic energy is in abundance. Perhaps the mysterious Bermuda Triangle lies in one such area. Along fault lines or in places of strong volcanic activity." Bering smiled. "Maybe your Superman cartoon wasn't too far off the mark, eh?"

Mike listened attentively, his wide-eyed gaze focused on the professor, who continued: "Think of the phenomena this could explain, Mike. Ghosts. UFOs. Mythology may not be so mythical. Angels.

Spirits. Flaming chariots in the sky. Higher dimensional beings can explain it all. And above all, it's all well within the realm of scientific possibility! So long as we don't diverge. So long as we press into the gnosis."

It was like a drug taking effect.

* * *

Mike spent the night at Dr. Bering's house. It was a pleasant night, full of warmth and deep slumber, an experience he cherished and accepted like a gift he had waited too long to receive. Bering's guest bedroom was small but held a full-size bed, bureau, and more book-shelves teeming with fairy tales, fables, and wonderful, spiritual poetry—books of dreams that seemed to fill the air in the room with a giddy comfort.

A strange current had swept Mike up, and he suffered it gladly. It was as if the collision with the lady's car had jarred his conscience loose inside him—jarred it free, he would have thought (had he been thinking)—freeing him from his obsessive and paranoid over-rationalization. Redirecting his gaze to north of navel. He was a man used to worry, despair even, and now he found the former departing (despite his ragged physical and emotional condition) and the latter leaving his disoriented mind susceptible to the professor's knowl-edge. The man was cocaine.

Before he had succumbed to sleep, though, he had quietly explored Bering's home and came upon a large vacant room down the hall from his guest room that resembled a ballroom with parquet floors freshly waxed. It was devoid of furniture, of objects of any kind. Two windows stared from the far wall like empty, black eyes.

Yes, the room was empty ... but somehow not unoccupied. A pleasant electricity seemed to fill it, coaxing Mike in, caressing him. There was something incredibly fantastic about the room, about the whole house. It felt like home. More so, even, than his own, especially since Molly had left. He spent many nights in that house, many sleepless nights. Alone. Aching for her touch. Her voice. Her breath. And she had left. And now, he was in a new place, perhaps a new home.

The room was indeed alive with mystical dreams.

* * *

Mike had no knowledge of the goings-on two floors below that night, in a room most uncommon in Houston homes. In that subterranean enclosure, the darkness hung thick and grim. The temperature was twenty degrees cooler than outside, a veritable meat locker compared to the rest of the house.

Bering summoned the visitor ...

... but the visitor did not come.

* * *

Four ambulances, three fire engines, and a long line of police cars crowded the scene in front of Tom's Hardware in Dallas. The eighteen-wheeler had impaled the store. Somewhere inside the store, in bits and pieces, lay the remnants of the Volkswagen. The flashing lights of the emergency vehicles cast an eerie kaleidoscope onto the walls.

The paramedics retrieved the limp body of the truck driver from the cab. He had broken twenty-nine bones, but it didn't matter. He had died on impact.

In the rubble of car and tools and glass and bricks and wood and gypsum drywall, they discovered the woman, broken and torn to shreds. They dug her out, placed her inert frame on a stretcher, and called for a body bag. They placed her in it, zipped it up, and carried her out.

Vickie Holland had created her last finger painting.

* * *

"Where are you?" the professor called.

Dr. Bering tried all night. He started in his chair, fully dressed, calmly calling for him. He beckoned in this manner for hours and gave up the approach by removing his clothes and lighting the candle. He knew his visitor dismissed the necessity of these practices, but Bering was desperate. Nothing worked. No sign of him at all. No shadows glided across his wall. No objects in the room moved with the aid of invisible hands. As the night progressed, the professor grew not more tired, but more frenzied. It was not until the early morning hours that his wildness began to fade, and he felt weak and lame.

"Where are you?" he yelled again. His voice began to taper. His throat was sore, and his tongue was dry. Finally, he collapsed to the floor in a heap, no strength left at all.

Outside, dawn began to climb up into the city. It was the tiny crevice between night and day. The time of magic.

There was a sound like a rustling of leaves, and a familiar voice.

"Samuel. Samuel, whatever are you doing, chum?"

Dr. Bering pushed himself up with his hands and looked about the room. He could not see his visitor. "Where are you?"

"I'm here. Don't worry."

"I've been … I've been calling all night. Didn't you hear me?"

"I've had some business to attend to. I can't be two places at once, you know."

"But I thought you would come. I've been calling all night."

At this, the visitor appeared, his face smoldering with anger. He leaned in close to the professor, who was petrified and still lying on the floor. Bering opened his mouth to speak, and the visitor covered it with a large, rough—almost scaly—hand. The dark one exhaled a foul breath, a long, smoky sigh that reeked of bittersweet decay. His eyes narrowed into slits. His brow furrowed into a menacing crease. "You already said that, and I told you, I had someplace to be. I'm not a pet, chum. I don't come, tail wagging, every time you blow your whistle. Understand?"

"Y-yes." He felt the visitor's fingernails piercing the flesh on his cheek.

"Good."

The visitor disappeared as quickly as he came. Bering put a finger to his face to massage his wound and, when he removed it, found it tipped with a fresh drop of blood.

CHAPTER EIGHT

Bering cracked the door to the guest bedroom and said, "Mike? You might want to get up now. Don't forget we have class today."

The form underneath the covers grunted an incoherent reply and slowly rose to life. Mike had been asleep only a few hours, but it had been a good, hard sleep, and he had a vague yet confident intuition that as soon as the initial daze was gone, he would feel totally refreshed. He turned over and glanced at the clock on the antique nightstand.

"Isn't it a little early?" He yawned.

"Yes," came the reply, "but I thought we might go by the Regal Theater to pick up your car."

"Oh, yeah." Glimpses of the previous evening shot through Mike's head in fuzzy and eerie flashes, mental daguerreotypes imprinted on his consciousness in grotesque still-life panels. "Sounds good," he said.

Mike sat up, rubbed his eyes, and dressed in his clothes from the previous day, still dirty and torn from the night's adventure. He would have to make a stop by his own house to change before class. Oddly, his bruises had lost most of their soreness, and his cuts did not sting half as bad as when he had retired to bed. His thoughts went to the chance meeting between himself and Bering in the street outside TransCo. But was it chance? What had Bering said? *A little bird told him.* Mike resolved to ask the professor just what he meant by that, but later he forgot, and so he never did.

"I feel like an idiot. I can't believe I actually pulled a gun on someone."

"It's okay," Bering said. "You can hardly blame yourself, considering your mental state at the time. Let's just be glad everything worked out like it did." And then he added, "And that the gun wasn't loaded."

"Even if it had been," Mike said, "I'm not much of a marksman. I doubt I woulda even hit the car."

"That poor lady didn't know that."

An electricity was passing between them, joining them, binding them.

Mike believed he owed Bering something, and though he was not sure what it was, he wanted to devote himself to searching it out. Protégé. Assistant. Whatever the case called for, he would be it for Bering. And more. He made this resolution with willful surrender completely foreign to his character. But he was tired of the mental agony of pondering the excruciating minutiae of life, tired of the stress it put on him. He was tired of checking every thought against his own tender sensibilities. He was tired of worrying, tired of caring. He was tired of being timid and of being neurotic. He was tired of assuming control; his personal sovereignty only offered pain. He could do nothing but give in.

Bering's car pulled into the Regal's parking lot.

"See you in a few hours," Mike said.

"Right you are."

Mike got into his own automobile, and for a while, it refused to start. But after coaxing it some, he was on his way home. Once there, he showered, changed clothes, and began his new day.

The battery on his phone had long since died, so he didn't get the voice mail.

✳ ✳ ✳

Jimmy Horn rested on the ash-stained carpet of his tiny bedroom and practiced opening his butterfly knife with one smart flip of the hand. Loud rock music blared from the huge speakers on the dresser. A cigarette faded out in an ashtray next to his knee, sending up a thin, disintegrating smoke signal. His eyes watched the blade of the knife fly out of its handles as he opened and closed it repeatedly.

Jimmy was seventeen years old and had been in and out of juvenile correctional facilities since he was old enough to leave the house to avoid the violence.

When Jimmy's mother had found the courage to say enough was enough, she moved the two of them to Houston, and that's where Jimmy began to get into trouble. "Hanging with the wrong crowd," as his mother would say. She would never believe that Jimmy himself constituted "the wrong crowd." Alcohol. Shoplifting. Vandalism. When he was thirteen, he got caught holding up a convenience store. The gun was unloaded, but it was the first in a line of serious crimes for Jimmy Horn. Sometimes he got caught. Sometimes he didn't. He had set fire to Percy Wheeler's house and never got caught. He even hid in the shadows of some trees across the street, eating sunflower seeds and watched it burn for a while. Jimmy had burned his own conscience to ashes. The rage intensified.

Trouble just seemed to fit Jimmy Horn, and that was fine by him. He liked to be feared. He saw the way people looked at him as he passed by. The way teachers and principals even seemed to be scared of him. In juvie everyone feared him. Even the bigger prisoners were afraid of Jimmy Horn. The meanest residents, many of them gang members, stepped out of his way and went to extremes to secure him cigarettes or drugs. Securing their own safety, of course. Most didn't even know his name. He knew that they spoke of him in hushed reverence, calling him Mr. Black, because when he could get ahold of the polish, he painted his fingernails that color, and because his black hair hung down into his face like a drawn cowl. Because everywhere he went, a dark cloud seemed to hang over him. He knew they called him that name, always whispering it so as not to anger him. He knew, and he liked it.

Jimmy Horn lived with his mother now. And the voices.

He didn't know what they were or *who* they were, but for two years he had listened to them and did almost everything they asked him to do. He once told his friend Kurt about the voices.

"That's crazy, man," Kurt said.

"What?"

"*You're* crazy, man," Kurt said. "You hear voices? Like, in your head? You're crazy."

Jimmy promptly stabbed Kurt in the arm with a fork.

No one called Jimmy crazy and emerged unscathed. The voices were not an issue of sanity to him. The voices were real—very real—and though Jimmy didn't fear any man, he was definitely afraid of the voices. He couldn't see them, for one thing. And they asked him to *do* things. Things he didn't really mind doing, but it was the principle of the matter. Whether he enjoyed doing these things or not, he didn't enjoy being ordered around by anyone. But he always listened, and he always did the things they asked. And as they asked for more and more things to be done, Jimmy himself began to fear that he was indeed crazy.

Jimmy would lay on his bedroom floor, playing with his knife, and keep telling himself, "I'm not crazy. I'm not crazy. I'm not crazy ..."

And then the voices came. Echoing in his ears. Pounding in his brain. "Do us this favor," they said and kept saying.

"Do us this favor."

"I'm not crazy."

"Do us this favor."

And then, the conversation slipped into his mind. The conflict began.

Jimmy! A favor!

I'm not crazy!

Do us this favor!

I'm not!

Please!

Do you hear me? I'm not!

Jimmy ... please do us this favor.

His mother was peeling potatoes over the kitchen sink. The blare of music from Jimmy's room drowned out his approaching steps, but somehow she'd sensed his presence.

She turned. She looked at the unfolded butterfly knife in his hand strangely, as if it were something she'd never seen before.

She dropped a potato.

"Jimmy?"

Jimmy, please just do us this one crazy favor.

* * *

One thing Steve Woodbridge knew without a doubt was that the early-morning call from Graham sounded important. With no hesitation, he raced past rows of new family restaurants and strip malls, the ever-creeping tendrils of Houston's northern urban sprawl, to the little diner near the Houston-Trumbull border. He arrived first, so he took a seat in an out-of-the-way booth and ordered two scrambled eggs, toast with butter, and black coffee.

He had finished his first cup by the time Graham found him.

The two men ate and shot the breeze about sports, weather, the biography of Truman that ran on A&E, and how they thought things were going in the church Steve pastored and Graham attended. They finished their breakfasts before moving on to more serious matters.

"So what's been going on, Graham? You sounded a little off in your call this morning."

"Well, I'll tell ya—this place is going crazy."

"How do you mean?"

"Hard to explain. Last couple of days—well, starting last week, I guess. With all this UFO business. I got reporters out the wazoo. It died down for a while, but then this crazy farmer has his other cow killed, and all of a sudden they're all back. He's got TV crews out there at his place. Got some parapsychologists scanning his barn for energy fields and whatnot. I went over there to check it out. You know, right after he found it. It was a mess, let me tell ya. Guts all over the place. We found some death card or something—"

"Death card?"

"Yeah, some kinda card. Got a Grim Reaper on it. One of my boys said it was a *tarrow* card or some sheesh like that." Graham rolled his eyes. "And I'm thinking, *This is all I need,* you know? Whole town's caught up in it. We get reports of lights in the sky every night, and you can't even suggest to them it was an airplane. No, an airplane's too unbelievable. But they're gonna believe some alien's trying to get their attention. The whole thing's just getting weird."

"It'll blow over. How many cows the guy got?"

"None now."

"See? It's over already."

The men laughed.

"Yeah," Graham said, "but he's got a whole pen full of chickens. And if it ain't that, we'll be getting people comin' in sayin' *they* were attacked or abducted or whatnot." The captain paused and cast his gaze down to his empty plate. He fiddled with the handle on his coffee mug.

"Something wrong, Graham?"

"Yeah. I don't know, Steve, but it's more than all that. It makes me mad to have my whole town stupid like this, but there's something else. I don't know. I just get this feeling. I've been having these headaches for over a week now. And this cold weather's unlike anything I've seen here. Not that it's so cold, but that it's so cold for so long and so early in the season. And it all kinda came together somehow in that old man's barn. I was looking at that card, and somehow it all came together. Not real clear, you know? I mean, I couldn't put my finger on it, but I just felt something. Some kind of ... *pressure*, I guess. No, I know what: oppression. It felt oppressive. It's just really strange. I guess you could pray for me, Pastor, that I do my job well. If we can catch our cow killer, maybe we could put a stop to all this. And also, that my headaches go away. How are you?"

"Well ..." Steve shifted in his seat nervously. "I've been having kind of a hard time lately. I don't know, I guess doubting myself. You haven't noticed anything different about me?"

"A little," Graham answered. "You seemed a bit upset in our meeting last week. And I could tell something was bothering you during the service. During your message. You weren't quite yourself, I guess."

"Well, you're the first person to be honest about it. I heard, 'Good sermon, Pastor' so many times, I thought I was gonna throw up. Truth is, I have been a little upset. I guess my mind's been someplace else."

The student-teacher relationship had been enhanced. Now that he was high on Bering's preternatural charm, the classroom became a place of marvels for Mike, a whole new dimension itself. The lectures became all the more mesmerizing. There was a new bond between Mike Walsh and Dr. Samuel Bering, and Mike's morning in class was by far his favorite. He was disappointed when Bering announced that he must leave the class early to take care of some business, but on his way out, he paused at Mike's desk and quietly said, "Sorry I've got to step out. Stop by my office afterward for a chat if you've got the time."

"I'll be there," Mike said.

Forty-five minutes later, he walked down the hall and knocked on Bering's office door.

"Come in, please."

Mike opened the door and found Bering speaking with another man, who was sitting in one of the wingback chairs, his legs crossed. He was an older man, probably quite a bit older than Dr. Bering. His hair was completely white, as was a thick mustache nestled under his nose. He wore a brown tweed suit and horn-rimmed glasses, and he looked altogether more professorial than even Bering. With his rosy cheeks, though, he reminded Mike of a thin Santa Claus.

"Mike," Bering said, "let me introduce you to Dr. Leopold Sutzkever."

Sutzkever rose and shook Mike's hand.

"Nice to meet you, Dr. Sutzkever."

"Very pleased to meet you," Sutzkever responded with a heavy French accent.

"Mike is one of my students and a good friend," Bering said.

Mike smiled at the words *good friend*.

Bering continued: "Dr. Sutzkever was just telling me a ghost story."

"Actually, I was just leaving," Sutzkever said. And with that, he restated, "Mike, it was a pleasure to make your acquaintance. Thank *you*, Samuel, for your time." He began to leave.

"Good-bye, Leo," Bering called after him. "Perhaps we could take some tea together tomorrow."

"That would be wonderful," Sutzkever said, and he turned the corner and left.

Mike sat down. "He seems cool," he said.

"Yes, he certainly is."

"What was the ghost story?"

"What?"

"You said he was telling you a ghost story."

"Oh, *that*. Just a story. Dr. Sutzkever's a very peculiar fellow. He and I have become pretty good friends, despite our differences in interest and opinion. He seems to disregard science, which of course is my bread and butter. He teaches several religion courses here at Landon, and he has several courses at the theological seminary across town. Yes, opposite poles. That's what we are, I suppose. But as they say, opposites attract. I call his religion 'mythology,' and he calls my science 'irrational faith in rationalism.' But we share a great passion for literature. I tell you, Mike, many a discussion on Shakespeare or Milton has saved us from arguing till our mouths dropped off."

FROM THE JOURNAL OF DR. LEOPOLD SUTZKEVER:

Had a brief conversation with Dr. Bering this morning. At the mere mention of my experience with the light originating from his office, he noticeably turned very nervous. I daresay that he almost jumped in his seat upon the relation of my discovery of the broken vase. He laughed it off, of course. It's an amazing admission for him, but he did tell me that he was dabbling in some experiments of a paranormal nature. I did not relay my suspicions to him, but the indication of his "dabblings" very much confirms them in my mind. He took me to task for being concerned about him. (He noticed this on his own. I did not say I was concerned about him, nor did I say anything to that effect.) He was not specific concerning his "experiments" but vigorously cited several scientific research findings about the unified field theory and how it relates to psychic phenomenon. Then he admonished me to "get my head out of Augustine and Aquinas, and put it into Hawking" and another name I don't recall. I very much like Dr. Bering. He is an altogether agreeable man, but he strikes me to be like those Saint Paul wrote Timothy about who "are always learning but are never able to acknowledge the truth."

✳ ✳ ✳

Mike left Landon University and drove downtown to work. As expected, it was a cold day, but not a dreary one at all. The sun shone unobstructed and cast its glory across the metal and glass of the Houston skyline. At his cluttered desk in *Spotlight's* offices, Mike poured himself into someone's piece on rodeo clowns.

You were miserable with her anyway, came a stray thought.

It flew in from parts unknown, and a feeling of guilt immediately struck him. It passed, though, and he spent no time examining the mental statement. He simply accepted its sentiment and went back to work.

Robbie took him to lunch to discuss possible assignments. Mike suggested a bio on Dr. Bering. Robbie, despite being the one who had originally pushed Mike to do the UFO story, nixed the idea. "Aliens are so last month," he joked. Mike insisted that the newest cow mutilation would renew interest and that Bering wasn't a believer in UFOs in the strictest sense.

"Listen," Robbie responded, "we did the history of UFOs as a serious piece, but printing this stuff about other dimensions and wormhole travelers would put us right there on the bull pile with all the pulp magazines."

Mike arrived home later and connected his phone to the charger. After a few minutes, it lit up to life and buzzed the announcement of a message.

Somehow he knew it was bad news.

Maybe Molly found a job.

Maybe she wants a divorce.

Maybe she hates my guts.

The moment before he pressed the PLAY button, he attempted to wipe his mind clean of depressing forethought. *It'll probably be*

Robbie with a final decision. Maybe it'll be Dr. Bering with an invitation for coffee. He clicked.

A woman's voice played back, soft and hoarse. It was a voice he would have found sweet had the message been anything other than her sobbing, quiet words: "Mike ... Mike ... This is Molly ... Mike, are you there? It's ... I ... I don't know what to do ... It's Vickie, Mike ... I don't know what to do. Vickie's dead, Mike. Vickie's dead she's dead she died"—his wife's frantic outpouring continued, sounding like a plea for help—"she's dead she died oh, Mike, she's dead they say she died—" The message cut off.

Mike wanted desperately to call her and console her. To tell her everything would be fine. That he would have it all under control. He knew he would have to.

Molly and Vickie grew up as orphans. They didn't have any family. He was it. Molly had one sister, and now she was dead. And she had one husband, and she had left him.

He returned the call.

* * *

The phone was ringing, but Molly Walsh was in a state of shock. She stared at Vickie's painting—the finger-painted lady—and blocked out the world around her. Her cheeks were a vivid red and streaked with dry lines of mascara, the riverbeds of tears. The phone rang, and she did not hear it. Whoever was calling was persistent, though, and eventually her mind cleared to the recognition.

"Hello," she whispered.

"Molly?"

She raised it a little bit, but it was hard. Crying for hours makes the vocal cords sore. "Mike?" She began to cry again.

"Tell me what's happening."

"The police called … they said Vickie died last night. They want someone to …" She broke down, sobbing loudly into the telephone.

"To do what, Molly?"

"To … to …"

"Just take it easy."

"… to make sure it's her."

"Make sure it's her," he repeated. "Molly, listen to me."

"Uh-huh?" she whispered.

"I'll be there as soon as I can."

✳ ✳ ✳

Evening seeped into the sky, drawing chalky curtains of clouds with it. The moon hung high and full. It was bone white, a huge celestial snowball overlooking the winter scene in Trumbull. Abby Diaz cupped her tiny hands to her mouth and blew into them like she had seen Daddy do. Her breath provided fleeting warmth. It grew darker, and she began to cry, not for any particular reason, but because she was a little girl walking home at night all alone. The tears cascading down her rosy cheeks felt hot against her freezing skin. She sniffed and sobbed, puffing foggy breath into the air.

Abby had spent the afternoon at her friend Elizabeth's house. They played "school" (always more fun than the real thing) and Barbie dolls and then watched cartoons. Elizabeth's mother noticed dusk approaching and suggested Abby head home. There had been the usual childhood petition by her daughter, begging that Abby be allowed to stay for dinner. The answer was no, and Abby was urged on her way.

Abby Diaz, bless her heart, was a slow walker. A real stop-and-smell-the-roses little girl. She petted a stray dog, pausing long enough to give it a good scratching behind the ears. When the dog fell into utter delight at the attention, lying down and thumping its hind leg on the ground, she was love struck and petted him longer than she intended. She spent a considerable amount of time trying to get the mutt to follow her home. He would not budge, though, and eventually Abby gave up. She resumed her journey, stopping to look at horses standing around in a neighbor's field. She climbed up onto the wooden fence and thought, *I bet they're really cold.* Then she realized that *she* was really cold, and she hopped down to be on her way.

The sky was not black. It was a soupy midnight blue, and the gauzy wisps of clouds and the full moon reminded Abby of nights in the scary movies Daddy let her watch with him. She always hid her eyes when the monster appeared, or buried her face in Daddy's neck. She remembered how the sky always looked in those movies— haunted, just like the night sky looming over her at that very moment.

She made the right turn off of the paved street that led to Elizabeth's house and onto the gravel road that led to her own. It was the home stretch. On each side of the road ran two long rows of bushes. They were three or four feet high and very thick. Open fields lay beyond the bushes on the left side. She walked on the right side of the road, closest to the bushes backdropped by woods. The trees stood close to each other, their branches gnarled and twisted together in conspiratorial embraces. Woods always looked frighten-ing at night. The trees seemed alive, tall wooden ghosts with hideous faces of bark and shadow and knotty eyes that frowned, and long, stick-arms with claws that reached out and down. Out and down to snatch up little girls and eat them. She started to cry now, and she barely noticed the chilly air because she was sweating and burning up with fear. She tried not to look at the trees. The huge, ghoulish trees.

Something in the bushes behind her moved, and she jumped. She wanted to scream, but all that came out was a soft whimper. She increased her pace. Tears streamed down the front of her pink winter coat. Her feet crunched against the gravel. She concentrated on that sound, the grinding crunch of rocks beneath her little shoes, and tried to block out any other noises around her. The nearly silent rustle of a breeze swirling through the foliage. The steady whistle of the crickets. More movement in the bushes. The sound of her own footfall overcame all. She began to count her steps.

"One, two, three, four, five, six ... "

She counted each step, and when she got to forty-six, she heard *it*. She was not far from where she began to count. Little girls have little strides. Her bones began to quiver, vibrating in terror. She kept walking, listening to her footsteps, but they were echoed by another's. Echoed by *it*. There was a second set of footsteps behind her. She was sure of it.

She stopped. She heard nothing.

Slowly, she started out again, listening intently, and after a few steps, the crunching behind her resumed. The noise was louder than her own. Whatever was there was certainly larger than she. It was too loud to be a figment of her imagination. It was too real.

She wanted to run, but her fear paralyzed her. *If you just stay still, it will go away.* Abby kept walking, but she didn't run, *couldn't* run. She knew that if she did, *it* would run up behind her and that would be the end of that. Her entire body trembled, and her tears ceased, the ducts clogged by absolute shock.

Then the footsteps behind her stopped. Abby kept going, all the while thinking about sleeping between Mommy and Daddy, safe and secure in Mommy and Daddy's big bed from the trees and the monsters and the *it* behind her. She hoped that *it* had gone away. She stopped, and then she did something that she never thought she would have the courage to do. Slowly, cautiously, she began to turn around. She intended to look behind her, to look at the road she had traveled, and she prayed to God that she would find it empty.

Please Jesus please Jesus please Jesus, she prayed. *Please, Jesus, don't let …*

She was halfway there.

anything

She closed her eyes for a moment.

be

The turn complete, she opened them.

there!

Nothing. The path rolled on into the darkness.

She turned back and continued the stroll home.

In the bushes, to her right and not far behind, *it* watched her with wide-eyed intensity. A young girl. Little girl. Six, maybe seven years old. It saw that she was shivering, and it was shivering too. She had almost seen it. She must have heard it walking behind her.

Carefully, it crept along in the dark shadows of the woods, staying close to her. Tracking her. But it placed its footsteps cautiously, avoiding leaves or twigs, so as not to make a sound. It hunched over, bending its knees, and used one hand for balance. The other held a butterfly knife.

He was not sure if he had killed his mother. Everything went blurry back at the house, and the voices had been screaming so loudly in his head that his ears rang. All he knew was that he was freezing (and probably had the beginnings of frostbite on his fingers) and that he had decided to do whatever the voices said from here on out.

The girl walked very fast now. She was practically running. He scrambled along the brush, trying hard to keep up and forgetting all about stealth and silence.

Jimmy? One more favor, please.

The girl walked briskly, and he began running after her. She tried to scream, but the cold flesh of his rough hand covered her mouth, pressing tight against her teeth. He was upon her.

CHAPTER NINE

Robbie Jensen and his wife, Teri, sat at their antique breakfast table and ate dinner. Robbie gulped down the last bite of his second helping of lasagna, and the phone rang.

"Robbie. This is Mike."

"Hey, Mike, good to hear from you. Had dinner yet? Teri made lasagna, and you can come over if you want. There's plenty left."

"No, man. Thanks, though. Look, I need a few days off from work. Something came up, and I need to get out of town for a while."

"You all right?"

"Yeah, I'm fine." Mike sighed. "Molly's sister died last night."

"Oh, man, I'm sorry." *How exactly does one follow that?* "What happened?"

"It was a car crash, apparently. Look, Molly's not taking it too well—"

"How could she?"

"Right. Anyways, you know they grew up in foster homes—in an orphanage, for God's sake—so I'm really the only family. Molly's just too broken up. I'm gonna have to take care of the arrangements."

"Sure, sure, Mike. I understand. No problem. No problem at all."

"So I can have the time off?"

"Of course. Yeah, it's no problem at all, man. Is there anything I can do?"

"Well, there is one thing. Do you go to church?"

The question seemed to come out of nowhere for Robbie. "Do what?"

"Church. Do you go?"

"No. No, not really. Christmas and Easter," he said, almost apologizing

"I'm just looking for a minister. You know, to do the service. I'd look for one in Dallas, but it'd just be eeny-meeny-miney-moe. I wouldn't know one from the other. I guess I could go with whoever the funeral home suggests, but it wouldn't be the same. Molly was going to church a lot, so I'm sure she would want a real minister doing the funeral, if you know what I mean. Somebody with a connection somehow."

"Yeah, yeah, I know exactly what you mean. What about the church she went to here in Houston?"

"I called already. All of their staff is away at some conference for the week."

"Well," Robbie said, "Teri goes every now and then. Let me ask her."

He did and returned. "She goes over to that church on Jones Road. She says the pastor's nice. Name's Steve Woodbridge. Hold on a second. Teri's getting his phone number for you."

"Thanks, Rob. I really appreciate this."

"Like I said, man—no problem at all."

"Hey, Rob. You think maybe you could come up for the funeral? Molly's got no family, and some of mine will be there, but it'll look really empty. I'd really appreciate it if you could maybe come up."

"Sure, Mike. I'll be there."

* * *

Pops Dickey retired to bed, satisfied but angry. Attention from the media had kept him busy all day. Even the Houston local news showed up, though they seemed a bit unhappy to be there. A little ashamed, too. Representatives from newspapers and magazines swarmed, camera-toting moths drawn to a dying flame, and Pops figured most of them were still hanging around town after reporting the first cow's death. Waiting for further developments. Mysterious lights in the sky, maybe.

He did not feel guilty for making up his story. He knew that aliens had killed his cows, and he knew they came from outer space, and just because he didn't actually *see* them didn't mean the story wasn't true. He didn't care if the police found a tarot card in his barn. He didn't care if the second death looked entirely different from the first. Aliens had killed his cows, and he knew it.

Gertie didn't believe him, but what did she know, anyway? She hadn't seen the flying saucer. *Well, neither did I, for that matter*, he thought. *But at least I know it happened.*

Pops lay alone in the bed, the quilt pulled up to his chin for warmth. Gertie got so put out by all the goings on that she went to stay at a friend's house. She had never done that before. She called Pops a "crazy old man," and she up and left. He was alone now, nobody to believe in him. To believe his story. *Stewadell would*, he thought. *He'd stand right there beside me and tell 'em he saw the aliens with his own two eyes.* But in reality, he knew that Stewadell would probably laugh at him. Stewadell would call him crazy, just as Gertie had. They all thought he was crazy. Including Lattimer. That guy aimed to stop the show. He didn't believe in aliens or flying saucers. He believed in coyotes or teenage vandals or tarot-card readers. He wanted to stop the show.

Pops loved the spotlight. The day had satisfied him. But he hated Graham Lattimer, and underneath his sense of satisfaction ran a current of rage.

Maybe somebody will have to stop him, then, won't they?

* * *

Lisa Diaz clutched the dish towel to her breast tightly and peered out the window. She stood in the kitchen, which lay in the front of the house and looked out upon the street. Night fell, and she could see nothing beyond the front yard. She expected to see the headlights of the neighbor's pickup truck come blaring down the road. The expectation had turned to hope, and then to worry. Abby should have left Elizabeth's thirty-or-so minutes ago if she planned to walk, and she definitely would have arrived home by now. The walk was short. The walk was easy. Abby had walked the distance many times before, and she had never taken this long. Lisa chewed on her bottom lip and wrung the towel in her clenched fists, her knuckles turning white. She thought of her child, her little girl, walking home in the darkness. Scared and alone. *She should be home by now.* She called Melody.

"Melody, this is Lisa. Is Abby still over there?"

Melody did not answer immediately, and the hesitation ignited panic in Lisa's hands. They began to shake uncontrollably.

Finally, Melody responded: "She's not home yet?"

A chill ran through Lisa's body. Her mouth went dry. She hung up the phone without saying another word to Melody, ran to the foot of the stairs, and called up to her husband, who was watching the news in the bedroom. "Carlos! Carlos!" Her eyes began to gush with huge torrents of tears, and her lungs heaved rapidly, her sobs quickening until she hyperventilated.

Carlos came bounding down the steps. "What's wrong?"

Lisa struggled to get it out. "Abby ... Abby ... She left from Elizabeth's a while ago and she's not home yet ... It's so dark, Carlos ... Something's happened."

"Okay, okay," he said. "I'm sure she's fine. Probably stopped to look at the Baileys' horses or something. I'll go out and get her."

He turned toward the door—but then it opened, and Abby walked in.

Lisa jumped up and rushed to her daughter, embracing her triumphantly, but she was horrified. Abby's hair was disheveled and her blouse was torn. Her knees were skinned and bleeding, and she was filthy with dirt. But there was *something* ...

Something odd ...

She was smiling.

"Abby!" Lisa said. "What's wrong? What happened to you?"

"It's okay, Mommy."

"What happened to you, sweetie? Who did this to you?"

"The bad man," Abby replied.

Her father rushed out the open door and ran into the darkness of the road in search of the monster who had attacked his little girl.

"What happened, Abby? What happened?"

"The bad man came out of the bushes and grabbed me, Mommy, but don't worry, it's okay. I'm okay. The bad man couldn't hurt me."

"How did you get away?"

"The good man."

"The good man?"

"The good man came and grabbed the bad man before he could hurt me. The good man took the bad man away."

Lisa Diaz picked up her daughter and clutched her tightly to her chest. She turned back to the phone and called the police.

Outside, her husband walked up and down the street, looking for the bad man, but he never found him.

* * *

Taking a late-night flight to Dallas with such a foreboding thought as death in his mind aggravated Mike's already omnipresent paranoia. The fear of having to identify Vickie's body set a firm foundation for more irrational fears. *The pilot has a stroke, and the plane goes down. Lightning strikes the wing, and the plane goes down. A crazed terrorist leaps up from his seat and announces that a bomb is ticking in the cargo hold, and, of course, the plane goes down.* When you're on a plane, every imaginative scenario ends with the fiery plummet of the plane. Airplanes were not ideal environments for the nervous imaginations of men like Mike Walsh.

Stereo headphones sprouted from the arm of his seat, and he adjusted them over his ears. The classical music bubbling from Station 7 soothed him a little. He glanced across the aisle and noticed that a woman in the middle seat held the latest issue of *Spotlight Magazine.* He supposed she had read his article on UFOs already. He smiled, and his nervousness settled down a bit further.

Still, he could not help thinking of the duty awaiting him. He knew it was just a formality. Obviously, the authorities knew for a fact that the body they had on their hands was Vickie Holland. He would need only to glance at her. Perhaps he could even fake it somehow.

Close his eyes quickly or look at her hair instead of her face. All they wanted from him was the assurance—the words: "Yeah, that's her."

The thought of his chore terrified him, but not for the obvious reason. The thought of seeing the corpse did loom over him—he fixated on it—but something existed beyond fear of seeing a dead body. He had never been very close to his sister-in-law. He could say that he was sad she had passed away, and he could mourn her loss for his wife's sake, but if he was honest, she was not a personal loss to him. It was not dreadful to say that he would not miss her, because he hardly knew her. No, he did not fear Vickie's dead body. He feared what it meant. It meant confronting DEATH.

He had confronted DEATH, or rather, it had confronted *him*, a long time ago. He still had nightmares of that encounter, and now it seemed that those nightmares were slipping free from the shackles of sleep. They became conscious. They became true. They became real.

He did not fear the physical action of viewing death, but rather DEATH itself, and despite recently finding a friendship that seemed to offer hope, feelings of his own nothingness swallowed him once again. Once again, life was meaningless.

He rented a car at the Dallas airport and drove to Vickie's house. On the way, his fear spread to a wholly other situation in his life—Molly. The notion that Vickie's death would bring him and his wife closer together was fleeting. In theory, after losing her only blood relative, Molly would rush into Mike's arms and cling to him, the only family she had left. But both rational thought and his own pessimism convinced him of the converse. She would surely drift further away. He knew about the statistics showing the strains death had on personal relationships, strains that often led to separation or divorce. Heck, he'd probably written an article about it at one time or another. But their strain had already been there. They were already separated. They could only grow more apart.

He still looked forward to seeing her. Deep down, though he didn't explore the thought fully, Mike believed there was still a chance at reconciliation.

Mike pulled into the driveway of the modest one-story home. As he removed his overnight bag from the backseat, he realized that Dallas was not as cold as Houston.

He rang the doorbell, and Molly answered. She smiled when she saw him, and it made her look pretty despite the obvious signs of heavy crying on her face. She looked altogether unflattering with her eyes red and puffy, her hair disheveled, and her face devoid of makeup. The figure he often admired in secret was obscured in the fluffy folds of a gray sweat suit. Mike loved this woman, and the distance and his desire covered her multitude of cosmetic sins. The emptiness of not seeing her every day made her appear as beautiful as she had been on their wedding day.

He stepped in, and she hugged him. Again, the thought that *this could be my chance* surfaced, but he stifled it and felt guilty. *Her sister died, you jerk!*

"I made some coffee. Do you want some?" she asked.

"Sure."

He set his bag down. Molly went into the kitchen, and Mike stepped into the living room. An abstract painting of a vague human form stared at him, though the person had no distinguishable eyes. He sat down.

Molly came in and handed him a mug that had obviously belonged to Vickie. It read: DON'T BUG ME! ARTIST IN CREATIVE TRANCE.

"Thank you for coming so soon," Molly said.

"Well, I didn't want you to have to be by yourself."

She smiled again. "I'm sorry to put all this on you. I just … I don't think I can handle it."

"I understand. It's okay. I called from Houston and made all the arrangements. The funeral will be the day after tomorrow. Tomorrow morning, I'll go down and … well, you know."

"Yeah. I'm sorry about this, Mike. I just wouldn't be able to do it."

"I know. It's okay."

"Did you find a minister?"

"Yeah. I need to head back tomorrow and pick him up. I just didn't know who to get here in Dallas. Robbie recommended this guy to me."

"You couldn't get ahold of Reverend Ayers?"

"He's out of town. Anyways, we'll be back sometime tomorrow night, probably late."

"Do you really have to drive all the way home and all the way back?"

"Well, I thought I should at least meet the guy and be able to tell him about Vickie."

Molly nodded.

Mike told her more about the arrangements. The service would be graveside at the Roselawn Cemetery. That would be in the obituary appearing in the next day's newspaper, but he asked if she would be able to call some of Vickie's friends to let them know. Molly answered that she would probably be able to do that, but as it turned out, the matter was not very pressing. Vickie didn't have any close friends—only a few acquaintances and admirers of her work.

They made small talk into the late hours of the night. When a lull came in the conversation, Molly rose and went in to turn off the coffeepot. When she returned, she said, "Mike?"

"Yeah?"

"Thank you for doing all this."

He smiled.

Meekly, she again said, "Mike?"

"Yeah?"

"Do you think maybe you could sleep in the bed with me tonight?"

"Sure," he said, and he smiled a calm and gentle smile, a reassuring smile, a comforting *everything-will-be-okay* smile, but inside his heart leaped for joy.

✳ ✳ ✳

Police car headlights brightened the road in front of the Diaz home. Hands that gripped flashlights were numb from the cold even inside the insulation of gloves. The lights' bulbous glares danced around, shining this way and that like mutant fireflies. Officers from the Trumbull Police Department, including Captain Graham Lattimer, searched through the bushes and the fields and the patches of woods for *the bad man*, but they did not find him. They found no trace of *the good man* either.

✳ ✳ ✳

The small Dart 'n Shop convenience store stayed open twenty-four hours a day, three hundred and sixty-four days a year in Trumbull, Texas. Daryl Worth hated that fact. He worked the midnight to 7:00

a.m. shift. The only thing that kept him awake was the expectation of a surprise visit from the store's manager (which he was still young enough to believe might happen) and the fear all graveyard-shift grocers have of gun-toting, homicidal thieves (which he was old enough to be paranoid about).

Daryl read a Silver Surfer comic book and sipped a soda, watching out of the corner of his eye the young kid who walked up and down the aisles. The kid's pants and shirt were dirty. Dead leaves clung to them. He looked like he had been rolling around in the woods, and Daryl supposed maybe he had. The red markings of skin abrasions covered his arms and face. And he had a wicked-looking tattoo.

Maybe he's been in a fight, Daryl thought, and not just because he looked like a kid who had been in a fight, but also because he looked like a kid who *would* get into a fight. The kind of kid you don't bring to your house to play after school, because he'd probably steal your stuff or convince you to play some stupid game like "Who Can Take the Hardest Punch?" or "How Close to Our Feet Can We Throw a Knife Without Cutting Off a Toe?" He also had that blank stare so common in neighborhood bullies and the high school tyrants they eventually grew into. The only thing that changed about these kids was the name of the rock bands on their T-shirts.

The kid turned a corner and headed to the big refrigerated coolers in the rear of the store. He stopped at the alcohol cooler, his eyes scanning the cans and bottles of beer. Meanwhile, Daryl scanned the kid. In the back pocket of the kid's blue jeans, a handle peeked out, and Daryl led himself to believe the handle belonged to a knife.

The cooler opened, and the kid pulled out a white-labeled can. He turned around and walked toward the counter. Only by accident, Daryl looked into the kid's eyes, but only briefly. They were black and lifeless and piercing.

In that splinter of a moment, Daryl's imagination went into irrational overdrive. *Maybe he's going to kill me.*

The kid placed the can on the counter.

"Is that all for you?" Daryl managed to ask.

The kid nodded.

Daryl did not want to say it, but he did anyway: "Can I see some ID, please?"

Nothing happened at first. The kid bore into Daryl with those dead eyes of his, and Daryl could feel them, though he didn't look at them. Then Daryl saw the arm reach around to the back pocket, and his first thought came: *He's getting his ID*, but then he realized, and *knew*—so quickly he froze in his place, eyes bulging and throat swelling—*He's going for the knife.*

It didn't seem irrational anymore.

The kid's arm swung back around, and Daryl wanted to jump but couldn't, and before he could even scream, the kid's hand lay before him, a cheap wallet dangling from his fingers.

"Here," the kid said, and he dropped it clumsily onto the counter. Daryl picked it up and opened it. It had a Velcro fastener, and the sound as it tore open amplified a hundred times in the cold, still air of the convenience store. The appearance of the wallet did not allay the terror quivering in Daryl's spine. He dug through it cautiously. No driver's license. No identification of any kind. Not even any money. Just a little, dog-eared photograph of a woman. Probably the kid's mother.

Daryl didn't want to say it. "There's no ID in here."

The kid looked blankly at the wallet in Daryl's hands. He snatched it back and reached around to place it in his pocket. He bowed over the counter, his face hovering inches from Daryl's own, and suddenly, the shining blade of the knife swept into focus, a cold steel shark fin slicing through the air.

The kid said, "Give ... me the ... m-money in the ... in the ... in the *thing.*" He poked his weapon in the direction of the cash register.

Daryl obliged, scooping up all the bills from the cash drawer into a neat stack, never averting his gaze from the knife trembling in the kid's hand. He offered the money, but the kid didn't accept it immediately. He stared at it, a quizzical look upon his face. He seemed to think, *What's all that for?* but after a few seconds, he grabbed it and shoved the bills into his pants—not into his pocket, but down the front of his pants. Then his glare fell onto Daryl, and Daryl felt it fall, hot and stinging and brutally intense. The clerk looked into the evil eyes for the second time and saw *something* in them. He saw the wickedness that dwelled inside; he saw it alive and screaming and squirming to get out and attack.

He's going to kill me.

In a broad roundhouse stroke, the kid swiped at Daryl's face with the knife. Daryl's immobility dissolved, and he jerked back, the knife barely missing the tip of his chin. He stumbled backward, tripped over his own feet, and fell down hard on his behind. The counter obstructed his view of the kid, and Daryl expected to see him lunge over it wildly any second, mouth drooling and fist clenching his instrument of death, eager for blood.

But the kid didn't attack. He fled out the door and into the night.

Daryl stood up, his knees knocking, and glanced around the store. He fumbled for the phone and called the police.

Jimmy Horn's days were numbered.

* * *

Yes, someone will definitely have to teach that Southern boy Graham Lattimer a thing or two, Pops Dickey thought, and he closed his eyes to get some sleep. A few minutes later, his drift into unconsciousness not yet realized, he heard a scratching noise from within the wall behind his bed. He opened his eyes, letting them adjust to the darkness in his bedroom. The noise came again—*scritch, scritch, scritch*—like something alive, not random like the brush of a tree limb. A mouse, maybe. And it was down low, at the base of the wall, and *in* the wall, not outside of it. Pops decided that it was a mouse, and it upset him a little, because he never had mice before.

He closed his eyes. The scratching came again, only this time much louder, resembling a tearing sound, more than a scratching. If there was a mouse in Pops's wall, it was a big sucker. It sounded like it planned on coming right through the wall itself! It sounded like—

The window over the bed began to rattle, and Pops almost thought it was caused by the wind, but the inside of the house began to rattle as well. The portrait of him and Gertie hanging on the wall swayed back and forth. The dresser shook, and so did the bed. He expected the pane above him to implode, drenching the bed with a glittering rain of glass.

"What in God's name?" he said aloud.

Then a blinding white light filled the room, invading every corner. The light was hot and fierce, an atomic blast emanating from somewhere outside and shooting directly into his bedroom, and the old man could not see a thing save stark whiteness.

"What's going on?" he cried.

The bed shook more violently, popping him up and down convulsively on the mattress. He thought his bones would snap at any moment, and his heart began to beat like a bass drum in his chest so hard he thought it might explode.

I'm going to have a heart attack!

He clung desperately to the mattress, not wanting to fly off. Gradually, in fragments, his sight returned. He could see only outlines of objects in the room—the rectangle of the dresser, the sloping back of the chair ...

... the small form of a person at the foot of the bed.

His aged and hardened heart tightened in his chest.

"Who are you?"

"Exactly what you wanted," came the voice.

Burning light still filled the room, and Pops could not discern any of the figure's features, but he thought the visitor was smiling. He didn't have to lie about aliens anymore.

The show must go on.

"Just what are you doing to find the monster that did this?"

Carlos Diaz's angry words had haunted Graham throughout the night. The man had a right to be angry. Someone had attacked his daughter, and Graham considered it a miracle that she'd escaped relatively unhurt. Whoever saved her could not be found, and no one had any explanation why. In the child's words, *the bad man* arrived, then *the good man* arrived, and then *the good man* took *the bad man* away.

Why, then, wouldn't the good man be hanging around? he thought. *Why isn't he basking in the adulation? Why isn't he looking for a pat on the back? Or reward money? Or his name in the paper?*

The answers to these questions eluded him, and he felt much like the girl's father, angry and helpless at the same time. Furious, both by what had happened to her and by the ease at which her attacker had escaped them. Graham expected Trumbull's new UFO aficionados would suspect an attempted alien abduction.

The girl did not have much of a description to offer. She hadn't seen her attacker, only felt him. And she had not seen her rescuer either, only knew that he took *the bad man* away. Graham assured Mr. Diaz that the police were doing the best they could. He told him that they would keep looking.

And they did.

Three hours later, with dawn approaching, Graham stopped in a fast-food restaurant for an early-morning coffee. He sat down, removed his gloves, and sipped his cup contemplatively, knowing full well that the caffeine would aggravate his headaches.

"Captain Lattimer?"

Graham looked over. Lewis Driscoll sat in a booth across the aisle.

"How ya doin'?" Graham asked.

"Not bad. Care for some company?"

"Sure," Graham said.

The veterinarian picked up his biscuit in its wax-paper wrapper and shuffled over to Graham's booth.

"Can you believe this cold?" Lewis asked.

"Pretty strange, huh?"

"Yeah. Folks out here aren't so used to all this cold weather for so long. Has something to do with one heck of an El Niño out there in the middle of the ocean, or so I've been told. Places all over the world are experiencing their fiercest winters in years. Decades, even."

"I thought El Niño made warm winters," Graham said.

"Oh. Yeah, maybe so," Lewis said.

Graham took several more sips of his coffee.

"You look like you been up awhile," Lewis said.

"Yep. A little girl was attacked last night."

"Jeez. What happened?"

"Don't know. Didn't find so much as a footprint."

"Hope you don't mind my asking, but how's it coming on the other incident?"

Graham knew exactly what Lewis was talking about. "Haven't found *him* either," he said.

"Maybe you're looking in the wrong place."

"Aw, sheesh. You gonna start with that alien business again? You shoulda seen that second scene, Doc. Woulda blown your whole theory to bits."

"Oh, I'm sure the second killing wasn't the work of the first killer."

"Yeah?"

"Yeah. I've seen the news stories, seen the pictures. They were two entirely different incidents. Anybody with half a brain could figure that out."

Graham raised an eyebrow.

"You think I'm crazy, don't you?" Lewis asked. "You think I'm one of those nuts out there like Pops."

"No. I don't think that. Petrie told me how you walked out of the press conference. How you said it was setting back serious research, or something like that."

"Yes—"

"But still. UFOs? Little green men? I'm sorry, Doc, but I just have a hard time believing in all that."

"Have you ever seen a UFO, Captain?"

"Have you?"

"Well, no, but—"

"And yet you're so darn sure they're flying around all over the place."

"Captain, have you ever seen God?"

Graham hesitated. "No."

"But you believe in Him, don't you?"

"That's a different subject altogether. Apples and oranges."

"Not really. You've never seen God, but you know He's out there. Well, I've never seen a extraterrestrial, but I know they're out there."

"No. I know God's out there because I've heard Him. I've felt Him. Because there's evidence all around us that He's out there."

"And what do you call Pops's dead cow?"

"Just a dead cow. That's what I call it."

"Okay, okay. Don't mean to get you riled."

Graham took another sip. "Sorry. Just a little wound up, that's all."

"No, I'm sorry. I didn't mean to ... Well, I'm sorry. I believe in God. I just happen to believe in UFOs. I believe they're visiting us all the time. I think they want us to know they're out there. I think they want to make contact."

"Well, why haven't they come on down, then? Why haven't they come on down and had a little chat with the president?"

"How do you know they haven't?"

"Sheesh." Graham rolled his eyes. "And what exactly do you think they'd like to tell us?"

"I don't know. Maybe they can teach us more about God. More than we can ever hope to know."

"Right. That's why they come down here and suck the blood out of farm animals."

A thin smirk spread across Lewis's face. "Touché," he said.

"Look, Doc—you seem to be a pretty smart guy. I can't say I buy your theories here or anything, but you seem to be pretty smart. If you want to believe aliens killed that old man's cow, that's fine with me. I just see what that kind of thinking is doing to this town. It's making everybody crazy."

"Captain, I agree things have gotten out of hand, but think about it. The town of Trumbull could be known throughout history. This could be one of the most important events mankind could encounter. Trumbull could have an important place in time along with Roswell, New Mexico."

"Roswell," Graham said. He knew about Roswell. Supposedly, a flying saucer had crashed in the desert there in 1947. Now they had UFO conventions. UFO parades. UFO museums. "Doc, that's exactly what I'm afraid of."

* * *

The Trumbull Police Department bustled with activity. Melody, the mother of Elizabeth, rested in a chair in one of the offices, answering the questions of two officers who weren't exactly sure what to ask. Daryl Worth sat in another office and talked to Sam Petrie. A laptop on the table played back footage from the Dart 'n Shop's surveillance video. They reviewed the whole incident over and over. Daryl looks in the kid's wallet. The kid takes the wallet. The kid pulls out a butterfly knife. Daryl gives the kid the money. The kid tries to cut Daryl's throat. Daryl falls down. The kid runs out.

To Daryl, the entire encounter seemed to take a fraction of the time on video than it had in real life, and he was already imagining what it would have been like to catch that kid's arm mid-swing and pop him one across the jaw. *Yeah! Just like Jason Bourne, man.* He wanted to interrupt that wide, deadly arc with a lightning-quick reflex action and do some real Jason Bourne karate-type stuff, and then maybe pull a few Liam Neesons on that kid, or maybe a few Vin Diesels. *Yeah, that would've been cool, all right.*

"Never seen this guy before?" Petrie asked.

"Naw," Daryl said. His arms still shook a little bit, and sweat still cascaded down his forehead. He couldn't remember Jason Bourne ever being this scared.

* * *

Graham arrived and noticed Petrie in an office across from his own, watching television with a young guy who wore what looked like a grocer's vest.

"What's goin' on?" Graham asked Kelly.

"Kid got held up."

"Get me some aspirin, please." He stepped into the office. "What's up, Sam?"

"This is Daryl Worth, sir. He works over at the Dart 'n Shop convenience store. Kid robbed the store last night and tried to take ol' Daryl here out with a butterfly knife. We're watchin' the store video right now."

Graham sat down and watched the scene play out with them.

"Scary lookin' kid," Graham said.

"Yes, sir, he sure was," Daryl said.

"All dressed in black," Graham said. "Thinks he's Johnny Cash or something. Never seen him before?"

"Naw."

Petrie said, "He may not be from Trumbull, Cap. I've checked our recent juvenile mugs, and we ain't had him before. He might be from Houston."

"Have a copy of this video sent to the Harris County Sheriff's Department and HPD. They'll probably sit on it, but you're more than likely right. If he's got a record, it's with them."

Graham stood and turned to leave, but he turned back and looked at the TV screen.

Petrie said, "Sir?"

"Sam, how far is this store from our other crime scene last night?"

"Pretty close, Cap."

"That so?" Graham sat down again. "Look at the kid's clothes. Torn. Dirty. Lookit right there." He put his finger on the screen where the kid's elbow hovered. "What's that?"

"Looks like a leaf."

"You dang right that's a leaf. Looks like Johnny Cash here's been rolling around in the woods or somethin'. Looks like he got roughed up a little."

"Man, we even had a patrol car drive by the area of the store last night when we were looking for the assault suspect. We musta just missed him. He musta wandered in there after we left."

"Petrie, we catch this kid, and maybe we kill two birds with one stone," Graham said. He smiled, and then the smile vanished. His eyes widened. "Pause it!"

Petrie did.

"What's that right there?" Graham placed his finger on the kid's forearm.

"Looks like a tattoo," Petrie said.

"I don't believe it," the captain said.

"What?"

"Can you blow this frame up?"

"Not on this program."

"Well, get one that can."

Twenty minutes later, Graham and Officer Petrie sat in another office. The surveillance video played through another program on another computer, and Petrie was struggling to find the right menu with the right commands to do what Graham wanted. Finally, he managed to get the right frame frozen in the window. With a few clicks of the mouse, the kid's tattoo grew larger and larger. And clearer.

"Sheesh," Graham said. "Tell me that's not what I think it is."

"Looks like the Grim Reaper to me, Cap."

* * *

Two men led Mike down a brightly lit corridor. Everything was dressed in white—the men, the floor, the walls, everything. It seemed so pristine, so virginal. Why, then, did it seem so terrifying? The grim specter of what he walked toward made it all appear so dark. He had not prepared for this. He'd escaped from the black shadow of DEATH the night before by, once again, sharing a bed with his wife, and though she mourned the loss of her sister, it felt good to be with her. He'd nearly forgotten why he was there, why he'd gotten to reunite with her in the first place. But the morning came, and so did the anticipation of what lay ahead. It struck him like a cold wet splash in the face.

The two men steered him to the right, and they walked through a pair of swinging doors, stainless steel batwings, like the entrance to a grocery store's butcher shop. These images made Mike nauseous, for he knew that was exactly where he was headed. A butcher shop. A meat locker.

A fresh flop of warm nausea gurgled in his stomach.

They passed through a second set of doors. Sweat beaded on his scalp and in his armpits. The fuzz on the back of his neck prickled. The mingling of scents bombarded his nostrils. He smelled cleaning fluids and something like incense, only very faint, and a light burning scent and other chemical aromas, chemicals used for … well, he didn't know exactly what for, but probably for dealing with—

A bitter acid rose in his throat, and he fought it back down. He belched, tasting the nastiness on his tongue.

"Are you okay?" one of the men asked.

Mike nodded.

They walked the home stretch. The scents lingered more heavily there. It was the smell of DEATH. Not the rotting, bloated stench he expected, but the pungent chemical mask that covered it and became just as horrid. The clean smell of DEATH. Overhead, he heard the whish and whir of huge air conditioners.

They stepped through the final door, a huge, thick door on hinges with a long push bar, not a handle or a knob. They led him inside a small room. The air was freezing inside, and there, up against the wall, stood a table with steel legs. A white sheet draped over it, and beneath the sheet, lay the form of a person, a body. His sister-in-law, the corpse. Vickie Holland, the dearly departed.

Mike felt his knees wobble, and his legs began to give out. He tensed them.

"Are you sure you're okay?"

"Yes, I'm fine."

"Sure?"

"I'm fine."

"This'll only take a second," one of the men said.

They didn't bring him to her. They brought *her* to *him*. The table had wheels, and they rolled it over to him. He couldn't even look at the sheet at first. He stared at the white wall across the room. Then he tilted his head down slowly, fearfully. The white sheet gave away Vickie's features. Her head, chest, legs, feet. Her nose rose up, a tiny hill in the white snows of the covering. It reminded him of something from his childhood. His mother had taken him to church when he was a little boy, and one Sunday, the congregation celebrated what they called the Lord's Supper. A wooden table rested near the altar, below the preacher's pulpit. A white sheet lay over silver pans of crackers and grape juice—"the flesh and the blood," the preacher said. "This is the body of Christ." Mike was only five or six at the time. He thought an actual body lay sprawled beneath that sheet. Underneath that sheet laid the dead body of Jesus, and Mike closed his eyes when they whisked the sheet away.

And here he stood again. The table. The white sheet. The body. This time, an *un*holy communion. DEATH.

One of the men began to pull the veil down to reveal Vickie's face.

Just look at her hair! Just the hair!

He looked at her eyes. They were closed, but Mike saw them open and moving, pupils dilating, lids fluttering. He wanted to scream. It was only Vickie, but it wasn't. It was DEATH. The room grew very warm very quickly, and Mike stood not in a tiny white room, but in the shallow waters of a riverbank, and Vickie did not lie before him. Someone else floated where she had been. The corpse. The body. DEATH. And DEATH came alive and grabbed Mike at the biceps with rotting, bony fingers and squeezed and clawed and pinched. Mike gritted his teeth. Sharp spurts of tears popped from his eyes.

The corpse pulled Mike in close, nearer and nearer to the decomposing face, white and bloated and green with moss, and through the yellow teeth and brown gums and white, swollen tongue, the corpse wheezed and, with a sour-breath voice, said, "Now I've got you, Michael Walsh."

The words oozed out, riding the waves of ancient wind exhaled from ancient lungs, and seemed to envelope Mike's face with vaporous tendrils, velvety smooth but wretched, fetid but intoxicating. The sky above Mike swirled out of focus. His eyes rolled up into his head, and his legs buckled. He collapsed, striking his head on the tile floor, but his hand clutched the white sheet, and he pulled it down with him. It covered him completely.

FROM THE JOURNAL OF DR. LEOPOLD SUTZKEVER:

Something is happening here. Something big. Something like before. I don't know if it is the weather or Dr. Bering or if it's both, but I know something is happening ... is going to happen. I remember in 1979 how the days preceding the confrontation seemed so different. There was the unexplainable phenomenon. At least, unexplainable before the confrontation. But I could feel it happening then, before it actually happened. During the day, I could feel the darkness. It was heavy upon me. The oppression. I want to cherish this gift of mine, but it is so hard not to see it as a curse. I do not enjoy exercising it, despite the joy it brings when I use it fruitfully. I could not have guessed the outcome of that confrontation. And I can only hope that I am wrong now, but I do not think I am. Something is coming, and I cannot guess the outcome of this either. I can only pray that it diverts its course from here. I can pray that one who is more worthy be chosen to exercise his gift. I can pray that everything works together for the good, and I know that it will, but ... I suppose I am in the flesh right now. Something hovers over this place, and it is malevolent. It is not of the Spirit, but of the other.

CHAPTER TEN

Bright light. *Too* bright. Blinding …

… my eyes.

"Mr. Walsh?"

What's happening? Why is it so bright in here?

"Everything's …"

So bright. And … what is that? Diamonds? Black diamonds shining sparkling glittering in the deep thickness of black orbs … Black diamonds …

"… going to be …"

No. No, not diamonds. Moving twitching shaking … frowning? Eyes. Eyes!

"… all right."

The eyes! The dead rotting diamond eyes of the man of the body of the dead body of the rotting corpse floating to me and grabbing me! Get this man—

"—off of me!" Mike screeched, and he swung his fist wildly above him and connected with one of the two men who had led him to Vickie's body. Only it hadn't been Vickie's body. They took him to see *it*. To see the body from his nightmares. The body from his childhood. They took him to see DEATH. And now it all streamed back to him. He knew where he was. "I'm … I'm sorry about that," he offered.

"It's okay," the man said, rubbing his cheek. "You gave us quite a scare back there."

You think you *had a scare?* Mike thought.

"Do you remember what happened?"

"Well, I guess I must've fainted or something." *No, that's not it. Vickie wasn't Vickie. She was the corpse I saw when I was a kid, and he reached out and grabbed me and spoke to me, but I can't exactly say that to you, now can I?*

"Yeah. You fell down and hit your head pretty hard on the floor. Are you sure you're okay?"

Mike felt the back of his head. It didn't hurt a bit. "Yeah, I'm fine. Just a little spooked, I guess."

"That's understandable. We just need you to sign a few papers, if you could."

"Sure. No problem."

FROM "UFO HOT SPOT IN TEXAS" BY PATTY MEITZEN IN *ENCOUNTERS MAGAZINE*:

With several UFO sightings to its credit and two documented cases of mysterious cattle mutilation, the small town of Trumbull, Texas, is fast becoming one of America's premiere UFO hunting grounds. Residents have reported fifty-six sightings, most of them lights in the sky, but several have claimed to see disc-shaped objects. One Trumbull man's own livestock have suffered. Lucas "Pops" Dickey found his cows murdered, their bodies cut with surgical precision, drained of blood, and missing certain organs. Are extraterrestrials visiting Trumbull? The town's chief of police declines to comment, and the captain investigating will only adamantly deny the claim, despite the insistence of many eyewitnesses who have yet to come to terms with whatever is taking place in their peaceful country town.

Jimmy lay on his back in the cold grass, not one hundred yards from someone's back porch.

Clear memories of the previous days' events eluded him. He had rushed to the little girl at the ruthless insistence of the voices, with the intention of killing her. He knew that. But before he could bring his blade down and into her, someone (or some*thing*) grabbed him roughly by the neck like grabbing a puppy by the scruff, and he flew away from the girl and landed on the road.

Even less of a memory was his encounter with the employee in the Dart 'n Shop convenience store. But he was sure he had slit the man's throat.

And then there was his mother. He still couldn't recall what had occurred in the kitchen the day before. The screaming of the voices covered it all, blinding him with sound.

He assumed the police were looking for him, but he didn't concern himself too much with that. He didn't consider himself at fault for his actions. To him, it was kill or be killed, and it all started with that night on the old man's farm.

Jimmy stared at the sky, watching the clouds slither by like ghosts. He saw pictures in them, images formed by their cottony folds. A dog with fangs and foam bubbling from its mouth. A white raven with a hooked beak. A skull.

He rolled onto his side and looked at the fence in the distance. He could see the peak of a roof jutting out above it.

The voices came, tickling his ears with the sweet whispers of sin.

That's the house, Jimmy.

"What house?"

The *house, Jimmy.* She *lives there.*

"Who?"

The girl. The girl you let slip away. She's laughing about it right now.

"She is?"

She's laughing at you, *Jimmy.*

Jimmy began to cry.

She thinks you're crazy.

"But I'm not," he sobbed.

But she thinks you are, and she's laughing at you right now. She's saying to herself, "That crazy Jimmy. He thought he had me, but I got away. He's just too weak." Too weak and just too plain ol' crazy.

"Is that true?"

Nutty as a fruitcake. Of course it's true, Jimmy. We've never lied to you. We like you, Jimmy. We don't want her to laugh at you like that.

FROM THE *DALLAS MORNING NEWS* OBITUARIES:

HOLLAND, Vickie Lorraine. Age 38. Dallas-area artist. Survived by sister, Molly Walsh, of Houston. Graveside funeral service 10:00 a.m., tomorrow, at Roselawn Cemetery, conducted by Reverend Steve Woodbridge of Cypress Creek Baptist Church, Houston. Roselawn Funeral Director, 555-2088. The Ferber Center for the Arts on Ross Avenue will

have a weekend memorial display of Ms. Holland's
oil paintings beginning Friday.

Mike pulled his rental car into the driveway of the Woodbridges'
brick home in suburban Northwest Houston and debated whether
to honk. He really didn't feel like meeting the family if they happened to be home. He really didn't feel like meeting a minister, for
that matter, but he also realized that honking would more than likely
be considered rude. After all, this was not a good friend like Robbie
who would think nothing of being honked for, but a preacher who
would probably condemn him to everlasting hellfire for not having
the courtesy to ring his doorbell, despite the fact that ringing the
doorbell served pretty much the same function as honking the horn.

His internal debate was interrupted momentarily when Mike
noticed the Woodbridges' neatly manicured lawn. It looked so green,
so lush, even in this harsh winter weather. He couldn't see a single
brown patch. His thoughts drifted to his own yard, which he had, at
one time, cared for almost compulsively. He had let it go for at least
a month. He figured his neighbors probably noticed the difference
and thought he had lost it, and he thought they wouldn't be too far
off in thinking so.

Mike's hand began to rise to the steering wheel, but before he
could sound the horn, a tall man emerged from around the corner,
a garment bag slung over his shoulder and a blue Nike duffel bag in
his other hand. Steve Woodbridge? The man's appearance startled
Mike. With brown hair and boyishly handsome face, the minister
was practically identical to Mike himself. Mike thought that anyone

would mistake them for brothers. And the minister was not wearing a suit as Mike had expected, but blue jeans, a black winter coat over a gray sweater, and tennis shoes.

Mike had not been looking forward to sharing a long drive with a preacher. The thought of it made him very uneasy, but his initial exposure to the casually dressed minister disarmed him. And when Steve threw his stuff in the back, settled into his seat, and reached over and shook Mike's hand with a "Hi, how are ya?" Mike felt a whole lot better.

"Pretty good," Mike said. "Steve, right?"

"Right," Steve said.

"Or should I call you Reverend Woodbridge or—?"

"No, no. Steve's fine."

"Okay. I'm Mike Walsh."

"Good to meet you, Mike."

"Same here."

Mike backed the car out and headed for Interstate 45.

"This is a pretty nice car," Steve said.

"Yeah. It's a rental, but I don't think I want to give it back."

Steve chuckled, and Mike smiled.

"How long a drive you think we got ahead of us?" Steve asked.

"Well, it took me a little over five hours to get down here, so I figure it'll probably be a good six heading back, 'cause we'll probably get into some traffic with people getting out of work. I'm sorry I didn't send you a round-trip ticket. Thought it might be important for you to, you know, ask whatever you need to of me—as Vick's family, I mean—before just throwing you into the ceremony."

Six hours. Mike didn't know what kind of conversation he could have with a minister for six hours. He began to sweat.

"What do you do for a living, Mike?"

"I write for a magazine. *Spotlight*."

"Really? My wife reads that all the time."

They traveled in silence for a long while after that, their only exchange consisting of Mike asking Steve if he minded if he turned the radio on, Steve saying, "Not at all," and Mike (nervously selecting a station that wouldn't offend his Christian companion) tuning in to 87 FM—classical—and asking, "This okay?" Steve said, "Sure."

He enjoyed the music for a while, but the lack of conversation began to worry him. He wondered what the minister was thinking about him.

"Your plane ticket's in the glove compartment there. I'll drive you to the airport tomorrow night. I think your flight leaves at seven. I hope Continental is okay."

"Yeah, that's great," Steve said, taking the ticket from the glove compartment. He looked it over. "I've never flown first class before." He slipped it into the inner breast pocket of his coat.

"Also, I've got a room reserved at the Hilton for you tonight, if that's okay."

"That's great, really. You didn't have to do all this. I'd be fine anywhere."

There was more silence until Mike said, "The funeral will be at ten tomorrow morning. Did I tell you it would be graveside?"

"Yeah."

"Okay. I'll pick you up at the hotel around nine, I guess."

"Okay."

Steve said, "I'm real sorry about your sister-in-law."

"Thanks. Really, though, we weren't very close. I barely knew her. Actually only met her a few times."

"I assume your wife's already up there?"

"Yeah. She's been in Dallas for … well …" Mike hunched his shoulders. He felt uncomfortable. Should he tell this man that Molly had left him? "… We're kinda separated. She's been in Dallas for about a year now."

"Oh," Steve said.

Mike couldn't tell if that was a condescending "oh" or an indifferent "oh."

"She must be having a pretty tough time," Steve said.

"Yeah. She was real close to Vickie."

They entered Huntsville and passed the huge stone statue of Sam Houston. It reminded Mike of the Paul Bunyan statue in that Coen brothers movie, and Sam looked just as ominous, although his pose was more regal. Vivaldi's "L'Inverno" concerto from *The Four Seasons* began to play on the radio, and Mike immediately noticed the beginning's similarity to the theme from *Psycho*. He almost jumped when his companion said, "You go to church anywhere?"

A-ha! Now we get down to the nitty-gritty! "Uh, no," he answered. *All right! Here it comes!*

It never came.

Mike said, "My wife goes."

"You know where?" Steve asked.

"Wood Glen Community."

"Oh, yeah? The pastor over there and I are pretty good friends. Brian Ayers."

"Yeah. My wife really likes him a lot."

"He's in Chicago this week for a church conference. I'm assuming that's why you've got me instead of him, right?"

"Well, yeah," Mike said.

"He's a great guy. I hope I'm a suitable replacement."

"Oh, yeah," was all Mike could say. He turned off the radio halfway through the Allegro.

✳ ✳ ✳

"What in the world happened there?" Patty Groden asked.

She maneuvered her long white Cadillac into the Dickeys' gravel driveway and stopped. She and her passenger, Gertie Dickey, had seen the boards nailed over the bedroom window from down the street.

"Pops expecting a hurricane?" Patty asked.

"Probably kids," Gertie said. "Baseball or something. Thanks, Patty. See you in church Sunday."

Gertie got out of the car and walked up to the house, hoping her husband's mania had dried out. She had heard enough about flying saucers and alien killers. She climbed the steps to the porch, held the screen door open, and put her key into the door. She stopped and looked into the front window. The shade was up, the curtains spread, and Gertie noticed that no lights were on in the house. She turned her key, twisted the knob, and stepped inside.

The afternoon sun cast a pale light into the living room. She could see particles of dust dancing about in its subtle glow.

"Pops?" she called. The area of the room farthest from her, where the couch sat, lay in darkness. "Pops?"

She took a few steps forward. The silence frightened her, despite the high probability that Pops was working outside or had gone into town. But for some reason, Gertie believed Pops was in the room, or at least in the house. And he wasn't answering.

"Lucas, are you in here?"

Yes, he was, and she could hear him breathing.

"Lucas Dickey, you answer me!"

His voice came soft and low. "Quit your jabberin', woman."

"Pops, you monster," she said and wanted to say some more, but as she moved toward him, he became more visible, and she froze when she saw that he was sitting on the couch with his shotgun in his lap.

"What's wrong?" he asked.

"Why do you have your shotgun out, Pops?"

"You wouldn't believe me if I told you, Gert."

"What happened to the bedroom window?"

"You never did believe me," he said.

"Pops, what's going on?"

"You're just like that policeman, Gert. You never did believe me, did you?"

She began to shake. "What are you talking about?"

"Stewadell would tell you. He'd back me up. I could always count on ol' Stu. But you—well, you've been against me since the beginning. And I told you, Gert. I told you what I'd seen, and you just laughed at me. Went and stayed with your old hag friends, and they probably laughed at me too. But they won't laugh for long. Nope."

Gertie's purse dropped from her hand and plopped onto the floor. "I ... I don't understand."

"Sure you do. You just want to stop the show. And, Gertie, I love you, but I just can't let you do that."

✳ ✳ ✳

Abby Diaz had not been outside since she'd been attacked. Her mother told her it was much too cold and she didn't want Abby to catch pneumonia, but there were other reasons. Lisa was still scared. All day, she repeatedly checked all the doors and windows in the house to make sure they remained locked. She would not let Abby go play at Elizabeth's. *For goodness' sake, that's where it all began the first time,* she thought. She had also begun to think that something was wrong with Abby. Her daughter didn't seem frightened at all. She seemed to have forgotten the entire incident.

Lisa rinsed some dishes in the sink and stared out the window. Abby sat at the dinner table and connected the dots in a coloring book, her innocent eyes wide with anticipation to see what picture would form. The phone rang.

"Hey, hon. It's me," came Carlos's voice.

"Hey."

"Would you mind getting some logs from outside and putting them on the hearth? I'll make a fire tonight and we can relax."

"Okay."

"See you around six-thirty, okay?"

"Okay."

Lisa replaced the phone and looked over at Abby. The little girl's lips clenched the straw protruding from her mug of chocolate milk, and she was admiring her connect-the-dots creation (a clown).

"Abby?"

"Yes, Mommy?"

"I'm going to go outside and get some wood for the fireplace, okay? I'll just be out for a few seconds. I'll be right back. Okay?"

"Okay." Abby turned the page and began coloring a frog red.

"I'll be right outside, okay? I'll be right back in. It won't take long at all."

"Okay," Abby said again without averting her eyes from the page.

Lisa's brow furrowed with disappointment. *Why isn't this girl as scared as I am?* "All right," she said, and she walked into the living room, paused to put on her coat, and moved toward the door into the backyard.

She stopped at the door, her hand on the cold knob, and looked around the yard. She craned her neck against the window and tried to peer down the far ends of the house. She glanced back at Abby and then unlocked the door.

Outside, the wind greeted her with chilly apathy. Lisa turned to her left and walked around the corner to the woodpile on the side of the house.

If the woodpile had been on the other side of the house and Lisa had taken a right turn, she would have walked right into Jimmy Horn, who was leaning against the brick, trying to get warm in the winter coat he had stolen from a car parked at a Burger King.

Jimmy heard the back door open, and he poked his head around the corner to see Lisa Diaz walking to the opposite side of the home and disappearing around the corner. He slipped his hands into his pockets. The butterfly knife felt cold. He stepped out into the backyard, paused, and then walked to the door. He saw that it was open a crack. He noticed the little girl inside, coloring in a book at a table. She looked different in the daylight. He opened the door and stepped inside, heading straight for the stairs.

FROM THE *HOUSTON CHRONICLE*:

Police authorities in Trumbull are investigating the holdup of a convenience store and the assault of a young girl who was walking home from playing at a friend's house. Investigators believe the crimes are related. Surveillance cameras in the Dart 'n Shop convenience store in Trumbull caught the suspect on film. He is described as a white male, age fifteen to nineteen, with black hair and black eyes. He was last seen wearing black denim jeans and a black T-shirt. The suspect is considered armed and dangerous.

If you have any information about this suspect or about either of the crimes, please contact the Trumbull Police Department or call CrimeStoppers at 222-TIPS.

Watch Channel 2's CrimeStoppers segment tonight at six o'clock for further information and exclusive video.

✳ ✳ ✳

"I have no idea where I am."

Mike and Steve had entered Dallas.

"Are we still on 45?" Steve asked.

"Yes," Mike said. "But I don't know where we are."

"Look, here comes a sign."

"30? How did we end up on 30?" Mike asked.

"You got me. I was sleeping. Don't believe in GPS?"

"We have one, but Molly took it."

He had been. The minister had slept for more than three hours. It didn't bother Mike much, though.

"Here," said Steve. "Why don't you take this exit and we can turn around or something."

"Sounds good to me." Mike turned onto the exit ramp.

"Take a left here," Steve said.

Mike took a left. "Can you read that street sign?"

"Uh …" Steve squinted. "Yeah. Elm."

They drove west down Elm Street. Steve looked at all the buildings. Mike read every sign that came up. He hated being lost. He was about to retrieve his phone to use the maps feature when he recognized a familiar landmark.

"Hey, there's a sign for the museum," he said. "Vickie's house is in this area." He drove on. "Okay, I think I know where we are. The Stemmons Freeway is up here, I think."

"Mike, do you realize where we are?"

"What?"

"Stop the car," Steve said.

"What?" Mike braked to a halt. "Why?"

"Look out my window."

Mike did. Outside Steve's window, he saw a grassy hill illuminated by the streetlights. Cement steps ran up the hill and led to some trees around an unidentifiable concrete structure.

"Yeah," Mike said. "What is it?"

"This is Elm Street," Steve said. "Didn't you see that sign back there?"

"Which one?"

"This is Dealey Plaza."

Suddenly, Mike understood.

Steve said, "Don't you recognize this?"

"Yeah, yeah I do," Mike said. "This is where Kennedy was shot." And immediately, he felt as though his rental car, motionless in the far right lane and directly below the infamous grassy knoll, was sitting in the exact place that Kennedy's presidential limousine, a blue Lincoln convertible, had been that horrible moment when the sniper's bullet ripped through his skull.

"I've never seen this before," Steve said, but Mike didn't hear him.

Transfixed on the grassy slope, Mike's eyes glazed over. He looked into the shadows of the trees atop the incline.

"I think I wanna get out and look around," Mike said, and he opened his door.

"I don't think we should, Mike. We can't just park here in the road."

"It won't take long." And with that, Mike hopped out of the car and began walking up the steps to the knoll. Had he been thinking clearly, he would have seen these actions as further steps contrary to his natural timidity.

Lisa Diaz, arms cradling a small pile of wood, carefully took the step up from the back patio into the living room and pushed the door shut with her heel. After setting the firewood down on the hearth, she returned to the door, locked its dead bolt, and peered once more into the back lawn. She walked all over Jimmy Horn's impressions in the carpet, obliterating the telltale signs that *the bad man* had returned.

At the table, Sesame Street's *The Monster at the End of This Book*, starring Grover, held Abby's undivided attention.

Lisa smiled. "Abby, why don't you go upstairs and wash up for dinner?"

"Okay, Mommy."

✳ ✳ ✳

Mike was crouching down at the base of a tree, resting his back against its coarse trunk. Steve wandered around, peering over the fence and into the railroad yard and looking up the street toward the former Texas School Book Depository. An assassination museum now occupied the sixth floor. Down on Elm Street, cars swerved around Mike's rental, and some honked. Steve thought it wouldn't be long before a cop showed up, telling them to find a suitable parking place, maybe even ticketing them. He looked at Mike sitting down in the evening shade. He appeared deep in thought. Steve walked over to him and knelt beside him.

"What's going on?" Steve asked.

"Oh, nothing," Mike replied.

"You look like you're in outer space."

"I don't know. I was just thinking. There was a murder here," Mike said.

"Yeah. Feels kinda weird, huh?"

"Yeah. I mean, we're sitting in history right now. A man, a president, was shot and killed right here. The man that did it was right there," Mike said, pointing at the fence.

"Well … I guess. Government said from right there," Steve said, pointing down Elm toward the sixth-floor sniper's nest.

"Yeah, but you get my point."

"I gotta be honest here, Mike. I don't think I'm following."

Mike looked at the minister. "If I tell you something, you promise not to think I'm crazy?"

"Sure," Steve said, intrigued.

Mike opened his mouth, acting as though he wanted to say something, but he didn't. He waved his hand in the air, erasing words unspoken. Steve watched his face gather into angst and saw the man begin to shiver. The Dallas evening was cold but oddly not as cold as it had been in Houston.

"You ready to go?" Mike asked.

"Yeah."

The two men walked down the hill, got into the car, and drove on.

✳ ✳ ✳

In the State Farm Insurance office on Louetta Road, Darla McKay sat in her chair at her desk, biting her nails and wondering what to do. She had already called the house four times every day the last couple days. Every time, an answering machine received her calls. Every time, she left a message: "This is work. Just wondering where you've been. Mr. Knox is getting pretty mad. Call me."

Darla had just left one of those messages.

Now she picked up the phone again and dialed another number. The answer came: "Sheriff's Department."

"Hi, my name is Darla McKay and, this might sound stupid, but there's a lady who works with me who hasn't been to work in a couple days, and I can't get an answer at home. I was wondering if, well—"

"Would you like us to drive by the residence and check in with her?"

"Yes, that'd be great. I'm getting kinda worried here," Darla said.

"Okay. Name?"

"Darla McKay. Oh, *her* name. Right. Okay … Maggie Horn."

* * *

Officer Mark Lane hurried into the Trumbull Police Station and walked briskly to Graham Lattimer's office. Kelly stopped him.

"Hope you have good news," she said.

"Why?" Lane asked.

"He's pretty upset."

"The protesters?"

"Yeah. Among other things."

By "protesters," Lane meant the sixteen people gathered outside the station, holding signs that read, TRUMBULL POLICE COVER UP THE TRUTH, LATTIMER'S A LIAR, and UFOS ARE REAL! Even more people had congregated outside the mayor's office.

"So you don't think I should bother him?" Lane asked.

"Up to you," Kelly said.

Lane thought for a second. "I think he'll want to hear this."

"Your call."

Lane rapped on the window of Graham's office door. Inside, the captain looked up from a pool of aspirin on his desk. He nodded at Lane, and the officer entered.

"Sir?"

"Yeah?"

"I think we've got some good news."

Graham arched an eyebrow. "Well, that'd sure be a switch," he said.

"Yes, sir," Lane said. "HPD found a match for our holdup suspect."

Graham stood up. "You don't say."

"Yes, sir. Name's James Horn. Lives in Houston," Lane said.

"Well, get someone out to his school and his house. Pick him up."

"Already done, sir. Harris County Sheriff's got a man going by the home as we speak. Seems the boy's mother hasn't been to work in a few days and nobody's been able to reach her."

"Sheesh," Graham said, and he grabbed his coat.

✳ ✳ ✳

The rental car zipped up and down suburban streets.

Mike had felt very strange sitting beneath the tree in Dealey Plaza. He wanted to explain it to Steve, but he could not find the words. When the pastor crouched down beside him, Mike sensed genuine interest in his face. Genuine concern, as well. He wanted to tell the man how he felt, how the grassy knoll affected him, but chose not to. Mike had a wealth of things on his mind. He wanted to tell Steve about seeing a dead body in a river. He wanted to tell him about having that same body reach out to grab him in the morgue that morning. He even wanted to tell him about pulling an unloaded gun on an unsuspecting driver. These events were fresh on Mike's conscience. Visions of animated corpses aren't easily shaken.

In the end, though, he decided not to say anything. He still didn't know Steve all that well, and he could not be sure that this man, a preacher, wouldn't think him crazy, devil possessed, or worse (whatever worse might be). He realized that Steve saw *something* was going on with him in the Plaza, but Mike just didn't have the words to describe it. In a way, he had felt a morbid curiosity in walking around one of history's most famous murder scenes, but he also found himself in a peculiar confrontation with that which he had been programmed to fear most. DEATH. He felt it all around him. In the car, on the hill, and under the tree. He felt it crawling on his skin like an invisible animal. A predator he feared but could not bring himself to shake off. In an odd way, he felt *good* about being there, about feeling it claw at him, as if this was the beginning of shedding his fear. It felt like the sort of nightmare that is terrifying but so compelling, one almost fears waking up. He also felt that, somehow, Steve's presence made this confrontation easier.

Mike managed to find Vickie's neighborhood.

Mike introduced Steve to Molly, and they sat down to have cake and coffee. The table in the kitchen almost bowed under the weight of numerous desserts and snacks. Mike remembered how Molly always seemed to occupy herself with cooking when she was upset.

Steve told Molly that he and Brian Ayers happened to be good friends, and she seemed to enjoy hearing that. If Reverend Ayers couldn't conduct the service, at least a friend of his could. They spent a long time talking and eating. Molly asked Steve about his church. He asked her about Vickie. Molly showed him some pictures of her sister and showed him around the house, so he could see some of her paintings.

When the conversation turned to more spiritual things, Mike excused himself and went to the bathroom. He wasted time, wanting to be sure all the religious talk was good and over by the time he emerged. He could hear them talking. Molly's voice sounded wet. He heard her sniffling. When he couldn't hear them anymore, he came out and found them praying.

Shoulda stayed a little bit longer, he thought.

Mike looked at them. He watched his wife, her beautiful auburn hair flowing down her back in waves, her thin hands clasped, her eyes shut. Even in pain, even in grief, she was radiant. He wanted so badly to be the one next to her at that moment.

On the way to the Horn home, the police officer's radio broadcasted the latest news. The home of Maggie Horn was also the home of her son, Jimmy Horn, who was wanted for assault with a deadly weapon and armed robbery. Proceed with caution, the radio said. Four other cars were en route.

Upon pulling up to the curb outside the home, the officer first noticed that lights inside the house were on. He radioed that he was approaching the home.

He knocked on the door. He rang the doorbell. He knocked again. He pounded on the door. He called out, "Harris County Sheriff's Department. Anyone home?" He walked to the window and looked in. He could see the dining room and, beyond it, the living room. He rapped on the glass. "Hello?" he yelled. On the dining room's right wall, he could see an entrance to what he presumed was the kitchen. Lights shone in this room. He rapped one more time, then noticed something. He squinted. He could see flies buzzing in and out of the entrance to the lighted room. Not a lot of flies, but enough. Not a good sign.

He walked back to the door. Two police cars pulled up to the curb. The other officers jogged up to the door.

"Doesn't look good," he told them.

All three drew their guns. The first knocked one more time and shouted, "Sheriff's Department! We're coming in!" He kicked the door, budging it a little. He kicked again, putting all of his weight into it, and the door exploded inward. The three men, pistols readied, stepped inside. The first called out one more time, "Sheriff's Department! Anybody here?"

The first thing to hit them was the smell.

They entered the kitchen, and the sight was even worse.

* * *

Molly gave Mike directions to the Hilton, and he drove Steve to the front door of the lobby.

"Room's already paid for," Mike said. "You shouldn't have any problems."

"Thanks, Mike. I appreciate it."

Steve gathered his bags from the backseat.

"See you around nine," Mike said.

"Okay," Steve said, and he nodded.

Mike watched the preacher walk into the hotel lobby and approach the front desk. He seemed like a nice guy. Mike enjoyed his voice, earnest and sincere, and the way Steve made him feel at ease despite his profession. The only ministers Mike had ever known were overbearing types, intimidating presences, loud and obnoxious. They always talked about themselves or told unfunny jokes. Steve didn't seem that way at all. He seemed like an ordinary Joe. A guy you'd want to hang out with. Get a pizza. Grab a beer. Okay, maybe not a beer, but coffee.

Mike found his way back to the house. He walked back to the bedroom. Molly had already fallen asleep. What to do? He wanted to get into the bed next to her, pull her close, hold her, and be a husband to her again. He wanted to cradle her in his arms and comfort her. But he didn't know if she wanted him to do that. Yes, he had slept with her last night, at her invitation, but now was not the time to assume anything. Now was not the time to offend.

He walked back to the kitchen and poured himself a cup of coffee. Sitting at the table, he toyed with a dish of pecan pie, plucking off the pecans. In the stillness, in the dim light of the kitchen, with no sound but the wind outside and an occasional car, Mike sat there, eating what was now brown sugar pie, and felt very alone.

He began to think about Dr. Bering. The old man had saved his life. So what if he seemed a little bit crazy? So what if he believed in another dimension? He was a friend, and in a time like this, a lonely, aimless time, a man could use all the friends he could get.

"What're you doing?"

Mike turned around to see Molly standing in the hallway, leaning against the wall, in pajamas he hadn't seen before.

Probably Vickie's, he thought. *What am I, crazy? They're probably hers. For crying out loud, we haven't lived together in a year! She couldn't have gone out and bought a pair of pajamas? Of course she did! And she probably did a lot of other stuff too. She certainly wasn't hanging around waiting for me to call her up, that's for sure.*

She sat down at the table, noticing the pile of pecans on his plate. "You never did like those things, huh?"

"Nope," Mike said. He took another bite of the pie and followed it with a swig of coffee that had grown bitter cold. Glancing around, he realized that half of the desserts had been eaten—most of them probably by Molly.

This has something to do with grieving, right? What's that short story by Raymond Carver? Some boy gets hit by a car on his way to school, and he dies. His parents never tell the baker who's already made the kid's birthday cake, so the baker makes repeated phone calls, asking about the kid, but never telling them who he is. They keep hanging up on him, believing the guy's making some pretty sick jokes. The baker gets angry. I mean, he's got a perfectly good cake sitting in his shop with this kid's name on it, and nobody's called him. Nobody's come to pick it up or pay for it. Finally, the baker's calls become pretty threatening. The parents realize who the guy is and go down to his shop to confront him. They argue. Then they tell him: "Our kid's dead." He never knew. He realizes what he's done. He apologizes. Then—and this was Carver's main point, I guess—he starts feeding them. I mean, really stuffing their faces with bread and cakes and rolls and biscuits and whatever else he's got. They eat and talk, but mostly eat, and it helps them grieve. The baker keeps saying, "Eating's good at a time like this," or something like that. A good ending. It never happens that way in real life.

He leaned back in his chair and looked at her. "What did you think of Steve?"

Her face softened. "I liked him. I liked him a lot. I'm glad he's a friend of Reverend Ayers."

"So I did okay?" Mike asked.

"Yeah. Yeah, you did great." She was wringing her hands, and she looked down at them. "Thank you for everything you're doing."

Mike didn't answer. He watched her pale face. Her eyes were puffy from sleeplessness, her cheeks blushed from weeping. Her lips were thin and peach, no longer pink, no longer luscious. She seemed to have aged a great deal since their meeting at Lily's. But, he admitted, so had he in the last year. His hair had a little more gray. His eyes had gone bloodshot. At least hers were still blue and gleaming, and he'd give anything for her to look into his at that moment. He wanted her to see his thoughts.

Can't you read my mind, Molly?

Her head rose a bit, but she did not look at him. She said, "What have you been doing?"

How can I answer this one? Should I say what I've really been doing? I've been working. You know, the thing you said I did too much of? That's what I've been doing. I've been working my tail off and going to school. That's right! Me. A grown man going to school. I have homework and textbooks and tests and everything. But that's just the tip of the iceberg! I've been into loads of trouble. I've stolen my father's gun. I've gone to movies in the middle of the night and can't remember what I saw. I tried to shoot a lady who tried to run me over with her car. I've been wallowing around in the gutter. Basically, I've lost my mind. I've lost my wedding ring, and I've lost my mind. I'm crazy. You know why I think I'm crazy? Not just because I'm a gun-wielding maniac, but because I've become friends with a college professor who's a UFO expert and who believes in aliens from other dimensions right here on earth, and you know what? I believe him! I really think I believe him! So that's what I've been doing, and it might seem like a lot, or it might not, but I can tell you one thing: I wouldn't have done any of it if I hadn't lost you! Is that what you want to hear? What do you want to hear? Please tell me, 'cause I want to say it! Believe me, I want to say it.

Mike looked at Molly, and she looked at him, and for an instant, their eyes met and locked. In that brief, shining, ecstatic moment, sadness and loneliness were forgotten, blurred like buried dreams, and she was beautiful and he was attentive, and they both were in wondrous love. Mike felt like he had that life-changing day he met her.

"I've been missing you," Mike whispered so low that he couldn't be quite sure she had heard him.

Molly leaned forward and thrust her arms around him, burying her face in his shoulder. He took her gladly, pulling her in close and embracing her. He felt her tears, warm and moist through his shirt.

"I miss her so much, Mike," she cried.

He almost pushed her away, not in anger, but to interrupt the moment he almost believed they had shared. *Oh. Are the tears for me or for her?* His heart sank, but he wanted to console her, and so he did.

One ambulance and a dozen police cars lined the street outside the Horn house. They had already taped off the area as a crime scene when Graham Lattimer arrived. He knew when he drove up that someone had been murdered. He also knew that this was a Houston homicide and, therefore, was Houston's jurisdiction, but he figured that they would allow him inside. After all, the kid who lived there happened to be a suspect in two Trumbull crimes, maybe three.

His uniform got him into the yard, his badge got him into the house, and his explanation got him access to all rooms within. He slipped on the latex surgical gloves they handed him.

He walked into the kitchen. Two men dusted the counter for fingerprints, and one man held a camera focused on … well, it was hard to tell. From the hair, Graham assumed the body belonged to a female. Probably the kid's mother. Everything else—her face, her arms, her entire body—was … indistinguishable. Congealed blood covered everything with its black stickiness. It looked like someone had poured out buckets of it onto the linoleum floor. Graham watched his step. A detective approached him calmly, his hands in his pockets as he smacked on chewing gum. Graham nodded toward the body.

"Stab wounds," the detective said. "Too many to count. Practically sliced her face off."

"Any ideas—?"

"Had to be the kid," the detective said.

"Think so?" Graham asked.

"Check out the kid's room. It's Halloween, brutha."

Graham walked out of the kitchen and down the hall. He looked into the first door he came to. Police officers were dusting a dresser, a mirror, and a stereo. One man had a pair of tweezers poised over a pillow on the bed. He snagged some hair and placed it into a plastic bag. Graham stepped in and looked around.

Posters of rock groups lined the room's walls. An ashtray sat in the middle of the floor, and the tan carpet had hundreds of cigarette burns. He walked over to the dresser and scanned the spines of the books on a shelf above it. Mostly horror novels. A couple fantasy books. A *Choose Your Own Adventure* book. A copy of the Bible. Graham picked the Bible out and examined it. A pentagram had been carved into the cover. He flipped through the pages and found the majority of them torn or marked on with black and red ink. *Halloween, brutha.*

"Excuse me," he said to one of the men. "You mind if I look through these drawers?"

The cop shrugged and continued looking through some comic books by the bed.

Graham opened the top drawer. Underwear. He opened the middle. T-shirts (all black). He opened the bottom. Junk: some baseball cards, a couple packs of cigarettes, some cheap grocery store cigars, some CDs, some socks (all black), *Tales from the Crypt* comic books, a roach clip, an old *Fangoria* magazine, dice, hundreds of loose matches, a handful of jawbreakers, and …

Graham immediately grabbed the deck of tarot cards. They were bound with a rubber band, and he quickly yanked it off. He noticed that the cards' backing bore the same design as the one found in Pops Dickey's barn. He went through them all, and when he had finished, he had not found the death card.

As far as Graham Lattimer was concerned, the mystery of Trumbull's mutilated cows was solved.

"Can I hold on to these?" he asked, showing the man the deck of cards.

"Have to sign them out," the cop answered. He motioned toward the hallway and added, "Check with them."

Graham left the room and walked back to the kitchen. "Sure, no problem," the detective said. Before leaving, Graham looked once more at the mess. He thought about the little girl who had come very close to meeting the same end.

✳ ✳ ✳

The CrimeStoppers telephone hotline received thirty-two calls after Channel 2's airing of the Dart 'n Shop holdup video. More than half of the people calling were teenagers identifying the suspect as Mr. Black.

* * *

Abby Diaz rose from the warm bubble bath, dried off, put on her underwear and pink Powerpuff Girls pajamas, and brushed her teeth at the bathroom sink.

From downstairs, her father called, "Are you brushing your teeth?"

"Yes, Daddy," she yelled, spraying toothpaste foam onto the mirror. She giggled.

She spit, rinsed, spit again, and strolled to her bedroom. She climbed into bed, pulled the covers up to her chin, and waited for her mother to come read to her, which had been their nightly custom since Abby was three. *The Lion, the Witch, and the Wardrobe*, a book they were halfway through in their third consecutive reading of The Chronicles of Narnia, rested on her nightstand to the right, between the bed and the wall.

Abby glanced around the room, admiring the posters of puppies and kittens and one she had bought at the elementary school's book fair of an orangutan wearing swim trunks and "floaties." They all hung at girl height, all personally tacked to the pastel pink walls by Abby herself.

In the corner, a dozen dolls sat on top of each other in a child's rocking chair. In the middle of the night, with the lights off and the moon glowing eerily through the window, the shadow of those dolls looked like a monster hovering in the corner, watching.

Abby remembered that her nightlight bulb had burned out. Her mother had showed her how to replace it, and she'd put a package of new ones in Abby's top dresser drawer, the junk drawer that held rubber bands for her hair and batteries for her toys and marbles and extra dice for her board games. The little girl climbed out of bed and shuffled over to her bureau. She opened the top drawer. It squeaked, but within that squeak, she heard something else …

A thump? A rustle? Hard to tell with the drawer's squeal drowning it out. She looked over her shoulder at her closet door to the left of the bed—right next to it, as a matter of fact. The door was shut. Abby turned around and faced it.

It seemed like she always heard sounds in the house. Especially at night. Creaks and squeaks. Thumps and bumps. The occasional scraping sound. Her mother always told her those were the sounds a house makes when it's settling. This explanation never satisfied Abby very much. She remembered a *Brady Bunch* rerun where the kids kept hearing noises and their parents told them the house was settling, and in the end, the house turned out to be haunted by ghosts. (Okay. *Really* at the end, the haunting was all a hoax carried out by the boys, but Abby had been so scared, she had stopped watching before that could be revealed.)

She didn't want to get back in bed. She heard footsteps approaching from the hallway.

"Abby, why aren't you in bed?" her mother asked.

Abby shrugged.

"Go ahead," her mother said. "I'll be back in just a second to read with you. Where are we tonight?"

"Chapter Nine: In the Witch's House," Abby said matter-of-factly.

"Oh. Okay, I'll be right back."

With that, her mother turned around and walked away.

Abby looked again at the closet door and her bed that lay right next to it. She *could* get in that bed. She *could*. But then she'd be in arm's length of anything that happened to lurk in her closet and wanted to reach out with a gnarled, spider-hairy hand and grab her with sharp, dirty fingernails. The hand of *the bad man* felt like that, and at that very moment, Abby knew that he had taken up residence in her closet, had made her room his lair. Behind the curtain of clothes, in a pile of shoe boxes and toys and puzzles and Baby Sitter's Club books, *the bad man* crouched, knife in hand, waiting for her to climb into bed and fall asleep so he could slither out and pounce on her.

"I'm coming up, so you'd better be in bed," her mother yelled.

Abby Diaz tiptoed to her bed, never averting her eyes from the closet door.

CHAPTER ELEVEN

He had crouched behind the row of hanging clothes to the right just inside the closet, waiting in their shadow for hours. His knees began to cramp, and he thought she would never come upstairs. He heard the front door downstairs close and assumed her father had come home. They stayed down there for a long while, probably eating dinner or watching a little television. But Jimmy knew that the girl would be up sooner or later. Little girls have bedtimes, and those bedtimes come fairly early.

He had his butterfly knife out and had been swinging it open and closed, open and closed, until he heard footfalls on the stairs. He placed his ear against the door. He heard the sound of running water. The girl's bath. He wanted to kill her now. Mommy and Daddy would be downstairs watching *CSI* or some stupid cop show, and she'd be left all alone. The sound of the faucet would cover the noise. And then he could clean his hands in the sink …

Just like at home.

And then Jimmy remembered what happened to his mother, what *he* had done to her. She'd screamed when he approached her. And then he brought the blade down and in and across and up what seemed like thousands of times. He remembered walking to the bathroom, cleaning his knife in the sink, and taking a shower, mesmerized by the swirl of blood spinning down the drain. The memory of his deed, and even the understanding of it, had drained away as well, but now it came back. It backed up like sewage, and Jimmy remembered it—the foulness, the evil—vividly. Too late to go back. And yes …

He wanted to kill the girl now, while she shampooed and scrubbed and maybe had soap in her eyes. Jimmy grinned. She would be playing with rubber duckies, and he would walk in, and she would look up and, with bubbles on her face, would mistake him for Daddy. "Hi, Daddy," she would say. And then Daddy would reach down and do a very bad thing. Yes …

The time had come.

No, Jimmy.

"Who's there?" he said aloud.

Shh, Jimmy! Are you crazy? They'll hear you, you idiot!

"I'm not crazy," Jimmy whispered.

Then just shut up and listen.

"Okay."

See, there you go! Talking after we told you not to!

A sharp pain pierced Jimmy's skull. He winced, tears squirting from his eyes, but he did not say a word.

Now, just listen. We don't want her now, Jimmy. We want her. Make no mistake about it, we want her, and we want her good. Better than your mother, Jimmy. And you know why? Because this little witch has already escaped you once. She's gotten away from you, and she laughed about it. So now she's got to pay.

Thoughts of that night drifted into Jimmy's mind. What about …

Don't worry about the other one, Jimmy. He sneaked through last time, but he won't do it again. That's all taken care of. But you have to be patient. You have to wait until bedtime. The others will be asleep, and she will be too. She'll be asleep in the bed right outside. And then, Jimmy—and then, you come out. Just like in her nightmares. The thing that goes "bump" in the night. The monster in the closet. That's you,

Jimmy. So just do us this favor: just stay right where you are and wait for her to turn her light off and go to sleep.

Jimmy heard the water's rushing cease. Bath time was over. He leaned back against the closet wall. His crouch cut off some circulation in his legs, and they went numb. Clutching the knife to his breast, he waited, just in case someone happened to open the closet door. If that happened, all bets were off. Forget about the voices. He would jump out and kill anything that moved. He heard a man yell, "Are you brushing your teeth?" and a reply—"Yes, Daddy."

Footsteps now, coming down the hall. Little footsteps. The girl. Then, the bed springs creaking. Only a wall separated them. Jimmy thought he could thrust his knife through the sheetrock and probably get her. But he would follow the instructions of the voices. Killing her in the middle of the night would allow a better getaway, anyway. No one would be downstairs to see him steal away.

The little girl sighed.

The bed creaked, and he heard two tiny, pajama-padded feet strike the floor. He heard her shuffle across the carpet. He leaned forward, peering through the wedge of light at the door's side. She walked over to a white dresser with pink trim. She opened a drawer. Jimmy lost his balance and fell forward, his right knee thumping on the floor. He froze.

The girl looked over her shoulder. Jimmy thought maybe she could see his eyeball in the sliver of space between the door and doorjamb. She turned around.

All right; this is it. If she knows I'm in here, I come blazing out. I'm Mr. Black, and I ain't afraid of no little brat in pink pajamas. I'll take this little chick out.

She remained staring at the door. Something in her face told Jimmy that she was toying with the idea that the sound in her closet was "just a noise." He thought she was thinking, *Maybe I just imagined the whole thing. There wasn't any sound at all.* He heard footsteps. *If it's Daddy, and she tells him she heard a noise, it's all over.*

"Abby, why aren't you in bed?" Mommy asked.

He watched the girl relax a bit, and she hunched her shoulders.

"Go ahead," Mommy said. "I'll be back in just a second to read with you. Where are we tonight?"

"Chapter Nine," the girl said. "In the Witch's House."

Jimmy thought, *You got that right.*

"Oh. Okay, I'll be right back," Mommy said, and she left.

The girl looked at the closet door again. He saw a swallow trickle down her neck. She was afraid. She took a step forward.

That's right. Come to Mr. Black. Mr. Black will make everything "ay-okay."

He decided to go ahead and burst out, maybe give the little chick a coronary before he sliced her up, when the voices said, *You do it, and we kill you, Jimmy!*, and her mother yelled, "I'm coming up, so you'd better be in bed."

He shrunk back but kept his line of sight through the crack. He watched the little girl move slowly toward the bed, watching *him* through the closet door. She silently climbed in, and he thought it might be cool if he reached out and grabbed her by the neck as she cozied up. He could hear her breathing, every tiny inhale and exhale.

Mommy returned and sat on the edge of the bed. Her body blocked Jimmy's view through the crack. She said, "Do you want to read, or me?"

"You," the girl said.

"Okay," the mother said. "Chapter Nine: In the Witch's House. 'And now of course you want to know what had happened to Edmund,'" she began.

Jimmy reclined against the closet wall, rubbing his legs silently, and listened to the little girl's mother read her a story. The event lasted only about seven minutes, but might not have lasted that long, if the girl hadn't stopped her mother several times to ask questions.

Finally, the mother read, "'Make ready our sledge,' ordered the Witch, 'and use the harness without bells,'" and the story was over. "Good night, baby," Mommy said, and Jimmy heard the sound of a kiss. "I love you."

"I love you, too," the girl replied.

The bed creaked, he watched the woman walk out the doorway. The lights went out, and he heard her walking away down the hall.

Just two hours, the voices said. *Just wait two more hours, and she's yours.*

Those two hours crawled by. In the silent darkness, Jimmy could hear the faint sound of snoring coming from another bedroom. He didn't know how he would know when two hours had passed, but he assumed the voices would tell him. They had guided him this far; they would take him the rest of the way. He almost fell asleep in there, but the moment came.

Now, Jimmy. Now's the time. But be quiet about it.

Mr. Black stood up. His joints popped, and his legs groaned as blood coursed freely through them again and feeling rushed back. He felt light-headed. Sweat gathered on his brow, though his body shook with chills. He reached out and grasped the doorknob. Mr. Black was about to meet the girl for the second time. And this time, someone would die.

Holding his knife with his right hand, he twisted the knob with his left.

✳ ✳ ✳

Pops Dickey sat on his rear in his backyard grass, something he normally wouldn't do. It was too difficult to stand his old bones back up again. He didn't think about it. He started a cozy little fire, and he sat up close to it, feeding on its heat. The flames lit up his face like a grotesque jack-o'-lantern.

Gertie had fainted dead away. The sight of him sitting on their couch, shotgun in hand, rambling on about UFOs and aliens and Graham Lattimer and people who wanted to stop the show, was probably just too much for her to handle.

He smiled into the fire. The shotgun lay across his lap. He looked into the distance, into the darkness of the woods, and then looked up into the sky. A full moon. He felt like howling. He wanted his visitor to return, maybe to take him away to its far-off planet. He thought about that, what it must be like. How long would it take to get there? Was it in the Milky Way? He saw a pair of blinking lights, knew they belonged to an airplane, and almost cried.

Hoping it could sense his psychic energy, he began to pray to whatever had visited him the night before.

A light drizzle began to fall.

✳ ✳ ✳

Something woke Abby Diaz up. Not a noise. Not a nightmare. A realization. She had never replaced the bulb in her nightlight. The room slept in haunting darkness. The autumn moon, full and glowing, squeezed its aura through the open blinds, casting strips of ghastly light on the floor and illuminating the room with an eerie alien shimmer. She listened to the darkness …

… and heard *something*.

She knew immediately that *the bad man* had come for her, so it was not a great surprise to see, when she rolled her head to the right on her pillow, the doorknob on the closet twisting.

She sat up and looked again, wiping the dryness of slumber from her eyes. The knob turned.

"Mommy Daddy!"

Inside the closet, Jimmy, inspired by the girl's screams, finished turning the knob and pressed against the closet door.

"Daddy!" Abby jumped out of bed and ran down the hall to her parents' bedroom.

Jimmy pressed against the door, but it would not open. *Locked!* He cursed and fumbled on the knob …

… There *wasn't* a lock.

Stuck! He banged against the door, fully expecting to explode out into the room and come face-to-face with the girl's father. The door wouldn't budge. He hurled himself against it.

Carlos and Lisa Diaz met their daughter in the hallway.

"What's wrong, sweetie?" Lisa asked, but she knew. She could hear the banging coming from Abby's room.

"Lisa, take Abby right now," Carlos demanded. "Take her right now and go downstairs and call 911."

"Carlos—"

"Now!" he yelled.

"*The bad man's* in my closet," Abby said through her tears.

"Come with me, honey," Lisa said, and she grabbed her daughter by the arm and dragged her down the stairs.

The banging in Abby's room continued.

Carlos headed for his daughter's bedroom. "Run to Melody's, Lisa," he shouted.

Inside the closet, Jimmy Horn was going berserk. He cursed the door, and he cursed the little girl. The voices began to jeer.

Come on, Jimmy! We thought you were Mr. Black! We thought you had it all under control! Why can't you even open a simple door? Do we have to do everything for you? Are you so crazy you can't even open a door?

"Leave me alone!" Jimmy wailed, and he threw all of his weight against the door. Nothing. He began to cry heavy tears of rage. He turned the knob again. Nothing. He pressed against the door. What could be holding it? *Who* could be holding it? The girl! The girl had undoubtedly pulled her bed against the door.

You're an idiot, Jimmy! How could that little girl pull that heavy bed three feet over to block the door? You must be out of your mind!

"I'm not out of my mind!"

You must be, Jimmy! You must be! No sane person would ever think that a little snot-nosed girl could move her heavy bed!

"What, then?"

Think, you fool!

Jimmy didn't want to think. He wanted to ram the door open and kill everyone in the house. He leaned against it with his shoulder. Nothing. Okay, she couldn't prop anything against the door, and even if she could, he would have already pushed it away. No, whatever held that door closed was not an object, but a force. That was the only way to explain it. Some force pressed against the other side of the door.

This door's about to eat it, Jimmy thought, and he backed up until he touched the closet's back wall. He tightened his grip on the knife. *Mr. Black's comin' out blazin'.*

On the other side, Carlos, a baseball bat in hand, crept toward the closet. For some reason, whoever happened to be in there couldn't get out. And for some reason, he had stopped trying. He reached for the handle, holding his Louisville Slugger aloft. "Who's there?"

Jimmy's mind raced: *Just like* The Shining, *man. Heeeeeeere's Johnny! Well, get ready, you little witch, 'cause heeeeeeere's Jimmy!*

Jimmy sprang forward with furious speed and strength and hit the door like a cannonball. The door flew open, smashing into Carlos Diaz's face and shattering his nose. He dropped the bat and put his hands to his bloodied face. Jimmy's momentum threw him right into Carlos's body, and the man flew back, hitting Abby's dresser with the small of his back and slamming it into the wall. The mirror on the wall fell on the top of the dresser and tipped forward, crashing onto Carlos's head and sending shards of glass to the floor.

The dresser propped Carlos up, prevented him from falling, and Jimmy, who had already taken a step back to regain his footing, moved in swiftly, ripping the butterfly knife across Carlos's face between his nose and upper lip. The man screamed and leaped onto his attacker. He caught Jimmy in the ribs with his knee, and the kid doubled over, gasped, and stumbled back, but he did not fall down and he did not lose hold of his weapon. Carlos, blood pouring from his face, darted for the bat. The coppery taste of his own life in his mouth, on his lips, and on his tongue, drove him quickly, and he reached it. His hand squeezed around it, and he righted himself, but Jimmy had caught his breath and was bringing his knife down once again. He stabbed Carlos in the forearm, the one attached to the hand that held the bat, but the man didn't drop the slugger. He winced, stepped back, and gripped it in both hands. Jimmy stabbed him again, this time in the chest, and he twisted the blade before pulling it out.

Carlos groaned, dropped the bat, and retreated to lean against the wall behind him. *The bad man* moved in, striking like lightning. In wild, dramatic swipes, Jimmy slashed Carlos across the chest and stomach, managing to nick the man's arms in the back swings.

Carlos pushed forward with his remaining strength and knocked Jimmy down. The man picked up the bat and brought it down onto the kid's hip. But the man's power was draining with each drop of blood. He hit Jimmy several times, some of the hits hard, but not hard enough to do any damage. Jimmy smashed the bottom of his foot into Carlos's shin, and the man dropped like a rag doll, screaming in pain and terror.

The bad man, Mr. Black, Jimmy Horn, pounced on the fallen man and killed him.

* * *

Lisa and Abby Diaz made it to the house down the road, but it took seven minutes for anyone to answer the door, despite Lisa's frantic screams. Chris and Melody Taylor let them in, and Lisa ran to their phone.

"What's going on?" Chris asked.

"*The bad man*," Abby said solemnly. "He's in my closet."

"What?"

Lisa dialed 911 and got through. Hysterically, through sobs and sniffs, she cried into the phone, "There's someone in my house! ... Yes! Please! ... 457 Derry Road, please hurry! ... No, I'm not there, I'm at the neighbor's! ... Please! My husband is still there! Please hurry!"

✳ ✳ ✳

Jimmy Horn must have been crazy, because, before leaving the house, he walked into the bathroom down the hall and washed all the blood off of his hands and arms. He wiped his blade clean on Abby's bath towel, which still hung over the shower curtain rod.

He knew the girl had escaped.

Again!

He took his time walking down the stairs and left through the back door, scaling the backyard fence and sauntering into the woods. The first thing to greet him was the wind, freezing and without mercy. He had taken the stolen coat off in the little girl's closet, and he regretted that move immediately.

He began to run, for the most part sure-footed, although a few hanging branches and vines scraped against his face. A light drizzle began to fall, and the wet, bitter wind burned into his skin with its coldness. His ribs hurt, but he would have traded a broken arm for that warm coat.

He ran for miles on the pure adrenaline of fright and insanity. He came out of the woods onto a road and looked around. He could hear sirens in the distance, but they came from far enough away for him to take it easy for a while. Inside his chest, his lungs raged with a suffocating fire. Scanning the street, he noticed only one house and, behind it, a tiny flicker of light.

As he approached the house, he realized he had been there before but couldn't quite remember when and under what circumstances. He climbed over the property's wood fence and bypassed the house in favor of the fire burning behind it. He walked into the open and saw the shadowy figure of a man sitting on the ground. He had his back to Jimmy, his face to the fire.

Jimmy's hand felt immediately for the knife in his jeans pocket. He walked slowly and quietly, but he didn't know exactly what he should do. For some strange reason, he didn't feel as if he needed to kill the man. He pulled his hand from his pocket and walked right up to the fire, circling it and looking into the man's face.

Pops's expression remained blank. The old man acted as if he had been expecting the boy any minute. Jimmy saw the shotgun resting across the man's lap but didn't feel afraid. He hugged himself, rubbing his hands up and down his arms, trying to get warm.

"Got a coat on the back porch," Pops said.

Jimmy walked to the back porch and put on a dirt-brown coat that waited for him on the steps. He walked back and crouched down next to the fire.

"Are you gonna shoot me?" he asked.

"Do I need to?" Pops replied.

"No."

"Okay." Pops placed the gun on the wet ground next to him. "One chilly night, huh?"

Jimmy didn't say anything.

"With the wind, it's gotta be in the teens," Pops said.

"Should we go inside?" Jimmy asked.

"No. Gertie's in there. Passed out, you know. Wouldn't want you to be tempted to ... well, you know."

"What?" Jimmy asked.

"Well, you're a killer. I know that."

"How do you know?"

"Don't know how I know," Pops said. "Just do, that's all. You killed somebody tonight, didn't you?"

"Maybe."

"Yeah, you did. Don't worry about it, son. I'm sure whoever it was had it coming to 'em."

Jimmy said nothing.

"They'll be looking for you, I'm sure," Pops said.

"Yeah. So?"

"Well, we couldn't let them take you away."

"I've been in jail before," Jimmy said. "It's no big deal."

"We can't let them take you away, son. We're supposed to be together, you and I," Pops said.

"How do you figure?" Jimmy asked.

"I was told," Pops said, and he pointed a bony finger at the sky.

Jimmy looked around him and noticed the barn in the distance. It all came rushing back. He said, "I've been here before."

"Yeah?" Pops said.

"I killed your cow."

Pops looked at the boy through the dancing tongues of the fire. "I don't think so, son," he said.

"I did. I killed your cow."

"No, no, you didn't. *They* did," Pops said.

"Who are you talking about?"

"Aliens, son. The grays."

"The grays?" Jimmy asked.

"Yeah. Three feet tall. Large round heads with big black eyes. Long arms with long skinny fingers. Gray skin. The grays."

"You seen 'em?"

"Yeah," Pops said. "I've seen them."

"Sometimes I hear voices," Jimmy said.

Pops smiled. "Why don't we get on inside before we freeze to death?" he said.

"What about your wife?" Jimmy asked. "You know I'm a killer."

"You won't touch her," Pops said.

"How do you know?"

"'Cause I'll blow your head off."

They rose and began walking to the house.

"What about the fire?" Jimmy asked.

"Let it burn."

✳ ✳ ✳

No one turned on any lights, but they kept knocking. Pops could hear the voices of Graham and Petrie out on the porch, commiserating.

Mr. Black looked at Pops.

After their meeting by the fire, they had come into the house together and found Gertie still lying in the same spot as before. Pops became a little worried at the sight of her, but after checking her vitals, he picked her up in his wrinkled arms and carried her into the bedroom. He gently laid her on the bed and drew the covers up to her neck, pausing before he left to plant a kiss on her forehead. "One of us may be dead before this is all over," he whispered, and despite her unconscious state, he believed she heard him.

He and Jimmy (who Pops had begun to call Mr. Black without any prompting from the boy at all) were just walking into the kitchen when the knock on the front door came.

"They're here for you, Black," Pops whispered.

"Who?"

"Who do you think? The cops. You killed somebody tonight. Didn't you think they'd be looking for you? I'm sure they're checking every house in a fifteen-mile radius, maybe more."

"I ain't going," Jimmy said.

"'Course you're not," Pops replied.

Graham knocked again. "Hello?" he yelled. "Anybody home?"

"Just a second," Pops shouted. He looked at Jimmy. "Get in the closet and don't do anything stupid."

Jimmy took a peek at the closet. "I ain't getting in no closet," he said.

Pops whispered, "Then go get in the tub in the bathroom down the hall. Make sure the light's off and you close the door."

Jimmy hesitated.

Another knock came. "Mr. Dickey! This is Trumbull Police! Please open up!"

Jimmy retreated down the hallway and hid in the Dickeys' bathroom.

Pops opened the door. Graham Lattimer. That Southerner. That *show stopper*. It was hard to keep from vomiting. Heck, it was hard to keep from dashing into the kitchen, grabbing his shotgun, and blowing a couple of holes in the man.

"What's going on?" Pops grumbled.

"Mr. Dickey," Graham began, "I'm Captain Lattimer. This is Officer Petrie—"

"I know who you are. What do you want?"

"Been outside, Mr. Dickey?" Graham asked.

"Call me Pops."

"Okay. You just get back from somewhere, Pops?"

"Why?"

"Your hair's wet."

"What's it to ya?"

"Do you mind answering the question?" Graham asked.

"I don't gotta answer nothin'. What's it to ya?"

"A man was murdered tonight."

"So?" Pops said.

"So, a man was murdered about four miles from here, and the clothes you got on looks like you been outside awhile. Have you?"

"Yeah," Pops said.

"Where you been?" Graham asked.

"In my backyard," Pops said.

"What were you doing out there?"

"None of your business."

"Do you mind if Petrie and I come in?"

"Am I a suspect in this murder, son?" Pops asked.

Graham leaned in close. "Well, no, no," he said, "except that, well, everyone's a suspect. Pops, you gonna let us in?"

"You got a warrant?" Pops asked.

"No."

"Then I'm not gonna let you in."

"Why not? Just a friendly visit," Graham said.

"I've never had a friendly visit with *you*."

Petrie asked, "What happened to your window, Pops?"

"What?"

"Your window," Petrie said. "It's boarded up. What happened?"

"You wouldn't believe me if I told you."

"Pops, c'mon, let us in," Graham said.

Pops turned around and looked behind him. *Let's hope Mr. Black finds a little common sense in that bathtub and stays there.* He faced the men at his door. "All right," he said. "Just be quiet. Gertie's sleeping."

The two officers entered and sat down on the couch. Pops sat down in his chair and hoped the house was too dark for them to notice his shotgun on the kitchen table behind him. He crossed his legs, tried to look at ease, and hoped Mr. Black stayed put.

"What were you doing in your backyard?" Graham asked.

"Wouldn't you like to know?"

"Yes, I would. Very much."

"Okay," Pops said. "I made a fire for warmth, and I was waiting."

"Waiting for who?"

"The grays," Pops said.

"What are the grays?"

Petrie said, "Cap, the grays are a term given to aliens. On account of their gray skin."

Graham gave a *what're you, an idiot?* look at Petrie. He turned back to Pops. Graham squinted, had an unease in his face, looked like he'd tasted something sour. He asked, "That true, Pops? You were waiting for aliens?"

Pops noticed the cop nonchalantly lower his arm onto the bulge of his holstered pistol.

"Yeah," Pops said. "I'm sure you think I'm crazy, but you know what? I don't give a flying fugazi what you or anybody else thinks."

Something was definitely wrong.

"Mr. Dickey, do you mind if I use your toilet?" Petrie asked.

The old man righted himself. *Okay, Pops. What do we do now?*

"It's pretty urgent," Petrie added.

Graham looked at him disapprovingly.

"Sorry, Cap." Petrie stood. "Pops?"

Pops watched him closely. *What to do, what to do?* "First door on your left," he said.

"Thanks," Petrie muttered, and he jogged down the hall.

Pops got up. "Gonna make some coffee. Want some?"

"No, thank you," Graham said.

Smart thinkin', you redneck. A little coffee—cream, sugar, some rat poison, maybe. Pops didn't turn on the kitchen light. He stayed within arm's reach of his shotgun. *Any second now. Any second, Mr. Black will come bounding down the hallway—after killing the kiddie cop, of course.* Pops supposed the kiddie cop was dead already, or close to it.

An odd sensation of dread overcame Graham. Suddenly, the house seemed darker than when they had first entered. And why didn't Pops turn on the kitchen light?

In the bathroom, Officer Petrie stood over the toilet and read the cross-stitched poem hanging framed on the wall over it. He whistled. The tub lay to his right, its curtain drawn.

In the bathtub, Jimmy remained motionless and alert. He thought it might be the old man, but the man cleared his throat, and it sounded like the voice of one much younger. Jimmy wanted to jump out and kill him. *In a shower, man! Just like* Psycho! He felt for his butterfly knife.

Graham strained his eyes to discern what Pops was doing in the kitchen. It didn't sound like he was making coffee. And, for goodness' sake, how long does it take a grown man to go to the restroom! Graham suddenly felt as if there were more people in the Dickeys' house. More than just him and Petrie and Pops and Gertie, who was apparently still sleeping in the bedroom. He believed the house crawled with people. People he couldn't see.

Be assured.

He began to sweat, and he placed the palm of his hand on his weapon. "So, you still into this alien stuff," he said to Pops, not really asking—just trying to get a sense of the old man's mood and where he stood in the kitchen. Graham couldn't see him.

"Yeah," Pops said warily. "Why?"

Graham heard steps coming down the hallway. *Finally*, he thought. *Petrie's done his business, and we can get out of here.*

Pops heard the steps too, and he picked up the shotgun, bracing its butt in his armpit. His finger fondled the trigger.

Graham rose to his feet, turned to the hallway, and Pops took a step forward, aiming the gun at Graham, and Petrie emerged into the living room.

"'Bout time," Graham said.

Pops skidded around, stuck the shotgun between the refrigerator and the cabinet, and called out, "You want some coffee, kid?"

"No, thank you, Mr. Dickey," Petrie said.

"I think we've seen enough," Graham said. "Thank you for your time."

"Sure," Pops said.

The officers left.

CHAPTER TWELVE

Graham and Sam Petrie walked up the path away from the Dickeys' front porch and exited through the gate. The captain could feel the burn of watching eyes on his back, and more than anything in the world, he wanted to get away from there. Fast.

Graham noted that the windshield of Pops's pickup was frozen over.

The two officers climbed into the patrol car, Petrie driving.

"You think Pops killed Carlos Diaz?" Petrie asked.

"Naw," Graham said. "If his truck's cold, he ain't been nowhere. 'Cause if he did, he ran. And if he ran, he's in pretty good shape for a seventy-one-year-old man. Seem out of breath to you?"

"No."

"He's been out, but I don't think he's been *that* far out. Still … I think he's hidin' somethin'," Graham said.

"Could get a search warrant for his place."

"With what evidence? He's acting really creepy? That sheesh don't hunt."

Having completed their visits, they drove back to the Diaz home. The two-story house looked like a beehive with all the uniformed officers, detectives, and paramedics buzzing in and out and around the property. The flashing lights of the police cars and the single ambulance swam across the house in a kaleidoscope of emergency colors. Sadly, the paramedics were of no use.

Graham asked, "You mind gettin' a ride?"

"Nope. You're not coming in?"

"Naw. I'm gonna head back to the station."

"All right," Petrie said. "See you later."

Petrie got out and walked up to the house, doing the limbo under the yellow police tape stretched across the front lawn. Graham settled into the driver's seat and drove to the station.

* * *

8:00 a.m. The phone rang in Steve Woodbridge's hotel room, ripping into his sleep and sending him rolling across the bed and nearly onto the floor. He reached over and answered, "Hello."

"This is your eight o'clock wake-up call, sir."

"Oh. Right. Thanks." He hung up.

Why did hotel beds always feel so snug? Steve didn't want to get up. He lay in the bed and stared at the ceiling for a while. His own phone buzzed.

"Hello?" Steve answered.

"This is Mike. Just wanted to let you know I'll be over in about forty-five minutes."

"Okay, sure. See ya then, Mike."

Steve sat up, perched on the edge of the bed, and scratched his chest. That always felt so good in the morning. *Time to get up, Steve*, he thought. *Got a funeral to do.* He managed to rouse himself, and he shuffled into the bathroom to brush his teeth and shave. He splashed cold water onto his face. *Okay, big guy. Gotta wake up.* He looked at himself in the mirror. It appeared to him that he had aged so much in the past few months. He could see the fine etchings of wrinkles in his once-childish face. His eyes seemed so ... what's the word? *Old* was all he could come up with. Looking into his eyes, he felt so old. Or maybe it wasn't his eyes, but what lay behind them. He hadn't been very happy with himself lately. Okay, for a long time he hadn't been very happy with himself, but he was just now facing the music. He didn't much care for the man in the mirror.

He removed his suit from the garment bag and examined it, making sure it, unlike himself, was wrinkle free. He got dressed, grabbed his Bible, and rode the elevator down to the lobby.

Steve had just finished his second cup of coffee when Mike strolled in.

"You ready?" Mike asked.

"Yep," Steve said.

They got in Mike's rental and drove out to Roselawn Cemetery, neither of them saying a word.

✳ ✳ ✳

Roselawn's staff had set up two sections of folding chairs, with five rows per section. Seventy chairs total—more than enough. The first two rows of the sections lay in the shade of the canopy resting Vickie's coffin, the open grave, and the wooden pulpit from which Steve would conduct the funeral. Every person attending enjoyed the shade, for only fourteen people came. Mike sat with Molly in the front row of the right section, with Robbie and Teri to his left. Mike's parents sat to Molly's right. On the front row of the left section sat a few of Vickie's friends, six artists and one lady who directed the gallery that displayed most of Vickie's paintings.

A cool morning breeze flowed through the cemetery, and the sun was shining.

Steve assumed his place behind the pulpit and asked everyone to stand for an opening prayer.

"Heavenly Father," he said, "we are here this morning to mourn the passing of Vickie Holland. A beloved sister, a dear friend, and a beautiful lady. God, we know it's not easy when someone so close passes on, so we want to ask You right now for Your gentle touch. We want to ask You for Your loving hand. Your peace that passes all understanding. We can't understand what has happened, Lord. We can't begin to understand it. An accident that seems so unjust, so undeserved, and just so unexpected. It breaks our hearts, God. She was loved so much. All we can ask, Lord Jesus, is that You show us how to remember her. Show us how to learn from her, Lord. Show us how to love those that we have more dearly. And, Lord, through this, somehow, draw us closer to You. We pray this in the name of Your precious Son, Jesus. Amen." Steve opened his Bible, pressed it firmly down to hold it open, and said, "You may be seated."

That's a whole lotta "Lords," Mike thought.

Everyone settled in, but the metal seats of the chairs challenged comfort. Mike noticed that several of Vickie's friends were already crying. Molly was not, but he put his arm around her. He did not like being in the cemetery. For Mike, a man whose ultimate fear was DEATH, the graveyard seemed a haunted hell. He could not bring himself to look at Vickie's casket. He half expected to see the lid pop open and the river corpse spring up like a Jack-in-the-Box, saying, "Now I've got you, Michael Walsh." He kept his eyes on Steve.

"It's very hard," the minister said, "to talk about death. For one, it's just not something you or I like to think about. But, in a time like this, it's even harder. Losing a loved one is perhaps the most difficult aspect of the human experience. Nothing can really prepare us for it, even when it is expected. And then, to lose one so young and without warning … it just kinda knocks your breath out. The least we can do is to remember Vickie, to cherish her life in our hearts.

"Vickie Lorraine Holland was born in Dallas, Texas, in 1975. Two years later, her mother passed away giving birth to Vickie's sister, Molly. Two years after that, their father passed away. Vickie and Molly grew up in an orphanage and in several foster homes where, even at an early age, others could see Vickie's talent for art. While the other children played with dolls or read books or played make-believe, Vickie would not leave her drawing and coloring and finger painting. Vickie was an introvert. She was shy and very intellectual. She loved the world around her, immersed herself in it, and then reflected it with her paintings. With her God-given talent, Vickie managed to make quite a living from selling her work, and she has some of her paintings displayed in a few art galleries here in Dallas. Vickie was a woman who loved life and had others who loved her. And miss her. Molly wanted me to read this poem this morning. It was a favorite of Vickie's."

Steve began, reading: "Nothing Gold Can Stay" by Robert Frost:

"Nature's first green is gold,
Her hardest hue to hold.
Her early leaf's a flower;
But only so an hour.
Then leaf subsides to leaf.
So Eden sank to grief,
So dawn goes down to day.
Nothing gold can stay."

Molly began to cry, and Mike handed her his handkerchief, thinking how stupid the Frost poem was and how stupid and obvious Vickie was to have it as her favorite. Molly leaned over and placed her head on his shoulder. Mike's mother patted her on the knee.

"Nothing gold can stay," Steve repeated. "For those who held Vickie's life so precious, that seems so painfully true. Let's pray."

The mourners bowed their heads.

"Father, we thank You for being here with us this morning. We thank You for comforting us in our time of need and sadness. Help us to make sense out of this tragedy, and if not to understand it, to get a glimpse of You and Your love for us. In Jesus's name we pray. Amen.

"I'd like to speak for a little bit about death and what it means for us. This morning, and for mornings to come, it means a time of grieving over the loss of Vickie. At times like these, we wish life wouldn't work that way, but there is a time to be born and a time to die, and so, every day, babies come into this world and others leave it. It's such a mystery, isn't it? We really don't understand it. We really don't. But that's the way it happens, and the good news is that there *is* good news. God, for reasons mysterious to us, has set up life to work with births and deaths, but He has also provided an escape from eternal death for us. Romans 6:23 says, 'For the wages of sin is death, but the gift of God is eternal life in Christ Jesus.' See, death has come into our world because of our sin, and while escape from death is impossible, escape from eternal death is *possible*. The Bible says that 'it is appointed one time for man to die, and after that, the judgment.' Because we are born into sin, we face separation from God for eternity after we die. But God loves us. It's hard for me to fathom sometimes, but He really does. He loves me, and He loves you very much. So He's provided a way for us to spend eternity with Him in Paradise after we die.

"First Corinthians 15:53 through 57 says, 'For the perishable must clothe itself with the imperishable, and the mortal with immortality. When the perishable has been clothed with the imperishable, and the mortal with immortality, then the saying that is written will come true: "Death has been swallowed up in victory. Where, O death, is your victory? Where, O death, is your sting?" The sting of death is sin, and the power of sin is the law. But thanks be to God! He gives us the victory through our Lord Jesus Christ.'

"God loves us so much that He sent His Son, Jesus, to die for us—to pay the debt we owe and can't pay ourselves. And, Jesus, God in the flesh, came to earth and faced a terrible death. He may have feared the pain, just as we do. The Bible says He sweated blood on the eve of His crucifixion. That's how anguished He was about what He was about to do. He cried and prayed and sweated blood, but He allowed them to kill Him. Why? Because He did it for you. And so He let them torture Him and spit on Him and slap Him and curse Him and hammer nails through His hands and feet into a cross, when He could have said, 'Okay, I take it all back. I won't bother anyone anymore. I won't teach, I won't preach, and I won't tell people that I'm the Son of God. I'll just go away.' He could've said any of those things. He could've run away in the middle of the night and just disappeared. But He didn't. He died because He wanted to.

"So make no mistakes about death and God's position on it. He understands our grief. He understands our sadness better than we do, because His loved one was murdered. His grief, like ours, was real. And in His dying, Jesus defeated death. He rose from the dead three days later to claim victory over death, and now that victory can be applied to us.

"John 3:16 says, 'For God so loved the world, that He gave His only begotten Son, that whoever believes in Him shall not perish, but have eternal life.'

"Today, we face death with all of its sadness, but I want to offer you a hope. A reason to live. And a reason not to fear death and, beyond it, eternal death. Accepting God's free gift of love will give you eternal life. Perhaps Vickie's passing has got you thinking about these things, and maybe you'd like to know more about what I've said this morning. If you want to, please feel free to approach me afterward, and I'd be glad to talk to you about whatever you'd like to talk about.

"I'd like to close with this quote. Many years ago, a preacher by the name of Dr. Arthur John Gossip lost his wife. In the sermon he preached the very next day, he said, 'I don't think you need to be afraid of life. Our hearts are very frail, and there are places where the road is very steep and lonely, but we have a wonderful God. And as Paul puts it, "What can separate us from His love? Not death," he says immediately.' If you know Jesus Christ, you have put on the imperishable and the immortal, and not even death can separate you from God's love. Let's pray."

Steve prayed, and friends and family who had gathered to mourn the loss of Vickie Holland unanimously agreed that it was the most beautiful prayer they had ever heard. When he finished, he allowed for five minutes of quiet reflection. Although she had been touched by Steve's closing prayer, Sandra, one of Vickie's friends, leaned over to her neighbor during the quiet reflection and whispered, "Just like a preacher to bring Jesus into everything."

The truth had been clearly proclaimed here, plainly before Mike for the grasping. It was punctuated by the boxed corpse of Vickie before him, a shining emblem of his ultimate fear. But just the notion of death now, even in the context of escape, prompted his tuning out. He had caught bits and pieces of the message almost subliminally, primarily the parts about "not fearing death," but his mind had already drifted to other concerns. His attention, by choice, had been diverted, occupied wholly with thinking about Molly and what she planned to do. He wondered if she would come back to Houston. He hated to think that it took the death of her sister to drive her back home to her husband, but to him, that possibility was the bright light at the end of this dark, dark tunnel.

After they lowered Vickie Lorraine Holland's body to rest, her friends congregated around the hole in the earth, paid their respects, and thought their last thoughts. Then they each approached Molly, some hugging, some crying, and told her how much they loved her sister and how close they were to her and how such-and-such a time they went to the zoo or the park or the movies or out on a double date. Molly thanked them all and invited them to the house for snacks. All of them declined.

Thirty minutes later, the rest were sitting in two groups in Vickie's home on Poplar Drive. Mike, his parents, and Robbie and his wife, Teri, sat in the living room. Mr. and Mrs. Walsh watched CNN with the volume muted, and Robbie and Mike talked business.

"Sending you to Utah in January," Robbie said.

"Oh, yeah?" Mike replied, his eyes glued to the floor.

"Yeah. Movies all day. Get a little skiing in. You might even see Redford out there. He runs the festival, you know."

"You don't say," Mike said.

"Yeah. But you need to come up with something in the meantime, okay? Take your time, but I'll need some ideas in a couple of weeks," Robbie said.

"No problem." Mike looked up at the TV. Soldiers were saluting a coffin draped with the American flag.

In the kitchen, Steve and Molly sat at the table and talked. Mike could see that Molly was crying. Every now and then, they both closed their eyes and prayed.

Mike got up to go to the bathroom, and his mother followed him down the hall.

"Mike," she said in her tender, maternal voice.

"Uh-huh?"

"Are you all right?"

"Yeah. I'm fine." He smiled, but he knew a mother could always tell when her son's smile was fake.

"Have you gotten a chance to talk to Molly at all?" she asked.

"A little bit," he said uncomfortably.

"Do you know if she's …?"

What? Do I know if she's what? Decided she does or doesn't need me? Decided to stay here in her dead sister's house for the rest of her life, because she'd rather be anywhere than with her louse of a husband—her soon-to-be ex-husband? I really have no idea, and frankly, I really don't think I want to know. "If she's what?" Mike asked.

"Well," his mother said, "are you two all right?"

Mike shook his head. "I don't know, Mom."

She put her hand on his arm. "Your father and I love you very much."

"I know. I love you, too." He began to turn around, but his mother said, "Mike?"

"Uh-huh?"

"Your father's missing one of his guns. You didn't, by chance, borrow it or anything, did you?"

Suddenly, Mike *really* had to use the restroom. *Oh, sure. I used it at the movie theater. I waved it at some lady who tried to run me over with her car.* "No," he said. "I don't know what happened to it." His lie burned in his mouth.

✳ ✳ ✳

Graham Lattimer sat at his desk, popping aspirin like candy and watching Sam Petrie talk on the phone in the main office. Graham had spent the night at the station. He hadn't seen the throng that had gathered outside in the early hours of the morning to protest the department's handling of the evidence that Trumbull was being visited by UFOs. They held signs. They wore WHAT ARE YOU HIDING? T-shirts made especially for the protest. One man wore a mask of an alien, a replica of those Pops Dickey referred to as the grays.

Petrie hung up the phone and entered Graham's office without knocking.

"Well?" Graham said.

"Got a match, Cap. Prints pulled from Abby Diaz's closet door-knob match those found all over the Horn home. They belong to Jimmy Horn. Also, the medical examiner I spoke to said he couldn't be positive right now, but he thinks the same murder weapon—or at least, a very similar murder weapon—was used on both victims. We know who we're lookin' for."

"Well, let's find him," Graham said.

FROM "HOUSTON AND TRUMBULL MURDERS LINKED, OFFICIALS SAY" IN THE *HOUSTON CHRONICLE*:

Homicide investigators in the Houston Police Department and the Trumbull Police Department have verified early reports that the murder of a Houston woman discovered in her home yesterday is connected to the brutal attack and murder of a Houston businessman in his Trumbull home last night. John Dickerson, an HPD detective, announced this morning that fingerprints lifted from the Houston crime scene match those lifted from the scene in Trumbull. The suspect's name is Jimmy Horn, the son of the woman found slain in her kitchen. He is also wanted in connection with a convenience store robbery and the attempted kidnapping of a child.

Authorities say that the child is the daughter of the Trumbull man found murdered last night after the man's wife called 911 to report a break-in. Trumbull police say that Horn, 17, had probably been stalking the girl for a while. The reasons are unclear. Horn has been in previous trouble with the law and has served sentences in juvenile correction facilities. He is considered armed and dangerous. If you have any information concerning Jimmy Horn's whereabouts, please contact the Trumbull Police Department or the Houston Police Department, or call the CrimeStoppers hotline at 222-TIPS.

✳ ✳ ✳

5:15 p.m. Mike and Steve stopped at a fast-food chicken place on their way to the airport. Steve's plane left at six fifty-five.

"Mike," Steve said.

"Yeah?" Mike said, mumbling through an Original Recipe chicken leg held to his mouth like a harmonica.

"Do you mind if I ask you a question?"

"No, I guess not." *This isn't gonna be about Jesus, is it?*

"Yesterday. Back on the, uh, grassy knoll. What was going on?"

"Oh. Well, you know, like I said. I was just thinking."

"Oh," Steve replied, but his tone said, *That doesn't exactly answer my question.* "About what happened there?"

"Yeah," Mike said. "About what happened there. And … well, other stuff, too."

"About Molly?"

Mike looked at the minister. *Do I know you? Can I tell you things? Are you a friend?*

Steve said, "Back on the knoll, you started to tell me something, but you stopped. Was it about Molly?"

"Yeah … Well, no. No, it wasn't about her. I don't want you to think I'm crazy or anything."

"I don't think you're crazy."

"Okay, but I don't want you to think I'm a sinner or a heathen or whatever," Mike said.

"Okay. What's on your mind?"

"I've been having these dreams about … Well, it started when I was a kid. I was out fishing with a friend, and we found this dead body in the river. It just kinda floated toward me, you know. Like it knew exactly where it was going. Like it wanted to come to me. Like it wanted me to see it. And, well, I've been seeing it ever since. I just … I guess I feel like what you talked about at the funeral today. You know—fearing death. I guess I feel like death is haunting me."

Mike scooped up a spoonful of mashed potatoes and placed it in his mouth, letting his words sink in. He didn't enjoy saying any of it but felt as though a heavy weight had been lifted from his shoulders. He swallowed the potatoes. "Forget it," he said. "I know it sounds stupid. It's too hard to explain."

"No. It doesn't sound stupid," Steve said, and the pastor looked like he meant it.

On the way to the airport, the two men talked about the Texans' playoff chances. "Who knows?" Steve had said. "As long as they keep wanting it bad enough."

They talked about their parents, about the Astros (sports are a staple of men's conversations, especially when two men don't know each other that well), and about other random news of note until Mike asked, "Do you believe in UFOs?"

Steve laughed. "UFOs? Hmm. I guess I never gave it much thought. You talking about the deal in Trumbull?"

"Well, yeah, but in general," Mike said.

"Well, I guess people are seeing *something*. I mean, that's why they're unidentified, right? But as far as them being, like, flying saucers?"

"Yeah."

"Nah."

"You don't think so?" Mike asked.

"Nah," Steve said. "I don't believe in 'em." His eyebrow arched. "You?"

"No, I don't either. Still … like you said, they can't all be liars."

"That's not what I said. I said they're seeing something. But that doesn't make those somethings flying saucers."

"So what do you think they are?" Mike asked.

"I have no idea. Planes. Stars or planets. You can see Venus sometimes when the sky's real clear and it's the right time of year. They say it looks like it's flashing."

"What about people who say they've been visited by aliens?"

"Hmm. I'll tell you what, I think that if those encounters actually occurred, they were hoaxes or ..."

"Or what?" Mike asked.

"Or ... well, I guess ... encounters with demons."

"Demons?" Mike chuckled.

The pastor seemed amused by his own statement. "Yeah," he said.

"You actually believe in demons?"

"Well, yeah, I guess. I mean, the Bible talks a lot about angels and other spirits. They may not be as prevalent today, but I believe what's in the Bible, so if someone told me they had a visit from some creature in the middle of the night in their bedroom, I would think it was a trick, a dream or hallucination, or a demon," Steve said.

Mike smiled. "I didn't know you guys still believed in that stuff."

"Well, I've never actually seen one or met anyone who has, but yeah, I believe they exist. Somewhere."

"What about parallel dimensions?" Mike asked.

"What?"

"Parallel dimensions. Another dimension here on earth that we can't see. A whole other world. With people like us living in it."

"Sounds like science fiction to me," Steve said.

"What if I told you there are scientific principles and theories to support a belief in it?"

"I'd say that any scientist who believes in something can come up with something that will support his belief and make it into a theory. Like starting your research with an already-drawn conclusion. Whoever came up with that theory knew where he wanted to go, and he made sure he got there when he was done."

"Maybe," Mike said.

"You know," Steve said, "even Carl Sagan wrote a book talking about the popular myth of UFOs and such."

"That same book talks about the myth of demons."

"Well, okay. You got me there. All I'm saying is that maybe the truth of the Bible can explain sightings of aliens and people from other dimensions," Steve said.

"Or maybe interdimensional beings can explain some of the stories in the Bible."

"I guess you could look at it that way, but there's only one truth. And everything else has to be false."

Mike said, "I think that I would agree with that."

They drove on, exiting onto the road into the Dallas-Fort Worth International Airport. Steve gathered up his belongings.

"Hey, Steve," Mike said.

"Yeah?"

"What made you want to become a minister?"

"Well," Steve began, "I had supportive parents ... And, I guess, I knew when I felt God calling me into it."

"You mean God told you to?"

"Well, not exactly, but sort of. I mean, God called me into ministry, but being a pastor is sort of where He led me." He had an anguished look on his face. "Does that answer it?"

"Sure," Mike said.

Steve started to get out of the car.

Mike said, "Hey, thanks for everything. Thanks for today. I know Molly was really glad you came, and she was really pleased with what you said at the funeral."

"I was glad to help. I'll be praying for y'all."

"Yeah, well, thanks. Here." Mike handed an envelope to Steve. "Hope you have a good flight. Maybe I'll see you around."

"Yeah, hope so," Steve replied. He took the envelope and placed it in his pocket. "Bye."

"Bye." Mike hoped he had paid him enough. He didn't know what the going rate was for funerals. He figured paying for the man's plane fare and hotel stay and meals went without saying. But what do you pay? He didn't want to offend him. He'd written Steve Woodbridge a check for four hundred dollars.

Forty-five minutes later, on the plane, when Steve finally pulled the envelope from his pocket and read the amount written on the check within, he spit out his Pepsi.

✳ ✳ ✳

Gertie seemed catatonic. When she finally began to regain consciousness, she struggled against the restraints. He had tied her to a chair. Tightly. She called out from the bedroom she shared with Pops, "Lucas! Lucas! Where are you?"

Pops could hear her calling, but he ignored her. He was outside, sitting in the backyard with Mr. Black, enjoying the fire crackling in front of them, and staring heavenward. The old man knew Black had a weapon tucked into his coat. Pops kept one bony hand on his shotgun.

"I'm f-freezin'. C-can't we go inside?" Mr. Black asked.

"Not yet," Pops said.

"Think they'll come tonight?" Mr. Black whispered.

"Yeah. They'll come," the old man said, and he turned and spit on the ground. The cold wind irritated his chapped lips.

The night was angry, cradling the town into its bitter fold. The black sky was an opaque ceiling, allowing no moon, nor the glimmer of stars. A few minutes passed, and Pops's neck began to tighten. He lowered his head and watched the fire.

Flaming ribbons lapped at the air, flickering and snapping. And then the entire blaze puttered out, as though a great gust of wind had swept down from directly above it. Pops didn't feel any downdrafts. The fire appeared to die down, and then ... the night grew darker. A huge shadow shifted over them, and the temperature dropped several degrees.

Pops looked up.

"Open your eyes, Black!"

Jimmy looked up. He cursed.

Above them and their fire, hovering at no less than one hundred feet, was a large round object. Fierce lights, a hot white and a neon blue, blinked slowly around the disc's perimeter. The disc didn't move. It seemed fixed in the sky.

"I don't believe it," Jimmy said.

"It's the grays," Pops said. "You can forget your voices, boy. The grays are your gods now."

✳ ✳ ✳

"What are your plans, Samuel?"

Dr. Bering rested in his chair, facing the visitor across the room. He called only once and the visitor appeared, now floating against the wall like a phantasm.

"My plans?" Bering asked.

"Concerning the man you have befriended."

"Michael?"

"Yes. Michael." A crooked smirk crinkled on the visitor's face. "What are your plans for him?"

"I was hoping that he could join us. If it pleases you, of course. He's an empty soul. I think he would bring you great pleasure," Bering said.

"Perhaps. Or perhaps *you* need him, Samuel. You need him here with us so you don't have to, as you say, 'go it alone.' Am I right?"

"Please do not be angry with me."

"Angry? Hardly, chum. If bringing him into our circle pleases you, it pleases me."

CHAPTER THIRTEEN

Halloween morning came, bringing a day of new hope for Mike Walsh.

He woke with his arm draped over Molly, who slept soundly in the bed next to him. He smiled.

After a long shower, he got dressed and found her in the kitchen, nibbling on a piece of dry toast, her head raised, her eyes staring into space. Mike stepped up behind her and tried to see what held her attention. It was one of Vickie's paintings.

He leaned over and planted a light kiss on her forehead.

"Good morning," he whispered.

"Good morning," she said.

He placed a hand on her shoulder, hoping she could feel his love. Her head drooped.

"Want me to make some breakfast?" he asked.

"No." She shook her head. "Thanks."

"It's no problem. I'm gonna scramble some eggs anyway."

"I'm not really hungry," she said.

"Okay." *Let me do something for you. Please.*

In this muted state of relational limbo, every response felt like rejection to Mike. He began a search for a frying pan. Molly walked back to the bathroom. Mike could hear the water running in the bathtub.

She's avoiding me, he thought.

He ate his eggs and had some milk before attempting a talk with her. She sat on the bed, wrapped in a bathrobe, her hands folded neatly in her lap. Mike stood in the doorway, wondering whether to cross the threshold or not.

"Molly?" he said.

She looked up at him.

Mike crossed the room and sat next to her on the bed.

"Will you be coming back with me?" he asked. He almost didn't want her to answer.

"Mike ..." A look he couldn't identify appeared on her face. It wasn't sadness. And it wasn't quite disappointment. "I ... I don't think so," she said. "I need to take care of some things here, I think. And ... I still need to be alone for a while. I need to think about things." She took his hand.

Take care of things? Mike thought. *Just two days ago you couldn't handle any of these things! I had to take care of things! Now you've got everything covered?*

He closed his eyes, feeling the hot sting of tears stalled at the floodgates. He fought them back. He felt her thin fingers tracing over his hand. It felt good, but he blocked incoming assumptions with better judgment.

Molly ran her fingers over the back of Mike's hand, over the knuckles and up and down the length of his fingers.

She looked down.

"Where's your wedding ring?" she asked.

"What?" Mike said.

"Your wedding ring. Where is it?"

"Oh." *Well, one night I was so depressed I got a little drunk and went out and saw a movie and then tried to shoot somebody with a gun I stole from my dad and that somebody ran over me with her car and when I tried to get away I collapsed into the street and my ring's probably floating in the Houston sewers somewhere right now.* "I lost it."

"You lost your wedding ring? I thought you never take it off."

"I don't; I didn't. I mean, I guess I did and it got lost. I looked for it. I really did."

Molly released his hand.

✳ ✳ ✳

It was Halloween morning, and outside the Trumbull Police Department, the demonstrators carried out endless tirades against the government conspiracies involving extraterrestrials. Several protesters, perhaps for Halloween alone, milled about among the masses in costumes—most of them patterned after the most commonly reported aliens, the grays.

Inside the station, Sam Petrie sat in Graham's office, watching the captain stare at his desk. Petrie had a pen in his hand, and he nervously drummed it against his knee. This annoyed Graham to no end, but his mind lay elsewhere. The topic of conversation was Jimmy Horn.

"We could get a chopper up here," Petrie said. "Get a bird's eye of the area."

"Naw," Graham said. "We've combed the woods. We took the dogs out. If he was out in the woods somewhere, we would have found him. And if he's been outside all this time, he'd be dead of hypothermia or exposure by now."

"So you think he's dead?" Petrie asked.

"Naw, he ain't dead. If he was dead, we would have found him, I think. He's gotta be stayin' somewhere. See if you can find out if there's any empty houses around. Get some of the guys to check 'em out. He could've shacked up in an abandoned house or in an empty one up for sale or somethin'."

The phone intercom buzzed, and Kelly's voice came through. "Captain?"

"Yeah?" Graham said.

"Mr. Woodbridge called. He wants to know if you've got lunch plans."

"Tell him to name the place. I'll meet him around eleven-thirty."

"Yes, sir."

Petrie said, "Sir? What about Pops Dickey?"

"Run by his place, Sam. Make sure you talk to the missus. Make sure everything's on the up-an'-up."

The young officer rose to leave.

Graham said, "And Sam—after that, go home and get some rest."

Petrie smiled. "Would you?"

"No."

"Then I'll be back in an hour."

✳ ✳ ✳

Mike returned the rental car (though he hated parting with the superb automobile), downed a dose of Nyquil, and slept through the flight back to Houston.

When the plane landed, he checked his voice mail. No messages. At home, he watched some TV. He ate some cereal. He picked up his phone and dialed.

"Dr. Bering?" Mike said.

"Yes?"

"Dr. Bering, this is Mike."

"Mike! I've just been thinking about you."

"Good thoughts, I hope," Mike said.

"Of course, of course."

"Dr. Bering, I was just wondering if maybe … well, if maybe I could come over and talk."

"I would love for you to come over. I'll put on some coffee."

* * *

Officer Sam Petrie's police cruiser sped through the Trumbull streets to the back roads and flew onto Trace Road like it was the Daytona 500. He grinded to a stop in the Dickeys' driveway, sending up a cloud of dust. He let himself in through the gate, walked up the porch steps, and knocked on the screen door.

Mr. Black, with Pops's shotgun firmly in hand, answered.

FROM THE JOURNAL OF DR. LEOPOLD SUTZKEVER:

October 22, 1978

It appears the nastiness is over. For now, anyway. I will be forever indebted to Dr. Silverman, Jonas's physician. The ailments Jonas suffered were first treated medically, and no blame should be placed on the boy's parents. They did what they thought best and what any other parent would have done. Jonas was sick—very sick. So they called their family physician. Dr. Silverman did what he could but found himself in quite a predicament. The boy's illness would not go away, and the good doctor's treatments, both medical and psychological (for Silverman has told me he spent a great deal of time with Jonas, playing chess and, as he put it, "just shooting the breeze"), had no apparent affect. It was only after serious talks with Jonas that Dr. Silverman discovered that the boy's problems were not of a physical nature, but a spiritual one. Thank heavens the man is a believer! If not, I fear Jonas would still be suffering to this day (and I pray that he doesn't!). Silverman knew me from church and knew of my reputation. He had heard about my gift. But he was reluctant to approach me. As he said, "I never lent credence to this sort of thing." He had seen that awful 1973 movie, and he regarded it as fantasy. "Besides," he told me, "the movie offended me on account of my religious beliefs." I was quick to assure him that I had seen the film and responded in much the same way. In my opinion, it does a severe disservice to the reality of its premise. Silverman had outrun his options, though, and a mutual friend of ours suggested he meet with me. The rest, of course, is recorded within this diary.

If only Jonas had had the wisdom to see the potential danger from the outset. In his eyes, it all started harmless enough. From talks with the boy, I learned that he had become involved with astrology and reading the tarot and the writings of Crowley. He began to dabble. To seek enlightenment. That was all the foothold they needed.

"Beloved, believe not every spirit, but try the spirits whether they are of God: because many false prophets are gone out into the world. Hereby know ye the Spirit of God: Every spirit that confesseth that Jesus Christ is come in the flesh is of God: And every spirit that confesseth not that Jesus Christ is come in the flesh is not of God: and this is that spirit of antichrist, whereof ye have heard that it should come; and even now already is it in the world" (1 John 4:1–3).

Indeed. But in the words of Saint Paul, "The God of peace shall bruise Satan under your feet shortly" (Rom. 16:20). Praise God!

The wonderful aroma of fried food wafted through Goodson's on State Highway 249, between Houston and Trumbull. As always, the place was busy with lunchtime patrons, most of them from the computer plant several miles down the road. The waitress delivered two plates of chicken-fried steak to Graham and Steve's table. Graham's steak was drenched in gravy.

"You look like you ain't got much sleep," the captain said.

"So do you," the pastor said. "How're things going?"

"Well, we're gonna do a door-to-door today. It'll take a while, but we got everybody out. Most of 'em will work around the clock."

"No ideas, huh?" Steve asked.

"He's gotta be stayin' someplace. It's just too dang cold for him to have lasted outside all this time. I got a guy checking empty homes."

"How's the family holding up?"

"I guess okay, considering," Graham said.

"Did they see the guy?"

"Nope. But we lifted his prints all over the place. We know who we want. Findin' him's the problem."

"How are *you* holding up?"

"Okay, considering," Graham said with a smirk. "I've got a murderer on the loose we can't seem to find, and on top of that, I've got these killer headaches, and every time I walk outside I have to deal with protesters convinced we got a flying saucer tucked away in the station house. And somehow these kooks have gotten around."

"What do you mean?"

"A psychologist working with the Diaz family handed over some of the little girl's crayon drawings as evidence."

"I thought they never saw him," Steve said.

"They didn't, but the little girl's convinced she knows what he looks like."

"And?"

"Skinny black body. Large gray head. Looks like an alien."

"You gotta be kidding me."

"I wish I was. It sounds stupid, I know," Graham said.

"Didn't you say she was nearly abducted once before?"

"Yeah. On her way home from a friend's."

"And someone saved her, right?"

"Oh, yeah. She calls him 'the good man.'"

"What does he look like?" Steve asked.

"Don't know. She hasn't drawn him yet."

"Aliens," repeated Steve, stifling a grin.

"Yeah, laugh it up. I'm just trying to catch the kid. It's hard enough with all the whackos around screaming about cover-ups and sheesh."

"Well, you'll have to pardon my bad timing, then," Steve said. "But I need you on something."

"Okay," Graham said.

"I've been doing a lot of thinking and praying, and I think I've decided to resign."

"Say what?"

"It just doesn't feel right, Graham. It never has."

"Who knows about this?"

"Just my wife and now you."

"You're gonna step down?"

"Well, I'm not positive yet. I just … well, you know. I need you to pray about this for me."

"You know I will. But I have to be honest, here. My selfish prayer will be you change your mind."

* * *

Winter fury cleared the streets on Halloween night. The trick-or-treaters stayed indoors for costume parties or harvest festivals in church and school gymnasiums. Only a few brave souls (with coats covering their Power Ranger or Spider-Man or clown or hobo costumes) ventured out with bags in hand and Mom and Dad in tow, constantly asking, "Are you ready to head back now, sweetie?"

Mike drove to Dr. Bering's house, and the two rested in armchairs, facing each other in Bering's study. Outside, the wind howled against the house and rattled the windows.

"Looks like a storm may be kicking up out there," Mike said.

"I wouldn't be surprised. We've had some dreadfully foul weather lately. I mean, *really*, with this cold of an autumn, I wouldn't be surprised if our Christian neighbors begin predicting Armageddon," Bering said.

Mike chuckled and took a long gulp of coffee. The temperature in Bering's study wasn't exactly warm. He wondered why the professor didn't turn up the heat.

"I hope everything came off well in Dallas," Bering said.

"It went all right," Mike said. "The funeral was real nice. The minister I found was a really nice guy, and he did a good job."

"Good to hear it."

"It's just … well, with Molly, things didn't go exactly as I'd hoped."

"Sorry to hear that, Mike."

"Well, I don't mean to make it sound bad. We didn't fight or anything. I guess I was just hoping … Oh, I don't know—"

"That she would come back with you?" Bering asked.

Mike nodded. "Yeah, I guess so. And she still might, but she saw my wedding ring was gone, and I don't think she believed I lost it."

"Why would she think you would lie about that? Especially since you were trying to get her to return with you?"

"That's a good point. I don't know. I guess she was still upset about Vickie and … well, I wouldn't expect anyone to think very clearly under those circumstances."

"That's very fair of you, Mike. You don't think she's giving you a raw one?"

"A raw one?" Mike asked.

"Yes. Treating you poorly, I should say. Haven't you made it obvious that you want her back? That you're willing to make it work?

You haven't pressured her at all. Don't you think she should recognize this?"

"I guess. What are you trying to say?"

"I'm not trying to say much, Mike. I don't know your wife, nor do I know much about your relationship, but it just seems to me that she has no intention of salvaging your marriage."

"I … I don't believe that."

"You don't have to," Bering said with a smile. "I'm just an old fool trying to be a friend. Please don't measure my counsel any greater in these matters than any other friend of yours."

Mike swallowed more coffee, thinking, *What friends of mine? Robbie? He'd probably say the same thing.* "No, you might be right. I just think that I love her. I can't imagine living without her."

"Well, then," Bering said, "I suppose that would certainly be love." The professor crossed his legs and hunched over slightly, peering into Mike's eyes and smiling. He said, "But you didn't come to visit to discuss your marriage, did you?"

Mike squirmed in his chair uneasily. How did Bering know?

"No," he said. "That's not exactly why I came."

"Well, then. Let's hear it."

Was he ready to make this leap? He had already made it, really, but perhaps there was still time to turn back. *Surely this man is a lunatic, a fruitcake. What he's hinted at all along cannot possibly be real. It can't be true.*

"It's the hyperspace stuff. I've read your article over and over and over again, and each time it becomes clearer. More understandable. And I got to thinking. I mean, you describe things in there that can't possibly be researched scientifically. You say so yourself in the article. We don't have the means or the technology or even the understanding to explore another dimension. Yet your work has such an insight. Like you're so sure of yourself and your theories. I was wondering: how can you know so much about it? You just don't seem like the kinda guy who would be so obsessed with the purely theoretical."

"You tell me, Mike. How can I obtain knowledge of the impossible?"

"Well, this is gonna sound crazy. I don't know if I even believe it myself, but your article just seemed to be almost a personal narrative in some places. Hypothetically, I guess, the only way you could understand the impossible is if you had experienced it firsthand. If—this sounds ridiculous—you had made it possible somehow."

✳ ✳ ✳

Gertie, still bound to the chair in her bedroom, screamed herself hoarse.

Pops's seventy-one-year-old legs sprung him forward and crashing into Jimmy. They'd been arguing for what seemed like hours over Petrie's corpse until Pops couldn't take it anymore. Something had snapped inside. The two went sprawling, knocking over an end table. Jimmy rolled the old man over and pounced on him, punching and pounding with a demonic fervor. Pops, with strength beyond his ability, grasped the kid at his forearms and pulled him over and off his chest. Pops rolled with him, sitting atop the kid's stomach. The old man grabbed the shotgun and lodged the barrel under Jimmy's chin.

"You idiot!" Pops said. "What are we supposed to do now?"

"Who cares?" Jimmy asked, his eyes firmly locked on the gun barrel pressing into his Adam's apple.

"How long do you think it will take before they realize he's missing and come looking for him?"

In one swift motion, Jimmy knocked the shotgun away from his throat and managed to wrestle it from Pops. He thrust it into the man's belly, sending him doubled over to the floor.

Rising to his feet, Mr. Black said, "I don't care what you do about it, gramps. It's your mess. You clean it up."

Flying saucer or no, a shift of power was taking place. Pops wanted to believe his sheer belief had willed it all into existence, made the lies true—the grays, the saucer, and even his dominance over his youthful comrade. But the kid wasn't susceptible to the old man's will. He had his own ideas, his own plans, and he had come to see Pops as *his* sidekick. Not vice versa.

"But ... but, the grays," Pops wheezed. "The grays told us to stay together."

"I ain't going nowhere," Mr. Black said. "We can stay together, but get this straight. You do things my way, or you end up like the cop. I don't need you for what they told us to do. I can do it on my own, and they know it. They'll see we never needed you at all."

"You're crazy," Pops said.

An unearthly anger spread over Mr. Black's face. His eyes narrowed to slits, sleek as daggers.

"No one calls me crazy." He sneered. He kicked the old man in the hip. "Now get up and clean the mess. I'll take care of the car."

"What are you going to do?"

"Don't worry about it," Jimmy said.

Pops's eye landed on the Grim Reaper branded on the kid's forearm, and the most horrible feeling of dread took root in the old man's stomach.

✳ ✳ ✳

"I don't believe it."

"Don't you?" Dr. Bering replied. "I have a feeling you knew exactly what you believed when you came over here."

"It can't be true," Mike said.

"If you say so."

Mike laughed good-humoredly, but he was nervous. As fluid as these new thoughts were, they were nonetheless pervasive. He was drowning in them and reaching for the safety of any explanation. Strange things had happened to him. Vickie's corpse came alive. The odd sensation of DEATH in Dealey Plaza. This sort of thing grew more and more possible every passing day. Maybe it wasn't so much that he believed Dr. Bering, but that he *wanted* to believe Dr. Bering.

"So you actually communicate with hyperspace?" Mike asked.

And so it began.

"Yes, but *they communicate with me* would probably be more accurate," Dr. Bering responded. "Mike, compared to our visitors from hyperspace, we are nothings. Less than ants. You have to understand that Kaluza-Klein and all that goes with it do not even penetrate the surface of this. Those are our feeble grasps at understanding. With all probability, our world will never, not in a hundred millennia, be able to bridge the gap to other dimensions. But, as you will see, we don't have to as long as the gap is bridged from the other side."

"Yeah, okay, okay. You're saying you actually see these people?"

"Oh, yes. Well, I speak to one of them, and he to me," Bering said.

As if repetition would secure its plausibility: "Okay, one more time: someone from another dimension comes here, *to your house*, and talks to you."

"Yes."

Plowing forward: "What about?" Mike asked.

"Anything and everything. His mind is limitless, and so he is limitless in what he can teach us."

Already breathless: "I think I need a drink."

"Would you like to meet him?"

Apprehension: "What? You mean now?"

"No better time than the present," Bering said. "Would you?"

Surrender: "Absolutely."

Dr. Bering eased out of his chair, almost slinking. Mike followed him, eyes wide, mouth open, and watched Bering kneel on the hardwood floor. The professor's eyes were shut, and Mike believed he was about to pray. What followed sounded very much like prayer. Bering whispered a long string of words, uttering them so softly that Mike could not make them out, but somehow they sounded very, very sweet.

Bering continued, and Mike half expected him to suddenly hop up and guffaw, and the whole thing would be a joke. A cruel charade.

But Mike knew it wasn't a joke. He believed Dr. Bering, believed in what the professor claimed to have access to. He believed because he wanted to, because he had to, and because his heart, his empty shell of blackened heart, yearned for it to be true. He was tired of the darkness and of death. He was ready to step into the light. To live.

Mike craned forward, concentrating on Bering's incantations. The room seemed to grow darker. And colder. Was it an illusion?

He could hear the words slipping from Bering's lips. Bering said, "Please come to us. We want to see you. Please show yourself ..."

Two hours later, Bering lay facedown on the floor, muttering into the wood, and Mike fended off sleep. Nothing had happened.

He rose from his chair and left the professor alone, without saying a word. He closed the door quietly behind him and walked through the yard to his car. Dewdrops of ice glimmered in grass like sparkling crystal, lending a sense of magic to the house. Mike still believed, despite Bering's failure to provide proof.

He almost had his safety belt buckled when a great exultant cry resounded from within Bering's home. He jumped out of the car and rushed up to the door, flung it open, and dashed inside, heading for the study. In the doorway, he froze, and the color in his face bled away. His heart seized up. His flesh prickled with chills, the tickles of ghosts. Before him:

The most frightening ...

... and the most exhilarating thing he'd ever seen.

Though all the switches were off, Bering's study sparkled with an array of dancing lights, tiny bubbles of brightness swirling about the room, shining seeds of light onto the walls from an invisible mirror ball. There seemed to be a stirring, a forceful breeze that came from nowhere and rushed back and forth through the room, sweeping over the floor. It stirred the cuffs of Mike's pants. The room had grown colder, but Mike's chills slid away from him, and warmth bathed him inside and out. The most marvelous rush took his body, making him high, kindling within him the fires of pleasure and enlightenment, almost erotically so. His flesh tingled as he watched the room come alive, activated from beyond and lit up with the electricity of phantoms. It was beautiful, and Mike had the sensation of standing in the middle of a golden field with the winds of spring filling his lungs and the sun bathing him with its warmth. Before him lay an altar, an ancient ruin of stone and the flesh of gods, waiting for a sacrifice.

Bering, in the center of the room, embraced by the field and the winds and the dancing lights, said, "Welcome to the otherworld."

Mike said, "It's the single most beautiful thing I've ever seen."

"Would you like to meet him?" Bering asked.

"Who?" Mike nearly shouted, since it seemed that music was seeping from the otherworld.

"Malcam," Bering said.

The breeze picked up speed, its waves becoming a whirlwind of energy circling the room. The spheres of light, caught in the current, spun around ever faster, and a small tornado of wind and light blossomed up between Mike and Dr. Bering. In the center of the twister, the form of a man took shape, at first appearing smoky, a weak projection, but then appearing very solid, very real. The spinning funnel did not affect him in the least. He faced Mike and smiled.

The tornado shrunk slowly and was swallowed up in a portal in the floor. The winds died, the lights vanished, and Malcam stood where Mike had previously seen the altar.

Dr. Bering switched on a lamp.

Malcam wore a black suit over a black shirt. His hair was black and combed back.

Bering said, "Mike, allow me to introduce you to Malcam."

Mike swooned, felt nauseous, lost feeling in his body. Before he could collapse, Bering caught him under the arms and hoisted him upright. The professor held him there until the stiffness returned to Mike's bones and he recovered his balance and senses.

Mike peered at Malcam, suspecting that he was a hallucination but not really caring.

"What do I say to him?" Mike asked through feeble lips.

Malcam spoke: "My dear friend. Samuel and I do not share a secret language. You may say to me anything you'd like, and you may say it directly."

"Are you really from another dimension?" Mike asked.

"From your position, yes," Malcam said.

"And from yours?" Mike asked.

"I'm afraid you'd have no means of comprehending things from my point of view."

"Can I ask you anything?"

"I'm not an oracle. I cannot predict your future. While I am immortal and have even witnessed your world's evolution, our time runs much the same as yours. There is no time traveling for us. Only world traveling."

"But what about the link between hyperspace and time travel?" Mike asked.

"Your scientists have accomplished a great deal in their attempts to understand hyperspace, but the possibilities of exploration are limited to hyperspace alone. The future is being made every second. Tomorrow does not exist yet. It doesn't take a scientist to understand that. You can't go to a place that doesn't exist."

"But what *can* you tell me?" Mike asked.

"Whatever your heart desires, chum. Consider me your friend. I want to give you your life back."

* * *

The new morning of November cleansed Houston of Halloween night.

Steve Woodbridge met with the church's Personnel Committee in the conference room attached to his study. The committee consisted of five men, two of them church deacons, all of them considered pillars of the congregation. Most of them served on other committees, and they all made the church's business *their* business, for better or worse.

Steve found himself at the table with these men, allegedly the best of his flock, the leaders of the church. He did not trust most of them, and he did not like any of them. He knew that several of them had said some pretty harsh things about him behind his back. He figured they would feign dismay over his announcement but would secretly rejoice.

The pastor said, "Why don't we start with prayer? Don, would you do the honor?"

Everyone bowed their heads, and Don prayed: "Heavenly Father, we thank Thee for Thy many blessings. We praise Thee for Thy lovingkindness and Thy mercy. We worship Thee with our hearts and mouths. Thank You, Lord God, for Your Son. Thank You, Lord God, that we are not like those who do not know You. We know that we find favor in You. Thank You for bringing us men here this beautiful morning to set about the business of Your church. Guide us, O Lord. Guide our hearts, hands, and minds, that we may best serve Thee, and let our plans be diligent and holy. We pray these things in the name of Your precious and holy and wonderful Savior-Son, Jesus. Amen."

Everyone awoke, grumbling amens and opening their notebooks and manila folders, pens ready.

"Well, okay, Pastor," Mr. Leeds said. "What's on the agenda?"

"Well—" Steve began.

"You leavin'?" Simon interrupted.

How could he know? "Well—" Steve said.

"Well, are you?" Bob asked.

Steve took a deep breath. He looked around the room. He'd already lost control. He found on each face a frown. Why wasn't it easy to do this? He looked out the door that led into his study. He could see some of his cherrywood shelves, filled with his books (Lewises and Schaeffers and Bonhoeffers, oh my!). The church had built him the study as an extra incentive to get him hired.

"Fellas," Steve said, "I've been doing some thinking. And this comes by a lot of prayer. I've really sought the Lord on this, and I ..."

The frowns remained, permanently pressed.

"I've decided to step down as your pastor. I feel like God is leading me into another ministry."

"What ministry?" Bob asked. "Where? Here in Houston?"

"Well—"

Dave asked, "Mills Road Baptist? They're looking for someone. You going there?"

"No," Steve said.

"We've never had a pastor quit before," Mr. Leeds said.

"Well, yes, I know that," Steve said. "You've fired them all."

"Well, I wouldn't exactly say fired," Don said.

"You asked them to leave," Steve said.

"There were very good reasons for those dismissals," Bob said.

"Okay, but that's beside the point. I'm not going to another church."

"Where you goin'?" Bob asked.

"I don't know. Wherever the Lord wants to take my wife and me."

Simon rolled his eyes.

"You just leavin' for the heck of it?" Mr. Leeds asked.

"No, not for the heck of it."

"Something wrong with this church?" Bob asked.

"We too small for you?" Simon asked.

"No, it's none of those things," Steve said.

They were bombarding him, keeping him unfocused. He could already feel them sucking away his resistance like telepathic leeches.

"You unhappy here?" Dave asked.

"Yes. I mean, no. Not exactly."

"What is it, then?" Dave asked.

Steve didn't respond. He felt the heat of their intrigue on his face. His forehead began to perspire.

What's going on here? These guys don't care about me, and they never have. Why aren't they shaking my hand, faking disappointment, and offering to help me pack my bags?

He looked around at them, trying not to stare at each for too long. Despite a persistent sadness, Steve almost felt like laughing. He was surrounded by caricatures.

Two minutes seemed to pass. Silence. Don Figaro pretended to pray. Finally, Mr. Leeds said, "How can we change your mind?"

✳ ✳ ✳

Graham could not get an answer from Sam Petrie's house. Petrie had not checked in at the station since leaving the day before either.

"He's probably sleeping," Lane said.

"Maybe," said Graham. "I'm gonna run by his place, see what he's up to. Give me a whistle if he shows up here."

"Will do."

Graham drove out to Petrie's one-bedroom home. Petrie's cruiser was not in the driveway.

✳ ✳ ✳

Mike spent the night at Bering's home, and the two of them stayed up talking to Malcam. It never really hit Mike that he was conversing with a hyperspatial being. The visitor was friendly and charming. He brought Mike in. Reality wasn't questioned; Mike's previous doubts were forgotten. Malcam told Mike as much as he could about his world. That is, as much as Mike could understand.

"You would die instantly if brought into my world," Malcam said. "Your three-dimensional body would not mesh with a higher dimension. Even if you did survive, you would not be able to see anything. It would be limbo. All would be a void."

"How do you come into our world?" Mike asked.

"You would not understand how we do it, but let me put it this way: could a fish survive out of the water?"

"No."

"The fish is chained, so to speak, to its habitat. But you may go into the water as much as you like, and sometimes for as long as you like, provided you have a breathing apparatus. The fish's world is, in a sense, a lower dimension to you. You can exist in its world, because you are a higher species in a higher dimension, but it cannot exist in yours. Look at my visiting here as a type of scuba diving."

"Why do you look like a man?" Mike asked.

"What should I look like?" Malcam asked.

"Oh, I don't know. Just a question. How do you look in your world?"

"That is something I cannot explain in three-dimensional terms, and if I described myself in ten-dimensional terms, you either would not understand it at all, or your brain might explode. Care to take a chance?" He smiled.

"I think I'll pass. How did you come to visit Dr. Bering?"

"Throughout your world's history, my people have taken quite a shine to the thinkers among you. The philosophers, the scientists, the poets and professors. Samuel is one of many I have befriended out of sheer admiration for his intellect. Also because I take pride in assisting these great thinkers in their pursuit of higher understanding. My world regularly watches yours. There was a time when I saw Samuel struggling with the theories of hyperspace, with Kaluza-Klein, and I thought I might give him some firsthand experience."

"How often do your people visit?"

"We can assume that there are at least one hundred visits with different people around the world every day," Malcam said.

"UFOs?" Mike asked.

"When they are real, it is us," Malcam responded.

"Why haven't you made yourselves known publicly? Why haven't you met with governments?"

"Influencing thought interests us, not influencing government. Besides, we have yet to see a world leader who would respond well to one of our visits. You have to understand that we select only those we feel can handle our sudden appearances. And at the same time, we are not in the least interested in superstitious and spiritual men, who may regard us as ghosts or spirits."

"Is there no truth to the spiritual realm?"

"Any spiritual reality lies with us. If a man's ghostly encounter is a true story, you can bet he met up with one of my colleagues. The same goes for so-called angels. Michael, there are no extraterrestrials, no spirits, and no angels. There is only you and me."

"Religion?"

"Poppycock."

"Sacred writings?"

"Of noble intention, but misguided nonetheless. Most are rubbish."

"The Bible?"

Malcam chuckled. "A good book, but not *the* good book."

"Jesus?"

Malcam seemed to wince at the name, but a grin cut through his face. "A nice fellow," he said. "Still, He had it in His head to stir things up. You might say He almost deserved His fate."

"What about life after death?" Mike asked.

"My, my! You do have all the questions, don't you? God and Devil; life and death. Heaven and hell. But that one, Michael, I do not know if I can answer in the way you would like. There is no death for my kind. And as for yours, I cannot say what lies beyond your last night on earth. I would suspect nothingness. My supposition is that death is the end of existence, the end of consciousness."

"Then what is the point of anything?"

"Why, life, of course! This life. Make what you can of it. Enjoy it. You are, in your basest form, an animal. Therefore, hedonism is human nature's truest and highest art."

"Hedonism?"

"Pleasure is the highest good, and the only moral duty is fulfilled through pursuing our appetites."

Through this entire exchange, Dr. Bering remained silent, sitting in his chair and beaming. Somehow, the introduction of Mike to Malcam pleased him greatly.

Mike asked more questions about life. Malcam's words soothed him and reassured him. Perhaps DEATH was really just death, and he had feared it needlessly all these years. Animating corpses and recurring dreams were figments of his paranoid imagination, grotesque fantasies that were really portrayals of his subconscious fears. Life and death were separate, were intended to be separate. For now, all that was, was life. This eventually led him to the inevitable: Molly.

"I have a wife," Mike said to Malcam.

"I had a feeling you'd get to this," Malcam said. "Samuel has told me you're quite taken with her and are troubled by her absence."

"Well, yes—"

"Do you love her?" Malcam asked.

"Of course," Mike responded.

"Are you sure?"

"Yes. I do. I love her. I'm empty without her. I need her and want her to need me. I'm not the same alone."

"So it may not be that you need *her*, but that you feel empty without someone to share your life with. Allow me to suggest, Michael, that it is not your wife you crave, but the sharing of a relationship with a woman. I'm guessing you miss her warmth, her tenderness, her companionship, her affection. Perhaps the intimacy of sexual intercourse?"

"Well, yeah. All those things," Mike said.

"And couldn't you find those things in another?"

"Yeah, I guess. But it's Molly I want."

"Ah, yes. Emotional attachment. Quite understandable. But believe me, given time, you can develop the same attachment to another. I am by no means suggesting you hop right out and find yourself a lady friend. Take what time you need, but realize that if she's been gone this long and shows no signs of returning, it is probably best that you sever that bond. There is no such thing as *meant for each other*. Only what she and you and anybody else wants."

This all sounded so right to Mike. It sounded so right and so true. How could anyone actually believe that two people were destined to be together? And how could anyone believe that divine providence brought people together? It never made sense, and now Malcam was saying that it didn't because it didn't happen.

"Mike," Dr. Bering said, "are you all right?"

"Huh?" Mike mumbled.

"You look very, very tired."

"I guess I could use some sleep."

"Sure you could. Malcam understands. This is a lot of exposure all at one moment. You probably should go home and get some rest. That would be all right, wouldn't it, Malcam?"

"That would be fine," Malcam said.

"We'll still be here when you're ready to have another go at it," Bering said.

"Okay," said Mike. "I'll just go home and rest up a little. Maybe we could visit again tomorrow?"

"All in good time, friend," said Malcam.

CHAPTER FOURTEEN

The next morning, Graham Lattimer went to church. Steve's sermon was an adequate one, an able exposition of the second half of Romans 7. He seemed back to his old self. He paced and waved his hands and had the congregation hanging on his every word. Perhaps he had found a comfort in his congregation's passive acceptance of performance rather than proclamation. Going through the motions never fazed them, Graham realized. He wondered if Steve would make his announcement at the conclusion of the service. The message ended, Don Figaro prayed, the offering plate made its way through reluctant hands, and everyone rose to sing "The Bond of Love." No announcement.

On his way out, he shook Steve's hand, telling the pastor to give him a call if he needed anything. Graham drove back out to Trumbull, heading straight for the station. Once inside, his first words were, "Any word from Petrie?"

"No, sir," Kelly said.

"I'm headin' out to the Dickeys'," he said.

Still dressed in his Sunday best, he took his police cruiser out to Trace Road. Pulling into the driveway, he noticed that the house seemed different. Darker, maybe. He glanced up at the sky. In the entire expanse, there hovered only one cloud, seemingly directly over the Dickeys' house. But it was not blocking out the sun. The image of shade didn't come from the cloud. There was just a shadow. Or at least, what looked like one.

Be assured.

The same feeling he had during his last visit to the Dickeys' returned. Was it fear? Nervousness? Something about the house or someone who lived in it wasn't right, and Graham knew for the first time that the sensation was a spiritual one. The aura of the house afflicted his spirit. There was an evil presence about the place.

He tucked his hand inside his coat, feeling his pistol strapped securely into his shoulder holster. The gun made him feel better but didn't make him feel good. He strode up to the house, scanning the windows for any signs of danger. He knocked on the door.

Pops opened it.

"What can I do for you, Captain?"

"We're missin' an officer," said Graham.

"What's that got to do with me?" Pops asked.

"He was last seen on his way out to your property. You know Sam Petrie, don't you?"

"Yeah. He the guy who checked out my cow? Tall, gangly fella?"

"That's him."

"Yeah. I know him. Nice fella," said Pops.

"Have you seen him?" asked Graham.

"Well, no. Not since the last time the two of you came by together."

"'Cause he said he was coming by your place. And Sam don't lie. So if he said he was, he did. Or at least tried to."

"What's that supposed to mean?" Pops asked.

"That means I believe something happened to him, and since he was last seen headin' out here, you got some questions to answer," Graham said.

"Well, go ahead and ask."

"For the record: you see Petrie yesterday?"

"Nope."

"You sure?"

"Yep."

Graham peered over Pops's shoulder, trying to look into the house. Pops stepped over, blocking his view.

"You charging me with anything?" Pops asked.

"How's Gertie?"

"Gertie's fine."

"She here today?" asked Graham.

"No. No, she's out today."

"Where's she at?"

"With a friend."

"Friend got a name?" Graham asked.

Pops flushed with anger. "She didn't tell me, okay? You wanna quit beating around the bush and come out and tell me what's going on?"

"Mind if I come inside?" Graham asked.

"You got a warrant?"

"Why are you so concerned about warrants, Mr. Dickey?"

"'Cause I don't want you in my house, that's why!"

"Got something to hide?"

"No."

"Then why can't I come in?"

"Because I don't like you."

"Fair enough. But listen to me, you old fool: Petrie's my friend, and if something happened to him, and if I find out you had something to do with it, I won't need a warrant to come crashing through your door and beat your face in."

"And I'll be waiting for you," Pops said, and he slammed the door in Graham's face.

Stepping away from the Dickey home, Graham felt safer. The air didn't seem as cold outside the gate.

He drove back down Trace Road, the way he had come. As he neared its intersection with Rolling Lane, he let off the gas and leaned over to turn on the heater. He played with the knobs, setting it just right. When he looked up again, back at the road, he caught some movement in the woods out of the corner of his eye. He slammed on the brakes. Turning his head, he managed to catch a glimpse of a figure, clad in black, disappearing into the brush.

Graham put the cruiser in park and hurried out, running up to the edge of the woods. A narrow ditch separated the road from the brush. He heard a branch snap beyond the brush, from deep inside the dense thicket.

"Who's there?" he called. But he had a vague intuition he knew who it was.

Graham pulled his firearm out of his shoulder holster and surveyed the ditch. He walked cautiously into the brush.

"Trumbull Police! Come on out," he yelled.

He could hear footsteps, faint and rapid, in the dark woods ahead of him. He waded through the bushes. They were wet with melted frost, and they dampened his suit. Pistol extended, he crept out of the brush and to the edge of the trees. He squinted, trying to make out anything in the dense foliage. He froze. He couldn't quite tell, but it appeared as if a person stood next to a tree about thirty yards ahead of him. Shadows overwhelmed that distance, but he could feel the figure watching him.

"Who's there?" he shouted.

Graham jogged forward and hid behind a large tree. He peeked around. The figure had disappeared. He listened. He could hear the sound of leaves crunching beneath footfalls. He swung around the trunk and ran five yards to another.

"This is the police! Come on out, now, with your hands raised!"

The distant footsteps stopped.

Maybe he's too far away for me to hear.

Graham walked forward, making sure to keep behind trees, keeping his eyes focused on the darkness ahead. He stepped into a clearing and paused. He listened. Something moved in the grass behind him, and he spun around to see the branches of a bush rattling. He pointed his pistol.

"Who's there?" he shouted.

A wicked laugh erupted from the woods behind him, slicing through the air and into Graham's head, and he turned around again. A wind began sweeping through the trees, swaying the branches and whistling eerily.

"Come on out where I can see you!"

Footsteps to his left.

He whirled around. Nothing.

Again, the stirring behind him.

He turned around. Nothing.

Okay, Graham. Just relax. You're getting paranoid here. Just a little frazzled. Get it together.

With his pistol steadied in both hands, he started walking purposefully into the darkness. He made it ten yards, when he heard a laugh. It stopped him in his tracks. His blood ran cold. Gooseflesh broke out on his arms. The cackle was different than before. It was deep, guttural, and sounded simultaneously human and inhuman.

Be assured.

"Who's there?" he called, but his voice lacked the usual authority.

His air of command left. Cold fear set in.

Yea, though I walk through the valley of the shadow of death, I will fear no evil, he thought. He holstered his pistol, closed his eyes, and prayed.

When he opened his eyes, he ran back to his car and radioed for backup. He wanted the woods searched.

Mike slept on and off for a good seventeen hours, but when he awoke, he felt more tired than he had the previous day. He drank some juice and tumbled back into bed.

The previous day struck him as a fantastic dream, but he looked forward to venturing into that dreamland again.

There is no such thing as "meant for each other."

Malcam's sharp words resonated in Mike's mind, haunting and peculiarly charming. And despite the words' seemingly mystical source, they were undeniably unromantic. Even worse: they somehow made sense.

There is no "meant for each other," Mike thought. *And ...*

Did he really love her?

... there is no meaning.

Could he love another?

No meaning to anything.

Thoughts sailed in like whispers from foreign tongues. He could conceive the inconceivable. Perhaps their love was not meant to be. Perhaps Mike belonged to greater things. Perhaps he was meant for something else. Or, perhaps ...

... someone else.

* * *

Consciousness stole back into Mike's head, stingy with its clarity, so he did not fully realize (or accept) its arrival. The effects of stepping into the otherworld swam over him, the aftershocks of a maddening adventure. And when he looked up and saw a man sitting in a chair at the foot of the bed, he didn't jump. Not at first.

He merely stared, squinting his eyes into focus. His mind swallowed the last drop of consciousness, and he awoke. Then he jumped back, slamming his spine into the headboard of the bed. The back of his skull knocked against the wall. He winced.

"Who's there?"

"Don't be afraid, chum. It's only me."

I'm still asleep, Mike thought. *I'm still dreaming. And maybe ... maybe this whole thing's been a dream.* "Are you real?" he asked, not really thinking.

"As real as you."

Mike didn't like the answer. "Malcam?"

"Aw," he mocked. "You guessed it."

"What ... what are you doing here? Where's Dr. Bering?"

"The professor and I aren't joined at the hip, friend," Malcam said. "I come and go as I please, and it would be in your best interest not to assume that the old man has the monopoly on fellowship with my kind."

Mike squirmed uneasily. An uncomfortable realization arrived: he had removed his clothing during his sleep.

"Our dreams reflect our lives, Michael. Oh, how they do. You don't understand this yet, but I can help you understand it."

"Wh—?" Mike began.

"You are naked."

Mike blushed. He pulled the covers further up, pressing them to his chest.

"You are naked and ashamed," Malcam said. "In your sleep you have wrestled off your clothes, and now you are naked." He rolled his eyes. "The symbolism is rich. You are vulnerable. And you are ashamed."

Mike scanned the floor for his clothes. "Why are you here?" he asked.

"To make you unashamed! To give you your life back. Don't you see, friend? You are naked. You are weak and afraid. I can make you strong again. I can make you unashamed. You have only to let me in."

"I … I don't understand. I want these things. I know I do. I want to be different. I want to be free—"

"Free!" Malcam shouted. "Yes!" He floated toward Mike and whispered, "I can set you free, chum." His breath hit Mike's face and sizzled with a bittersweet warmth. "Your freedom is in *me*."

Mike's eyes swelled with tears and overflowed. "Let me dress," he said.

"Of course, friend. But soon, you will be naked and unashamed. Just as your kind was before. Malcam only cares for your restoration," he said. But Mike sensed beneath Malcam's paternal facade an obvious mockery. And for some reason, he did not feel consoled at all.

FROM "TEXAS HOT SPOT UPDATE" BY DON MONTAG IN *U.F.O. REPORT MAGAZINE*:

In the pale light of early morning, Trumbull looks like any other small town. But this tiny Texan burg has attracted UFO researchers from all over the country. And a few from points beyond.

Reynaldo Esperanza, a photojournalist from Mexico City, is here, and he tries to blend in with the folks at the local McDonald's, in the hopes that someone will give him a story … any story about what is going on here. Esperanza lost his photographer's job with a Mexico City television station after he spearheaded a campaign to get footage of UFO sightings in the city skies on the air. "The people of Mexico City, the government in particular, were very afraid of what that might mean for the city," he says. "They feared rioting. Now, the sightings are commonplace. They are as much a tourist attraction as anything else. Still, I cannot get my job back."

So Esperanza took his equipment and became one of Mexico's most respected ufologists. His grainy photographs of what may be the creature known as the *chupacabra* are considered the best around and have withstood all charges of photographic trickery.

The UFOs keep him in business, though, and in Trumbull, Texas, business is booming. Esperanza already has pictures of several night sky phenomena that, for now, remain unexplained. "There is definitely something occurring here," he says. "Even the weather here seems to suggest a difference. A psychic I know flew in from Argentina, and he immediately said that there is an energy here, an aura he has felt only a few times before."

2 Timothy 4:3–4:

For the time will come when they will not endure sound doctrine; but wanting to have their ears tickled, they will accumulate for themselves teachers in accordance to their own desires; and will turn away their ears from the truth and will turn aside to myths.

* * *

"Hey, Margaret. Listen to this!"

Potter Adkins scratched his ear, leaned over his spit-cup, and let loose a load of sunflower seed shells and saliva. The load sprang back on a spittle bungee cord, and he spit it back down. Bulls-eye.

"Margaret? You listenin'?" he called.

Mrs. Adkins switched off the blender and waddled to the kitchen entryway. "What?" she asked.

Potter held up a *National News* over his head.

"Yeah, so?" his wife said. "What's it say this time? Another cyclops baby born? Oil drillers tap into hell again?"

"No," Potter said, frowning. "It's about Trumbull."

"Now, Potter. I told you to stop reading that rag."

"But they got pictures, honey," he whined. "Pictures and expert testimony and all."

"Of the UFOs?" Margaret looked doubtful but curious. "Hand it here, nutty," she said, and before he could, she swiped it away from him.

"Second page," Potter said.

"It's all smudgy. Cheap newsprint."

"You can read it. Go 'head."

Margaret scanned the article. When she finished, a look of complete amazement spread over her face. "Well, I'll be. Looks good, Potty."

"I hate it when you call me that."

"Looks pretty good," she said, ignoring him. "Potty, this looks bona fide."

"You don't even know what that means," Potter said, grabbing the tabloid back.

"That looked real. I mean … those pictures! And here! In our little town."

"There's a rally tomorrow night out front of the courthouse. Nate told me about it. Everybody in town's gonna gather and figure out what to do. We may even see one!"

Margaret's mouth gaped. "You think? Oh, Potty, you think?"

"Maybe," he muttered. He hated being called Potty.

"But it's so cold. We'll catch pneumonia out there."

"Hmmph," Potter grumbled. "That's the government's doing."

"What?"

✳ ✳ ✳

"That's the government's fault."

Digger Thomas patted the arm of his rocking chair, hoping to add illustrative support to his claim. He shook his head.

Digger's maid, Rosey, stopped dusting and turned around. "Excuse me?"

"The government. This weather. It's their doing. That's what I think."

"I think you've plum lost your mind, Mr. Thomas," Rosey said. And then she added, "If you don't mind me saying so."

Rosey had worked for the Thomas family for fifteen years, and she had grown accustomed to eighty-year-old Digger waxing philosophical about everything from AIDS and cancer to Waco and Ruby Ridge (and they were all connected, mind you). Everything, he claimed, was the government's fault. Rosey usually nodded, then rolled her eyes when his back was turned. Just a paranoid old man. But this ... well, this was something different. The weather? The idea that the government could control the weather was just ludicrous.

"Think what you want, Rosey. Mark my words. It's the government."

"Uh-huh," Rosey said, not at all agreeing.

"One of these days they'll come cart me away and label me a nut."

And they'd be right, she thought.

"But they'll really be following orders to silence me."

Why do I even bother? "Okay, Mr. Thomas. I'll bite. Why do you think the government's controlling the weather?"

"They blew it in Roswell. Didn't count on the story getting out. Now they spread disinformation in every continent to refute UFO claims. They know Trumbull's being visited."

"And the weather?"

"Come on now, Rosey. The government's been conducting weather experiments since the founding of our great nation. And part of those experiments have been attempts at manipulation. Even back when Jefferson and Franklin joined the secret demonic brotherhood, they tried to use witchcraft to harness the weather. Now they have technology. They've withheld rain from poor white farmers, and now they use their satellites and lasers and whatnots to make it unbelievably cold in Trumbull. Keep us ice-a-phobic Texans indoors while they intercept our visitors."

"Oh." Rosey chuckled. "Yeah, that makes perfect sense."

"You wait and see," said Digger, and he patted the arm of his rocking chair again. "You'll see. You'll see when they come to get me."

✳ ✳ ✳

"They'll come to get all of us."

Ruth Bloker kicked her cat and plopped down onto her plaid couch.

Mittens slinked away, tossing a hurt glance back at her owner.

Ruth sneered at the animal. "They know that I know, kitty," she said. She picked up her cross-stitch. "They know I know, and they'll be here soon."

✳ ✳ ✳

"They'll be here very soon."

Rick Bardwell and his son, Matt, stood in the driveway. Matt practiced his free throws.

"To come get us?" Matt asked.

"Yeah. But we won't need to be afraid. They're peaceful. They'll come down and invite us up. It'll be fun."

"My teacher says there's no such thing as aliens."

"Well, Matt, I'm sure your teacher's a nice lady. But I'm your father. You believe *me*, don't you?"

"Well ... yeah."

"And you know I wouldn't lie to you, right?"

As unhappily as possible, nine-year-old Matt said, "Yeah."

"Okay, then." Rick retrieved a rebound. "My shot?"

Matt began to cry.

* * *

Still bound head and foot in her own bedroom, believing that, any minute now, her husband or his crazy new friend would come in and decide it was time for her to die, Gertie Dickey began to cry.

* * *

Huge clouds gathered and froze over Houston and Trumbull, placing a polar cap on the city sky. And while a small minority of Trumbull citizens blindly suffered the crush of paranoia, others saw things ... differently.

Unsolved murders lay fresh on their minds. No amount of delusional hoopla could divert them from the overwhelming sense of fear, the gradual descent of what could only be described as oppression.

There was Matt Bardwell's teacher, Francine Skinner, who more and more felt like moving out of town every day. *Something's very wrong here*, she thought.

There was Abby Diaz, who knelt down beside her hotel room bed and clasped her tiny fingers together. She closed her eyes, eyes that were tired from mourning her father.

"Dear Jesus ..." she prayed.

✳ ✳ ✳

And there was Captain Graham Lattimer. Gruff, seemingly sour Graham Lattimer, who unknowingly joined his spirit with many others in his small town as he prostrated himself beside his bed and wet the carpet with tears.

This man would appear unrecognizable to his daily acquaintances had they the opportunity to see him in this moment. Graham, a man normally commanding complete authority without a word, a man often thought of as emotionless, so foreign to helplessness both in demeanor and deed, buried his face into the floor, gripping it as if it might give way. As if the very earth underneath it was seconds from dissolution.

"Dear God!" he cried, and aloud too. It seemed the only fitting way to pray now. "What is happening here? What is happening?"

His cries burst out, poured forth from a mouth so known for its unintentional frown (the "Lattimer frown" passed down from Graham's father), his heartfelt prayer the culmination of days upon days of pressure and desperation.

"Please help me!" He echoed the plea over and over, digging his fingers farther and farther into the floor. And then his words gurgled out, rushed out, a river raging with depression and insatiable need. And as he screamed out to God, his headaches returned with a vengeance, like the pounding of nails into his skull.

He howled in pain but continued praying nevertheless, working his throat-wrenching warbles into petition.

And if he could have seen into the other world—*the otherworld*—at that moment, he might certainly have died, for standing over him, drenched in darkness and dripping evil, was a dark emissary, its arms thrust downward, its muscled claws drilling into his head.

He groaned and tried to lift his head but found it paralyzed. "Dear God! What can I do?"

The big man, the strong man, strained beneath the weight of things unseen and was a child tugging at the cloak of the Father. A spirit stooped down to whisper a message: "It will be over soon. Be assured ..."

✳ ✳ ✳

Malcam followed Mike around the house as Mike prepared for their trip to Dr. Bering's home. Malcam's presence made Mike uneasy, but the excitement over what lay ahead kept him from entertaining the suspicions he should have had.

Malcam said they would have their "session" at Bering's place. Mike thought Malcam held the keys to the meaning of life, but he wondered why the being had to study him as he put his clothes on. Malcam's movements were smooth, effortless. He glided about the house, sometimes seeming to pass through the walls.

When it was time for Mike to leave for Dr. Bering's house, Malcam simply said, "See you soon," and disintegrated. Mike noticed the air seemed warmer after his departure. *I can't believe this is happening*, he thought.

But it was, and he had given himself over to the fantasy of it all. Real or not, he embraced the experience as real *enough*. He'd tried to wake himself up from his own life a thousand times, but it was a dream world of shocking permanence. He hoped this new adventure would eradicate the nightmares.

He didn't know that the real nightmare lay ahead.

✳ ✳ ✳

The crushing weight of evil ascended from Graham and into nothingness sometime during the night, but he had long since passed out. The morning broke through his bedroom window, the light sneaking in and bathing him in warmth. Slowly opening his eyes, sore from tears, he realized first that his headache was gone.

He rose from the floor, from the indention his body stamped in the carpet, like a man waking at his own funeral, perplexed by the proceedings. He crept to the bathroom. The shower revitalized him, and he decided to return to the Dickey farm. This time he wanted in the house.

Pulling into the driveway, he noticed that Pops's truck was gone. He knocked on the door. No answer. He peered through the porch window. He could barely see through the tightly drawn curtains, and there were no lights on. The living room looked empty. He knocked again. Nothing. He yelled, "Hello? Is anybody home?" Nothing.

Graham walked around the side of the house. The broken window sat high above his head. It was still covered, but not completely. Graham rose on his toes, tilting his head up. He lacked a good six inches. Looking around, he noticed a bucket a few yards away under a faucet. He set it on the ground under the window and stepped up.

The slits between the wood covering the window were wide enough to see through, but the room inside was as dark as the living room. He cupped his hands to the sides of his eyes, trying to let his vision adjust. He focused his vision afar, and when he could actually see, he could make out the numbers on a clock on the far wall. He adjusted his focus, bringing the rest of the contents of the room into his line of sight.

When his vision processed the outline of a person, he froze. A lone figure sat in the room. Graham placed a hand on his gun. He leaned closer, trying to make out the face. He ultimately realized that he was staring at a person's back. He saw a mess of white hair. Graham couldn't be sure if the person was alive, or even real. The figure remained motionless, almost frozen in space. Not a hair rustled, not a muscle twitched. He pulled his gun from the holster. Resolved, he asked, "Who's there?"

The figure immediately burst into wild spasms, throwing itself against restraints Graham couldn't see. Graham jumped, tumbling off the bucket. His gun discharged, sending a bullet into the ground. He landed on his back but quickly leaped up. He heard the figure groaning, practically squealing. He shouted, "Police! Who's there?"

More squeals. A thumping sound came from the room, wood knocking against wood.

Graham ran back to the front door. "Police! Coming in!" He kicked the door hard, shattering its lock into fragments of twisted metal. He was welcomed by a gun blast.

✳ ✳ ✳

Steve Woodbridge's wife, Carla, awoke in an empty bed. *If he slept on the church lawn again, I'll kill him*, she thought. But she remembered Steve at the previous night's dinner, complaining about not having any meat. *Threw it out*, she explained. They hadn't gone to bed together. Carla retired early, leaving Steve to read in his office. She rose, dressed, and went to brush her teeth. Steve was sitting in the bathtub, fully clothed.

"Steve? What are you doing?"

He was awake. He lifted his head, and Carla gasped at the redness of his face. His eyes were puffy. "Steve, what's wrong?" She crouched next to the tub, slipping an arm around him.

"I—" he began, but sobs stepped in and interrupted his thought.

"Steve. Tell me what's wrong."

Steve gulped. Taking a deep breath, he rolled his head over, nestling it between her chin and shoulder. "Do you ever look at our life and wonder how we got here?" he asked. It sounded more like a statement than a question.

Carla paused. "I'm not sure what you mean," she said.

"Is this how you imagined our life?"

"I don't know how to answer that."

"Just answer it. Yes or no."

"Well, I thought we'd have kids by now."

"Is that it?"

"No, I guess not. I mean, I never thought we'd live in Houston, but I'm not upset about it. Are you?"

"You don't have any regrets?"

"No, no. Why would I? I married the man I love, we've got a nice house with nice things, and we have lots of friends."

"*You* have lots of friends," Steve corrected.

"Is that what this is about? You've got friends, Steve. What about Graham?"

"No, that's not what this is about."

"What's wrong? Are you depressed?"

Steve sat up. He sat cross-legged, his knees rising up to his chest. "Probably," he said.

"What's wrong?"

"I can't really say. Isn't that depression? I don't know. I don't know anything except that something doesn't feel right. I think somewhere along the way, I disobeyed God and I've been wandering aimlessly ever since. I have this weird feeling I'm supposed to be doing something else. That I'm supposed to be somewhere else."

Carla didn't say anything. She wrapped both her arms around him, kissing him lightly on his cheek. She could taste the salt his tears had left behind.

* * *

A blast of hot, acrid air attacked Graham, blazing by like lightning. The shotgun fired its death at him, narrowly missing his neck. He felt the sting of its wake before he heard it whiz by. His ears had gone deaf, his face hot with the flash.

He tumbled onto his back, his head dangling freely over the porch steps. Scrambling to his feet, he returned fire, shooting wildly into the open doorway. He shot his gun dry and crouched outside the door to insert a fresh clip of ammunition. "Who's there? This is the police! Drop your weapon and put your hands up!" He listened. The air was still, the silence unnerving. He thought he could hear the sweat bubbling from his pores. "Drop your weapon!"

Again, no answer. He could hear the other person moaning from the bedroom. Graham cautiously peered around the corner, his pistol ready. No one was there, and he noticed the shotgun on the floor, still smoking. A long white string ran from its trigger to the doorknob through a strange mass of boxes and duct tape, Pops's violent approach to a Rube Goldberg contraption.

Graham quickly spun into the living room, still crouched low. He looked around the room, scanning for more booby traps. He slowly stood, his gun held out perpendicular to his body. His muscles tensed. He walked to the bedroom, keeping his back to a wall with each step. The door to the bedroom was closed. "Who's there?"

The moaning continued. Graham slowly turned the knob, keeping his body to the outside of the door frame, lest another gun await him on the other side. With a flip of the wrist, he popped the door inward. It swung in slowly, carried by minimal momentum, uncovering the room and revealing Gertie Dickey gagged and bound to a chair.

At the sight of Graham, she screamed through her muzzle, a wide strip of duct tape. She rocked back and forth. Her eyes bulged, vibrating in terror. Graham rushed to her, pulling the tape from her face. Her words came out in a torrent: "My Pops is crazy he's gone crazy I don't know I don't know he's gone crazy what's happening he's crazy he's crazy I don't know ..."

Graham wrapped his arms around her, hugging her close. "It's okay. It's gonna be okay."

"He's gonna kill me," she cried.

"Nobody's gonna kill you. It's okay. I got you. You're safe now," Graham whispered.

She wailed, "Ohhh!"

"It's okay," he whispered. "Let's get these ropes off."

He untied her, but exhaustion kept Gertie from standing on her own. Graham scooped her up and headed for his cruiser. She was emaciated, thin beyond the thinness of old women. She shook all over, and Graham held her rattling bones and loose flesh close. On the way out, he noticed a blood stain on the baseboard. *Someone wasn't very thorough*, he thought. Gertie was hyperventilating when they reached the car, but she forced out, "They killed him. They killed him."

✳ ✳ ✳

At the station, Gertie was given coffee and a blanket. Kelly sat in the briefing room with her, tissue in hand, doing her best to console the shaken woman. Officer Lane spoke to Graham quietly in the hallway.

"No sign of Petrie, Cap."

"Yeah," Graham said. "I got a bad feeling about this. I think Dickey has something to do with it."

"With Petrie?"

"Yeah."

"You don't think—"

"I don't know, Lane." He said it firmly, almost but not quite angrily.

Lane dropped his eyes from Graham's. "You, uh," he said, "you said Mrs. Dickey said *they*?"

"Yeah," Graham sighed.

"What does that mean?"

"I think Dickey is with our murderer."

Kelly stepped into the hallway, tears in her eyes. "I can't do this stuff, Captain. It's not my job."

"She needs a woman to talk to, Kelly. It's a lot better than us cops awkwardly pawing at her, saying, 'There, there.' Sheesh."

"Then find a friend of hers. I'm a secretary, and I can't handle this." She said it more from grief than insubordination. Gertie's body was light, but her experience was heavier than Kelly could bear. "Her husband almost killed her."

"Did she say where they went?"

"Can I go now?"

"Did she say where they went?" Graham demanded.

"No. No, she didn't. May I go?"

"Yeah. Go find a friend of hers to come get her." He turned to Lane. "Stay with her, you."

"Aw, Cap," Lane protested.

"You don't have to talk, Lane. Just keep an eye out for Dickey. Make sure you go to the friend's house. We have a crime scene unit at the Dickey place."

Graham hoped to God the blood on the baseboard wasn't Petrie's.

* * *

Pops and Mr. Black didn't know where they were, but they walked with purpose, as if their destination would announce itself. They felt drawn, pulled by the gravity of dark forces to the epicenter of an unknown disaster. Keeping to woods and backstreets, they headed southward toward Houston.

Pops held his shotgun under a long coat. (The one he had used to create a booby trap at the house was an older one, a gift from Stewadell, actually. He'd never used it.) Jimmy kept his right hand on his pocket, the joints of his fingers closed tightly on the closed sheath of the butterfly knife. Compared to Pops, he was out-experienced and out-armed, but they both knew he was in control now.

The midday sun hid behind a dreary curtain of clouds. A chill wound its way through the concrete landscapes of Houston.

* * *

Lane escorted Gertie and Betty Leverett to Betty's house.

At the station, Graham waited for a call from the forensics team at the Dickeys' house. When the phone rang, he answered to hear the voice of a frantic woman instead. "Who's this?" he asked.

"They transferred me to you," the woman said quickly.

"Okay," Graham began, not quite understanding.

"There's a police car out here behind my house."

Suddenly, Graham was very interested.

"You have to come quick," she said. "My kids, my kids."

"Slow down. What's happening?"

"My kids were out playing in the backyard. It, uh, it slopes down to the ditch, and, uh, they found a police car."

"Where are you?"

* * *

Graham was too late. Had been, actually, for quite a while.

A handful of Trumbull's finest were gathered behind the house. Graham could see them in the distance, small lonely figures pacing aimlessly around something he couldn't see. He could see the yellow tape, though, and he almost vomited. Officers Bill Roberts and Mark Garrison met him in the front yard. Graham was moving quickly, practically jogging. Garrison stopped him, holding his arm. Roberts blocked his way, saying, "It's too late, Captain."

"No," Graham whispered. He tried to move away, but he felt too weak to move.

"Cap," Roberts said simply, and Graham looked into his eyes and saw that said it all.

"No," Graham said again, and he dropped to his knees in the grass.

"The unit's on their way, sir," Garrison said. "They'll take care of it."

The men didn't seem to know what else to say. Graham closed his eyes. Garrison offered, "Kids were out playing. They found him about forty minutes ago."

Now it was said. The word *him* came crashing down on Graham. The pain returned to his temples. The fear was real. One of his best cops, one of the few men he considered a friend, was dead. This reality hung in the air, suspending all time, ripping a hole in space, a vortex sucking him into its icy void.

CHAPTER FIFTEEN

FROM "SNOW POSSIBLE, FORECASTERS SAY," BY ERIC GUEL IN THE *HOUSTON CHRONICLE*:

Winter may be a month away, but you might want to keep your coat and mittens handy. The cold front continues to linger, and we may have record lows this week, forecasters say. There is even the chance of snow tonight and tomorrow morning. For notice of any school closings, watch your local news or call your school office in the early morning tomorrow.

* * *

Mike found Dr. Bering sitting on the floor of his study. "Dr. Bering? The, uh, the door was open."

Bering sat motionless, eyes closed. He looked contemplative, like the Buddha. His arms lay limp at his sides, his hands curled on the floor. "Shut the door," he said quietly, calmly.

Mike did so and sat down on the floor opposite the man. No sign of Malcam.

Without opening his eyes, Bering cooed, "Ah, it's so wonderful, Mike. It is so freeing." A smile of utter delight spread across his face. "You just have no idea. This is what it's like to be alive, to be really alive. To achieve the gnosis."

Mike said, "That's what I want."

"Good," responded Bering. "Close your eyes, Mike. Close them tightly, but don't tense yourself. Relax your body. Let your muscles rest. Breathe very slowly."

Mike did all of this.

"Good, good," the professor said. "Now let your mind go. Try to cleanse it of all thoughts. Empty it out. Let down your guard."

Mike found it hard to obey these instructions. His was a mind used to scrutinizing every nanosecond of daily life. It was even more experienced lately in worrying about larger problems. Molly, for one. This whole bizarre episode, for another. He tried to let go. He thought of Malcam's visit the night before and that very morning. The visitor's promises echoed in his head. They held allure, mystery. Mike felt himself giving his mind over to them. He ignored the tiny doubt struggling for its own place inside.

Bering coaxed, "Yes, yes. Give yourself. Let it in."

Then Mike heard Malcam, inches from his ear, whispering, "Care to take a little trip, chum?"

Mike's eyelids lay heavy, and he thought he could feel the weight of his eyes. They were too heavy, and his head rolled forward. His shoulders slumped; he faced down, sitting loose like a rag doll.

"Yes. Let's," Malcam answered himself. "Come with me, Michael, to a place of comfort and wonder. It is a world apart from all others."

Hypnotized, Mike asked, "Is it your world?"

"No, no. It is much better. It is more fit for beings like yourself. It is a world of magic and scintillating spirit."

The room grew warmer. Mike felt a light breeze on his flesh. The breeze rolled back and forth, traversing the room in long, rhythmic waves much like the ones he'd felt at Malcam's debut. His limp body swayed in the current, and he suddenly had the overwhelming sensation of sitting in the shallow waters off an ocean shore. Malcam continued to woo him, slipping feather-light temptations into his ear.

"Feel the waves around you, chum. Move with them. Let the current take you out, far out. Far out to sea. Just let go and float away. Everything is glorious."

A sizzle ran through Mike's body, setting his nerves alight. Gooseflesh rose over his skin. His hair stood on end. He felt very, very drowsy and sensed an impending entrance into sleep. All the while, Malcam continued his invasion of Mike's consciousness.

"There you go, friend," he said. "Just let go. You're very close now. You're almost there. It's not much farther."

Inwardly, Mike felt himself tumbling down and through a seemingly bottomless tunnel. The water continued to swirl around him, and he was submerged now, but in no danger of drowning. He continued down, plummeting into a mind-tickling chasm.

He entered the otherworld.

✳ ✳ ✳

"Where are we going, Black?"

Pops was out of breath and tired of following the kid. The cold air hurt the man's lungs, and, every now and then, the pain would send his brain the full weight of what he had done. The signals were just flashes, though. Brief sparks of remorse flickering like cinematic freeze frames.

"Shut up," was all Jimmy said.

"I gotta stop," Pops said, and he did.

Jimmy continued walking, leaving Pops behind him.

"Just a minute, Black. Just let me catch my breath."

Jimmy didn't stop.

"We're not even following the grays," Pops called out.

Jimmy kept walking but retorted, "When you got the grays inside, you don't need to see no stupid spaceship."

✳ ✳ ✳

Lisa Diaz didn't expect to find the captain at her hotel room door. "Mr. Lattimer?"

"Uh, hi, Mrs. Diaz. I was wondering if we could talk a little bit."

"Sure. Come in."

They sat at a little table in the kitchenette. Abby was sitting on the bed, watching cartoons on television.

Lisa shifted nervously. "What brings you here, Captain? Have you found the man who murdered my husband?"

"No, ma'am," Graham said. "We think he killed one of my men, too."

Coldly, Lisa responded, "Well, maybe you'll know how I feel now, Mr. Lattimer. Maybe that'll force you to find him."

Graham sat upright. "Yes, maybe so."

"Have you ever lost anyone, Mr. Lattimer? Besides your cop friend, I mean. Have you?"

"Well, yes, actually," Graham said. "My parents and the grandfather who raised me."

Unprepared for such an answer, Lisa meekly said, "Oh."

"Reason I'm here, Mrs. Diaz, was I just wanted to check on Abby."

"Abby?"

"See how she's doing, that sort of thing."

"She's doing okay for a little girl with no daddy."

"May I talk to her?" Graham asked.

"I s'pose."

Graham nodded and rose. He approached the bed. Abby held a doll in her lap, and while her eyes remained on the TV, she was methodically undressing and dressing the doll over and over, pausing from time to time to place a tiny bottle in its mouth.

"Hello, Abby," Graham said.

Abby neither turned her head nor answered.

"Can I sit down with you?"

Abby continued, her fingers operating nimbly on miniscule clasps, buttons, and Velcro fasteners. Graham approached, standing over the girl. "Please?" he asked.

Without looking up, she said, "Yes."

Graham squatted, sitting next to the girl. He sat on her right, his own right hip with its holstered gun out of view. "Do you remember me?" he asked.

"Yes," Abby said.

"I'm Mr. Lattimer, the policeman."

"I know," she said, still not looking up.

"I wanted to ask you about the other night."

"Daddy got killed," she said matter-of-factly.

"I know, I know. I'm very sorry. I want to ask you about that night you walked home."

"The bad man tried to take me away."

"I know. That was very scary. Can you tell me about the good man, though?"

"He was nice."

"Is that all you remember?"

"Yes," she said.

"Nothing else?"

"He was nice," Abby repeated.

"What about the bad man?"

"The Black Man," she said.

"He's black?" This was a new wrinkle for Graham. "He has black skin?"

"No, silly." Abby smiled and suppressed a giggle.

"What, then? He wears black, right? Is that it?"

"Yeah."

Graham repeated, "He wears black clothes?"

"Yes," Abby said. She put the bottle to the baby's mouth. For the first time, she looked up at Graham. "The Black Man is very scary, Mr. Lammer, but God is very big."

He smiled at the mispronunciation of his name. "He is, huh?"

"Yep."

FROM "HOUSTON KILLER TAKES ANOTHER LIFE," BY PHILIP SCHROEDER IN THE *HOUSTON CHRONICLE*:

Police authorities are saying today that the Trumbull police officer found dead in his car is more than likely a victim of the same teenage suspect wanted for the murders of his mother and a Trumbull businessman. Jimmy Horn, 17, is also wanted for the attempted kidnapping of a young Trumbull girl. She is the daughter of the murdered Trumbull man.

Children discovered the body of Samuel Petrie, a four-year veteran of the Trumbull Police Department, in his patrol car while they were out playing.

Forensic evidence has linked Horn to the murder, authorities say. The victim's blood also matched blood found in the scene of an assault in another Trumbull home.

Trumbull police found Gertrude Dickey, 68, tied to a chair in her bedroom, apparently by her husband Lucas Dickey, 71. Readers will recall Mr. Dickey as the source of Trumbull's recent UFO sighting claims, making this story stranger as it develops. Police believe Dickey and Horn are together, but they are unsure of their whereabouts.

The suspects are considered armed and dangerous. If you spot them, do not approach. Call your local police or the CrimeStoppers hotline at 222-TIPS.

✳ ✳ ✳

North of Houston, in a Dallas suburb, Molly Walsh wandered around her late sister's house. More and more, she identified herself with the finger-painted lady in the frame on the wall. The world was chaotic, unstable. She thought about her husband. How much she wanted to see him again! How she wanted things to be right. But she was floating in those finger-painted seas, adrift in the random dark hues of tragedy.

She began to pray for Mike.

And she began to realize that she was not the finger-painted lady. The expressionist portrait was not of a lady at all. Molly saw Mike more clearly than the painting displayed its floating figure, but the figure undoubtedly represented him. He was adrift; he was lost. He had been sucked into chaos, and this startling fact chilled her, touched something within her that provoked the response of guilt. For the first time, she thought not just of how her leaving affected him emotionally, but of how it had affected him spiritually.

This realization gave way to a fearful prescience. Her overwhelming concern had instantaneously created within her the knowledge that Mike was actually in great danger. And, perhaps, so was she.

* * *

Less north of Houston, Abby Diaz prayed a simple prayer in her playroom while her mother found new tears to cry.

"Dear God. Say hello to Daddy for me. I miss him a lot. Please let Mommy not cry. And please let Mr. Lammer find the bad man. He is very bad. Amen."

* * *

"The beginning of words is the end of all sadness," Mike heard Malcam say, and his cryptic proverb sounded as if spoken through a long tunnel. The sound was mechanical, amplified, but vibratory and tinny.

Opening his eyes, Mike found himself in an actual ocean, adrift in actual waves. The water was crystalline blue but translucent; Mike couldn't see his feet.

Stretched out ahead of him, not forty yards, floated the shore of a small island. Its sandy beach sparkled in the sun, an infinity of microscopic quartz crystals reflecting dazzling rays of light into the atmosphere. The entire effect was that of a giant halo hovering over the beach.

Energized by this beatific sight, Mike swam eagerly toward the shore. He found the task practically effortless. The waves carried him closer and closer ever so gently until at last he set his hands and feet upon the grainy ground. He crawled around on it a bit—scampered actually, dithering about like a playful child.

Engulfed by emotions both of the numinous and (oddly) of the primitive, Mike keeled over, squirming on his back in the sand. The sky looked closed somehow, a pale, fading water-colored blue on a stone ceiling high above.

Tilting his head backward, he encountered the upside-down vision of a gate in the distance and, before it, an expanse of emerald grass. He quickly rose and traipsed off, soon finding his bare feet pressing on a mossy lawn, spongy beneath his toes. The grass was short and curled oddly, the blades woven together. Looking up, he saw Malcam standing at the gate. He looked more like a man than before. The visitor wore a dapper black suit with a neatly knotted tie tucked into the coat's buttoned fold.

"Here is the place you have always dreamed of, my friend." Malcam stepped aside, opening the gate door dramatically.

Inside, Mike discovered a world of trees and plants, bushes and vines. They were greens of every shade with leaves of every shape and texture. The mossy lawn continued in the garden, and giant tree trunks rose out of it, rushing to the opaque sky. The trunks were all grays and rusty browns. The garden as a whole struck Mike as unreal, as a vision pale yet nonetheless inviting.

Strolling through the garden, Mike encountered people. They were milling about aimlessly and never seemed to notice his presence. They were spaced apart; no one walked with another. Alone, they paced, staring far ahead of themselves like pleasant zombies. Mike started to approach one, a lady with blonde hair. Like all the others, she wore normal "thisworld" clothing.

"Don't talk to them, Michael," Malcam said.

"Our presence doesn't disturb them?"

"No. They don't even know we're here."

Entranced by their behavior, Mike stopped and watched them a while. Doing so, he realized that each person seemed familiar to him. He didn't know their names or remember where he knew them from, but he recognized each face. Without Malcam's prompting, Mike knew these were all people he had encountered in his lifetime. He recognized his fourth-grade teacher. She walked mere feet from a teller at his bank.

"Beyond that wall is the inner garden," Malcam said, and he gestured to the right.

Excitement flooded Mike's soul, for he fully believed the secret to life's happiness lay inside that inner realm of the garden.

"To happiness," Malcam toasted with an invisible drink.

The first step was the hardest, but after taking that initial forward movement, Mike broke into a full trot, heading for the end of a great stone wall. Malcam trailed him closely, moving with little effort.

Etched on the smooth stones of the wall were the words: THE BEGINNING OF WORDS IS THE END OF ALL SADNESS. Mike remembered them as the mystery shared by Malcam upon his entrance to the otherworld.

Reaching the end of the wall, Mike spun around it and halted. The grass on the other side was the same as the outside, but its color was darker, less distinct. Mike saw before him a smooth expanse of bluish gray turf rising into a low slope. At the top of the small hill were a few trees. None looked real; that is to say, none looked as real as those in this world.

Reality ceased to exist for Mike. Malcam was taking him further and further into the dark hole inside himself. Mike always believed nothing lived inside. He now saw differently.

Excitement again overwhelmed him. Among the trees wandered more people from his life, but these were his closest friends. Robbie and his parents seemed to walk together, strolling side by side across the low ridge. Coming closer, Mike saw Dr. Bering who, in the "thisworld" sat across from the limp Mike in his study, but now scampered about the hill. Bering was the most animated of the few people, but Mike had not the curiosity to wonder why. He was more struck by how few his friends really were. Only four: his parents, Robbie, and the now dancing Bering.

Aghast at this sad truth, Mike eagerly scanned the landscape for Molly.

"Does Molly live here too?" he asked Malcam.

"Perhaps she's in the darker valley," Malcam said. "That is where we must go next. Here are your closest friends, chum."

"Everyone looks so distant, so vacant. Except Dr. Bering, I mean."

"Remember that Samuel is, for all intents and purposes, on this journey with you. He is not actually inside as you are, but he's the only soul in touch enough to talk to."

"Excellent place, isn't it?" Bering suddenly said. He danced a little jig.

"Land of my dreams," Mike responded cheerfully.

"All dreams are imagined, my dear Michael," Bering said. "This place … this place is real."

"Now you have a picture of the only truth that exists," Malcam added. "Your life is all that matters. As Samuel has discovered, it is up to you to find joy within yourself."

"Do I stay here forever?" Mike asked.

"Really," Malcam answered, "this is merely the starting point. We are in the beginning. Your entire life, your entire world, is this garden. What you choose to do here is your choice for your life in the day-to-day world."

"And the dark valley?" Mike asked.

"Across the ridge, on the other side. That is where you will make your choice. We shall travel there shortly," Malcam said.

"Now?"

"Do what thou wilt," Malcam answered, a sneer forming on his lips.

Plodding forward, leaving Bering behind, Mike ascended the hill to its apex. Looking down, he noticed the grass darken before him. There were more trees in the dark valley, which wasn't really a valley at all, but a wide ditch. It was really just the other side of the hill.

Approaching the edge, where the grass's blue gray moss became slate blue, rough-edged turf, he saw a raised altar made of granite a few yards off. He recognized it as a replica of the one he'd seen in his first dizzying encounter with Malcam.

"Right there," said Malcam, "is where your choice is made."

"Are you going to show me where Molly is?" Mike asked.

"Do you really want to see her, Mike? Think carefully about this. This woman, this person you say you love abandoned you, wrote you off. You stand on the verge of something greater now. You can

have the life you know you really want. Free of fear and worry. Full
of pleasure and liberty. Able to do whatever you want. Do you really
want to trade the end of all sadness for the person who has cultivated
the most sadness within you?"

"I want to see her," Mike insisted.

"See for yourself," Malcam said with a disappointed sigh. He
gestured toward a cluster of trees.

Entangled in their intertwining branches hung a motionless
Molly. Mike ran to her. He tried to wrestle her free to no avail.

"Lower the branches," Mike said to Malcam. Tears flowed from
his eyes.

"Our journey is almost done, chum," Malcam said. "Worthless
tasks are steps backward."

"Save her!"

"The riddle is over. The end of words is here. Now is the beginning of all sadness."

Malcam's voice grew more sinister. He grasped Mike by the collar
and dragged him wriggling back to the altar. Mike could not break
free, and he watched helplessly as the branches writhed, tightening
their thorny hold on Molly.

"No!"

"Hush, hush. It will all be over in a jiff," Malcam said.

The visitor propped Mike up in front of him, facing the altar.
Mike saw himself lying on top. His otherworldly twin was naked.

"This," Malcam instructed, "is naked and unashamed. Don't
listen to the others. They will insist it can't be this way—at least, not
in your time. But we can end all that, can't we, chum?"

Malcam placed a dagger in Mike's trembling hand. Try as he
might, Mike couldn't thrust it away.

"The knife can only complete one service, Michael. Don't be afraid." Malcam grabbed Mike's wrist. "It's easy. Trust me."

The air grew thicker, and Mike heard a multitude of voices all around him. They were saying nasty things, things he couldn't understand, but he knew they meant him harm.

"Easy now," Malcam hissed. Something like the forked tongue of a snake tickled Mike's inner ear. "Easy now. Just step forward."

Mike resisted.

"Just step forward. It's ever so easy, chum. Nothing to it."

Mike inexplicably raised the knife over his replica on the altar. Malcam smiled. "Easy does it," he said.

The cacophonous drone of voices intensified, filling the air with a litany of unholy words in unknown tongues. Mike cast a terrified glance around. What once looked mysterious now struck him as miserific. The unreality of the garden, once a curiosity, appeared freakish, exaggerated, a horrific impostor of a real land, a real garden someplace else.

"Now bring that handsome arm down," Malcam said, "and free yourself."

Before he could obey, Mike's will broke free. At the same instant, a blinding light broke in from above, splitting the ceiling of the otherworld's finite sky. In a dazzling unity of movement and happenstance, Malcam shrunk back from the light, grabbing at the ground and wincing in pain, while Mike dropped the dagger and screamed, "No!" The light filled the otherworld, disintegrating it. Mike felt himself tumbling back through the tunnel through which he had entered.

When he opened his eyes, he found himself back in Bering's study. He was alone, but he heard the imprecation of an invisible presence. Mike pitched forward and vomited. Shaken, sweating, he rose to his feet and fled the room, fled Bering's house completely. Leaving his car behind, he broke into a terrified sprint all the way home.

He never noticed the very real dagger he had left behind on the study floor.

✳ ✳ ✳

Back in Trumbull that night, Graham confronted an angry crowd of protesters on the steps of the courthouse.

"You've got to take us seriously," shouted Rick Bardwell. "We've had enough of the lies!" His son cowered behind him.

The others echoed those words, hurling accusations and wild theories Graham's way. The man reached his breaking point. "Listen, here, you idiots. There is no UFO, and there never was. You all need to go home."

"Stop avoiding the truth, and do your job," yelled a woman.

"You listen to me! All of you!" The ferocity of Graham's emotion quieted the crowd instantly. Even the unrighteous know righteous anger when they hear it. He continued: "We've got a murderer on the loose. He's killing people from our community, from our town. He tried to get a little girl. And all you care about is lights in the sky. And none of you's really seen 'em. Admit it, if only to yourselves. Now you can keep on grousin' on about aliens and sheesh, or you can go home and be with your families. You all got kids who are probably scared to death. Or don't you care? Now, put your stupid signs away and go home. Go! I've got work to do, and I can't catch a killer if I gotta mess with y'all."

With much grumbling under their foggy breaths, the protesters slowly ambled off. Graham felt pleased. He had just delivered a giant, waking slap to the collective face of Trumbull's disgruntled citizenry.

That's all it would take to squelch the UFO madness in Trumbull. Private complaints carried on for several days, but there were no more protests, no more angry calls or letters. No more reports of UFO sightings. The whole episode would eventually become an obscure footnote in Trumbull history. Many of those involved would later speak ill of others, denying their own involvement. But the whole UFO mess was merely tangential to the darker goings-on in areas nearby. That episode was not over yet.

Graham knew this. A still, small voice recited a familiar refrain: *Be assured.*

FROM "UNCLEAN SPIRITS AND THE ACTS THEREOF" BY DR. LEOPOLD SUTZKEVER IN THE *JOURNAL OF CONTEMPORARY THEOLOGY*:

… [S]o I must address, of course, the fellows in my own camp who have made a virtual mockery of the dealing with unclean spirits. They, in essence, see demons in every bush. Every disease, every catastrophe, every misfortune of any kind sends them to binding and casting out. They give our Enemy far too much credit. Even more unfortunate, they believe him more powerful than he actually is. They endorse the literal equivalent of the American comedy routine catchphrase, "The Devil made me do it." This approach is not without humor but is theologically suspect (at best). We are to emulate Christ's ministry, not Flip Wilson's. So the demon hunters cast out spirits of disease and handicap, and all the while lend support to the critics of *ekballistics* in general.

Let me be clear: I do not see good coming from the attribution of all problems to the working of demons. This teaching creates fear where there should be confidence, doubt where there should be faith.

Nevertheless, I cannot join the general critics. They are like the rider who, in fear of falling off one side of the horse, falls off the other. There are two dangers in our understanding of the Enemy and his minions. One is that we become obsessed with them; the other is that we take them too lightly. The Devil is real, and though the physical proof of demonic manifestations is rare in the West, to disbelieve in them is to grant the Devil his greatest goal—the disbelief in the Devil himself.

Malcam hadn't noticed Bering leaving the room. The creature was too consumed with Mike. He found the professor upstairs in a corner, seething. "What have you done, you?" Bering said. "You ... you *mutant!*"

Malcam sighed. His brow spilled downward, his eyes narrowed. "Tsk, tsk, Samuel. Such insolence." He said it calmly but sternly, conveying a warning.

"What's so great about him?" Bering asked. "Why is he so special?"

"Didn't you answer that question yourself?" Malcam replied. "Didn't I ask that of you? Let me remind you that Michael's involvement was your idea."

"Was it? Was it? Didn't you put it in my head? Didn't you?"

"I don't like your tone, chum."

"You said you would teach me things, teach me about reality. You would enhance my science. Teach me the secrets of hyperspace. But this is all mystical gobbledygook. You haven't taught me anything."

"You're missing the big picture, Samuel. Don't you think there's a greater purpose to my visits than expanding your mind? Can't you see outside yourself? It will all come together soon."

"But Michael? I had no idea—"

"Don't tell me you're jealous," Malcam said. "You're a little too old for that."

"I brought you here," Bering insisted.

Malcam's smile disappeared. Rage boiled over. He grabbed Bering by the neck, his leathery hand wrapped full around, his razor-sharp nails piercing flesh. "I don't think you know what you're saying, Samuel," he said through gritted teeth. He squeezed. Ignoring Bering's gasps for breath, he continued: "You have no power over me. The power is mine, you understand? If I want to come or if I want to go or if I want to plant daisies in your forehead, I will do it."

He released his grip. Bering flopped down, his red face smacking the floor, his purple lips wheezing deep breaths into the carpet. Malcam stood over him, smiling once again. "Relax, chum. I have the same plan for both of you."

✳ ✳ ✳

Mike couldn't remember how he made it home. His hike from Bering's house to his own passed for him in a state of conscious unconscious, like sleepwalking. But he remembered his trip into the otherworld vividly. Its synthetic landscape, voiceless friends. Its inner garden. Its hold upon his wife. He remembered how her face looked as she hung in and against the thorny branches restraining her. He remembered the hold upon himself, Malcam's strong hand unbearably tight on his arm.

He remembered the altar. He remembered realizing that Malcam wasn't offering an awakening but a horrible sleep. Mike had never lost his fear of death. The one thing that had drawn him to Malcam ended up moving him away. Oddly, his experience didn't send him spiraling into his previous madness. Despite his catatonic stagger home, he sensed a clarity stealing into his mind. He saw the otherworld not as an entrance into something, but as an exit into nothing. And as this clarity cultivated hatred of Malcam within him, he could not help but think differently of Dr. Bering. Converging with his gradual awakening was a growing line of concern. He saw Bering in his true place—not as Malcam's conjurer, but as his captive.

Mike couldn't see everything. Not yet. But he could see that the otherworld was more danger than delight. And he knew he wanted to get Bering out of it.

He thought better of returning to Bering's house alone and decided not to continue attending classes. He located the number of the only friend of Bering's he knew and made a call.

"Ah, Mr. Walsh, nice to speak with you again," Dr. Leo Sutzkever said.

"It's about Dr. Bering," Mike said.

"Oh, yes," Sutzkever said in a serious tone. "I had a feeling."

Mike said, "I'm not sure really what to say."

"Just tell me what's wrong."

"I want to, but I'm not sure how. I don't know if you'll believe me."

Sutzkever chuckled. "I think you will find, Mike, that I am hard to shock."

"But this is weird. Real weird."

"I don't doubt it. But there's no reason to hem and haw now, is there? Out with it. I'll promise not to think weird thoughts about you, if you like."

Recent history for Mike contained experiences of inconceivable occurrence. How he ever started believing in Bering, or hyperspace, or the otherworld, or how he ever decided to test its waters, he could not fathom. They were the decisions of a desperate mind—a lunatic mind, to be truthful—yet their recent occurrence could not tell him why he felt, at this moment, years from them in understanding. But he remembered the relative ease of those wild decisions. Somehow, just talking about them was harder.

He did talk about them, though. He began with his first intro-duction to Bering, recalling the chance encounter in the library and his reading of Bering's articles. He tiptoed around meeting Malcam but finished with the unbelievable trip Malcam had taken him on. All the while, Sutzkever remained silent.

When Mike finished, the professor said, "You interact with this Malcam."

It wasn't a question, but Mike said, "Yes."

"That is extraordinary."

"It is?" Mike mistook the comment for praise.

"Oh, yes," Sutzkever responded. "It is much worse than I thought."

"What do you mean?"

"Mike, you have stepped into a place as interesting as you think it is, but more dangerous than you can ever know. It is not hyperspace or a parallel dimension; at least, not the way Dr. Bering believes those things to be. It is the spirit world."

"You mean, like ghosts?"

"No, no. Spirits. The stuff of angels and demons."

Mike recalled his conversation with Steve Woodbridge in Dallas. Steve attributed real alien sightings to demons. Mike found that very superstitious then. It seemed very prescient now. "Are you saying Malcam is a demon?"

"Yes. You've gone too far for him to be a hallucination. The fact that you and Dr. Bering both speak to him, and he to you, says to me that he is real. And he obviously means you harm. Therefore, he is a demon."

Mike was troubled.

"Do you not believe in demons, Mike?"

"Well, I can't say for sure anymore. If we had had this conversation months ago, I would have chalked it up to religious hoo-ha. Now I don't know. Dr. Bering's claims had so much science to back them up."

"How can I express to you the seriousness of your experience?" Sutzkever asked, primarily to himself it seemed. He finally said, "I am going to ask you some questions, Mike. Make some guesses, all right?"

"Shoot," Mike invited.

"You have other problems, correct?"

"What do you mean?"

"It is my experience, Mike, that completely happy persons, people otherwise fulfilled by what their lives bring them, do not usually interact physically with demons. What, for lack of a better word, *problems* do you have?"

All of a sudden this guy's a shrink, Mike thought. "My wife left me."

"Hmm. That so? Very interesting. And so, of course, you feel empty, perhaps?"

"Well, yeah."

"That can't be all. I don't mean to downplay your problem, but lots of men's wives leave them. Perhaps I can approach it this way: what is your greatest fear?"

Mike leaned back in his chair. Again the scene felt very reminiscent of a previous one: his chat with Steve in Dallas. *These religious guys really cut to the chase. My greatest fear?* He held the phone away from him for a second, contemplating whether to drop it on the ground and walk away. He slowly brought it back to his ear. "I don't know," he said. But he did know. After a pause, he offered, "Death?"

It actually felt good to Mike to finally verbalize it.

"Hmm, yes, classic," Sutzkever said. "Fear of death. But not of actually dying, right?"

"The whole deal," Mike responded. "But more than that, yeah."

"You think about it a lot."

Mike nodded.

"You are, as they say, neurotic?"

"Yes," Mike said.

"You worry a lot."

"Yes, about everything."

"It is practically debilitating. It interferes with your thoughts. And you probably have related childhood trauma. Stop me when I'm wrong."

"No. No, you're right. You're so right, it's scary."

"I'm an old man given to fanciful speculation. Don't let me put words in your mouth, Mike."

"No, no. I … I saw a freaking rotting corpse when I was a kid."

"Yes, I suppose that would do it."

"And I've been seeing it ever since."

"Extraordinary. I am no psychologist, Mike, but allow me to suggest something. Wave it off, if you must. It is not necessarily death that you fear, but what death brings. At least *for you*. I'll come back to that in a second. But you are afraid of ceasing to exist."

Mike felt that earlier light, the one that came with his first inkling of comprehension of Malcam's intent and the otherworld's dangers, shine a bit brighter and warmer in his head. It wasn't just that he was afraid of ceasing to exist. No, not exactly. More like, he was afraid that right now, walking around and talking and living and breathing, he already did not exist.

Something was happening. Dr. Sutzkever continued:

"Yes, that's it, I think. Nonexistence. You are afraid of that, because it means insignificance, really. This is why you worry about anything and everything. Every action is a step toward or away from significance, meaning. Your early childhood encounter puts a face, if you will, upon your neuroses. You worry about what others think of you, because you are afraid that if they disapprove, they will write you off and you will, essentially, cease to exist. And your fear of death is a fear of losing the opportunity to matter to someone."

Mike nodded. He wondered if Sutzkever really understood how true his words were or if he was still just speculating.

"But of course," the professor resumed, "this necrophobia of yours is more than a scapegoat for a projection of your worry. It is a more obvious manifestation of the need common of all men. The need for God."

"God?" Mike couldn't help assuming some of that talked-about worry. "Until just then, I was about to say you were going Freudian on me."

"Freud? Good heavens, no. Bah. I'm talking Augustine here, and Pascal. 'Our souls are not at rest until they find their rest in Thee.' 'Every man has a God-shaped hole.' That sort of business. I'm afraid attributing your problems solely to the misfiring of synapses in your brain or repressed sexuality would only throw you further back into them. We are talking demons here, Mike," he said, "and so we must talk about God."

Superstition and religious hoo-ha. That's what Mike wanted to believe it was. But he'd never tried it out. It made sense, in a strange sort of way. And even though Dr. Bering could probably draw the mathematical formula for hyperspace on a blackboard, the other-world seemed to be the world of superstition itself. It was an image, but a faux one. It pretended *to know*, but it was as much a mirage as Mike wanted to think religion was. He decided to accept Pascal's Wager. At least for now. "So what do we do?" he asked.

"For now, I suggest you stay home and rest—"

"No way," Mike interrupted. "I don't want to be left alone."

"It is probably safer for you to stay put."

"I'm not too thrilled about going back to his house, but my car's still there. I'll have to get it eventually."

"You're worried for Dr. Bering, aren't you?" Sutzkever asked.

"You could say that."

"This worry of yours may save the day. Why don't you come down to the university? It is late, I know, but I suspect Dr. Bering will be there. I will meet you in the faculty parking lot."

Mike paused.

"Come on," Sutzkever encouraged. "At least you don't have to go to his house right away."

* * *

The two men walked down the hall, their shoes squeaking on the tile floor. This time, Mike's squeaky shoes weren't alone. The air around Sutzkever felt warm. It reached to Mike, who immediately found comfort and a tiny bit of courage. He could tell that Sutzkever held secrets like Bering, but he suspected the former's secrets were more promising.

They found Dr. Bering in his office, and though the man was sitting still and silent, doing absolutely nothing, he started as if being caught red-handed in the middle of a crime. "What, uh, what's the—?" He tried to gain some composure. "Leopold. What brings you by?"

Mike stepped in. "Dr. Bering, are you all right?"

"What? Yes, of course. Why do you ask?"

"Well, after—"

"Samuel, the man's concerned," Sutzkever said.

"I don't remember asking you," Bering responded. It wasn't Bering, though. Not really. The voice matched; the face remained.

But in the eyes, in the spirit—in the undiluted venom of the tone—they recognized another. Bering turned to Mike. "What's the big idea, Mike? What have you told this man?" He reached for Sutzkever's arm and held it tightly.

"Ouch, Samuel. Unhand me."

Mike placed his hand on the doorknob. "We're, we're …" He stepped back. "… just a little concerned, that's all."

"Samuel," Sutzkever scolded. He removed his arm from Bering's grip. Pouting, he rubbed it softly.

"Oh, Leo, don't be such a baby," Bering said.

"We just want to talk, Samuel," Sutzkever said.

"I have nothing to say to either of you. I'd like you both to leave. *Now.*"

✳ ✳ ✳

"We're going to have to stage an intervention."

"What, like in AA?"

"I'm sorry?"

Mike and Dr. Sutzkever had retreated to the professor's home. Mike found it resembled Dr. Bering's a great deal. Same old-world charm, wall-to-wall antiques, countless books in just about every room. But Sutzkever's house lacked darkness, coldness, and pesky interdimensional visitors.

"Never mind," Mike said.

They sat in a cozy study, stuffed into plush armchairs facing each other on an intricate Persian rug.

"An intervention," Sutzkever continued, "is an attempt at rescuing our subject from the hands of the evil one."

"Whoa, whoa. Evil one? This is getting way too Amityville for me. I mean, I'm still an agnostic here. I can't, uh, be slaying some evil one and playing exorcist."

Sutzkever spoke sternly: "What has happened in the last few days that makes you think anyone is playing?"

"It's just too much. My life was fine—complicated, but fine. This I don't need. I can't get into this."

"But you already are into this, boy. Do you want out?"

Mike, sarcastically: "Uh, *yeah.*"

"And you want Dr. Bering out?"

Mike, sincerely: "Yes."

"All right, then."

"I don't wanna be casting out demons and whatnot, though," Mike said, half-joking.

Sutzkever responded with a blank face. His eyes said it all.

"You're kidding," Mike said.

"I don't usually kid. You'll find a poor sense of humor one of my many flaws in situations like these. Now, first things first. We need to contact your minister."

Had Mike a drink, he would have delivered the world's finest spit take. "Contact my what now?"

"Every agnostic has a minister, Mike. Otherwise, they'd be atheists."

"Poor sense of humor my—"

"Mike. Time is of the essence."

Mike sighed. "Yeah, I guess I know a guy."

✳ ✳ ✳

"You want me to *what?*"

Hours later, Steve Woodbridge would wish he had never taken the phone call that woke him from more daydreams.

Graham (and the infamous church committee) had convinced him to postpone his resignation. *Mexico*, he thought. *Thousands of Mexicans want into Texas. I want a better life in Mexico.* He wondered if it would be the same as it had been so many years ago on that mission trip. "The poor you'll always have with you," Jesus once said, and so had Steve's father in his ongoing campaign to divert Steve's mind from the mission field. The campaign succeeded. For so long, his mind had been anywhere but Mexico. But he had left his heart behind.

Now this phone call. This crazy, stupid phone call. He should have gone shopping with his wife. He should have never done that funeral, never got sucked into Mike Walsh's paranoid ramblings. *What was it again? He'd seen a dead body or something? What a freak.*

In came Dr. Leopold Sutzkever, swooping into the conversation with his diverting French accent, speaking of God our King and God the Mighty Warrior and fighting for the souls of men, and Steve Woodbridge did the thing Steve Woodbridge does. He caved. "You mean, like an exorcism? Spiritual warfare type stuff?"

"If that helps," Sutzkever replied, obviously annoyed at Steve's poor reception. "Have you ever participated in a deliverance before?"

"Uh, no. But I've done some reading."

"Yes, reading," Sutzkever said, unimpressed. "The Lord uses His children despite their inexperience."

"Okay."

"We'll need a fourth, Reverend."

"Oh, call me Steve."

"Right. We'll need a fourth, the best prayer man you know."

"That may be a little difficult. My best, uh, *prayer man* has been a little busy lately."

"This is urgent, Steven."

"Right, urgent." *Did I say yes to this?*

"Call him right away," Sutzkever directed.

✳ ✳ ✳

Captain Graham Lattimer hadn't gone home that night. After dispersing the protesters, ending their lunatic charade, he settled into his patrol car and made his way from the north side of Trumbull southward into northwest Houston, scanning the shadows, the alleys, the woods, all for signs of Jimmy Horn and Pops Dickey. He kept his mind awake, playing word and number games in his head. *Pops is seventy-one. Jimmy is seventeen.* Graham tried to remember that word, that term used for reversible characters. Petrie used to point them out to him—Otto, Eve … *What are they called? Palindromes. Seven is the perfect number, the symbol of the divine. (I think.) Add a one. Subtract a one. You can't add to or subtract from perfection. You cannot hinder or improve upon the divine. The Devil tried. He got his sheesh tossed out.* He was still free-associating when his phone rang, singing shrilly from his pocket. He was already in Houston, mere miles from the home he'd been directed to by Steve's instructions.

Once there he was surprised to encounter the reporter but even more curious about the old man introduced to him as Sutzkever. They wasted no time filling him in.

The story was bizarre but it felt … right. He felt as though the information, strange as it was, was a key unlocking a stubborn door.

✳ ✳ ✳

Soon enough, the four men sat in the professor's dining room, each guarding his cup of coffee. Graham and Mike exchanged looks several times, trying to place each other.

"You two know each other?" Steve asked.

"Kinda."

"Yeah, kinda."

"Naturally," Sutzkever interjected. "It's providence. The four of us have been called into this."

Mike and Steve shifted nervously—Mike, because the whole thing still seemed so unreal, and Steve, because he was still uncomfortable with the concept of a "calling." Graham, who could only remember being nervous in the last two days, sat unmoved. Sutzkever unloaded the whole story, most to Mike's embarrassment and some to his astonishment. He recounted from the beginning to the very moment the four entered his dining room.

"This is *way* Peretti," Steve quipped.

Sutzkever winced. "When we go in, we go in confidently. Greater is He that is in us, right? The Lord has not given us a spirit of fear, right?"

"Sure," Steve said. "What exactly are we doing?"

"We pay a visit to Dr. Bering. We insist upon entering. We begin praying."

"And what then?" Steve asked. "His head starts spinning and pea soup shoots out of his mouth?"

"Bah! This isn't a joke. You have to get this right, get yourselves right. And forget all that Hollywood nonsense. The man is afflicted for real, and without divine intervention he will be lost."

"But what do we do?"

"Mr. Lattimer here will pray nonstop. You will stay with Mike, tending to his spiritual needs, praying also. I will confront Samuel, and, if God wills, the spirit of his oppression."

Malcam, Mike thought, and he shuddered.

"If a spirit manifests itself, be prepared for an onslaught of tricks. It may move from threatening you to tempting you to begging you to grant it mercy. Never assume you can trust it. It comes from the father of lies, and that's all it knows. It will harass you, shame you, taunt you. Call on the name of Jesus, rebuke the spirit in Jesus's name, and claim victory with the power of the blood of the Lamb."

Steve asked, "You're serious?"

Mike, the only irreligious man in the room, said, "I can't believe none of this sounds weird to me."

It didn't sound weird to Graham either. In fact, it made perfect sense. The UFO hysteria, the killings, even his headaches. A man of prayer knows the world of the spiritual more intimately than others. This just made sense. *Be assured.*

"So, yes? We begin tomorrow night. Sixish?" Sutzkever asked.

"What about Mike?" Steve asked. "He's not, you know, a Christian."

The professor turned to Mike, who was not at all offended by the remark and suddenly felt oddly at ease. "Mike?" Sutzkever said.

"I just want my life back."

"Would you settle for a new one?"

"That's been promised before, if you remember."

"Yes, but this one is life, and life abundant."

"I have no idea what you're talking about."

✳ ✳ ✳

Later, as the midnight moon hovered high in the Houston sky, still and watchful, Mike lay in bed, thinking of Molly and of the mess he'd gotten them both in. Forget the dead body, forget Gary Newsome, the pains of his childhood. He'd been a self-victimized moron. He'd been an inattentive husband, a jerk. Selfish, stupid. That's where these problems started. He ran her off and looked for her everywhere but where she was.

I'm so stupid.

He pulled the covers to his chin. Had the room gotten colder?

Now all of this demon stuff. It makes sense, but it is just so ... out there.

Why can't my life be normal? If God's there, why does He make everything so hard? It's like He's trying to scare me off. Did I leave that window open? Am I too old to run away?

A dog barked next door.

Man, it's cold in here.

Mike rolled out of bed and moved to the window. He slid it down slowly, afraid of his own incidental noise. Turning back—

What's that?

He squinted. Something on the other side of the bed. He squinted. Dirty clothes? His jacket? Yeah, his jacket.

Mike climbed back into bed, seeking warmth within the quilts.

Molly made this one. He smiled.

What was that? The dog again?

The jacket was gone. *Just a shadow, then.*

No.

Something was at the foot of the bed.

Who's there?

Did I say that out loud?

"Who's there?"

"Tsk, tsk, chum."

Mike felt his bowels rumble. Feeling drained from his flesh.

"M-Malcam?"

The thing laughed. It moved over him.

"Malcam?"

"You've ruined everything, Mike."

Bering?

"You've messed it all up."

"Dr. Bering?"

"Righty-oh," the professor said, and he pounced on Mike with a ravenous fury.

Mike saw the blackness of Bering's eyes before feeling the blow to his temple. Then, all was black.

CHAPTER SIXTEEN

Under the veil of night, a murky lunar eye as witness, two dark figures crouching in the bushes watched a car pull into the driveway and an old man moving with unnatural strength to pull a sleeping figure from the backseat into the house.

"What was that?"

"Them, stupid."

"Them? What *them*? What are we doing here?"

"This is the place."

"The place?"

"That's what I said, so shut up."

"Who was that?"

"The ones we want."

"What?"

"Old man, if you don't shut up—"

"What do we do now?"

"I think the house next door is empty. We crash there. Tomorrow's the big day."

"I want to go home."

"Shut up, I said. Tonight?"

"Are you talking to me?"

"Shut up. Tonight?"

"Who are you talking to?"

Tomorrow. Tomorrow, one last favor.

"Tomorrow."

"What's tomorrow?"

"Tomorrow, I do someone a favor. Then I'll take you home myself."

CHAPTER SEVENTEEN

My head hurts where am I? Where am I ouch.

Ouch.

Are my eyes open?

Where am I? So dark in here and cold. So cold in here. My head's pounding. Something sticky there. Blood? No way blood NO WAY. Taste it? Is it blood? Taste it are you crazy? Hurts so bad.

This isn't home.

Am I dead? No way that's stupid no way.

Should I say something? Why not? Why not say something?

"Hello?"

That hurt. Mouth hurts. Jaw or something. Get this blood off my hand. It's not blood, don't be stupid. Yes it is, think about it.

Malcam! No, no. Dr. Bering. Smashed me. Man, it hurts. Can't remember anything. What am I supposed to do?

Wait, he smashed me. I'm not dead, don't think that. Head's cloudy. From the smashing. I'll kill him.

Gotta get up.

"Ahh!"

Not good. So sore. Bruises. He beat me up. I'm really gonna kill him, I mean. Kill him dead if I could just get up.

Listen. Can't hear anything. Am I outside? Feel the floor, Mike, touch it. Cold and hard. Not outside. It gives a little. Tile or something. Feel it, man, feel it. Oh, yeah. Tile. Feel those grooves, those squares. Inside I'm inside. Where am I? Bering's house. Yeah, Bering's house. What's the deal? What did I do? He said it yeah he said something. I've messed it up or something, ruined it.

Otherworld. Can't believe it. Flying saucers hyperspace Malcam the inner garden. No way can't believe it.

"Concentrate, Mike."

Ahh! Stop talking, stupid.

Oh, yeah. Okay, it's coming. The inner garden. Man, he wanted me to kill myself. Malcam was gonna kill me. Or Bering. One of them, I know it.

Molly. Oh-man-oh-man-oh-man. She was hurt in the thorns.

I've ruined everything? You tried to kill me, you goon! Gotta get out of here.

I can't. I'm gonna die here. I think this is it. Yeah. Man I did it I screwed up I did it good. What's the dill, pickle? Heh.

Focus, Mike. Write it out. Here we go, man, a day in the life. Lost Molly, oh man. I'm so stupid. Ignored her and everything. So dumb. Let her walk out. Something was on TV what was it? Pay attention, dummy. She left and you let her. Write it out, stupid. All right, yeah, write it out.

I was too selfish, too self-concerned. I got too comfortable, too complacent. My marriage was falling apart right under my nose, and I let it. She packed up her stuff and left me. She told me why, though; at least she did that. Like an idiot, I let her go without a fight. Typical, Mike, typical. Must have been a heck of a game on.

Remember that time in St. Louis at the mall? We squeezed into one of those instant photo booths. Two silly photos, and then she kissed me on the third. She was wearing that blue sweater, and her hair fell onto her shoulders and kind of swooped up or something. Man, that was great. That smile she gave me after the kiss. Wow.

What is this, blood? No, not blood. What is—oh, tears. I'm crying, I guess. Can't even feel it.

Am I lying down? No, sitting. This is crazy.

Okay, so she left. How much time goes by, can't tell. A year, maybe? Robbie sends me to Trumbull to cover a cow's murder. Believe it or not, Ripley, it's true. UFO farmer man out there. Poppy? Pops, yeah, Pops. Robbie sends me to school. That's hilarious. Reading UFO junk in the library and my own stupid professor walks up. "Hey, dummy, how about you and I summon a demon?" Heh, heh. Not exactly like that, but you know. Okay, I listen to him. All scientific mumbo jumbo. Dimensions and whatnot, Kahlua something. Kaluza. Gesundheit. Man, I'm losing it. Kaluza-Klein, man. And here's the trippy part: I ask him how come he knows so much. "I talk to them." Man, first clue right there. Bail out. Like an idiot: "Oh, yeah? Let me in on that." So stupid.

Wait, something else. Got run over or something. Dr. Bering was there. Took me home. Classic. Like Florence Nightingale effect, I fell for him and his stupid otherworld. People are dying, a killer on the loose, Robbie wants to send me to watch movies in Utah, and I'm talking to that, that thing. Malcam.

Head hurts really bad.

That thing tried to kill me. Sucked me into his fake world, hypnotized me or something.

Write it out, Mike. This helps. Write it, yeah.

Dr. Sutzkever shows up. No, I go to him, right? I visit Sutzkever and express my concerns. He lays the whole demon trip on me. Like Steve did in the car. Wait. No, that's right. Man, I told that guy way too much stuff. So, last night—wait, is it tomorrow yet?—we're all together. Four men: me, Steve, Sutzkever, and the cop. Gil or something. Gil? No, it'll come to me.

We're supposed to intervene, deliver Bering from evil or something. Steve says, "Mike's stupid; he's not a Christian." Words to that effect. Wish I was, preacher man. Woulda solved all of this. Right?

* * *

"Anyone talked to Mike today?" Steve asked.

He and Graham, perched atop bar stools at Prissy's Diner counter, shoveled eggs and hash browns into their mouths between conversation.

"Not me."

"He's our link to the professor. I wonder if we're still on for tonight."

"Why wouldn't we be?" Graham asked.

"Just hoping." Steve smiled guiltily.

"Yeah. How was work this morning?"

"I just holed up in my office, locked the door, unplugged the phone. You?"

"I'm exhausted, Steve. This Horn kid is out there, probably with Lucas Dickey, doing God-knows-what. I can't sleep because of the headaches. I was almost killed by some booby-trapped shotgun. I finally got the UFO freaks to crawl back into their holes. Even got that vet Driscoll to write up some piece for the paper, talkin' about how the cows were had by coyotes and the lights in the sky were gaseous somesuch. Petrie's dead."

"Yeah, I heard. Sorry. If you don't want to do tonight, I'm sure everyone will understand." Steve feared his face evidenced his hope.

"Nah. They's connected, Steve. All this mess is bigger than we realize. This is a spiritual oppression thing. I feel like, we jump tonight's hurdle, and the rest is waitin' on the other side to be fixed."

"Yeah, I hope you're right."

* * *

How long have I been in here? Don't count sleep. Or passing out. Or the pain that blurs the time. Can kind of see now. The tile is gray, I think. With white squiggles or whatever you call 'em.

Supposed to meet those guys. Save Bering. He needs a kidney. Man, I'm a riot. No, save me. Who's gonna save me? I need a brain, I guess. Oh, Bering needs a heart, that idiot violent freak-of-a-jerk guy.

Relax.

It goes way back, this thing does. Way back. Saw that body in the river. What's the big deal? Happens to lots of people. If I wasn't such a wimp, it wouldn't matter. If I didn't overanalyze every little stupid thing. And that kid shooting me in the back. Just BBs. Whatever. They hurt, man. I could've been a normal kid. My parents, man, they were cool. Got a cool wife, cool job. What's my problem?

This all got messed up.

Ugh, saw Vickie's body. Her face looked okay to have been through a wreck with a truck, though. No scratches or nothin', I don't think. Weird. Oh, yeah, passed out then, too. I'm just programmed for weakness.

Is that a light?

No, don't think so. Can kinda see, though. Gray tile, yeah. Squiggles. Can sorta see my hands. Light gotta be coming from somewhere. Try to move? Why not?

**FROM "POSSESSION: FACT OR FICTION?"
BY DR. LEOPOLD SUTZKEVER IN
THEOPHILUS QUARTERLY:**

Evidence remains to be seen as to whether believers in Jesus Christ can be physically possessed by unclean spirits, but against the majority opinion,

I am inclined to believe they cannot. Nevertheless, demonic possession as physical reality is no light subject for the believer. If it is suspected in anyone, prayer and fasting should become first order. Human beings have done extraordinary (and extraordinarily horrible) things under demonic control.

✳ ✳ ✳

"There's nothing to eat here, Black."

The old man and the teenager had been waiting for hours—all night and most of the day, in fact—hidden from the outside world in a vacant house yards from the home of their appointed target. The duo surmised that the family had fled Houston for warmer climates (how odd that sounded). Two o'clock crawled into being. Pops, hungry and irritable, watched television. Every now and then, the news would break in with an update on the search for him and Jimmy.

"Won't find us, I guess," Pops muttered every time. He was gradually regaining some sense, had even cried when he remembered what he'd done to Gertie. But he was still afraid of the kid, mainly because the kid never let the shotgun leave arm's reach. The idealized encounter with extraterrestrials was long gone. Pops couldn't believe the grays would talk to such a lunatic. He figured they wanted peace, like in that *Encounters* movie. Pops had just gotten out of hand, got wrapped up in the fame and attention. That alien visited him, he still believed, but this couldn't be what he wanted. Could it? *Somewhere along the way, things got plum crazy. That stupid show-stopping cop didn't help things much either.*

He could feel the kid staring at the back of his head. He figured the kid would walk up and slit his throat if he wanted to. "I'm hungry," Pops said without turning around.

"So?" came the reply a good distance away.

Boy, Stewadell would laugh it up, I'm sure. Taking guff from some whippersnapper. This is what it's come to, Pops.

The kid looked at him dumbly, staring through him with glassy, unblinking eyes.

∗ ∗ ∗

"Reverend Woodbridge?"

"Yes? Steve. Yes?"

"It's Leo."

"Sure. I'd recognize that voice anywhere."

"We are nearing the hour. Have you spoken to Michael today?"

"No. Haven't you?"

"No. I don't know where the boy is."

"That's weird."

"Yes, weird."

"What do you suppose has happened?"

"Oh, perhaps he's frightened and is sort of hiding. Can hardly blame him. Not to worry, however. Tonight may be too much for him anyway. We can carry on and attend to him later."

"Oh."

"Three hours till six, though, Steve. He may turn up."

∗ ∗ ∗

Okay, I know it's been, like, a whole day. Still can barely see. Can move, though. Head aches but doesn't pound. Try to stand? Why not? Legs weak, wobbly. Whoa, watch out here. Doin' it, doin' it. I'm standing. Can't see a blamed thing. Blind man walking. Arms out. Baby steps. Shuffle shuffle shuffle.

"Umph."

Wall. Hands out. Textured, but slick. Sidestep shuffle. Shuffle shuffle. A-ha. A corner. Gotta be a door somewhere. Sidestep shuffle.

The day brought a gradual enslavement of Bering's mind. He began to give himself over to his mania, and kidnapping Mike was an impetus toward his downward spiral. He spent the day, each wretched minute, tearing his clothes, tearing his flesh, calling for Malcam. "Please come, please come," he cried. He left a trail of sweat and blood all over the house as he moved from room to room, testing each one for its receptivity to the otherworld. He didn't consciously admit it, but Bering had stopped believing in the otherworld as hyperspace a long time ago. He had gone too far beyond the borders of science, too far even for pseudo-science. He swam past the breakers, was bobbing in the waves, toes tickled by the undertow. He knew Malcam for what he was. But he cared nothing for the danger. He wanted the *gnosis*. The power was an intoxicating lure. He had to have it, had to drink it in. He'd drown if he had to, enter the tenth dimension, the netherworld, a wormhole, hell itself if need be. He wanted in at any cost. If blood was the asking price, so much the better. He had a coward and a traitor locked in his basement, and his blood was cheap.

✳ ✳ ✳

Indeed, Mike labored in the basement, shuffling his feet inch by inch along each wall. The lightless room gave the impression of immeasurable vastness, and if it had a door, Mike couldn't find it. He made six or seven rounds, pivoting in each corner, fingering the walls with roving hands, straining to see any hint of light or life outside. He called out many times, banged on the walls, kicked them. His voice returned to him in taunting echoes. His body gained more strength by the minute, and his mind was getting more lucid. His anger grew as well.

He was angry with himself, with Dr. Bering, even angry with his three new friends (who he believed should have already arrived). He wouldn't let himself believe whatever plans Bering had for him would precede his rescue. Tired of trying, Mike slunk to the floor, squeezing his back into a corner.

"Bering!"

Where is he? What's he doing? How much time left? If I could get my hands on him ...

The cold began to get to him, penetrating the heat of his anger. He folded his arms against his chest and grabbed each shoulder.

Think, man, think. If he doesn't kill me, the cold will. I ain't freezing to death in Bering's stupid house. When he opens the door, I'm gonna grab his wrinkled neck and squeeze. If I could find the stupid door, I mean. I'll just rush him. I'm younger. Faster and stronger. I'll just take him out, take him down, the freak. I don't care if he is possessed. He did this. He asked for it. He invited that thing. I don't care. I'll take 'em both out.

I wonder if Malcam can hear me.

Don't say his name, stupid.

What happened to me? I just walked right into this. I invited Mal—that thing, too. Just like Bering. Ugh. Can I blame him? He didn't know just like I didn't know. He thought he was helping me. The key to the universe and all that. The wisdom of the ages straight from an eyewitness. We both bought it.

When I get out—if I get out—I'm starting over.

"Why not start over now?" said a voice.

Mike screamed and rocked back, banging his head on the wall. "Who's there? Who is it?" Mike yelled.

The disembodied voice replied calmly, quietly, "Go back and start over."

Mike swung his arms out in front of him, beating the air in search of a target. "Where are you? Who's there?"

No answer.

He continued for several minutes from his sitting position, flailing his arms and legs into the darkness, calling out.

No answer. Nothing.

Go back, he says. Mike figured Bering was playing games with him. *Start over, sure. Just open the door, and I'll start by beating your face in.*

Still, the words settled in.

Go back. Go back and start over. Huh. Yeah, I could do that maybe.

It didn't take long to transport himself to the riverside from his childhood's worst memory. A summer breeze caressed his cheek, rattled his pant legs. He stood alone this time. Ahead, the river ran smoothly. The sun dappled its gentle ripples with liquid glitter. Mike approached. The vision seemed so real. The faint smell of flowers and grass and the smell of mud and fish intermingled and coated the air. His feet squished in the gradual muddiness of the riverbank. He eyed the water suspiciously, expectantly. The whispery whoosh of the current barely registered in his ears. The bend obstructed his upstream view.

Any second now, he thought.

But nothing happened. He began to survey the river downstream. Perhaps it had floated by and he missed it. Straining his eyes, he still saw nothing.

Is this it? Is this starting over? Have I overcome—?

He couldn't finish his thought. He had the queer sense that he was being watched, felt a tingle on the back of his neck. His hairs stood at attention. Slowly turning, Mike expected to see Gary Newsome in combat stance, BB gun in hand, poised and ready. What he saw made his blood run cold. The corpse—that river-fed body of his youthful torment—stood six feet away, palms upturned and gray eyes focused on Mike.

The body wasn't alone. Walking up beside him, seemingly out of thin air, and taking a position shoulder to soggy shoulder with him, was Vickie. Her face was equally passive and equally disturbing. Like the mystery man, she was dead but awake.

Please go away.

The duo stood their ground, unblinking. Mike wanted to run. He'd follow his heart, which he was sure had leaped from his chest seconds ago and was hightailing it home. Before he could, though, a third figure appeared, like Vickie, apparently from the ether. It was a man, and the closer he came, the more Mike's horror grew.

It was himself.

"See anything you like?"

Malcam returned, descending from the summer sky and taking a position in front of the trio of animated corpses. The azure horizon folded in on itself, the river dried, the grass withered. Darkness fell hard and heavy like a showstopping curtain. Mike fell backward and landed not in the mud but on the cold tile of Bering's basement.

"Get away from me!"

"Just hear me out, chum."

"Wh-what is that? Why am I—?"

"Dead?" Malcam finished. He shrugged his ebony shoulders. In a blink, the bodies behind him vanished into the darkness. Mike and Malcam were alone with the eerie glow surrounding Malcam's floating form. "I believe in second chances, Michael. Would you like a second chance?" He was so close Mike could smell the fetid stink of his breath.

"Go away."

"Naked and not ashamed. Think about it. You don't want to pass it up again, do you?"

"You tried to kill me."

"Please. That was Samuel's doing, friend. Silly old goat, that fellow. Got a little spooked, I guess. But we're right as rain, you and I. We can leave the old man behind and start anew."

"Was that you?"

"Was *what* me?"

"Told me to go back and start over."

Malcam looked puzzled. "Never mind that," he said. "What do you say? You, me, and the universe makes three."

"No."

"I can give you happiness beyond your wildest dreams."

"No."

"Sex with beautiful women."

"No." Mike's resolve strengthened.

"Samuel's head on a platter?"

"I said no."

"Come now, chum; think it over. Let's just talk it out a bit. The beginning of words is the end of all sadness."

"I'm done talking."

"Well, then," Malcam countered, and he leaned in even closer. Mike felt the creature's strong hand stroking his neck. "I guess we go with sadness."

✳ ✳ ✳

Six o'clock came, and there was no sign of Mike. Steve even called Molly in Dallas. She was understandably upset to hear that he was missing, a response Steve hadn't the forethought to expect. He did his best to console her, reassuring her that Mike would turn up. He made no mention of their plans for the evening.

He sat in the back of Graham's cruiser, biting his fingernails and jostling back and forth as the captain navigated streets like a stock-car racer. Dr. Sutzkever sat in the front passenger seat, oblivious to the near misses occurring at every turn. His white-haired crown barely surpassed the headrest. Through the security bars dividing the front from back, Steve watched a few wisps of white hair bob up and down in the warm air of the heated cruiser. The old man looked so small, so unassuming, like a child, even. His little knees, tucked inside brown corduroy pants, poked up like thin, knobby mountain peaks rattling against the glove box. In his wrinkled lap lay a modest Bible, its leather obviously worn from use.

Steve white-knuckled the door handle to his left and poked his chest out, testing the give of the seat belt. Graham tested the limits of his car.

"Streets are kinda wet tonight," Steve said, trying to hint without hinting.

"Uh-huh," Graham said.

"No Mike, I guess," Steve said.

"That is probably for the best," Sutzkever answered. "One can never know how things will go. A bit too much for him, perhaps."

"Sure," Steve said.

Drops of water plunked onto the windshield.

"Is it raining?" Steve asked.

Graham gazed out into the distance. "No. No, I think that's … Naw, can't be."

"It's snow," Sutzkever said.

The three men sat in silence for the duration of the ride, each mesmerized by the sight of snow falling in Houston, Texas. Sutzkever seemed oddly pleased, a thin smile parting the beard on his pale face.

The cruiser careened onto Bering's street and raced toward the professor's house. The shadows hung more heavily over it than the others.

"Hey, I think I see Mike's car," Steve said. "Think he's here already?"

"I don't think so," replied Sutzkever. "I took him home yesterday from the university. He mentioned leaving his auto here."

Graham brought the car to a skidding halt inches from Mike's fender.

"Well, men, are we ready?" Sutzkever asked.

"Guess so," Steve offered.

"Yeah," said Graham. The brusque cop carried an air of anticipation

"Just remember you are a child of God," Sutzkever said. "Satan has no authority over you, and God will crush him beneath His feet shortly."

"How 'bout we pray before we go in?" Graham asked.

"Excellent idea."

* * *

As Graham did what he did best, the exchange between Mike and Malcam in Bering's sealed-away basement took a mysterious turn. Malcam's face became pain-stricken. He released Mike's neck and staggered back.

"What's happening?" Mike asked, not to Malcam but to whoever else could hear.

Malcam froze. A look of unimaginable rage invaded his face. His eyes burned hellish fire, and he bit into his lips. A flush of red boiled up and into his flesh. Mike noticed the cloth of his natty suit pulling taut as the muscles within flexed and strained. He vanished.

Mike cowered, alone in the darkness.

* * *

The three uninvited visitors made their way up the freshly iced path to Bering's front door. Graham walked with resolve, his strides long and sure. Steve shuffled forward, his eyes occasionally darting out suspiciously at the falling snow. Dr. Sutzkever led the way, an unmistakable spring in his step, a look of earnest compassion on his face, and his Bible cradled under his armpit.

Maybe he's not home, Steve thought as Sutzkever rang the doorbell. They waited a minute.

"I'm positive he's here," Sutzkever said, answering Steve's unspoken question. He knocked. Hard.

No answer.

The old man put his ear to the door.

"There's no lights on," said Steve.

Graham peered through the panes on each side of the entry. Sutzkever closed his eyes. He cupped his hand around his ear. "I hear something," he said.

"What?" asked Steve.

"It is Samuel. He's speaking to someone."

"Mike?"

"No. There is no one answering."

"Maybe he's on the phone."

"Maybe. I can't hear what he's saying."

"Knock again," instructed Graham.

"Very well." Sutzkever did.

They waited. Steve shuddered in the cold. Then a light appeared inside the house.

"Here we go, then," Sutzkever said.

The door opened inward, and Samuel Bering stood before them, a shell of a man overcome with aggravation. One hand held the door handle; the other hung at his side, balled into a white fist. The rips in his disheveled clothes revealed scratched flesh, dried blood. His gray hair stood out, frazzled as if electrocuted. "Leo," he said through gritted teeth. "Whatever can I do for you?"

"Are you all right, Samuel?"

"What do you want?" Bering said.

"What's happened to you?"

"Nothing," he said coolly. "Now, good night."

"We'd like to come in and talk awhile."

"This isn't a good time. See me in my office."

"No, I think we should speak now."

"I don't want to speak now."

"Samuel, this man's a police officer," Sutzkever said, waving a hand at Graham. "We'd like to come in and talk. He can take a look at you. You have some nasty cuts there."

Bering glanced down at his blood-spotted shirt. "It's nothing, really." He looked back up at Sutzkever, zeroing in on his eyes with a steely stare. "*Really.*"

Sutzkever remained convivial. "Nevertheless, we would still feel better if we could come in a while."

Bering hesitated. He turned back, looking over his shoulder.

"Is anyone else here?" Sutzkever asked.

Bering sprang back. "No," he said sternly. Then his nervousness became apparent. "No, of course not. There's no one here."

"Samuel, it's cold out here. Let us come in, and I'll make us some tea."

✳ ✳ ✳

Bering's clenched fist relaxed. Had he given it away? *Do they know? Why did Leo bring a policeman?* He looked over their shoulders and saw Mike's car next to the curb. The Trumbull Police cruiser was inches behind. *Why didn't I move Mike's car? They've come to get him and to put me away. What to do?*

"How 'bout it, Professor?" It was the cop.

Bering didn't like the man's look. He was big and obviously strong. Even worse, though, his face was unforgiving, all business. Bering was in no mood for someone so pedestrian. He probably had a gun tucked away in his coat, too.

Bering couldn't think of an out. If they knew, they would find a way in anyway. If they didn't know, perhaps he could give them some tea and get rid of them. He looked at Sutzkever, noticed the Bible under his arm. *This could get out of hand*, he thought. He looked again at the cop. *This could be trouble.* He looked at the third man, a stranger who hadn't said anything. *He'll go first.*

He said, "Sure, I suppose some tea would be all right."

In the house next door, Pops Dickey searched kitchen drawers for a can opener. The can of tuna in his hand proved too tough for the knife he had yanked from the cutting block. Jimmy Horn stared through the kitchen window, which happened to look out onto Bering's house. He periodically wiped condensation from the glass. Random images from his recent history of violence replayed in his head, flashing with strobe-like effect and twisting back onto themselves in a Mobius strip of memories. He saw his mother, the little girl, her father, the cop, and even the grocery clerk. Jimmy's brain contorted, playing the images in a loop, opening a mental vortex, sucking his consciousness into the otherworld.

Jimmy? Hey there, Jimmy. One more last favor. One last crazy favor.

"That's the one, eh?" Pops asked.

"What? Oh. Yeah."

"And when—?"

"Soon."

∗ ∗ ∗

The four men entered Bering's study, the three visitors seating themselves on a couch across from Bering, who perched alone on a loveseat.

Sutzkever asked, "Are you sure you're okay, Samuel? Those cuts look quite nasty."

"Quite," said Bering. "I mean, quite okay."

"If you say so."

"I'm fine."

An uncomfortable silence followed.

"How about that tea, then?" Sutzkever asked.

"Right, tea. I'll just put some on."

"If it's no trouble."

"No, none." Bering rose and exited into the kitchen, keeping a wary eye on the trio until he reached his destination, at which point he checked the basement door anxiously. The locks held secure. He hoped his soundproofing would keep Mike's calls for help futile.

∗ ∗ ∗

When he considered Bering sufficiently out of range, Sutzkever began his instructions. "Graham, you begin praying. Aloud but quietly. Quietly but not meekly. I'm assuming you know what to pray for. Reverend Woodbridge here tells me you certainly know how. Reverend, take the book here. Turn to Psalm 62 and begin reading aloud in the same manner Graham is praying. Keep reading each psalm following until I tell you to stop. Is everything clear?"

"Yes."

"Yes."

"Good."

Bering returned. "The kettle is on and—what's going on?"

"Begin," Sutzkever said.

Graham began: "Dear God, we ask for Your healing, we ask for Your wisdom, we ask for Your power ..."

"What is this, Leo?"

Steve began: "My soul waits in silence for God only; from Him is my salvation. He only is my rock and my salvation, my stronghold; I shall not be greatly shaken ..."

Bering began to shake. "Leo?"

"We bring healing, Samuel," Sutzkever said.

Bering's tremors increased. "Leo, what are you doing?"

"... how long will you assail a man," Steve continued, "that you may murder him, all of you?"

Sutzkever stood. "We've come to deliver you through the power of Jesus."

At that name, a quizzical expression conquered Bering's face, followed by a blushing of brilliant pink and a gurgling in his throat. He lurched forward, dropped to his knees, and vomited onto the carpet.

"Samuel!" Sutzkever darted forward.

"Stay away!" Bering barked, and as the man looked up, Sutzkever could see it wasn't Bering at all, not really. "I know who you are. Get away." The voice was deeper, malicious.

Leo saw that Steve was sweating, but the pastor pressed on. "... they have counseled only to thrust him down from his high position;

they delight in falsehood; they bless with their mouth, but inwardly they curse ..."

Graham was focused on Bering, but he kept praying: "Send Your power, Lord. Send Your freedom. Send Your angels and send forth Your word ..."

"Make them shut up!"

"Listen to me now, you. I want to speak to Samuel," Sutzkever said.

"Make them shut up!"

"I won't. We're here to do a job, and we intend to do it."

Bering growled, turned, stumbled. He spit onto the wall.

"We have command here, in the name of Jesus Christ."

Bering spit again. With his back to the visitors, he said, "I know who you are, and I won't go."

"I think we'll have to see about that," Sutzkever said.

✴ ✴ ✴

As the bizarre battle commenced upstairs, Mike, unaware of the spiritual melee, began a mental one of his own.

Got to take control here. Got to do something. Find the door, find a light, something. Can't die here, can't. Do something, do it. Do it!

What if Malcam comes back? What to do? What did Dr. Sutzkever say? He's a demon? Whoa, Nelly. Slow down here. You're getting ahead of yourself. Mike could feel the impressions left on his neck. *Still ...*

He stood up, facing the darkness with a burgeoning faith.

I want out. I want out now. God, if You can hear me, I want out, and I want out now.

✳ ✳ ✳

Jimmy woke Pops, tapping the barrel of the shotgun on the old man's whiskered chin. Pops jumped, his withered bones creaking. "Huh?" he said groggily. "What's going on?" Pops noticed the kid had shed his stolen jacket. A partially obscured Grim Reaper glared at Pops from the cover of Jimmy's black shirtsleeve. The tattoo smiled a crooked, toothy grin.

"Let's move out," Jimmy said.

CHAPTER EIGHTEEN

Bering convulsed against the wall, spraying bloody saliva from his frothing mouth in wild arcs. Drops plunked onto Sutzkever's Bible, but Steve kept reading, afraid to stop, afraid to do anything else. He entered Psalm 64: "Hear my voice, O God, in my complaint; preserve my life from dread of the enemy ..."

Graham continued praying as Sutzkever leaned over the trembling Bering.

"Leave me alone," Bering growled. He swung around, smacking Sutzkever across the chest with a blow that sent the old man reeling. Sutzkever landed on the floor, his limbs in the air like an overturned bug. Graham rose.

"No!" Sutzkever said to him. "Do nothing. Keep praying."

Graham did, but he didn't return to his seat. "Lord, we ask You to hinder the work of the evil one here, to bind him, and to cast him out."

A cry came from Bering like a yelp from a wounded animal. He scrambled to his feet and retreated to the stairs just outside the study.

"Follow him," Sutzkever commanded.

The three men trailed Bering, who was ascending the wooden staircase rapidly. He reached the landing and disappeared before Sutzkever, leading the others, had made it to the halfway point.

"He took a left around the corner," Graham said.

Steve stumbled, attempting to read as he climbed.

They reached the top and turned the corner, feeling their way in the darkness together. Only one door was open, and Sutzkever entered cautiously. He felt for a light switch, flipped it up, and discovered a large room paneled with wood on all sides. It looked like a ballroom. It was empty except for Bering, who was attempting to climb out a window. He thrust it open and began making his escape when his hand slipped on the wet sill, tilting him forward and down to the floor in a heap. Graham rushed to his side, quickly shutting the window as snow drifted inside. Bering leaped up, knocking Graham over and running into a far corner. He tucked himself into a fetal position and, seething, glared at Sutzkever.

Sutzkever walked toward him confidently. "You are from below; we are from above. You are from this world; we are not of it."

"I know who you are," came a voice from Bering's mouth.

"Yes, you know me, and you know where I am from. I am not here on my own, but He who sent me is true. You do not know Him, but I know Him, because I am from Him, and He sent me."

"Those words, those words," Bering gasped. "They are not your own. I don't understand."

"The light shines in the darkness, but the darkness has not understood it."

"Shut up!" Bering dropped his head.

The room suddenly grew much colder as an invisible wind carrying an unnerving chill swirled about. The pages of the Bible rustled.

"What's happening?" asked Graham.

"Just keep praying, Captain. We will see," Sutzkever said.

"This doesn't feel right." *Be assured.*

"Pray, man, pray!"

Bering slowly stood, contempt blazing from his body like radiation. Small orbs of light appeared at his feet and encircled him.

Steve began to cry but kept reading. "The righteous man will be glad in the LORD and will take refuge in Him; and all the upright in heart will glory."

Graham took the words as a cue: "Yes, we praise You, God. We ask for Your protection and Your shelter."

Sutzkever watched the action around Bering as it grew more fantastic, more ominous. "Yes, now we see who we're up against."

The lights dipped rhythmically, bouncing to a silent beat. Bering screamed and collapsed to the floor once again. In his place materialized a man. A tall, imposing figure with a black double-breasted suit challenged them with an icy glare. His face was ghostly white, almost translucent, including his thin, sharp lips.

Steve glanced up from the book and turned just as white. "What in the—?"

Graham took several steps back, but his hand went for his pistol.

"You won't need that," the man said to him dryly.

Sutzkever, unfazed, stepped up. "No, we won't."

✳ ✳ ✳

Malcam sized up the old man. He was actually afraid of him but didn't want to show it. He smirked and said, "My name is Abimelech."

"No, it most certainly is not, but we don't care what your name is anyhow," Sutzkever said.

Malcam paused, puzzled. "You fools are always jabbering for my name," he protested.

"Superstition. I don't need your name to hold authority over you when we come in the name of Jesus Christ."

Malcam winced. "I know why you're here. Are you so stupid that you don't think I expected this? It has been orchestrated. You are all here so that we may be rid of you all at once."

* * *

Jimmy and Pops approached Bering's door, making no attempts at secrecy. Jimmy held the shotgun out conspicuously, and Pops tagged behind.

"I left Wisconsin to be rid of snow."

"Shut up."

"What do we do now? Are the grays in this house?"

"There are no grays, stupid. Just kill everyone in sight."

"Okay," Pops replied. He seemed too afraid of Jimmy to disobey.

Jimmy turned the knob and, finding it unlocked, popped the door in and stepped into its retreating swing.

Okay, Jimmy. Do us this favor now. Everyone's here. The party's just begun. Time to get a little crazy.

"Don't call me crazy."

"I didn't say anything," Pops replied.

* * *

Down below, in the cold darkness of the basement, Mike was calling for the other voice, the one he decided was friendly. The one Malcam seemed so upset about. He somehow knew something extraordinary was taking place in the house, if only because he knew six o'clock had to have arrived by now. The voice didn't answer.

I am so dead. Dead as dead can be. Dead as a doornail. Dead as dirt. Dead as po' Lazarus. Who was Lazarus? He had leprosy or something, right? No, that's not right. He had leprosy and died? I remember the flannel story in Sunday School a long, long time ago. Flannel-backed Lazarus in that cave or something, as dead as dead. Way dead, man. These girls were crying. Jesus shows up and brings the dude back. Pretty cool.

Huh. I bet it was cold and dark in that cave …

✳ ✳ ✳

Sutzkever countered the demon's assertion. "It has been orchestrated, spirit, but by the Lord our God. And He will be rid of you."

The demon ignored him. He turned to Steve, who was blazing through Psalm 66, speed-reading like his life depended on it. "Bless our God, O peoples, and sound His praise abroad, Who keeps us in life and does not allow our feet to slip …"

"Naw," the demon said, rushing Steve in an effortless sprint and smacking the Bible out of his hands. The minister followed the book down, frantically scrambling for it to find his place. "I know you," the demon said to him. "You're the preacher. You're a coward." He grabbed Steve by the arm and lifted him upright. Steve shut his eyes and felt a sour breath on his face that made him wilt. The demon resumed, "You're a coward and a puppet. Everyone pulls your strings because you're weak. You're the weakest one here. You'll go first, preacher man."

Steve courageously opened an eye and then tried to reach the Bible with his foot.

"Let him loose, spirit," Sutzkever commanded.

"No."

"Steve, the Word is in you. Find it there," Sutzkever instructed.

The demon strengthened his grip. And then, somewhere deep inside, beneath the fears and doubts and frailty, Steve Woodbridge discovered what was hidden in his heart. It was small but powerful, exploding from him like a firecracker through a clenched fist. "But He said to me," he defiantly said, "'My grace is sufficient for you, for My power is made perfect in weakness.'"

The demon groaned and released Steve like dropping a hot coal. Steve hit the floor but continued: "Finally, be strong in the Lord—"

"No," Malcam cried.

"—and in His mighty power. Put on the full armor of God so that you can take your stand against the Devil's schemes …"

Graham started toward Steve to help him up.

"Get back!" the demon snarled. He held a hand out at Graham. Instantly, Graham clutched his head and fell, writhing in pain.

Steve continued: "For our struggle is not against flesh and blood, but against the rulers, against the authorities, against the powers of this dark world, and against the spiritual forces of evil in the heavenly realms …"

The demon released a bloodcurdling scream and sent a powerful blow to Steve's back. The minister struck the floor, sprawled out and wheezing. The demon turned to Sutzkever. "This is your doing?" he asked. "Are you in charge?"

"God is in charge."

"Bah!" He kicked Steve in the side with an incredible force, and the minister felt and heard a terrifying crack he assumed was a rib. The pain was immeasurable, like a repetitive stabbing.

Steve saw Graham, a few yards away, rub his head vigorously and try to stand.

Steve rolled onto his back. With short bursts of air, he persevered: "Therefore, put on the full armor of God, so when the day of evil comes, you may be able to stand your ground ..."

"Make him stop," the demon said to Sutzkever. "I command you."

Sutzkever actually laughed. "I will not. Greater is He that is in us than that which is in you."

Graham, despite his obvious pain, began to sing: "Blessed assurance, Jesus is mine ..."

"Make him stop!"

"Oh what a foretaste of glory divine. Heir of salvation, purchase of God. Born of His spirit, washed in His blood."

"Argh!"

"This is my story, this is my song: praising my Savior all the day long. This is my story, this is my song: praising my Savior all the day long."

"I will kill Samuel." Malcam gestured at Bering, who throughout it all remained in the corner, apparently passed out.

"You have no authority here," Sutzkever said. "You have no power to take lives."

"You are wrong, old man. I am the authority here, and I will take the lives of those who are mine."

With that, the demon vanished, and almost instantaneously, Bering sprang to life. Rising to his feet and waving his arms purposelessly, the voice of the demon said, "Samuel and I may just take a dive out the window."

"In the name of Jesus, I command you to stop," Sutzkever said.

Steve inched his way to the Bible and leafed to his stopping point. He resumed: "For You have tried us, O God; You have refined us as silver is refined. You brought us into the net; You laid an oppressive burden upon our loins."

Suddenly, a loud cracking boom exploded into the room, echoing off the walls. A hot blast of air rushed by Steve, knocking him down again and burning his cheek. The demon began to laugh from within Bering. Everyone turned to see a teenager, dressed head to toe in black, standing in the doorway, a shotgun in his hands. Over his shoulder peeked an old face.

The noise of the shotgun tortured Graham, whose headache had risen to epic proportions when the demon had reentered Bering, but he turned to the doorway. His first sight was of the kid's bicep and the unmistakable image of the Grim Reaper leering at him from the pale flesh. The demon continued to laugh as Sutzkever and Steve clutched the wood floor.

"What an odd turn of events," the demon said. And then, wistfully: "In the old days, you had to create a cow of gold to lead people astray. Now you just kill one."

Graham, fighting the blinding pain, reached inside his coat for his shoulder holster.

Mike heard the gunshot.

"I'm gonna die," he said aloud. *I'm already dead. I'm trapped and I'm dead and I want out!* "God, if You can hear me, I want out! I don't want to be dead; I want out!" *I want what Steve talked about at the funeral, what Sutzkever said in our meeting.* "I need You, God! I want out!"

✳ ✳ ✳

Jimmy saw the cop removing his gun and stepped back, bumping into Pops. The shotgun discharged, sending another deadly spray into the room. The blast flew into the far corner, clear of everyone in the room, but they all flattened out anyway. Pops crumbled to the floor. Jimmy backtracked, hopped over his fallen comrade, and disappeared into the shadows to reload. He saw the cop sit up on one knee, poised with pistol drawn. The gun was aimed at Pops, who was clutching his hip.

✳ ✳ ✳

At the sound of the second gun blast, Mike began to cry uncontrollably. "I'm sorry God I'm sorry so sorry so sorry don't let me die let me out so sorry let me out get me out please …"

✳ ✳ ✳

Sutzkever placed his hand on the prostrate Steve and pushed himself upright. "Sorry," he quipped. Fearing nothing, he faced Bering, whose mouth projected Malcam's smile. "This will soon be over," Sutzkever said.

Malcam seemed to read the purpose in Sutzkever's eyes. It was as if the demon's ego could no longer protect his fear. His weaknesses were exposed to this man—he knew it. The man had a gift, and he would not stop until he had used it against Malcam.

"This world will perish," Sutzkever intoned. "The Lord's enemies will be like the beauty of the fields; they will vanish. Vanish like smoke."

"No," Malcam muttered. Bering's face proved the spirit was shaken.

"The Lord helps the righteous and delivers them; he delivers them from the wicked and saves them."

"Let's talk this thing over," Malcam begged.

"There will be no bargaining," said Sutzkever.

"But, but," Malcam stammered, "the beginning of words is the end of all sadness."

Sutzkever countered: "The Word has no beginning. He has always been, even in the beginning. The beginning of *knowledge* of the Word is the end of all despair, not sadness."

"But that's different."

"Well, of course it is."

"No, no, no …"

"Now, I shall cast you out, foul creature."

"Do you blaspheme me, an angel?"

Sutzkever knew what Malcam was referring to and replied, "But even the archangel Michael, when he was disputing with the Devil about the body of Moses, did not dare bring a slanderous accusation against him, but said—as I say to you now—the Lord rebuke you!"

Bering's hands reached for his own throat, and his eyes bulged. Choking, he pleaded, "But I am Malcam. I am Malcam."

Sutzkever's eyes widened in surprise. "Ah, yes: Malcam. Malcam, son of Shaharaim."

"Yes, yes; that's me."

"Malcam, god of the Ammonites."

"The same."

"Malcam, known as Mileom."

"Yes, that's right," Malcam said, strangely pleased.

In the background, Steve struggled to his feet and recited, "From now on, let no man cause trouble for me, for I bear on my body the brandmarks of God."

* * *

In Trumbull, Abby Diaz clasped her hands, closed her eyes, and prayed, "Dear Jesus, stop the bad man, wherever he is tonight. Let the good man win. Amen."

* * *

In Dallas, Molly Walsh cried as she took down Vickie's finger-painted lady from the wall. She ran her trembling fingers over the sharp texture of the thick and hardened paint. She whispered a prayer: "Lord, save Mike. Wherever he is, please save him."

* * *

Sutzkever continued: "Malcam, son of Shaharaim, known as Mileom."

"Yes, that is me."

"Malcam, known as Molech."

"Yes!"

"You are a false idol, a false god, an unclean spirit."

"No!"

Jesus, stop the bad man—

Lord, save Mike—

God, let me out!

"Be quiet and come out!"

An explosion of light and power rocked the house as Malcam burst out of Bering. In the same moment, one floor below, Mike chose a not-so-random spot on a not-so-random wall of the basement and ran at it full speed, shoulder level. He found himself running up an incline and eventually crashing through the door into the kitchen. Temporarily blinded from the sudden exposure to light, he stumbled about, plowing into one counter and then another, his frantic hands searching for a hold and instead pulling a few pots and pans onto the floor. With a loud crash, he tripped over them and out of the kitchen and onto the first-floor landing at the foot of the imposing stairs.

Rubbing the stars from his straining eyes, he glanced up toward a commotion. Looking down from the higher level, meeting his gaze, was a thin figure in the shadows.

"Dr. Bering? What's going on?" he called.

Mike didn't comprehend the meaning of the silver barrels of the shotgun tilting over the second-floor railing.

Boom.

Mike dropped, screaming, and threw a hurried glance upward to see his would-be killer sprawled on the floor of the landing. One sneakered foot poked out through the railing. An old voice said, "What do we do now, Black?"

Mike crawled away, his belly rubbing the floor. Reaching the den, he took another look back. His assailant, a young kid in black, was coming down the stairs quickly. At the top of the stairs, Mike saw Graham Lattimer enter the fray, a gun of his own pointed at the kid's back.

"Black, look out!" came the old voice again.

Mike saw Graham lowering his pistol and noticed that the kid froze for a moment, stunned, clearly shocked that it could end like this. Mike bolted for the front door, jiggled the knob, couldn't get it open in the frantic rush of it all. The old man lurched for Graham's legs and knocked them out from under him. The kid watched Graham tumble down the stairs toward him, an avalanche of bent limbs and flapping clothes and a short, jutting pistol, and then backed down the remaining steps.

Mike managed to open the door, and he sprang into the cold night, slipping on the slick sidewalk and sliding into the frosty grass. The kid was chasing after him—he could hear him bang against the doorway—and then came a loud voice shouting, "Stop!" But it was not the kid's.

The sheer surprise of the order stopped them both. Mike turned around to see Jimmy whirling around back into the house.

The kid brought the shotgun to ready one hundred and eighty degrees around and fired.

Shock hit Graham first. He had been standing at the foot of the stairs, pistol extended. The kid was quicker on the draw. Now Graham was on the floor wondering why and how. And what was wrong? He couldn't feel anything. He squeezed the trigger of his pistol, but nothing happened. He looked down to see his right arm was no longer there.

Jimmy pointed the gun at Graham's head.

* * *

In the upstairs room, Dr. Sutzkever cradled Dr. Bering, who was twitching and sobbing uncontrollably. "Help me, Leo; help me," he kept saying. He leaned forward, a series of dry heaves lurching from his throat.

"Steve, resume your reading," Sutzkever said.

Steve could see Pops through the doorway, but the old man appeared incapacitated, so he searched out the Bible. The gunshots below unnerved him, but he had come too far to distrust Sutzkever now. Something was welling up inside of him, something fresh, something—yes!—*youthful.*

"Let God arise, let His enemies be scattered," he read. "And let those who hate Him flee before Him. As smoke is driven away, so drive them away; as wax melts before the fire, so let the wicked perish before God—"

"But let the righteous be glad; let them rejoice before God," Sutzkever interrupted, reciting from memory, "yea, let them exceedingly rejoice."

"Leo, what has happened?" Bering asked meekly.

"Breathe, Samuel, breathe. We have expelled that creature. But you must renounce him for yourself."

"Yes, yes; I renounce him."

"Ask God to free you and forgive you."

"Yes, yes; free me, God. Forgive me, God."

* * *

Jimmy squeezed the trigger.

Click.

Nothing.

Need to reload, Jimmy thought.

Jimmy? Jimmy? The one's getting away. Get him, Jimmy. He's the one we want.

He turned his back on the cop and saw his previous prey outside skittering toward his car. The fleeing man slipped at the edge of the sidewalk and slid into the narrow crevice between the car and the curb. Jimmy ran for him. The man squirmed up and out, pulled himself across the hood, and scrambled for the driver's side door.

Unlocked!

The man quickly secured himself inside as Jimmy reached the car. The kid banged on it, pounded on the glass.

✳ ✳ ✳

Inside the house, Graham was pondering the pool of blood quickly forming around him. He could hear footsteps descending the staircase behind him.

Be assured.

Pops reached him and grabbed his collar. Graham promptly turned and smashed Pops's face in with his left fist. The old farmer dropped hard and muttered something that sounded to Graham like "strudel." Graham managed to pull his handcuffs from his jacket pocket and lock an age-spotted wrist to the banister. He began to calmly look around for his missing arm and, more importantly for the moment, the pistol at the end of it. He was trying to avoid shock, but as his adrenaline rush started to fade, his head lolled. Dizziness set in. He started to hyperventilate. The nerves at his freshly shorn shoulder sent waves of intense, debilitating pain through his weakening body. Stubbornly, he tried to overcome, to will himself forward.

✳ ✳ ✳

Mike deftly plunked every lock he could reach down, and as he scoured the upholstery for his keys, his attacker was searching his pocket for something. Mike jabbed his numb fingers into the cracks of the seats. He jerked the glove box open, spilling an assortment of papers onto the passenger side floorboard. He flipped the sun visor down.

Glancing back up quickly, he could see the kid had a knife now.

Mike plunged his hand beneath his seat and discovered cold metal. *The keys!* He grabbed and withdrew. He glanced out his window. The kid was there, madness oozing from his oily skin, a glittering knife in his fist. Mike looked back down into his lap. He saw the word LLAMA gleaming back at him.

Before he could think, an explosion of glass shook the car. The kid's bloody knife-wielding hand swung in, swiping wildly. Mike leaned to his right, but the tip of the blade caught his left side, ripping a thin tear from his cheekbone to his jawline. He dashed into the passenger seat, holding the pistol firmly.

The kid pawed for the inside door handle. Mike raised the pistol. He could just see his predator's menacing face descending into view, the knife leading the way, when he impulsively, defensively, pulled the trigger.

Utter surprise struck the kid in unison with the forty-five caliber bullet. His chest caved in, and he fell limp.

✳ ✳ ✳

So this is how it ends, he would have thought, had he the mental capacity to philosophize. But he didn't, so he didn't. It ended with a bang. He ended with a whimper. He was dead before he knew it. *You blew it, Jimmy. Man, you blew it.*

✳ ✳ ✳

Mike screamed, dropped the gun, and screamed again as the door at his back gave way and an arm scooped him up. He toppled backward onto the icy cement and into the blood-soaked lap of the cop.

"Unloaded—it … it was unloaded," Mike sputtered.

"I need an ambulance," Graham said matter-of-factly.

The previous shots had already inspired the neighbors' calls. In the distance, the woeful warble of sirens pierced the air.

CHAPTER NINETEEN

FROM "SUSPECTED SERIAL MURDERER KILLED" BY
MICHAEL ASBELL IN THE *HOUSTON CHRONICLE*:

The teenage boy suspected in a string of recent murders and one attempted kidnapping was shot to death while attacking his latest victim, authorities say.

Jimmy Horn, 17, of Houston, was wanted in connection with the murders of his mother, Maggie Horn; Carlos Diaz, a Trumbull man; and Samuel Petrie, a police officer. Police say he also attempted to abduct Diaz's daughter.

Last night, Horn assaulted Trumbull Police Captain Graham Lattimer and, after attacking a Houston man in his car, was shot by the man. Police say the shooting was clearly in self-defense, and no charges have been filed against the man, Michael Walsh of Houston.

Lattimer, meanwhile, lost an arm in the attack and has been placed on administrative duty pending further investigation.

In a strange twist, Horn's alleged accomplice is Lucas Dickey, 71, of Trumbull, the farmer renowned for his involvement in the recent rash of UFO sightings. Dickey has been arrested for the aggravated kidnapping of his wife, Gertrude

Dickey, 68, of Trumbull, and for the attempted murder of a police officer.

A court date has not been set.

* * *

Steve Woodbridge was nibbling on a pumpkin pie and greeted Graham Lattimer with a smile as the captain entered the Dixie Shack and ambled over.

"Afternoon."

"Afternoon."

"How's the day been?"

"S'okay. Just got back from Petrie's funeral."

"Oh, yeah. You ... okay?"

"It's okay. It was real nice. People got up, talked about what a good kid he was. Everyone had a funny story to tell. He was a good kid, a good cop."

"Yeah. How you been?"

"As good as it gets, I guess."

"No more headaches?"

"Nope."

"What about—?" Steve poked his fork at the empty space that should have held Graham's right arm.

"Can't say as I miss it," Graham joked.

Steve chuckled. "What are you gonna do, ya think?"

"Not sure. Not much use for a one-armed cop. I'm not a desk duty kind of guy, anyway. Probably put in for early retirement, take a good, long vacation. After that, who knows? Thinking about PI work."

"In Trumbull?"

"Well, I s'pose not. How about you, Steve? Any *decisions?*" He emphasized that last word, knowing full well his friend could not have survived their experience without developing some resolution. Graham had seen the minister's confidence emerge under that pressure, under the threat behind all threats.

"I went ahead and submitted my resignation."

"Oh."

"Yeah. The committee will probably try to talk me out of it again, but my mind's made up."

"Where are you going?"

"I'd like them to send us into missionary training."

"Sheesh."

"And then to Mexico, if possible."

"They'll say no."

"We're going anyway. I've wasted a lot of years doing the wrong 'right thing.'"

"Mexico."

"Yep. Pray with me?"

"Absolutely."

FROM "OUT WITH THE COLD" BY STANLEY GRUENWALD IN THE *HOUSTON CHRONICLE*:

> After a prolonged cold spell, southeast Texas is enjoying the onset of an Indian summer. Record lows were set in the Houston area and there was even scattered snowfall, uncommon for late autumn in the area. The forecast now calls for early

spring-like conditions—mostly sunny and warm for at least the next five days.

* * *

Sutzkever allowed no shadows of significant size in his house, at Bering's request. This feat required a ridiculous number of lamps and lights, all recent and hurried purchases from the local home improvement store. Sutzkever shopped alone, as Bering had slept for two days without interruption.

When Bering awoke, his old friend had tea at the ready, and a friendly pat on the arm. Bering had wet the bed, and despite his natural embarrassment, he was too weak and too grateful to protest Sutzkever's tending to the soiled sheets.

"You are being good," Bering said meekly. It was an infantile statement, a matter-of-fact acknowledgement and thank-you from a mind recently freed from the heaviest of burdens. It sounded downright silly, but Sutzkever seemed not to care.

"You are my friend," Sutzkever said, words that would make the most sense to Bering, delivered in an equally sensible and simple manner.

Over the next few days, Bering's strength began to return. His embarrassment only increased as the exploits of the last few months came more to memory. Sutzkever watched over him constantly, called in to the university and arranged for Bering's sick leave, then prayed over his friend like every breath depended on it.

The great divorce between Bering's crimes and Sutzkever's reaction became more and more obvious in Bering's every waking moment. And all of Sutzkever's care and concern only increased

Bering's sense of guilt. For each time Bering secretly shrunk in the horror of his own sin, Sutzkever somehow intuitively built him up with a kind word or deed.

The response was crushing. The amount of apathy was almost too much for him to bear. *No, apathy is not the right word*, thought Bering. Sutzkever was smothering him to life with something for which Bering was at a loss for synonyms. He knew nothing of grace until now.

"I tried to kill you, Leo," Bering said suddenly one morning over breakfast.

"I know," Sutzkever said. "Eat your toast."

FROM THE JOURNAL OF DR. LEOPOLD SUTZKEVER:

God's strength is perfected in man's weakness. What an odd sort, that Malcam. He intended to do us evil, thinking he had drawn us all together for some strange mass murder. But God meant it all for good. We did not all escape unharmed, but we did emerge alive. And God claimed the victory.

Michael is seeking help for his problems, I hear. Reverend Woodbridge has referred him to a counselor friend. We have cleared up the matter of his eternal destiny with him. He no longer fears death, because he is for the first time alive. Death, where is thy victory? Where is thy sting?

Samuel appears well also. We have added theology to our list of debatable topics, but his heart isn't really in it. I believe he is exhausted mentally and spiritually.

When you devote your entire soul to a soulless enterprise, no matter how scientifically articulate you think it is, you come away a shell of a man.

We are reconciling religion and science together. He is finding that it is quite silly to believe in hyperspatial beings and to disbelieve in a Creator. Especially a Creator he knows saved his life.

I do not know where Malcam went, though I hope it was to hell. And I do not know if he will return, but I somehow doubt it.

Worthy is the Lamb that was slain to receive power, and riches, and wisdom, and strength, and honour, and glory, and blessing!

✳ ✳ ✳

The *Spotlight Magazine* office was as deserted as a ghost town except for two old friends exchanging secrets in an open copy room.

"That is the absolute weirdest story I've ever heard," Robbie Jensen said. "And I don't believe a single word."

"Scout's honor," said Mike.

"Mind blower."

"Tell me about it."

"You need some time off, man."

"Tell me about it."

"Call tomorrow. Talk to Tina. She'll set you up with a ticket—"

Robbie froze.

"What?" Mike asked.

"—or two."

Mike turned. In the doorway stood the loveliest vision he'd ever seen, a picture of grace and beauty, mercy personified. An object of desire, a purpose for sacrifice. His love, his life. His wife.

"Molly." Mike stood weakly, slack-jawed.

"Hi."

Too wonderful. Too glorious.

Don't screw this up. "Hi."

"I was worried about you," she said.

"I'm just gonna ... do something, uh, someplace," Robbie said, making his exit.

"About me?" Mike asked. *Can I hug her? Should I?*

"I missed you."

Mike walked to her, every step less loud than his beating heart. He looked into her eyes. *Those marvelous blue eyes.* "I missed you, too. So much."

Was she? She was! Reaching for him. She grabbed him, pulled him close. She felt so good against him, so right. Her hair smelled so sweet. Mike trembled.

"Oh, Mike, I'm so sorry."

The tears began to fall on both of their cheeks.

"No, don't say that," he said. "You have nothing to be sorry for. I'm the one. I am so selfish. I ignored you, took you for granted—"

"It's okay."

"No, it's not. It's not okay. I'm so sorry, Molly. Sorry for being a worthless person, a lousy husband, a bad friend. I was lazy, stupid. Please forgive me."

"I do, I do."

"Please forgive me." *Can't get her close enough.*

She leaned back, not to escape his embrace, but to look him in the eyes. With a delicate finger, she traced the stitches on his face. A soft gasp puffed through her lips.

"Mike, what happened?"

"I'm fine, I'm fine. I'll tell you all about it later. I've had the worst weeks ever, things you wouldn't believe. But I'm alive. For the first time in my life, I feel alive. Everything got made right. But I still need someone; I need you. I *want you*. I want to make you happy, to give you the love you deserve."

"Slow down, Mike, slow down."

"I can't, I can't. I have to have you. I can't believe you'd take me back."

"I love you."

"I love *you*. And I'm getting help, help with all of it—my problems, our relationship. I promise to love you more and be a better husband from this point on."

"I believe you. I believe you."

Should I kiss her? Can I? He did, and she let him, even kissed him back.

"Can we go somewhere and talk about all this?" she asked.

"Yeah." Mike was overjoyed. He felt like a lovestruck teenager, flushed and sweaty, blushing sheepishly, butterflies fluttering in his stomach, his knees wobbly. He managed to ask, "Wanna share a pizza?"

She smiled.

Wow, Mike thought.

"I'd love to," she said.

So they did. They left, walking together hand in hand into the autumn sunlight to share dinner. And after it, a lifetime.

CPSIA information can be obtained at www.ICGtesting.com
Printed in the USA
BVOW02s1747111213

338820BV00002B/47/P